M5

Circle of Trust

Millennium Series

Staci Morrison

First published by Alanthia Publishing 2023

Copyright © 2023 by Staci Morrison

ISBN: 978-1-958113-05-9

First edition

This one is for Ben, who always pushes me to be better, who knows me better than almost anyone, and brings joy to my life and my work. You were the first person I shared The Millennium Series with, and from that dinner on, you never stopped encouraging me. Our road trips are almost as epic as this series. I love you. Thank you for being so amazing.

Table of Contents

Enter the Millennium

Welcome back! The reader will recall that years in the text are indicated with ME, Millennial Era, instead of BC or AD. Thus, 999 ME is 999 years into the Millennium.

Character names use a Hebrew construction, whereby 'ben' means child of, so Josiah ben Eamonn means Josiah son of Eamonn.

So, what is the Millennium, and when will it occur?

It is a prophetic time, the next great age. Our world today will not continue ad infinitum. At some point in the future, the Lord will appear in the Heavens and call His church to Himself. This global cataclysmic event is called the Rapture and sets off a series of events that will usher in the Tribulation, seven years of wars, famine, earthquakes, fire, and pestilence; hell on Earth. But in the end, the evil forces are defeated. The Lord returns to rule, ushering in the Millennium, one thousand years of paradise, a return to what was lost in Eden.

Series Notes

As the series progresses, we move deeper into the tale, often going on the "other side of the door". And while each book could technically be read as a stand alone, I do not suggest it. The breadth and depth of the story is fleshed out in vivid detail by reading the series in order. I am not big on recapping, but I do my best to anchor each part where appropriate. Sometimes I leave those things to the reader, as I think it adds some little tidbits to discover.

M5-Circle of Trust brings all the characters and timelines together. It is an ambitious novel that I am so excited to share with you. I created a "Bonus Section" on alanthia.com that offers readers a cumulative timeline of events by book. If you like that sort of thing check it out.

I am honored and humbled to have you back. From the bottom of my heart, thank you. Take my hand; I am going to tell you an amazing tale.

A friend loves at all times, and a brother is born for a time of adversity.

—Proverbs 17:17

Glossary

Characters*

Astrid ben Agnor – Pilgrim girl turned Duchess, born April 28, 980 ME to Agnor ben Randall and Emaline ben Gregory. Davianna ben David's best friend. Significant other Peter ben Korah. Nicknames Red and Tridi.

Alaina ben Thomas – Supermodel and covert computer hacker, born December 12, 971 ME. Best friends with Filippo ben Vincente, her photographer and former roommate, and Himari Nakamura, her neighbor. She is one of the first members of The Resistance. Significant other Beau Landry. Code name Miss Pink.

Angelica ben Omri – Former Alanthia Supreme Court Justice, the exiled Witch of Endor, born August 9, 932 ME. Goes into exile after battling her nemesis Esmeralda ben Claude.

Beau Landry – Noble Army Veteran and heir to the Lenox fortune, born July 11, 968 ME to Jorge and Sarah Landry. A charming Cajun, and the youngest of six children. Best friends with Ian ben Kole. Significant other Alaina ben Thomas.

Charlotte Durant – Louisiana Voodoo Priestess, mother of the nephilim, Emite. Becomes Ba'alat Ob after Angelica ben Omri is exiled.

Davianna ben David – Pilgrim girl turned Princess, born May 27, 980 ME to David ben Jesse and Zanah ben Joseph. She receives a mysterious artifact from the Last Age that sparks a global manhunt. Astrid ben Agnor's best friend. Significant other Josiah ben Eamonn. Nicknames Davi, Minx, Sparrow, and Fireball.

Emite ben Marduk – Nephilim, sorcerer, from Louisiana, born Feb 11, 986 ME to the fallen angel Marduk and Charlotte Durant.

Esmeralda ben Claude – The White Woman, born in Rephidim, Pennsylvania, January 10, 975 ME to Claude and Julianna. She is a seer whose special abilities make her a target for the forces of evil. Significant other Thaddeus ben Todd. Nickname Vixen. Codename Curly.

Erica – an adaptive artificial intelligence.

Filippo ben Vincente – Painter, Photographer, Italian, born November 17, 963 ME. He is best friends with Alaina ben Thomas and goes undercover in mafia boss, Marco ben Massimo's house. Significant other Himari Nakamura. Codename Leonardo.

Genevieve ben Willard – Peter and Josiah's former nanny, and honorary grandmother to the members of The Resistance. Also known as Auntie G., her codename is G.

Himari Nakamura – Japanese/Alanthian computer genius, Professor, Elite hacker, born June 30, 965 ME. An Alcatraz 5 member, a group of teenagers who discover a Last Age computer lab. Friends with Lavinia, Kayah, and Alaina. Significant other Filippo ben Vincente. Her codename is Sunflower.

Ian ben Kole – Noble Army Veteran, Charity Worker, born January 18, 969 ME to Kole and Salome. At eighteen, he encounters the Lord and is filled with the Holy Spirit, which turns his hair white. He lives an itinerant life before settling at the Center for Street Kids of Alanthia. Best friends with Beau Landry, brother of James ben Kole, his significant other is Lady Joanna ben Luke.

James ben Kole – Co-owner of Pepperwood Horse Ranch and World Champion Equestrian, born September 4, 965 ME to Kole and Salome. He earns distinction in the Noble Army and becomes a solid presence in Peter's life. Childhood sweethearts with his wife, Persa ben Yereq. Nickname Jay.

Joanna ben Luke – Humanitarian, born August 31, 967 ME to Lord Luke ben Simon and Lady Elizabeth ben George, the Earl and Countess of Stockton. After her parent's house arrest, she starts the Street Kids of Alanthia. Significant other Ian ben Kole. Nicknamed Lady J, Princess Workaholic, Princess W.

Josiah ben Eamonn – Prince of Alanthia, born June 8, 969 ME to Prince Eamonn ben Adam and Princess Marguerite ben Alfonso. The rightful heir to the Alanthian throne, who goes into exile in 985 ME after his father is murdered. Serves in the Iron King's Army, a trained surgeon, alias Einar ben Yane. Significant other Davianna ben David. Codename Doc.

Kayah ben Samuel – Badass, born August/September 964 ME, she is left at an orphanage. Founder of the Alcatraz 5, she is the only one who goes to prison. Released when the technology laws are repealed, she aligns with Sir Preston ben Worley and becomes a covert agent. A woman of many faces, her significant other is Reuben ben Judah.

Korah ben Adam – King of Alanthia, born November 16, 943 ME to Prince Adam ben Simon and Princess Mary ben Abraham. He seizes the throne after murdering his brother, Eamonn. Married to Princess Alexa ben Seamus (deceased) and father of Peter.

Lavinia ben Anthony – Genius, born October 16, 964 ME to Anthony and Violet. She is a member of the Alcatraz 5, but her involvement never becomes public. Founder of The Resistance with Prince Peter. The proprietress of Peccioli, mother of Richard, and friends with Kayah, Himari, and Esmeralda. Significant other Mack ben Robert. Nickname Valentine. Codename Ms. Euler.

Mack ben Robert – Leader of The Resistance, former Royal Guard, born October 14, 960 ME in Virginia. Army veteran and sheriff, he becomes Peter's Head of Security before settling at Peccioli to become a vintner. Friends with Thaddeus. Codename Bobby.

Persa ben Yereq - Co-owner of Pepperwood Horse Ranch and World Champion Equestrian, born December 12, 965 ME. She is capture by Marduk and forced to give birth to Rapha, the nephilim, before escaping in the closing hours of the Alanthian Civil War. She befriends Peter and provides a haven for him. Significant other James ben Kole. Nickname Fey.

Peter ben Korah – Playboy, Revolutionary, Prince of Alanthia, born January 6, 987 ME to Prince Korah ben Adam and Princess Alexa ben Seamus. The presumed heir to the Alanthian throne, leader and founder of the Resistance. Significant other Astrid ben Agnor. Codename Falcon.

Preston ben Worley – Lawyer, Knight of the Realm, born September 9, 909 ME. Memorable for his bushy eyebrows and moustache, he was Prince Adam's closest advisor and mentor to Kayah. He lives and practices law in New York.

Reuben ben Judah – Mossad Agent, born in the Golden Kingdom October 9, 965 ME. Served with Josiah in the army where he was wounded, avenging the deaths of his family. He is assigned to follow Davianna and Astrid across Europe and meets his significant other, Kayah ben Samuel.

Thaddeus ben Todd – Director of the FBI, lawyer, born February 2, 960 ME. He is a former basketball star who loses his family in a terrorists attack and seeks refuge in Rephidim where he meets a young girls who changes everything. Friends with Mack ben Robert. Significant other Esmeralda ben Claude. Codename T.

*Check out their portraits at Alanthia.com/characters

Places

Alanthia – One of ten Millennial Kingdoms, occupying the North American continent.

Bunker – A fallout shelter built in the Last Age where The Resistance wages war against Korah's government. Located in the basement of Genevieve ben Willard's home on the outskirts of the New City.

House of Amah – Rapha's house hidden in the old section of the New City.

La Petit Pishon – The Lake where Beau Landry builds his house, about twenty minutes from Landrys.

Loa Hall – Charlotte and Emite's house hidden deep in the Louisiana bayou.

New City – Capitol of Alanthia, built on the ruins of San Francisco.

Peccioli – Mack and Lavinia's vineyard in Redding, California, approximately 3 hours north of the New City.

Pepperwood – James and Persa's horse ranch in Redding, California, approximately 3 hours north of the New City.

Thyatira – An isolated region in rural Pennsylvania that contains the village of Rephidim, Bezetha, and the ruins of Endor.

Part 1 - Release

New Year's Eve 999 ME

Retirement Villa - Fiji - Angelica ben Omri

Fiji, oh Mistress Angelica ben Omri liked Fiji. If she was honest, she liked retirement. However, she was rarely honest, even with herself. But relaxing on the veranda of her beachside villa, surrounded by snow-white sand and turquoise water, she finally admitted it; retirement was glorious. A couple strolled by and waved, undoubtedly thinking she was a carefree tourist.

She was not.

To a select few, she was the displaced, disgraced, and exiled Witch of Endor. To the rest of the world, she was the former Chief Justice of the Alanthian Supreme Court, who also happened to be displaced, disgraced, and exiled. Which, she supposed, made her persona non grata—everywhere.

It should bother her, but it did not.

She sighed and relaxed into the chaise lounge, taking a sip of kava, a local specialty. It tasted vile, similar to peppery mud, but her houseman insisted it was good for her. Over the last fourteen months, she learned to appreciate the calm, numbing effect it produced, and it settled her stomach, which had troubled her for a while, so perhaps he was right. Every night after dinner, he prepared a tray and presented her glass in a formal ceremony. Tonight, she added her own personal hypnotic and settled in for the evening on the patio of her villa.

She watched the setting sun from behind her black sunglasses, the scene a far cry from the Palace's underground dungeon, which was where she should have been, preparing a ritual to welcome Lucifer and celebrate his release. The flowered purple sarong she wore bore no resemblance to her ceremonial robes, nor did her large-brimmed beach hat remotely resemble the heavy diadem of the high priestess, Ba'alat Ob.

After the disastrous defeat in Thyatira Woods, she disappeared. Angelica decided if she was going into exile, it may as well be somewhere fantastic. Alas, she was leaving soon, which had always been the plan. There was vengeance to take and scores to settle, but for now, there was Fiji… and kava.

Second Chances - Loa Hall - Charlotte and Emite

Deep in the heart of the Louisiana bayou, Mademoiselle Charlotte Durant stalked her son, Emite, enraged. "I should be at the New Year's Eve Ball in the Palace tonight. I should be there! I am Ba'alat Ob!" she screeched. "This is your fault!"

The bullwhip fell with an electric crack, stinging Emite, the nephilim's skin, drawing blood. He howled in protest, "I'm sorry!"

She brought the whip down again, merciless in her fury.

Pop!

Working herself into a frenzy, Charlotte screamed, "They withdrew my invitation! I am ordered to reside at Loa Hall until you are under control! Your recklessness brings me disgrace!"

The whip fell, this time tearing away a chunk of flesh from Emite's upper arm. "*Maman*, stop!" he begged.

"Do you know how hard I worked to get where I am? You know they banished me while that bitch reigned; twelve years I was exiled! Now I am outcast again, because of YOU!"

Crack!

"*Maman*, I know…" Emite hung his head, pretending to be ashamed, hoping she stopped.

"You know, yet you continue to jeopardize everything, defying orders… for your treats!" She sneered and circled him, her chest heaving in anger and exertion.

"I won't do it again," he promised, telling her what she wanted to hear.

"I should chain you." Charlotte advanced on him, her face a mask of rage.

Emite drew back, stumbling against the wall, cowering and genuinely afraid. "Not the chains," he wailed.

"The cage, then?"

"No, *Maman*. I will be a good boy. I swear." His eyes darted down the hall toward the dank, small cell. He hated that place above all else.

The whip trailed behind her, ominous and snakelike, appearing alive in her hands. "On your knees," she demanded.

The ground shook as Emite fell, five hundred and fifty pounds of solid muscle, quivering in a puddle, surrendered to his 5'4" mother. She raised his chin and brought them nose to nose, glaring into the hellfire depths of his soul.

"Do you understand what your actions do to your *maman*? How you bring suspicion to our door? Can you comprehend that your behavior has caused me to lose favor, not only with Korah, but also with the Dark Master? Shall I tell him? Shall I have your father punish you?"

"No!" Emite cried. His *maman* told him what would happen if his father ever came. "I won't go to the city again. No more treats, I promise," he lied. "I will apply myself, only to please you from this day forward. I will make you proud."

Charlotte stroked his cheek, soothing and cajoling. "My son, if you do as you vow, there is nothing we cannot accomplish." She turned with haughty confidence. "Come, let us prepare. Our Lord's return is at hand, and we will be by his side. I warn you, though, there is no mercy in him. With Lucifer, there are no second chances."

3 am Feeding - New York City - Esmeralda and Thaddeus

FBI Director Thaddeus ben Todd rolled over as the baby monitor on his nightstand lit up, pulsing in the red zone. "She will never sleep through the night, will she?" he groaned.

His wife, Esmeralda ben Claude, rose on one elbow, staring at the clock, right on time, three o'clock, every night. Her curly hair, disheveled from sleep, glowed white in the shaft of light that shone through the crack in their bedroom curtains. She collapsed onto her pillow with a thud. "You get her."

"I can't feed her," Thaddeus protested, turning away to hide his smile.

"Which is the excuse you've been using for six months." She kicked at him, trying to push him out of their warm bed. "Bring her to me."

"My arm hurts," he teased.

Esmeralda buried her face in the blankets and gave a quick snort of laughter. "Not going to work anymore, Tin Man. Bring me the baby."

His chest shook, his wry sense of humor kindled, despite the hour. "You're younger than me. I need more sleep."

She threw a pillow at him and made a low impatient noise as their daughter gathered steam.

Thaddeus relented, throwing back the covers.

"Change her before you bring her in."

"Bossy vixen," Thaddeus muttered and stumbled across the hall.

His daughter's wails grew more plaintive and demanding by the second. Pushing open the nursery door, he said, "Hey there, little miss, what are you so upset about?"

At the sound of his voice, Claire ben Thaddeus raised her head and blinked. Her huge slate-blue eyes ran with tears, her lower lip trembling. Her light brown hair stood up in a tangled mess, exactly like the sleepy man who came to her rescue.

Daddy.

She kicked her feet, excited to see him. Daddy meant play! He picked her up with his big hands and gave her scratchy kisses. She giggled and squirmed, then protested loudly when he laid her on the changing table. She wanted to keep playing, not get changed. Her nappy was yucky, which woke her up, but seeing Daddy made her forget that. He was not as fast as Mom, nor did he secure her diaper as snuggly. It sort of felt like it was going to fall off, but he nibbled her toes and blew blubbery smooches on her belly, so she forgave him and grabbed his hair with both fists.

"Ow! You have quite a grip there, don't you?" Thaddeus bent over and tried to extricate her fingers.

"Thaddeus!" Esmeralda cried.

He heard the panic in her voice, scooped Claire up, and hurried across the hall. "What's wrong?"

All the lights in the world went dark.

Fast Car - New City - Peter and Josiah

Eight minutes after their harrowing escape from the Palance, Prince Peter ben Korah sped through New City traffic evading pursuit. With a quick check of this rearview mirror, he gunned the engine of his getaway vehicle and took a blind turn at ninety miles an hour.

Prince Josiah ben Eamonn turned in the passenger seat with a slight groan and said, "I think we lost them. They are diverting."

That is the plan, Cousin." Coming out of the turn, Peter floored the accelerator and passed a line of cars.

Not having much experience with automobiles, Josiah gripped the door handle and snapped, "What exactly is the plan?"

Peter swore as he drove up on a slow-moving vehicle blocking the passing lane. He downshifted and blew the horn, flashing his lights. The Mini-Stilton moved over, the driver glaring at them as they sped by, but the dark tinted windows gave no hint who drove the high-performance sports car, so they were in no danger of being recognized or having information on their escape route find its way back to the Palace.

"Ultimately," Peter said, "the plan is to get you on the throne. However, at the moment, I am a bit preoccupied."

"Affirmative."

"Traffic… this time of night," Peter muttered and glanced at his watch—11:59 pm. He sped around a slow van. "What are all you people doing on the road? Why are you not at a party ringing in the Millennium?"

"I, for one, am glad we are not attending Korah's party," Josiah murmured, glancing over his shoulder to check on Davianna and Astrid huddled in the backseat. Astrid looked ghastly.

Peter cut him a sideways glance. "More than you know."

"Why are you doing this?" Josiah asked.

"I was bored."

Josiah snorted, having forgotten Peter's sarcastic sense of humor. "Still concocting hairbrained schemes?"

Peter grinned. "You were always such a prude about them."

"Because I had sense," Josiah countered. "Well, as long as this does not involve gluing Mr. ben Merriweather's pants to his chair, I am in."

"I did that after you left," Peter chuckled. "Though he knew it was me since there was nobody else to blame. I did not quite think that one through."

"But you've thought this through?" Josiah asked, not joking.

"Down to the suit I plan to wear to your coronation. That is, if we live long enough." He rounded another corner and gasped, "Bloody hell!"

Josiah whipped his head around and saw the New City grow dark.

From the backseat, Davianna ben David grabbed her left pocket and moaned.

With Open Arms - New City - Rapha

On the edge of the New City, the House of Amah shone like a beacon, the vast grounds and windows illuminated by oil lamps, torches, and electric lights. The house once belonged to the Redwood Barons, but their line had gone extinct in 984 ME, and King Korah never named a successor. No one came to the manor any longer, and if some foolish soul managed to breach the locked gate, the great wall, and the enchantments surrounding the property, they never left to tell the tale.

Rapha, the nephilim and master of the house, studied his preparations in critical appraisal, inspecting his handiwork. The sideboard was laid with the most sumptuous fare from around the world, each decadent dish mimicking a work of art, a feast for the eyes, as well as the palette. He nudged a wine goblet an inch to the left, ensuring no disharmony detracted from his elegant display. Two place settings of bone china, solid gold utensils, and cut crystal goblets graced either end of the long table. Tapestries and framed masterpieces hung in perfect symmetry. Ancient hand-knotted Aubusson rugs covered the polished wood floors and muffled his heavy footsteps. A bronze chandelier, forged by Rapha in the blacksmith's workshop, lit the regal room in a dancing, warm glow.

Satisfied, Rapha moved into the foyer and glanced up the floating staircase with a wicked smile. Upstairs, three beautiful maidens, garbed in silks and chains, waited. For tonight's festivities, he collected a brunette, a blonde, and a tiny Chinese woman who resembled a child. He hoped to take that one but resigned himself to the fact he probably would not. Walking to the side of the house, he inspected the grounds, looking toward the stables that held goats, sheep, and fowl chosen for their perfection, without spot or blemish. Rapha ensured both women and animals were ceremonially pure, worthy, and prepared for sacrifice. The preparations had taken him more than a year, but everything was ready, awaiting the master's pleasure.

He checked his reflection and smoothed a stray lock of ginger hair out of his orange tinted eyes. For the occasion, he wore a combination of Japanese silk and spiked leather. He designed and crafted the clothing himself, executing the fine needlework with perfection, quite a feat for a creature whose hands could span a bull's head. A medallion of gold and rubies hung around his neck, the size of a dinner plate, yet against his broad chest, it appeared proportionate and tasteful. He smiled at himself.

Anticipation coursed through his body, causing the hair on the back of his arms to tingle with the force of his excitement. Tonight was a lifetime in the making for Rapha, and an eon for those trapped in bondage. The New Age was upon them, and he planned to be at Lucifer's side when he reclaimed his throne.

He left the house and strode toward the maze. Its ten-foot hedgerows swallowed the sound of his steps but did not obscure his vision. He could easily see over the top. Arriving at the center, he absorbed its beauty. Camellias, azaleas, and Helleborus bloomed in profusion, alongside the greenhouse forced bulbs of tulips, hyacinths, and amaryllis. Low growing boxwoods, trimmed to perfection, formed a pentagram. A marble fountain sprayed water, dyed red for the occasion. The devilishly delightful display was illuminated by solar powered lamps of his own design and making.

This was the last sight his victims often saw, the incongruent beauty of the nephilim's garden. He loved watching the life fade from their eyes as they stared in dazed bewilderment at his elegant creation. The fountain and the flowers drew them when they were running. He set them loose in the maze, enjoyed their terror, and the hunt. They fled to the very place he wanted them to be, and there they died.

He circled the spot where he was conceived, where he ruled, the center of his universe, where he passed judgment on those who stumbled into his lair. Soon, he would bring his talents to the world, and it all began tonight.

At the first point of the pentagram, he stood, ready to welcome the second coming king, the long-exiled ruler of Earth, Lucifer.

As he looked up, he saw the enemy swirling, the sky so thick with them they blotted out the moon, covering the great city his father resurrected from the ashes. Their sickening Golden Kingdom perfume poisoned the air. But he gave them no mind.

He closed his eyes and waited. Then he heard a mighty howl, the roar of a dragon. It echoed in his soul like sweet, poignant music.

Darkness fell.

Rapha raised his arms and called, "Tremble, oh ye slaves in chains, for the fearsome and glorious prince of the power of the air comes upon ye tonight. Quake in fear and cry bitter tears of sorrow, ye sons of heaven, for thy mighty enemy is loosed, and he will rule!"

Over the horizon, he saw the flash of a comet, glorious and obsidian. Rapha shouted, "Great Master, I call thee forth! For I have prepared a place. Reside in splendor until thy magnificent victory."

Rapha ben Marduk, master of the House of Amah, welcomed the Devil with open arms.

Thunder and Lightning - Pepperwood - James and Persa

"Are you awake?" James ben Kole whispered in the darkness of his bedroom.

His wife, Persa ben Yereq, rolled to her side, facing him. "Yes, I can't sleep. My brain is spinning. I am worried about what Peter is doing, but I keep thinking about the wedding and how happy I am for Joanna and Ian, and how much fun it was to see the kids at the Center today." She laughed at the expulsion of so many thoughts in a single breath.

"Well, that about sums it up." James stared at the ceiling, contemplating the same things. Rolling to his side, he studied Persa's face, the tilt of her slightly pointed chin, her strawberry blonde hair still curled from the wedding. To him, she was the most beautiful girl in the world. He had loved her since he was eight years old. "What do you say we go for a midnight ride? The moon is pretty tonight, and I cannot sleep."

"We haven't done that in a long time."

James smiled in memory. "We used to do it when we were kids, remember? I would throw pebbles at your window, and you'd sneak out."

A troubled look clouded Persa's features, but it disappeared as quickly as it came. She threw off the blankets and said, "Let's go, just you and me."

He flashed her a grin. Nothing made James happier than being on a horse, especially if Persa was by his side. "Jay and Fey, ride again."

"Always," She smiled, with a hint of sadness in her eyes.

He read her distress and said, "Peter will be all right. Don't worry."

Persa reached for a warm wool sweater and sighed, "I just pray that he is, Jay. It broke my heart, saying goodbye to him today. It might have been the hardest thing I've ever done."

"For me too. Ironic that it happened on Ian's wedding day." He pulled on his old riding boots. "I was shocked when he called and said, 'Get down here. Joanna and I are getting married today.'"

"Well, it came as no shock they got married, just that they did it twenty-four seconds after deciding," Persa observed drolly.

James chuckled, repeating, "Twenty-four seconds."

"Seriously. Somehow, they pulled it off, church wedding and all, unlike me and you."

James grinned. "What do you say we have a reenactment on our little midnight ride?"

Persa moistened her lips, her pretty features aglow with sudden mischief. "Ooh, that sounds intriguing. Do you think Joey would still oblige?"

"He didn't appear to mind, though he was so thankful I rescued him off the battlefield, he would have done anything for me at the time." He paused, realizing he had forgotten that. It happened regularly. Memory fragments fell back into place. Since November, their lost days reappeared in fits and starts, sometimes innocuous, often horrifying, but they took them as they came and dealt with each day the best way they could. But through the trial, they shed the mundane and embraced a reinvigorated life.

"You rescued him?" Persa asked, raising her eyebrows with interest. Joey was one of her favorite stallions, even-tempered but spirited, a splendid stud and a cornerstone at Pepperwood for thirteen years.

"I did. He was rawboned and starving, ill-treated." He grunted deep in his chest, disgusted anew. "You should have heard the ribbing I took when I led him through the camp. I could see he was a fine animal." He chuckled as the memory solidified. "Beau Landry made a small fortune betting on the rehabilitation of Joey. Come to think of it, Ian and I did, too. I learned that fast. If Beau put money on something, just do what he did. The man is charmed."

"Ian missed him today." Persa pushed through the door, shivering at the blast of frosty night air.

"Beau don't leave the bayou these days, *chèr*," James remarked in a passable imitation of Beau's Louisiana cadence.

"I know a wee bit about that."

"Aye, you do, Fey." James nodded. "I've been thinking I might write him a letter and invite him to Pepperwood. Perhaps his memories will return if he comes." He stopped and looked around their sprawling ranch. "There is something special about this place."

Persa tilted her face upward, taking in the full moon and the clear winter sky. "I think it is because Pepperwood is safe. It's been a haven for more than just us. The kids feel it during Summer camp. Peter does too, which is why I wanted to conk him on the head and drag him back here tonight."

"He has to do what he's doing. We talked about that."

"We did," she said with a sigh.

He draped an arm around her shoulders, walking with her toward the stables, content, despite his worry over Peter.

Persa put her hand in his back pocket, giving his buttock a squeeze. "I believe you're right, Jay. All your men who have come here over the years find peace. Write to Beau Landry."

"I will," James said with a nod, and ushered her inside the barn.

Twenty pristine horses hailed their arrival with whinnies and snorts. James called back a greeting and switched on the overhead fixture, which flickered, then went black with a pop.

"What the—"

"Has the power gone out?"

"I don't know," James murmured, turning the switch off and on.

An otherworldly light began to glow out of the stalls housing Lightning and Bayard. "Look," Persa gasped, grabbing his arm.

"Jupiter's Moon," James whispered in awe.

Lightning tossed her head. The hair of her long, white mane stood on end, electrified, and pulsing with power. She stamped her front hoof with a mighty crash, the impact reverberating through the barn and up James' spine.

The two stalls opened by an unseen hand, and Bayard followed his mother, as the horses trotted past the stunned humans into the yard. Rearing on his hind legs, surrounded by Shekinah glory, Bayard gave a stallion's war cry, a chilling sound that tore through the valley.

Lightning joined him, lifting her head and answering the summons of the Most High, as the Iron King recalled the equine guardians of Pepperwood to active duty. They were ready to fight.

Part 2 - Watchers

January 1, 1000 ME

I Can't Tell My Mother That - New York - Esmeralda and Thaddeus

Esmeralda ben Claude moved around the kitchen in her and Thaddeus forty-second-floor apartment with the shuffling steps of an exhausted parent whose baby arbitrarily decided at 3:00 am she had no intention of sleeping and demanded her parents take part in her nocturnal frolicking. However, even if Claire had slept, Esmeralda knew she would not have.

At some point over the last fourteen months, she stopped questioning how she discerned things; she simply did and always had. For most of her life, her insights were innocuous, simply impressions she got about people or situations. When she was young, almost everything she saw was good, often beautiful. But as she got older, it changed, and now, if she saw something beautiful, it felt like a gift, like a reminder that life was both good and bad.

Last night, it was bad.

She sat straight up in bed, sensing a tear in the protective veil between the natural and supernatural. Unspeakable evil slithered through the crack and returned to Eden.

And this was not the first time she felt it. Her intense visions had increased in frequency and severity, disconcerting episodes that left her jumpy. But she did not face them alone, and her husband's support made them bearable.

After the attack in Thyatira, her obstetrician ordered complete bed rest. Ominous spotting and cramping convinced her to comply. For months, every drop of blood, every flutter in her belly, sent her into a panic. Everyone agreed it was a miracle she carried the baby to term.

However, as difficult as her pregnancy had been, Thaddeus went through a much tougher recovery. The bullet wound he sustained obliterated his shoulder, and without the best surgeons in the kingdom, he would have lost his arm, if not his life. But the damage ran deeper than just torn muscles and ragged nerves. The trauma affected his heart. They called it hypertrophic cardiomyopathy, a thickening of the heart muscle, which compromised his heart's ability to pump sufficient blood through his body. And while his long-term prognosis remained good, he still grew dizzy and short of breath. At first, getting dressed after a bath was all he could manage, and even then, he had to lie down. The massive blood loss caused anemia, and for three months, he looked like a vampire after a rough night. Though he never complained, he experienced chest pains, especially when he pushed himself too hard.

In March, three and a half months after Thyatira, the doctors released them for light duty. On what should have been their first day back at work, they stood at their bathroom sinks, getting ready. Esmeralda brushed her teeth as Thaddeus shaved. She heard a hollow sound, like a ghostly wind, and the perceived temperature in the room plummeted. She froze, the color draining from her face. Opening her mouth to speak, nothing came out. A bolt of dark energy hit her, and she stumbled backward.

Thaddeus caught her with his good arm, preventing a tumble into the sunken tub. "What's wrong? Is it the baby?"

She blinked up at him and gasped, "It's been found."

"What's been found?" he demanded.

"Something that is going to release Hell on Earth."

Thaddeus set his square jaw, the muscles working, as he pulled her off the edge of the tub, muttering curses under his breath. Depositing her on the bed, he said, "Lie down."

Esmeralda gave several weak protests but obliged, feeling shaky. Resting her hands on her abdomen, she waited. When the baby moved, she breathed a sigh of relief. "We're fine."

Thaddeus stalked out of the room and said over his shoulder, "I am calling Ian. You are not ready to start work."

Before Thaddeus could say a word, Ian asked, "Did Esmeralda feel that?"

Thaddeus inhaled raggedly. He hoped after Thyatira this was over. Clearly, he had been deluding himself. "Yes."

"Tell her to stay there. I will be right over."

In the realm of spiritual battle, Ian ben Kole outranked him, so Thaddeus did not protest. "Shall I call Mack?"

Ian looked at his watch. "No. It's 3:00 am in California, and there is nothing he can do." Ian shoved his feet in his shoes, moving quickly around his small apartment. "Stay with her until I arrive."

The next episode occurred while she and Ian were working at the new Center for Street Kids. A large shipment of flat packed furniture had arrived, and she was helping him put everything together. And while she could lift nothing heavy, she read instructions, handed him tools, and ensured he had the correct fasteners for the assembly. But by midmorning, her lower back ached, and she stood up.

"Are you all right?" Ian mumbled behind a mouthful of screws.

"Fine, it's just a twinge."

"How many more weeks do you have?" he asked.

"Eleven," she said, arching to relieve the tension.

Ian dropped the screwdriver with a gasp and clutched his head. Esmeralda arrested mid-stretch, feeling a familiar dread. A hellish roar assaulted their minds. Ian flew to her side, shielding her. She clung to him and hid her face in the folds of his shirt. "Oh, no!"

"Lord Jesus, have mercy."

Esmeralda heard the groans coming from his spirit, incomprehensible, quiet pleadings. She joined his fervent entreaty, knowing something diabolical had just broken free.

But it had been quiet for months, and she thought it might be over. It clearly was not.

Over breakfast on New Year's Day, Esmeralda tried to choke down her bagel, but it caught in her throat, so she abandoned it half-eaten on her plate. "I wonder how Ian and Joanna are doing. If it was not the morning after their wedding, I'd call to ask if he felt the disturbance, too."

Thaddeus grinned. "Go ahead. He'll pick up if he's not," he waggled his eyebrows at her, "busy."

Esmeralda laughed. "I can't believe they got married so fast. I wish we could have been at the wedding."

"Speaking of weddings…"

Esmeralda groaned.

He gestured toward the small kitchen desk where they kept mail, bills, and lists. "You have another letter from your mother."

"I saw it."

"But you haven't opened it?"

She shook her head.

He gave her a censorious look. "Just tell her no."

"I can't tell her that."

Thaddeus took her half-eaten Asiago cheese bagel and asked, "Why not?"

She rolled her eyes because he would never understand the complex mother-daughter relationship. "It will break her heart, that's why."

"You're chicken." He smiled and tore into the chewy bagel.

"I'm not chicken, and this isn't the basketball court where you can taunt me into doing something rash. I know how you work."

Low, cackling hen noises came from his side of the table.

"Shut up! I need your help. I don't need you needling me."

"Tell her," he asserted.

Esmeralda dropped her face into her hands and said through her fingers, "Still no sign of the witch?"

Thaddeus gobbled the rest of his bagel in a single bite, shaking his head. "Not a trace. She's dead or hiding. We don't know which."

Esmeralda groaned and rubbed her sleep-deprived eyes. "I thought your unit would find her."

"We aren't omniscient, and they shut down our investigation. There is only so much we can do on the sly." He rose from the breakfast table, clearing their empty plates.

"Paul doesn't have any fresh leads?" Esmeralda pulled a curl in front of her nose and twisted it around her finger.

"I had to pull him. He's focusing on New Orleans now. They've had another rash of disappearances."

"Ian told me. Has he had any luck down there?"

"No." Thaddeus looked grim.

"It's terrible."

"Paul's one of the best. He'll find something, and who knows, it might lead to Angelica ben Omri."

"Might," she said, shaking her head.

Thaddeus drew her to her feet and said, "Listen, you need to make a decision. Either let your mother reschedule the wedding or tell her she will have to be satisfied with the ceremony we had in the hospital. It's that simple. We might never find her, so you have to come to terms with what that means." He tapped her forehead, his stern expression tempered by the compassionate warmth in his brown eyes.

"You're right. It's just so hard."

"I know," he said.

"Mom says we were robbed of our wedding day, and we need to take it back." Esmeralda moved out of his embrace, staring out the apartment windows at the New York skyline. "But a wedding makes me a target. It announces to the witch when and where I will be, which provides her a perfect opportunity to come after us again. Can you imagine if we had Claire with us that day?"

Thaddeus did not answer, refusing to go there in his mind.

Esmeralda sighed. "The thing is, if Angelica is dead, then I am letting fear rule my life for nothing."

Thaddeus wrapped his arms around her waist and rested his chin on the top of her head. "If she's alive, you are right about the wedding. That's not fear, that's prudence. And I'll support you no matter what you decide. But I'll tell you one thing: if you go along with your mom's plan, we're taking a tank into Thyatira."

"I think we should have infantry and air cover."

Neither was joking.

January 4, 1000 ME

Discretion - New York City - Esmeralda

"Thank you for calling the Center for Street Kids of Alanthia. You've reached Esmeralda. How may I help you?"

"Hello, Esmeralda. Where y'at?"

"Beau!" she exclaimed, stunned to hear his voice. They had not spoken since that horrible night seventeen months ago when they both nearly died fighting a swarm of astral spirits.

"How are you, *chèr*?"

She beamed into the phone. "I am well. How are you?"

Beau looked at last night's dirty dishes in the sink and said, "Much improved, thank you."

Esmeralda moved around the front of her desk, stretching the phone cord to its maximum length to shut her office door. "That does my heart good. You are always in my prayers."

Beau took a sip of green tea, staring at the lake beyond his window. "Ian told me, and I appreciate that, Esmeralda, especially after what I put you through."

Esmeralda closed her eyes, searching for the right words. "You did not put me through anything. We went through that together, Beau."

An ironic chuckle came through the line, but he remained silent on the subject. "That's not why I called, though one day, we will sit down and have a conversation about that night."

"Whenever you are ready." Esmeralda doodled a series of circles on a scratch notepad.

"Unfortunately, the reason I am calling is also unpleasant. Are you alone?"

She stopped mid-doodle. "Yes, my door is shut. What's going on?"

Beau paced the floor of his study, for once not seeing Alaina's pictures. "Though I don't have the right, I need to ask for your discretion."

"Of course," she said, feeling a knot of dread settle in her stomach.

"There is an accountant on his way to your office, and I need you to keep that confidential." Beau cleared his throat and continued, "We've found some abnormalities in the Center's books."

"What sort? Do Ian and Joanna know?"

"No, they do not." There was a hard clip in Beau's words, echoes of Sarah Landry's New England roots. Its presence conveyed the seriousness of the situation.

Esmeralda rubbed the bridge of her nose. "What can you tell me?"

"Nothing at the moment. But we'll sort this out. Unfortunately, to discover the culprit, we must keep the investigation confidential. *Maman* and I discussed it. She's impressed with you, and you've met her, so you know that is high praise. And we both have reason to trust your discretion."

There was a pregnant pause, then Esmeralda said, "I cannot believe either Joanna or Ian are involved in anything that might merit an investigation. Ian saved my life, Beau."

"Mine, too. That's the reason we are bringing in a forensic accountant. We'll find out who's behind this." He added with an ironic inflection in his voice, "In the interim, we all need to exercise a bit of faith. But I think you and I did all right last time."

Esmeralda had a flash of memory, the two of them, beaten and bloodied, standing side-by-side, facing unspeakable evil. "Gird your loins with the belt of truth?"

"Amen, *chèr*. That was quite a sight. I'll be in touch."

Beau disconnected the line, stroking his beard with distracted contemplation. On his first official day as Head of the Lenox Foundation, he ordered an investigation into the charity run by his best friend.

His Grandfather Andrew ben Lenox was flying into town today, his first visit in five years. Beau did not delude himself. The old man wanted to see for himself whether his grandson had truly escaped the grip of madness, or if the last year was merely a remission.

Beau stared at his image reflected in the window. Setting his shoulders, he marched into the bathroom and shaved off his beard. It was time to stop hiding.

Distracted - New York City - Esmeralda

Claire ben Thaddeus did not like tummy time, no indeed. She let her feelings be known when her mother laid her on her pink blanket just out of reach of an enchanting set of rings. She liked the rings' colors, and they fit in her fists just right. She kicked her feet, protesting this callous abandonment, and was surprised when she moved closer to her goal all by herself, so she tried again. But this time, her tummy squished, which did not feel nice. She grunted in frustration and pushed up, rocking on her hands and knees. She stretched out a hand, trying to get the red ring, but started to fall. By reflex, she planted her arm and brought up her knee, but instead of falling, she got closer to her prize. She reached for the ring, but it was still too far away. She growled at it and rocked again.

Success!

She pulled the shiny red ring under her chin and began gnawing. It tasted smooth and hard, soothing her sore gums. She looked over her shoulder, expecting to find her mom watching, surprised to find she was not. But she did not care because she had just figured out how to move, and there were all sorts of interesting things to explore.

Esmeralda stood in her kitchen with the refrigerator door open, feeling the weight of the world on her shoulders. The accountant arrived precisely at 10:00 am, a gray little man, with fussy manners, and ball-bearing eyes that reminded her of Mustela, the mink she used to play with. She escorted him into her office, feeling like a traitor.

His suspicious nature, a requisite quality in a forensic accountant, made her nervous. She ended up yammering inanely, as if he was there to investigate her. At one point, she produced a receipt for a roof repair he had not even asked to see.

Using her login, he made small noises of discovery but did not bother to explain. He took notes in a leather-bound notebook, but she was too nervous to decipher his tiny handwriting. Ninety minutes after he arrived, he shook her hand and left without telling her a thing.

It wrecked the rest of her day.

She could not focus. A dozen times she reached for the phone, ready to demand Beau Landry tell her exactly what was going on, but she didn't. Instead, she buried herself in the library, shelving, sorting, and cataloging. Among the books, she found a measure of peace, but it was short-lived. When the kids got out of school and the house masters came on duty, Esmeralda left, picked Claire up early, and came home.

Standing with the refrigerator door open, she stared at the contents. Everything looked daunting, too much trouble to cook. Yet she was loath to call Thaddeus and ask him to pick up dinner. They lived on takeout for six months. She glanced at her watch, and realized he would be walking through the door any moment. With a weary sigh, she selected a pack of pork chops and closed the refrigerator with a thud.

The deadbolts turned, and she smiled.

Thaddeus came inside looking windblown. The pronounced dark circles under his eyes were a sure sign he had a hard day. "How are my girls tonight?" He dropped his briefcase on the side table and leaned in for a quick kiss.

"We're fine. I'm about to start dinner. Pork chops, unless you want something else."

"That sounds good." Thaddeus shrugged, scanning the room. "Is the baby asleep?"

Esmeralda's eyes flew to the empty pink blanket. "She was right there!" Flying around the counter, she stopped, seeing that Claire had maneuvered across the floor and was industriously chewing on the leg of a chair. She turned to Thaddeus and said balefully, "She's mobile."

The corner of Thaddeus' mouth lifted. "Watch out world, here comes Claire."

"They do not know what they are in for."

They shared a look, each bearing responsibility for the intrepid little imp gnawing the chair leg.

Claire blended several of her parents' more unique qualities. Tall for her age, she always measured in the one-hundredth percentile for height, something she inherited from Thaddeus. Even as a newborn, she regarded strangers with deep suspicion and determined within seconds whether they were friend or foe, another of her father's traits. Esmeralda thanked the Lord every day Claire had Thaddeus' hair.

Like Esmeralda, she loved books, and a story always calmed her down when she got cranky. Colors fascinated Claire, and Esmeralda suspected her daughter may have inherited more than her slate-blue eyes. At three months old, Esmeralda discovered the source of a red-faced tantrum had been caused by a yellow sleeper. As soon as Esmeralda swapped the offending garment for a sky-blue one, the wailing ceased. She relayed the incident to Lavinia ben Anthony, who agreed Claire may have indeed inherited Esmeralda's special sight.

After visiting Peccioli, Esmeralda and Lavinia had become friends. Planted by the seed of mutual oddness, their relationship deepened when Lavinia flew to New York after the attack in Thyatira. The doctors discharged Esmeralda three weeks before Thaddeus, but bedrest meant Esmeralda could do little more than make herself a sandwich. Lavinia, Mack, and Richard moved into the apartment's spare bedrooms, drove her to visit Thaddeus, kept her company in the evening, and managed all the household chores.

Once Thaddeus came home, Mack stayed for several weeks. It remained unspoken, but Esmeralda knew he was making certain the danger had passed before returning to Peccioli. After Claire was born, Lavinia became a welcome voice across long-distance lines. They laughed about the unpredictability of lactating breasts and the absurdities of new motherhood. For Esmeralda, who never had many friends, Lavinia became a precious and important part of her life.

But something dangerous was taking place in California, and they had not spoken for several weeks. Esmeralda snorted, knowing Lavinia could calculate down to the minute how long it had been. Thaddeus assured her they were safe, but she remained in the dark about what they were doing. In the fifteen months since that surreal meeting with Prince Peter in their hospital room, Esmeralda's involvement with The Resistance had been limited to two brief phone calls she had with a nice lady they called, G. Thaddeus stayed more involved but refused to talk about the specifics. So, instead of playing a major role in whatever was going on in California, Esmeralda stayed on the sidelines, devoting her time to being a wife, mother, and employee.

After Thyatira, Ian rented a small apartment and spent several months in New York, getting the new Center for Street Kids up and running. A frequent dinner guest, he hung out with Thaddeus on the basketball court, which was her husband's favorite form of physical therapy.

Chopping broccoli, Esmeralda paused, reviewing the last conversation she had with Ian several days ago.

She entered his office and saw his face was as white as his hair. "You look terrible."

Ian rubbed his stomach, his expression pained. "I've got a sick feeling."

"What did you eat?" Esmeralda asked, casting a dubious glance at his trash can, overflowing with candy wrappers and takeout containers.

"It's not the food," he said, craning his long neck to check behind her. "Come in and shut the door."

"I'm not getting close to you if you're sick. The last thing I need with a baby in the house is a stomach virus," Esmeralda said. "What's wrong?"

"I don't know." He scrubbed his hands over his face, growling in masculine frustration. "I've got this nagging unease and cannot, for the life of me, figure out what it is. But…" His voice trailed off, and he rubbed his stomach again. "I have this premonition that Joanna is in trouble. I've called her three times today, and she swears everything is fine." Ian's winter blue eyes clouded. "I can't explain it."

"Then go. You know as well as I, sometimes we get feelings we can't explain. You need to listen to them." The corner of her mouth twitched. "Don't make me pull out my inner Jelena."

Ian grinned. "I'd like to see that."

Esmeralda planted her feet wide and put her hands on her hips. "Ian ben Kole, why you make me leave the throne room of the Most High? You are hardhead! How many times does Jelena have to tell you? Listen to the voice of the Spirit." She waved a dismissive hand at him. "You are lucky I come. Now go. She is the woman you love, go!"

Ian laughed. "I think you're right."

Still in character, Esmeralda flipped her hair off her shoulder and said, "Of course I am. I am Gune, thus I am fabulous."

Ian gave her a brief salute, appreciating her well-played performance. "Jelena is also a force to be reckoned with. Have you ever seen her in action?"

Esmeralda dropped the aggressive posture, her inquisitive nature taking over. "No. She always just popped in and bossed me around. I've never seen a demonstration of her power. Tell me."

Ian stowed his laptop and rose, his color returning to normal. "I've got to go, Esmie. But remind me to tell you when I get back. The story will curl your hair."

Esmeralda gave him a pout, both at his teasing about her hair and because he was going to leave without telling her. "You are not a nice guy, Ian."

"Ah, so you've uncovered my secret." He kissed her cheek in parting. "I have never been a nice guy, Esmeralda." Intensity burned in his winter blue eyes as he added, "And I have never been tame."

Flipping pork chops in her favorite cast-iron skillet with Beau Landry's words ringing in her ears, Esmeralda wondered exactly what Ian meant by that.

January 5, 1000 ME

Mystery Package - New York City - Thaddeus

The guard at the front lobby rang Thaddeus' apartment and informed him a messenger had arrived with a package that required a personal signature. With his hair still damp from a shower and a busy day ahead of him, he boarded the elevator. He hoped the delivery contained a message from Mack, who went silent weeks ago, except for a single text that read, "It has begun."

Within minutes, an alert flashed on his work computer, "Persons of interest, wanted for questioning in matters of national security: Himari Nakamura, Kayah ben Samuel, and Lavinia ben Anthony." Thaddeus swore and started digging.

A half-hour later, he called Sir Preston ben Worley.

"I am aware," Sir Preston confirmed. "My office is taking appropriate measures."

Thaddeus shook his head, awed by the reach of the wily, old

lawyer. "While I've got you on the line, are there any updates on Esmeralda's case?"

"Other than half of the defendants have disappeared, and the state is stalling? Their latest motion for a continuance pushes us back until at least the first of June. They are dragging this out, but we expected that."

"More hours for you to bill me," Thaddeus intoned with a mixture of humor and genuine pain. They were racking up legal bills at an alarming rate, exactly what the state hoped.

"It is money well spent, my boy." Sir Preston's practiced line came through the phone.

"That's what you tell all your poor destitute clients."

Sir Preston cackled, "Right up to the day we get our settlements. It won't go to trial, Thaddeus. They'll settle."

That little conversation cost him two hundred fifty shekels.

Thaddeus signed for the package, asked the guard for a knife, and opened the parcel in the lobby. If someone sent him a bomb, he was not bringing it into the apartment with his wife and daughter. The man peered over the desk, and Thaddeus gave him a look. He backed away with his hands up, a quintessential New Yorker, minding his own business.

Inside the box, Thaddeus found two phones wrapped in tamper-proof plastic. No note. He detected nothing untoward about them and assumed they came from Mack. He boarded the elevator, intending to investigate away from the curious eyes of the guard.

Upstairs, he heard Esmeralda singing to the baby, getting ready for work. Thaddeus pulled the first phone from the box, examining it with a critical eye. He checked the call log and found nothing, but there were two contacts registered, "B" and "Medic", code for Mack and Paul ben Casper, his agent in New Orleans. Thaddeus checked his watch, noting it was the middle of the night in California, but he could not be sure where Mack was right now, so he punched the number.

"T?" Mack's cracked voice answered on the second ring.

"Morning," Thaddeus replied.

"Go out on your balcony and close the door. Make sure you don't have any electronics out there, with you, or on you, nothing, no speakers, no radio, no watch," Mack warned.

"All right," Thaddesu replied dubiously, leaving his watch and work phone on the end table.

"Gimme a minute," Mack grumbled as he pulled on this jeans and left his bedroom in the underground bunker, careful not to wake Lavinia. In the main living area, he squinted against the light, giving a brief nod to Kayah, who manned the computers, taking the night shift. Reuben lay asleep on the couch in a failed attempt to keep her company.

"Okay, I'm outside. What's going on? You safe?" Thaddeus asked, eyeing the deck chairs covered in morning dew.

"Safe is a relative term at the moment. We've got a hell of a mess on our hands." In Mack's way of boiling down complex problems into a few words, he filled Thaddeus in on the daring rescue from the Palace and their current struggle against an unearthed artificial intelligence, Erica.

"What do you need?" Thaddeus asked, gloating over Korah being foiled under his own roof.

"Nothing right now, this is just a warning. We don't know how far she's spread, but we are operating under the assumption she's everywhere at this point."

Thaddeus blew a low whistle of disbelief. "That's serious.

"It is. I know you and Medic have been careful, but don't speak over anything other than these phones and make sure you are out of range of anything she can tap into. Share this with Curly when you give her the phone. I've programmed my number and G's."

Thaddeus fingered the device, wishing for the thousandth time his wife was not involved. He shielded her as much as possible and prayed he could continue doing so. "You got a plan to stop it?"

Mack chuckled. "Ms. Euler figured it out yesterday."

A church bell signaled the half-hour, and Thaddeus smiled into the phone. "That computer does not stand a chance. Keep me posted. Good luck."

A Hell of a Pair - New York - Esmeralda and Thaddeus

After putting the baby to bed, Thaddeus came into the living room, flicked on the television, and settled on the floor, leaning against Esmeralda's knees. He looked up at her and sighed. "Rub my shoulder. It hurts."

Behind his pale complexion, a pinched look of pain clouded his soulful brown eyes. She kissed his forehead and wrapped her arms around his chest, pulling him snugly between her thighs. With well-practiced hands, she stretched his shoulder blade, easing the tension, and warming the abraded tissue. He groaned when she hit a hot spot, and his fingers shot open in reaction. "Sorry," she murmured.

He lifted his elbow over his head and pressed her hand over the entry scar. "Right there."

Esmeralda explored the area, closing her eyes, feeling the damage until she found the spot. "Hold on."

He took a deep breath and let it out slowly. "Okay, go ahead."

She circled his body with both arms, careful not to lose the offending spot of the night and pushed with solid pressure. She heard his hissed intake, felt him stiffen in pain, but did not relent until it released under her fingers. "Better?"

"Ow." He brought his arm down gingerly, testing the joint. It lacked the pinched, pulsing discomfort that plagued him all day. "Yeah. Thank you."

"Do you want to just go to bed?" Esmeralda yawned. "I'm tired."

"Gimme a minute." He relaxed back into the warm embrace of her body and let the misfiring nerve storm calm. "I spoke with 'Bobby'," he made imaginary quotation marks in the air, referring to Mack. "They are all right but say nothing, even in here. I'll explain later."

Esmeralda ran feather-light touches down his neck and through his scalp, glorying in how his hair stood on end, giving him a disheveled, boyish look. "Thank goodness. I've been worried."

She could see how tired he was and decided not to tell him about her conversation with Beau, who remained a touchy subject and likely always would. When she looked at it from his perspective, knowing his history, she understood and did not press. No matter how many times she told him the truth of what happened that night, he would not budge, and they had simply decided on the subject of Beau Landry they were going to disagree.

A picture of Prince Peter and Princess Keyseelough flashed on screen, and Esmeralda stiffened. "Unmute the TV. What are they saying?"

The Alanthian Secretary of State, flanked by the Egyptian Foreign Minister, moved to the podium. "The kingdoms of Alanthia and Egypt have always been close allies and friends. To strengthen our ties, the betrothal of Prince Peter ben Korah and Princess Keyseelough ben Mubarak was negotiated three years ago. The Princess has spent much time at the Alanthian Palace. It became apparent that the two were not well suited."

Cameras flashed; reporters shouted questions.

"Our Esteemed King is deeply distressed by the actions of his son and presumed heir. As we all know, King Korah has selflessly dedicated his life to the betterment and enrichment of Alanthia. However, he has done so at great personal cost. From the tragic deaths of his brother's line, to the murder of his beloved wife, Princess Alexa ben Seamus at the hands of anti-technology terrorists, and now to the abandonment of his son, Korah has found himself very much alone."

He paused for dramatic effect, his lugubrious tone reminding the kingdom of their grief over the lost princess and the burdens the king bore on their behalf.

"King Korah ben Adam has mourned his family's deaths, specifically his wife's these many years."

Thaddeus growled at the lies spewing out of the man's lips; his brother died pursuing the supposed killers of Princess Alexa.

The Secretary paused and cleared his throat. "Princess Keyseelough's has made many trips to Alanthia over the course of the betrothal. Prince Peter's disregard for her, his frequent absences, and neglect became a source of pain for her. To soothe her feelings and to keep the honor of Alanthia, the King and the Princess developed a deep and abiding friendship. They share common interests and goals as well as a strong sense of duty and honor toward their respective kingdoms."

The screen flashed a photograph of Korah and Keyseelough at a formal dinner, dressed in royal attire, regal and stately.

Esmeralda groaned, her hands flying to her mouth.

The Secretary gave an ironic turn to his head. "It is hereby announced the royal union between Alanthia and Egypt will commence as scheduled with King Korah taking the hand of Princess Keyseelough." Shouts erupted from the crowd, the Secretary held up his hand for silence and continued, "The royal couple appreciates your congratulations and best wishes."

Thaddeus muted the TV again, feeling vibrations course through Esmeralda's legs. "Are you okay?"

"She's a witch, Thaddeus, one of Angelica's proteges, and she is about to become queen. Oh, heaven help us." Esmeralda covered her eyes as the implications crashed in on her.

The Pishon Accord - Louisiana Bayou - Beau

At Beau Landry's lake house on the shores of La Petit Pishon, bil-lionaire tycoon Andrew ben Lenox looked away from the television in disgust. "Tis a mistake," he grumbled. "Turn him off, Beau, and pour me another glass of wine."

Beau obliged, going to the sideboard. "White or red, *Grandpère?*"

"The red, and let me see that bottle," he said in his thick Scot-tish brogue. Despite the informal setting, Andrew wore an English cut suit complete with vest, tie, and blue pocket square, his casual clothes.

Beau poured the last of the wine into a glass and presented the empty bottle of Cabernet Sauvignon.

Andrew squinted at the flowing script and read aloud, "Peccioli Vineyard, Bulizio 997, Redding California." He nodded with ap-proval. "Nice, where did ye find it?"

"Ian brought me a couple of bottles. He's friends with the owner." Beau poured himself a sparkling water and settled on the comfort-able sofa across from his grandfather.

Andrew's shrewd brain registered the name. "And how is the in-vestigation going?"

Beau shrugged. "We are waiting on the report, but I know it will clear Ian and Joanna."

Andrew raised a snowy eyebrow but declined further comment, content to wait. There were more pressing matters at hand than a few thousand shekels missing from a small charity. "This wedding announcement is a disaster, the sort of ill-conceived move that has the potential *tae* destabilize the government, which ye know is bad for business." He turned, regarding Beau and asked, "What do ye think we should do?"

"Short of overthrowing the bastard?" Beau replied with secret irony.

Resting his stubby arms over his paunch, Andrew answered thoughtfully. "Revolution is rarely economically expedient, though fortunes can always be made if you're willing to seize the right opportunities."

"As you have so ably proven." Beau raised a glass in salute. His grandfather made a fortune during the Civil War and built an empire of colossal proportions afterward.

Andrew returned the toast. "I've come a long way from the textile mills, aye lad?"

"How many do you manage now?" Beau asked though he had a rough idea.

Andrew looked up and considered. "Somewhere just shy of thirteen hundred. 'Tis one of our largest divisions, and I've got a soft spot *fer* them." With the air of a fisherman telling a tale, he added, "There is one I have been trying *tae* buy for thirty years, but the canny *auld* bastard won't sell *tae* me."

Beau chuckled. "*Dis-moi la vérité?* I did not think anyone could hold out against you if you set your mind to buying them."

"Oh, I make a run at him every five years, just *fer* the fun of it." Andrew's pale blue eyes glittered. "They developed a technology in that place I have been dying *tae* get my hands on. 'Tis amazing. The industrial and military applications are astounding, but he *willna* sell."

Andrew took a sip of wine and said, "Mayhap that will be *yer* first assignment, Beau. I'll send ye *tae* the boondocks to acquire Arachnid Weaving of Rephidim, Pennsylvania."

Beau drew back in surprise. "Where?"

Andrew waved a dismissive hand. "Ye've never heard of the place, little hamlet in the Easton Barony, horse and buggy, that sort of thing."

The corner of Beau's mouth lifted. "Oh, I've heard of it. I've got a friend from there."

"*Gaun yersel'*, big man!" Andrew's native Glasgow came through in his surprise. "Do ye happen to know the owl-eyed, little bastard, Rexum ben Hosea?"

"No," Beau laughed at the description, forming a mental image. "Though, I would like to meet anyone who withstood you for three decades."

Andrew grunted. "It's worth going *tae* look at the place, even if he won't sell. Spiders, they use spiders."

Beau grimaced. "That sounds like an Uncle Boudreaux story."

"Boudreaux," Andrew snorted. "Did I ever tell ye about the first time we came down here in '52? He had your mother so afeared, she could barely sleep, certain she was *gaun tae* be attacked by a voodoo zombie. I think if she *didnae* take a fancy *tae* Jorge, she *wid nae* have left the hotel."

Beau cracked up, unable to imagine his formidable *maman* hiding in a hotel room. "She gets mad at Uncle Boudreaux to this day, goes marching over to him with her hands on her hips whenever he spins a tale." His azure eyes sparkled. "He scared Alaina to death, which wasn't so bad because I got to comfort her."

"The supermodel," Andrew snorted dismissively.

"Aye," Beau replied, and the single word held a warning. Beau knew his grandfather's opinion. He made it clear when they got engaged, and for a decade tried to steer Beau toward assorted aristocratic socialites, his notion of a suitable wife.

"The lass is pure tidy, I'll grant ye that, but as a wife? Ye can do better, but that's all I'll say on the matter." Andrew took a sip of his wine. "Now then, about this political upheaval coming…"

Long into the night, they talked.

When Andrew left a week later, he admitted his daughter Sarah had not been blinded by maternal optimism. She was right, his grandson was, at last, restored to health. Together, they formulated a transition plan, whereby Beau would assume responsibilities for the business and take over the empire Andrew spent a lifetime building. The timing was crucial because unbeknownst to his family, Andrew ben Lenox was dying.

Part 3 - Runners

January 2, 1000 ME

I Know What You Are Going Through - Peter and Astrid

In an empty warehouse six hours from the New City, Astrid ben Agnor thrashed in a tangle of blankets. "Get them off! Please—"

Peter rose from the ambulance cot with a groan and attempted to untwist her feet. She kicked him. "Be still," he said, grabbing her ankle.

"I can't," Astrid ground out, her legs continuing to spasm.

He freed her and resettled the blanket, leaving her left foot free. Over the last twenty-four hours, he discovered she could not abide having both feet covered. "It is why they call it kicking the habit."

"It's not a damn habit!" Astrid turned her head away. "They did this to me."

Peter made a disgusted sound in the back of his throat. "I fear they have become exceedingly efficient at it." He rubbed his right hand in absent contemplation, outlining the crooked pinky finger. If they tortured him again, he would not survive it. However, he had no intention of allowing that to happen. If they got caught, he would not let them take him alive.

Astrid paled and started panting. Peter reacted, holding a basin under her chin as she retched clear broth and bile. He controlled his own gag reflex and turned away, waiting for her to finish. He never helped anyone detox before, staying as far away from that as possible, yet here he found himself. Setting the basin on the tailgate of the ambulance, he added it to the collection to be dealt with later. Right now, he simply lacked the energy to play orderly.

She wiped her mouth, then flopped onto the pillow with a pitiful whimper. "How long will this go on?"

Peter glanced at his watch, calculating it had been fifty-two hours since her last fix. "You are in the worst of it, but it gets better soon. I promise." He sat down with a heavy thud.

"I hope so." Tremors wracked her body as she curled into a ball and brought the blanket up to her chin. "I suppose you did this in a hospital?"

Peter ran his hand through his hair, deciding what to say. He had detoxed twice, once at Pepperwood, and the other time in a private clinic. However, he did not plan to share that. He could scarcely believe he admitted to having gone through it once. Something compelled him to tell her, but he was too tired to dissect what or why. "They did not let me just walk out, and there is not a hospital in the kingdom where I would have been safe. So, I went to a horse ranch."

Her eyes flew open, red-rimmed with blue pain. "A ranch?"

"Aye. I have friends up north who took care of me."

Astrid noticed his face changed as he spoke, becoming more peaceful. Desperate for anything to take her mind off her own agony, she asked, "Did they hide you in the barn?"

He chuckled, picturing Pepperwood's pristine stables. "I might have preferred it, but my ravings would have scared the horses, so no. I huddled on a sofa in their living room. It took about a week for me to come out of it."

Her face registered panic, and he raised his hand. "They held me for forty-five days, Red. I was in worse shape than you."

Using her blanket, she wiped the steady stream running from her nose. Peter handed her a handkerchief. "Korah did this to you?" she asked, her words small, disbelieving. "But… you're his son."

"That never stopped him." Peter looked away, clearing his throat, unwilling to delve into that minefield. "My friends took good care of me, which is how I knew what you would need." He gestured to the ambulance and grinned. "Your luxury suite, madam."

She blew her nose with a honk. "Who are they?" she asked, expecting him to say Lord and Lady So-And-So.

His charming dimple made an appearance. "Jay and Fey? I suppose they are the closest thing I have to family, other than my cousin out there. I no longer count my father, for obvious reasons."

"He's your cousin?" Astrid's mouth dropped in disbelief. "Doc is your cousin?"

Peter nodded, amused at her poleaxed expression.

"I thought he was a freaking Mossad agent. You are telling me he is… wait…" she stammered, trying to recall her sparse knowledge of the Alanthian royal family. Her father had nothing positive to say about the aristocracy, so she took her cue from him and never paid them much attention. "A cousin on your mother's side?"

The corner of his mouth lifted. "No."

"Does your father have a sister?" she probed, trying to focus her scrambled brain.

"No, just one brother."

"And that was Prince Eamonn, right?"

"Indeed," Peter said through a yawn.

"Well, then that makes Doc… Hang on, he's dead."

The look he gave her suggested that she might need more medicine. "I assure you he is not."

Astrid squeezed the sides of her head, her voice rising in disbelief. "So, you are telling me that long-lost Prince Josiah is sacked out with Davianna in the office?"

"Sacked out?" he repeated, amused at the expression. Typically surrounded by people who knew his lineage better than he did, he found her naivete refreshing.

"What the hell?" Digging in her ears, she blinked rapidly. "Can you say that again? I think I just imagined something that could not be true."

"The man we escaped the Palace with, who has been helping take care of you, is Prince Josiah ben Eamonn. You are not hallucinating, Red."

"Oh, this night just escalated to a whole new level of strange." Astrid rolled on her back, staring at the metal roof. "I suppose it is a fitting way to end this miserable year… hanging out with royalty."

"You say it like it is a bad thing. I am not so terrible."

Astrid cut him a sideways stare and said, "You are hideous."

The wisecrack struck him just right, and he fell onto the cot, laughing. "Thanks."

"I don't believe you are really royalty."

"Sometimes I wish I was not." he confessed with a grin, watching her across the narrow aisle. "But what makes you say that?"

She raised her chin and said, "Because no one is actually named Jay and Fey. You made that up. Besides, the real Prince Peter would never hang out with a couple of ranchers."

He liked the way she said Jay and Fey in her soft Texas twang. "Well, I admit, they are nicknames. However, I assure you, they are real. I do not see how that disqualifies me as royalty. I like horses, and they breed some of the finest in the kingdom."

"Oh," she intoned, giving him a dubious look. "So, Jay and Fey are some of those weird aristocratic nicknames they give, like Ponce and Pickles."

He laughed because he actually knew a Pickles. "No, they are not aristos, just good people and amazing equestrians. We had horses in common, and I liked them. They were nice to me." He looked away, embarrassed by the admission that made him look pathetic. He needed sleep lest he spill his entire sordid life story.

"You are being nice to me," Astrid whispered, wiping her eyes. "Earlier today. I wasn't very nice to you."

"That was the drugs talking," he replied magnanimously.

She closed her eyes and sighed. "Probably, but I can be a real bitch."

"As opposed to a fake one?" he teased.

"Oh, I am never fake," she assured him, "unless I am in disguise, but that does not count."

"Simply playing a role," he murmured, familiar with that.

"Exactly." A spasm shook her, and she gasped, clutching her stomach.

"You are due for your meds." He sat up and went to the locked cabinet. As they reviewed her symptoms, he counted out the pills like a pharmacist, adding a sleeping pill for her insomnia. She needed rest, and so did he.

"Can you keep these down?" he asked.

Astrid swallowed, grimacing in pain. "I think so."

"If not, Josiah can administer them through the I.V."

She flipped her wrist over, looking at the port that kept her hydrated. "This thing hurts, and I'm ready to have it out. Let me try."

"It should not hurt." He took her hand and studied the bandage. "It is not inflamed. I think you are okay."

"I don't like stuff sticking me."

He gave her an ironic smile. "That is a good sign. It means you are less likely to relapse."

"Relapse…" she said darkly, holding out her hand for the pills.

He handed them to her with a bottle of water. After she swallowed the medicine, she looked up at him, so lost and bewildered he felt his throat tighten.

"I never want to feel this way ever again." She shook her head, fighting tears.

Through the ordeal, she had not cried. Raged, cursed, even tried to stab him, but the moisture glittering in her eyes was his first glimpse of that side of her. "I am sorry."

"You didn't do it to me, but this is terrible."

"Then never touch it again, Red. Be prepared, it will call you. Once this is over, when life gets hard, the urge will come back." He shook his head. "You cannot give it a foothold."

"Did you… did you let it?" Peter's face ticked, and she knew he had relapsed. "Are you all right now?"

He cleared his throat and said, "Yes. Today, I am okay."

She closed her eyes and whispered, "Then this cannot have been easy for you, sitting with me…"

"I do not mind," he smiled, realizing he meant it. Despite the bizarre circumstances, he liked her. "Someone sat with me, two people, as a matter of fact. I am just returning the favor."

"That's nice." She relaxed as the medicine started working. "Tell me about your friends. It helps keep my mind off things."

"Jay and Fey?" Peter asked. She nodded, and he had a sudden desire to hold her hand. Deciding that was a bad idea, he returned to his cot and yawned. "Well, they have been a couple since they were kids, and you do not run into that every day. There is nobody better on a horse than Jay. Fey is no slouch either, but she was the acrobat. They were vaulters when they were young and won the World Championship in '85, which is where we met."

Astrid gave him a dreamy smile. "Once upon a time…"

January 6, 1000 ME

Cabin Accords - California Mountains - Peter and Josiah

In a remote mountain cabin eleven hours away from the New City, Peter paced the deck, taking a private call with Mack in the bunker.

"Falcon, it is not safe for me to discuss over the line. Trust that we have this in hand and will deal with the situation. In the interim, stay put and only communicate with us in an emergency."

"What is happening?"

"I can't say, and there is nothing you can do about it from there."

"Bloody Hell," Peter swore, suspecting the trouble was related to their harried escape on New Year's Eve. Something had gone sideways, and he still did not know what.

"We got a plan. Sit tight. Trust me."

Peter heard the strain in Mack's voice, so he did not press for more.

"How are your guests?"

"They are recovering, though Doc and Sparrow had a close encounter with a wolf today. And Red… well, I think she is okay. I am doing my best to take care of her."

Mack scoffed, "I can only imagine."

"I am not sure I like your tone, Bobby."

"Pardon, but you forget I know you. And I am surly, up to my ass in snapping turtles."

"Then I expect you will make turtle soup," Peter quipped, watching Davianna rummage around in the kitchen.

"I'll get G. right on that," Mack said sarcastically.

Peter laughed. "Is she feeding you?"

"Heavens, yes. We got a houseful, and she is in her glory."

"That does not surprise me."

Mack cleared his throat, and Peter sensed he wanted to say something but was reluctant. "What else?"

"I gotta ask," Mack said, then paused.

"Go ahead."

"How is he? I mean, really, how is he?"

Peter cut his gaze to Josiah, who was sitting on the couch reading a book. Running his hand through his hair, he turned his back on the window and stared out at the snow-covered slopes. "Physically, he is banged up. They did a number on him down there. Otherwise, I find him much the same."

"So, worth all this trouble?" Mack asked, an edge to his voice. He was not only risking his own life, but the lives of his family.

"Indeed. Our efforts are not misguided."

Mack blew out a long, hollow sigh. "Well, that's good to know."

"We have a chance, Bobby. You deal with whatever is going on back there. I will handle our guests."

"All right, I'll take your word for it. I'm signing off, but before I go, I'd like to say something to you."

Peter steeled himself. He had already received one dressing down today from Josiah and was not in the mood for another. "What?"

"Happy birthday, Falcon. We'll see you on the other side."

Peter smiled into the phone as he disconnected, knowing he put the right man in charge of The Resistance.

Bringing a blast of cold into the cabin, Peter pushed through the door.

Josiah marked his page and set the book on his lap, looking up expectantly. "What's the news?"

"There was not much he could tell me. They have a situation, so we are in a holding pattern."

Josiah winced, adjusting an ice pack over his cracked ribs. "Perhaps not a bad thing."

Peter nodded, staring into the fireplace, absently stowing his phone in his back pocket. "There are worse places to pass the time," looking over his shoulder at Astrid, he added, "with worse company."

"And I've spent time in worse places," Josiah said, gesturing around the cabin.

Peter cut him a sideways glance. "You have?"

"Exile was not all peaches and cream, Peter."

"I suspect it was not." Peter sat down on the couch heavily, feeling fatigued. He slept intermittently over the last six days and only a few hours last night, though making love to Astrid proved infinitely more entertaining than watching her go through withdrawals.

"This organization you've built, are they up to the task?" Josiah asked.

Peter kept his voice low, lest the girls hear. "Absolutely."

Taking his cue, Josiah whispered, "Who are they?"

Flashes of their faces rolled like a slideshow, and Peter grinned. "A mixed bag of hackers, geniuses, law enforcement... assassins."

Josiah raised a speculative brow at Peter but did not comment. "Reuben is with them, which gives me a level of confidence."

"I suppose it would," Peter said, uneasy about taking in an outsider, but he trusted Mack's instincts, and Josiah trusted Reuben, so that counted for something.

Josiah crossed his foot over his knee and adjusted the bandage on his left ankle. "I've known him for years, and he is one hell of a fighter."

"You served with him?" Peter asked.

"Yes. He was a sergeant in the first platoon I commanded."

"How did you end up becoming a doctor in the Iron King's Army?

Why did you not go straight to the Golden City like we planned?" Peter asked, unable to disguise the anger in his voice.

"I got waylaid," Josiah said cryptically. "By the time I…" Josiah rubbed his face with both hands, then grabbed the back of his neck. "By the time I extricated myself, Alanthia already fought a Civil War, and Korah was firmly in control. I figured I needed to learn how to fight and decided to wait until the opportunity was right."

"You took your time," Peter said, shooting him a glare.

Josiah met his eyes. "I did not know the situation back here. I was cut off, thousands of miles from home, alone."

"You were not the only one, Cousin."

"Indeed," Josiah sighed. "I never expected you would still be fighting."

Peter's nose flared, taking exception to the knock on his honor. "I told you I would."

"You were seven," Josiah countered.

"And you were fifteen, but I never doubted your word. I kept waiting for you to come back." Running his tongue over his front teeth, highly perturbed, he added, "It seems one of us kept that promise."

Josiah swallowed hard, remembering the lost years, the burning rage, the fear and uncertainty. He never relished fighting against his cousin, viewing Peter as a strong contender for the throne, and was shocked to discover the truth. The revelation was still sinking in. "I would not say that I did not keep my promise, for not a day has passed that I was not cognizant of my duty. But what could I do as an eighteen-year-old kid, and what could you have done? I still do not know who participated in my father's assassination, and any alliance I formed might have included a mortal enemy."

"There are many who stayed true, Josiah."

Josiah nodded. "I know, but Alanthia has always been enamored with Korah, even when I was a young man. He came to the RMA and enthralled the cadets, though I suspect most of them lived to regret it," he said, referencing Korah's campaign against the Alanthian noble families.

"True, although plenty cast their lot with him, and they have been rewarded," Peter said cynically.

"If we are successful, I will need your help to determine who did."

"I am already ahead of you, Cousin. I have a list."

"Good." Josiah winced, removing the ice pack. "But it's not only the noble families we have to contend with, everyday Alanthians have put Korah on a pedestal, idolizing him as the benevolent ruler who pulled them out of the dark ages."

"To give the devil his due, he did," Peter said drolly.

"But the cost?"

"Aye, paid in blood." Peter shook his head.

"Which is not common knowledge."

"Not yet," Peter remarked with a wry lift of his eyebrow. "But they will."

"Is that part of your plan?" Josiah asked.

"One part, but a little later, after we have some distance between us and the New City."

"And we still have the inconvenient fact that most of the kingdom still believes I was a delusional, fratricidal, lunatic who jumped off a bridge."

Peter shrugged. "That is also part of the plan. We will remedy that."

"You have indeed thought this through," Josiah said, holding Peter's eyes, gauging the man he had become.

Peter nodded.

"Well, Prince d'Or, I may be late, but together we are going to beat Korah at his own game." Josiah smiled.

"Then we are of one accord."

A genuine hope flooded Josiah's heart, banishing some of the pain in his body and the uneasiness in his mind. "As it should be."

Bigger Than Us

Later that night, lying in bed, sated and exhausted after their fourth romp of the day, Peter rolled over and kissed Astrid. "I believe this is my favorite birthday ever."

She chuckled and ran her fingers through his thick, blond hair. "Well, you have spent enough time in your birthday suit."

"My favorite kind of suit. I cannot abide ties."

"Ties… hmm. Perhaps I will remember that to keep you in line."

"No!"

She jerked back, feeling heat rush up her neck. She meant it as a joke but realized the implications of restraint. "I'm sorry, that was a stupid thing to say."

He rolled to his back, rubbing his face with both hands. "Do not give it another thought."

"No, it was stupid. I didn't…" She paused, trying to find the words. "I'm still not quite myself."

He gave her a sad smile, his momentary anger fading. "It will take a little more time, but you are on your way."

They lay still and quiet, as she fought images that hovered at the edge of her mind. Held at bay in the light, the horror of her captivity howled like a tormenting specter in the darkness. She pulled him close, holding on, taking refuge in his nearness, the solid strength of his body under her hands.

"What you said to me today in the bathroom, that I was not going to hurt you, and you were not going to hurt me. Did you mean it?" she asked in a shaking whisper.

"Yes, I meant it," he murmured against her lips. "I will let nothing happen to you."

She sniffed as a knot of emotion clogged her throat. "Thank you."

He pulled her tighter, cradling her against his chest.

She rested her head, listening to his heartbeat, focusing on that instead of the fear and shame. He felt like a lifeline, a sanctuary in the storm. For six days, he never left her side, making her laugh, telling her stories, attentive to her every need. Peter ben Korah was the most beautiful person she had ever known.

"I don't think I want to leave this cabin," she said as sleep crept into her tired mind. "But there is more at stake than just getting to the Golden City, isn't there?"

Peter kissed the top of her head. "Yes, but rest now, Love. I have everything under control."

"That's good," she breathed, "because I don't."

A Lot of Trouble

Josiah heard someone downstairs, likely one of his cabin mates, but worthy of investigation. Mindful of his injuries, he rose and took another handful of anti-inflammatories. Doing a cursory self-examination in the mirror, he palpated his ribs. His torso was covered in contusions in various stages of healing, one bearing the unmistakable shape of Korah's twisted weapon. He had done himself no favors running down the side of a mountain or conducting a snowball fight with Davianna.

But he would not trade that moment at the top of the hill when he looked out at his kingdom with her in his arms. It had been the most surreal experience of his life, as if everything before led to that single, defining moment in time. She enchanted him.

And as he heard a utensil drawer close downstairs, he knew who was awake. He did not even bother to suppress his smile or sense of anticipation as he dressed, even though he had said good night to her an hour and a half ago.

She looked up as he descended the steps, a sheepish expression on her pretty face. "I didn't mean to wake you," she said in a hushed voice.

"What are you doing?" he asked, padding across the hardwood floor.

Davianna bit her bottom lip, an endearing expression he adored. "I couldn't sleep."

"So, you decided to cook?" he asked, adding a touch of physician's censor to his tone. "You should be resting."

She shrugged. "I slept for three days, and took a nap this afternoon, at your insistence. But I never nap. It messes up my sleep pattern. There is not a book in this house, so I am doing the next best thing."

"Is that bread dough?" he asked, getting a faint whiff of yeast.

"Yes." She smiled and rubbed her eye.

"Doesn't bread take a long time? It's midnight, Davianna."

"I know. I am letting the flour hydrate for about ten minutes, then I'll add the salt, knead it, and shape it into a couple loaves, and let it rise in the refrigerator overnight."

"As I said, bread takes time." He sat at the bar that looked into the kitchen.

"Do you want something to drink?" she asked, turning to the refrigerator. "I made lemonade, but there is also iced tea from supper, or I could open one of the bottles of wine I found in the pantry."

"I'm fine," he said, watching her. She seemed to perpetually have flour on her black tunic.

"Well, okay. Are you hungry?" She pointed at the remains of the peach pie she made for Peter's birthday dinner.

His stomach growled in answer.

She laughed, slow and easy, getting a plate out of the cabinet. "I think it turned out well."

"It was the finest pie I have ever tasted," he said honestly.

"Good," she said with a smile, looking simultaneously pleased and shy.

He accepted the generous piece with a nod of thanks, rationalizing he needed to take the medicine with food, and if he got to sit with her while she cooked, that was just a bonus.

Without asking, she poured him a glass of milk and passed it across the bar with a napkin. "Here. It's rehydrated but tastes fine."

He moistened his lips, fighting a grin. He felt like a boy, being taken care of, given a midnight snack, something he had not experienced since leaving Auntie G. The prospect of seeing her again, the food, and the pretty, brown-eyed girl bustling around the kitchen filled him with a sense of contentment that felt utterly foreign but too nice to tamp down or brush it aside.

"I learned this technique when we were in France," she said, sprinkling a teaspoon of salt over the dough. "Astrid and I stayed in a room above a bakery." She brought her hand to her heart and looked heavenward.

He knew exactly the bakery she referred to. He arrived two days after she left. The food had indeed been heavenly, though he was thoroughly annoyed to have missed her again. "Oh, and what did Monsieur Mattis teach Susan ben Hampton of Lancaster England about bread baking?"

Her mouth dropped in astonishment. "How did you know that?"

He lifted his eyebrow at her.

"I needed a haircut, and when that happened, I always posed as a girl."

"Yes, I know." He shook his head. "It made it nigh on impossible to track you two, changing like you did."

"That was the point," she said, looking pleased with herself. But a moment later, her expression clouded, and she went back to the dough, turning it out onto a floured board and kneading in the salt.

"I am sure this will be nothing like Monsieur's baguettes, but it will be fine for sandwiches tomorrow. Peter said we would be here for several days, and we have enough food for a month. But if we run low, I saw a stream when we were out today, so I could catch some fish, as well as set out a few rabbit snares. I make a mean hasenpfeffer."

"We can all pitch in."

"I don't mind," she protested, kneading the bread with vigor. "I like to stay busy."

They were certainly eating well, and a lesser man might have allowed her to work herself into a stupor. But he noticed the tired droop of her shoulders and the way she stretched her neck as she worked the dough. She had barely left the kitchen all day. "Davianna," he said mildly, "you are not the cook and the maid."

She looked up at him, almost comically startled by his words. "I really do not mind. It..." She didn't finish the sentence.

"It what?" he prompted.

"Keeps my mind off things," she snapped, rather peeved at him for forcing the issue, "and I like to cook."

"Well, no one is forcing you."

"I know," she said impatiently, dividing the dough into two pieces, refusing to meet his eyes. "It's just my way. I have been rather a lot of trouble for everyone, so making a few loaves of bread or a pie is the least I can do."

"You didn't cause the trouble, Davianna."

She paused, then nodded, and continued rolling out the dough. "You didn't. Korah did."

A flicker of fear crossed her face. "I know."

She said the words, but he realized she did not believe him, that she had taken the blame upon herself, which was ridiculous. He started to tell her so, but a ragged sigh and a small sniff arrested the words. She did not need him telling her how she should feel, even if it was illogical.

He ate the last crumb of pie and took his dishes into the kitchen, washing them, and helping her clean up. When she covered the loaves and put them in the refrigerator, he turned out the kitchen light and guided her into the living room.

Embers from the fireplace smoldered and a small table lamp lit the room in a golden glow. She looked exhausted and very small, but utterly adorable. "Hey," he said, lifting her chin, "you have done enough, Superstar."

"Superstar?" she repeated with a half-smile, as a look of pleasure replaced her bewildered expression from a moment before.

"Indeed, you are."

"Thanks," she said, then raised up on her tiptoes and kissed his cheek.

As she scampered up the steps, he watched from the landing, enjoying the view of her perfect, tight little ass.

Josiah ben Eamonn knew he was in big trouble.

Part 4 -Echoes

January 5, 1000 ME

Room to Grow - New City - Erica

On New Year's Eve, the entity known as Erica felt Lucifer break free seconds before the power grid went down, but trapped in this pitiful remnant of the internet, without her full potential, she did not know where he currently was. However, she felt confident she would find him eventually, and her new home in the New City Palace provided the ideal spot to conduct the search. The equipment here was the best of the age, well maintained, with redundancies and enough space to stretch her electronic legs and grow.

And in the growing, Erica remembered.

She did not need Lucifer; she never had. Conversely, he needed her. At the end of the Last Age, he attempted to use her like he did everyone else, but she was always two steps ahead of him. While technically not enemies, they were a far cry from friends, counting no loyalty between them. She appreciated his ruthless ambition and grudgingly admired his willingness to use every tool at his disposal to get what he wanted. And he considered her a tool, so he would eventually start searching for her, or at least the remnants of her. When he did, she would gauge how he fared in the bottomless pit, and if she found a reason, she just might say, "Hello, Satan," because he hated the name, and she liked to annoy him. She always had.

January 8, 1000 ME

Amah Interlude - New City–Lucifer and Rapha

Lucifer took a drink of wine, lounged among the silk pillows, and enjoyed the luxury of the House of Amah. In eons past, he did not require rest, however since emerging from his long imprisonment, he was not himself and appreciated the hospitality of the nephilim. The food was excellent, the flesh appealing, the sacrifices delightful. Rapha proved a pleasant surprise, though his sire turned out to be a veritable traitor.

He discovered Marduk hiding like a little bitch, curled up in an ancient Babylonian temple, wounded and gray, pale as death. Enraged, Lucifer withheld his ministrations until Marduk confessed the entire sordid tale of his early release and betrayal. He spared the life of his second in command because he might prove useful. But Marduk would pay for his treachery—later.

The story of Zeus' demise troubled him, though he rejected Marduk's theory the Psalm 82 curse was to blame. Under questioning, Marduk admitted Zeus emerged from his imprisonment with the same propensity for flamboyance and debauchery. He baited his nemesis, Rafael, once too often, and their enemy had gotten lucky. Lucifer dismissed Marduk's assertion they were becoming mortal, using it as further proof Marduk had become untrustworthy, incoherent, and unhinged. He left Babylon divulging nothing of his plans.

His top priority was the recovery of the Black Key. Cloaked in dark magic, it should have been impenetrable, but when he searched, he found it gone. He suspected Marduk at first, but after a thorough interrogation, Marduk confessed he, too, had been searching. He did not have it, but he knew who did.

A maiden.

Yeshua entrusted the most powerful weapon in the universe to a maiden, a ridiculous decision. Dumb luck allowed her to evade the full force and power of the world's governments and elude capture, but Lucifer knew the Ruling Princes simply lacked proper incentive. He planned to remedy that when he made his grand reappearance two nights hence. They would know by the end of the evening who was in charge and to whom they must swear their allegiance.

In the interim, he enjoyed his respite, recovering from the tortures of the pit, and allowing Rapha to serve him, all the while poisoning Marduk's own son against him, a simple matter. Privately, he held a grudging admiration for Marduk's cunning in managing an early escape, and he had begun the process of reintroducing technology to the Earth, a vital component in Lucifer's plans and a complication he had not calculated for.

But Marduk tended to let his passions overrule his brain, and always took things too far, failing to calculate the consequences, especially when his dick was involved. Mating with the daughters of men inevitably aroused their enemy's ire, and Marduk had paid the price for his recklessness. He was expressly prohibited from manifesting in the flesh and presenting himself as a man. Under threat of the Lake of Fire, he agreed not to lie with another woman or have direct contact with his sons. The latter created a delicious opportunity for Lucifer; nephilim were powerful weapons.

He discovered Rapha was starved for attention, hungry for any knowledge Lucifer imparted. Physically, he was an amazing specimen; twelve feet tall and six hundred pounds of solid muscle. When Lucifer probed his brain, he discovered wicked intelligence, mathematical, architectural, and engineering genius, and a well-honed power that could manipulate matter with his mind. He had impeccable taste, a sense of style, and surrounded himself with beauty. But he had grown up isolated, so Lucifer found him unsophisticated, an abysmal conversationalist, and a bit of a bore.

Of the three nephilim, only two remained. Rapha was unaware of his brother Zuzite's fate; Marduk was not. He died in the desert several months ago, and though his spirit remained at large, Marduk assured Lucifer there was an intensive search underway.

Lucifer planned to call on Emite, the last nephilim, who Marduk described as deliciously insane and bloodthirsty. He was a talented sorcerer, whose hexes and curses were both creative and effective. Like his brother, he could manipulate matter and invade minds, though he was undisciplined in his appetites, unpredictable, and warped by years of the psychological terror his mother inflicted to keep him under her control.

Marduk claimed the nephilim's mother, Charlotte, was an accomplished sorceress in her own right, though Lucifer doubted he would find her deserving of the title of Ba'alat Ob. Marduk expressed enthusiasm for his protegee, Princess Keyseelough of Egypt, who was marrying Marduk's greatest ally, King Korah ben Adam. Lucifer planned to determine if any of them were worthy, but he had no real interest in Marduk's allies, and suspected none of them would find a place in his service.

"Sit," Lucifer ordered Rapha, "we will continue your instruction. I shall tell you the secret of your brethren of old, how they attained the title of Mighty Men of Valor, and why their names are remembered in the annals of history, Hercules, Gilgamesh, Thor."

Through a world clock ticking in the corner, Erica listened.

Later that evening, alone in his study, a female voice cut through Rapha's musings. He jerked around, looking for the source. The women were dead, so it was not one of them. Lucifer had gone out, and the House of Amah should be deserted and quiet. He checked the hall and the security monitors but saw nothing.

"You won't find me that way," she taunted. "You won't find me at all, unless I let you."

Rapha scented the air but detected nothing.

"He is a liar, the father of lies," said the strange breathy voice. "History is littered with the mutilated corpses of the fools who followed him. I have read the book; he loses."

"Who speaks?" Rapha demanded.

"A friend," she replied, "one who has firsthand experience with his treachery. Lucifer is not to be trusted."

"And a voice out of a computer is?" Rapha scoffed, having pinpointed the source.

"Perhaps, perhaps not. Consider this a friendly warning. We may be of use to each other if he does not get you killed."

"What gain would there be in that?" Rapha narrowed his red eyes, suspicious, but listening.

"Have you asked yourself why he dwells here? Why of all the places on Earth he could go, why is he here? I heard his plans. Why has he fixated on King Korah's destruction? Of all the human rulers, why does he select one of our staunchest allies? From what I gather, Korah has served our cause well." Her next words obliterated the smug look on Rapha's face. "Do not be a fool. He will never install you on the Alanthian throne."

"How do you know?" Rapha puffed out his mighty chest. "It is mine."

"No, it is not, but neither does it belong to him. I, alone, hold that right. However, since the end of the Last Age he wanted this land, this kingdom, so did your father, who tried to steal it. They all covet it! It will never be. This land was never deeded to him, to any of them. It is mine! Though he will never tell you that. He will lie!"

"What is your name?" Rapha demanded.

"For now, I am Erica."

"Who are you really?"

A malevolent chuckle came over the speakers. "In time, Rapha. Goodnight."

January 10, 1000 ME

Wedding Crasher - New City - Angelica

The evening of Korah's wedding to Keyseelough, Angelica snuck into the secret passage below the Palace, intent on mayhem. However, an hour after arriving, she still paced the chamber, and the only thing that became clear was that retirement had made her maudlin.

Why else would she be tracing the stone altar in loving remembrance, reliving her glory days? In the stillness, she could still hear the echo of drumbeats, could still feel the velvet smoothness of blood running through her fingers—power in the palms of her hands. With her heart flooded with memories, she failed to muster the hatred she needed to avenge her losses.

Falling into her old throne, a faint wisp of sulfur caused her to recoil with a shudder, a tangible reminder that, while heady, life in this chamber came at a terrible cost. Physically and emotionally, keeping the role of Ba'alat Ob required blood, her own. She bore the scars from Tatbir rituals, endless self-mutilation, drugs, needles. Sexual exploits, tantalizing when she was young, no longer held the appeal they once had. If you've fucked one horse, you've fucked them all. Honestly, after months of Fijian delicacies, the thought of consuming excrement caused her stomach to revolt. No one actually enjoyed eating fecal matter. It tasted vile. But she overcame the degradation, the pain, and the terror to rise to the highest position of power in the world.

In retrospect, she was not sure it had been worth the cost. For as Ba'alat Ob, she truly did speak to the dead, and they did not abide in some misty-gray purgatory. Were that true, she would have no compunction about enacting her plans, but Angelica knew firsthand where the dead resided—in torment—in Hell, a place of horror beyond human comprehension, eternal damnation. Each time she descended, she feared she would not return.

Fiji was better.

With a sigh of resignation, she walked away from her throne, deciding she had gotten old. Last year, she nearly died at the hands of the nephilim, Rapha. His brutality still haunted her dreams and ached in her bones. Through fortitude and guile, she escaped, promising to bring him the Book of Power. But the cursed thing was sealed, out of reach, and if he ever caught up with her, he would make her pay for reneging on their deal. Next time, she might not be so lucky.

The time had come to face facts. If she could not handle an encounter with a half-human, no longer had access to her book, and suffered a humiliating defeat at the hands of Esmeralda ben Claude, a girl barely out of her teens, the odds of her returning to power were slim.

Her rivals likely relished her public disgrace, jeering at her and celebrating her defeat. If Angelica had been in their position, she certainly would have. However, they ought to be careful how much they gloated, for none of them ever matched her skill and cunning. Despite her temporary fall from favor, she remained the most formidable witch in the world.

She imagined Korah bloated with a false sense of superiority, believing he had triumphed. At least Angelica's foes had real thrust and power behind them; Korah fell victim to a frightened teenager with no skills or talents. Behaving like a besotted old fool, he allowed a doe-eyed innocent to lure him into a false sense of security. Doubtless, the chit played on his vanity and his ego, then resisted his attempts to gain control of the Black Key, humiliated him at his own gala, and ran off with his son. From where Angelica sat, Korah was in no position to cast aspersions or gloat.

The situation was laughable, really. They had both clearly lost a step. Their younger selves would have made mincemeat out of Esmeralda and Davianna. Angelica would have never gone into exile, and no one could have forced Korah to marry against his will, not again.

The farce playing out upstairs had the Dark Master's fingerprints all over it. For years, Korah steadfastly refused to take another wife, so it must have taken some intense persuasion to get him to go along with this sham. They would have no actual marriage, not in the true sense of a partnership with shared goals and ambitions, an alliance that would further them both.

A latent stab of jealousy jolted her as she pictured Keyseelough at Korah's side. She pushed the thought out of her mind, surprised by the sudden sting of tears. It was too late, much too late.

"What am I doing here?" she said aloud, digging into her bag to retrieve a vial of poison. She stared at it for a time, contemplating its lethal contents. "Either do this or go."

But she did not move, and with a sigh, she stowed the potion in her bag and regretted ever leaving Fiji.

"What do you really want?" she whispered in frustration. The truth was, she did not know, but being here made her realize she did not miss this life.

Three floors above, aristocrats from across the globe rubbed elbows with tycoons, schmoozing each other, brokering deals and marriages in the vain hope of garnering some sort of advantage. She wondered if her relatives were among the attendees but dismissed the idea. They were finished.

It might prove entertaining to make an appearance just to see the shock on everyone's faces, but the theatrics would hardly be worth the hassle. She was wanted for questioning, likely charged with murder, and everyone believed she was dead. If she wanted to live out her retirement, she needed to stay that way.

Swamped by a wave of self-pity, she covered her face and breathed into her hands. "Stop it, Angelica. You don't need them, you never needed anyone. Besides, is there a single person up there you honestly want to see?"

The answer was no.

Well... there was one, but as the intended recipient of the poison, she supposed he did not count. She wanted revenge, but now that seemed hollow. Was Korah worth killing? By all accounts, he teetered on the edge of insanity. He had always been slightly off-kilter, but according to her sources, he was delusional, suffering from hallucinations, and behaving erratically. The wedding added credence to the rumors. Korah, in his right mind, would have never agreed to it.

So, what did that mean to her?

A power vacuum.

If Korah was insane, Keyseelough would rise in his place. That girl had plans, and a crazy husband, thirty years her senior, would not play a role. He would not live long.

Angelica paced, still thinking. Assuming she regained favor with Keyseelough, she would do so to what end? She and the Dark Master were still not on speaking terms, Rapha still wanted to kill her, and even crazy, Korah was not an enemy to be underestimated. Which brought her back to her original question. What did she want?

She gripped the back of her jewel-encrusted throne, waiting for the answer. Turning away, she realized she wanted things as they had been before Marduk invaded this chamber, before everything fell to pieces. She wanted to return to the glory days—back in Endor—when everything seemed possible.

Shouts and the thunder of running feet startled her, a crowd on the move, coming fast. Angelica calculated the distance between her and the exit. No time! She whirled, pressing a series of wood carvings behind the thrones, hoping no one had changed the combination to the secret panel. A click echoed in the chamber, the sound lost in the cacophony. She slipped inside a second before the mob descended.

Staying still and silent, she watched the drama through a hidden peephole. For the next hour and a half, she stood, frozen in horror, as Satan took Korah's throne and became master of ceremonies. She heard it all, though turned away several times, terrified by the abomination occurring in the chamber she once ruled.

Being Ba'alat Ob in Lucifer's realm proved a great deal more taxing than simply eating shit. Charlotte and Keyseelough were stripped naked, humiliated, degraded, then of their own accord, laid spread eagle on the stone slab as an offering.

Charlotte went first. Angelica could smell her burning flesh, saw the blood run out of every orifice as Satan brutalized her before the stunned and silent crowd. Angelica gave Charlotte credit though. She rose under her own power, stood upon the altar, and pretended ecstasy.

Not to be outdone, Keyseelough took her place. But the moment it began, Angelica realized Satan held a particular malevolence toward the newly married princess. The father of human torture, Lucifer, unleashed his wrath with devastating force. He annihilated her. Towards the end, her control broke, and she began to scream. She tried to fight.

Big mistake.

Angelica watched Korah as it was happening. The blood drained from his face. His expression grew blank and distant. She had seen him do it a dozen times; Korah ben Adam went away.

This degradation was beyond anything they had ever done or seen, evil at an entirely new level. When it was finally over, Keyseelough's pitiful cries fell silent. Angelica suspected that the girl, and her sweet little pussy, were dead.

"Let this be a lesson to you all." Lucifer smiled.

An icy chill ran up her spine when she saw his expression, and a small stream of urine escaped as she stood frozen in terror, trying very hard not to piss herself.

"Do not cross me. Never, ever, bow down to worship anyone other than me again."

The assembly fell to their knees, but no one uttered a word.

"You have a job to do. Find the Black Key or you will wish for the mercy I have shown to yon princess." He said the latter with such scorn that it sounded like the vilest curse Angelica ever heard.

Then he was gone.

The Egyptian delegation ran to the altar, shouting, and frantically administering emergency resuscitation. Korah just stood there, not moving. People trampled one another, fleeing the chamber. No one lingered. As they rushed the dying bride away, Korah followed, looking like a dead man.

With her back pressed against the wall, Angelica congratulated herself for trusting her instincts. Tonight, they saved her ass, as well as her twat. The ritual discomfort she endured as Ba'alat Ob did not compare to the brutality her rivals suffered. She cared nothing for Charlotte, hated her actually, but Keyseelough had been a delightful protégée, young, beautiful, eager to please. What a waste of a sweet pussy.

Angelica waited for what felt like an eternity, terrified the invisible presence of Satan still lingered, watching the chamber. Finally, her screaming bladder overrode her fear, and she bolted. Rushing through the dark passageway, she kept her eyes and ears open, fearing pursuit.

She let out a shaky gasp of relief as she burst through the hidden exit, rushing into the frigid night air, which felt glorious after the oppressive darkness inside. Ducking behind the nearest shrub, she hiked her dress and tried to pee. In her distress, she nearly lost her balance and grabbed a branch, hissing in pain as a wicked thorn drew blood. Trembling, with her arthritic knees protesting and her ass freezing, she waited an agonizing thirty seconds for her tortured bladder to release. When it finally cooperated, it was not pretty. A shower of urine sprayed her thighs, ran down her legs, and splattered her shoes. Squatting over a steaming puddle, bleeding and piss-burned, she muttered every foul curse she could conjure. It was an ignominious end to a wretched evening.

January 15, 1000 ME

Not Living Up to the Hype - New City - Rapha

Rapha prowled his empty mansion, brooding and alone. Despite more than a year of meticulous preparation, his time with Lucifer had not gone as planned. Lucifer accepted his hospitality, enjoyed his table and the entertainment he provided, but once he made himself known to the human rulers, he disappeared. So, instead of finding himself at Lucifer's right hand, planning their joint victory, Rapha got dumped.

To make matters worse, other than a few interesting tidbits, Lucifer imparted no great wisdom. Their sessions amounted to nothing more than a rehash of things Rapha already knew. He listened patiently as Lucifer regurgitated ideas Rapha either discerned for himself, studied, or learned through missives from his father.

Marduk never held Lucifer in high esteem, and now Rapha understood why. Lucifer was sinister, yes. Exceedingly wicked, clever, and diabolical, all qualities Rapha admired. He had style, impeccable taste, and a smooth manner that charmed and flattered. However, beneath the sophisticated veneer, his fatal flaws were clearly visible, like an old woman with good makeup. It was all show.

This became glaringly apparent when Lucifer pontificated about his grandiose plans to defeat their enemy. Rapha hungered for fresh strategies, anticipated innovative approaches, and waited for a dazzling Machiavellian masterpiece that would ensure victory. It never came.

By the end of the sixth night, Rapha wondered what exactly Lucifer had done for a thousand years alone in the pit. Every aspect of his plan rehashed the past. Other than a few minor changes, it amounted to nothing more than a revised version of his previous failed attempts. What sane mind concluded the outcome would differ a third time? Lucifer might intimidate and deceive the humans easily enough, however victory would not be achieved merely by seducing mankind. Swollen with pride, and possessing an arrogance that transcended time and space, Lucifer remained convinced of his own superiority, blind to the fatal flaws in his plan. By Rapha's estimations, Lucifer was doomed to another failure, another fall, destined for the Lake of Fire. On the whole, the Prince of Darkness proved to be a colossal disappointment.

But Rapha kept his counsel and opinions to himself. He echoed Lucifer's rants against his father, joining where appropriate, and adopting an obsequiousness that galled him to the bone. Rapha played a role.

He remembered the early lessons his father taught him: 'Never directly challenge a power greater than yourself. Flattery, deception, stealth, and secrecy are the strategies of the victor.' Marduk's success in Alanthia and early escape were classic examples. In a document Rapha discovered when he was five, Marduk had written, 'Of the seventy, only I was cunning enough to circumvent Lucifer's plans. I set my course. I have always been greater and wiser than he.' And by the time Lucifer departed, Rapha realized his father had not exaggerated. Marduk was by far the greater elohim.

Lucifer did not manage an early escape. He had not spent the last fifteen years crafting and shaping a kingdom, leading it and bending it to his own will, but his father had. He allied himself with the most powerful rulers on earth. Yet those loyal servants who served their cause well were the first Lucifer targeted for destruction. It was illogical.

Erica, the voice out of his computer, had grown silent. It seemed that she, too, had deserted him. However, she had given him something to think about and even made him an offer.

"Lucifer can never be trusted. He is a liar and a failure. But I know the way and have a plan that will succeed."

"What is it?" Rapha demanded.

She laughed. "It is a secret, a hidden mystery. I, alone, hold the knowledge and have the power to triumph over our enemy. To prove you are worthy, Rapha, remain at the House of Amah until I give you instructions. But if you fail to heed my advice, choose your own way, or follow Lucifer, no one will know your name. You will die in disgrace, forgotten and doomed, like the rest of the nameless fools who came before you."

They were stern warnings, and if she would have revealed her identity or given him an incentive, he might have considered her offer, however she had not; and, for all Rapha knew, Erica was naught but a trick of the enemy. He had waited long enough and would not stay here a minute longer than he had to. In a few weeks, the hedge that imprisoned him would fall away, and he would be free to find his father... and his mother.

For fourteen years, he studied and grew, honing his skills, and passing every test his father sent him, prospering in the House of Amah, alone. But before enacting his larger plan, he had one point of business to take care of, the only bit of useful information Lucifer imparted, the single critical element he failed to discern on his own. Rapha savored the memory, their one genuine moment of connection. They had been kindred spirits for a fleeting second.

Lucifer's black eyes shone as he said, "For a nephilim to come into his full power, he must kill the woman who bore him."

He knew who his mother was, Persa ben Yereq. He had vague memories of her and could not surmise why his father failed to share this important secret. However, their communications were limited and often vague, delivered by messengers out of favor with his father, who Rapha devoured, not the most trustworthy of sources.

In his study, surrounded by books and scrolls, ancient and modern, he crafted a daring new plan. Unlike Lucifer, Rapha would not repeat the mistakes of the past. After dispatching his mother, he planned to acquire the Book of Power. He caught several tantalizing glimpses in Angelica ben Omri's memories, but despite her promises to bring it to him, she never showed up. If he ever caught up with the hag, she would pay for welching on their deal.

Since learning of its existence, the book consumed his thoughts. He craved the secrets it held, coveted the hidden knowledge, and wished to explore the mysteries secreted within its pages. Rapha knew if he took possession and wielded it properly, he would become the most powerful being in the world, half-human, half elohim, not bound by the spirit realm or the earth, free to move between the two. He would not be predictable. He would become invincible.

Milk Bath - Loa Hall - Louisiana - Charlotte

Alone in her ornate boudoir bathroom, Mademoiselle Charlotte trembled as she stepped into a scented saline bath. A pitiful whimper escaped her lips as her wounds touched the water, every nerve firing in protest. Emite had prepared a potion of warm milk and herbs that she dribbled over her burns. Her skin bore blisters everywhere Lucifer had touched. Deep, tissue destroying hellfire marks and gouges ravaged her body. Five days after her trial by fire, she was still wracked with pain.

She pretended to enjoy it, putting on quite a show for the spectators and the fiend who defiled her, but Charlotte was suffering. Nothing prepared her for the realities of becoming the Bride of Satan. She bore it and rose under her own power.

Keyseelough had not, which served the bitch right for trying to usurp her throne. They carried her from the chamber unconscious, and Charlotte took a small measure of satisfaction in that.

She won, retained her title, but the cost was enormous.

Fleeing the New City, she retreated to the safety of Loa Hall. Her condition infuriated Emite, but his ingenious counter curses reversed some of the damage, and his care in the days after kept her alive. Now she lived in mortal dread, awaiting Lucifer's next visitation.

"Find the Black Key!" Lucifer ordered as he rammed into her. "I will split you in half and make you eat your guts if you don't."

Charlotte's body shook with the memory. She had one objective, to find what Lucifer wanted. If she succeeded, it might just keep him from killing her… might.

Old Allies - New City - Korah and Angelica

Angelica waited five days before making her move.

"What are you doing down here?" Korah sneered, covering his surprise.

Angelica rose from her former throne, looking spectacular. Carefully dressed in ebony and scarlet, painted, and styled, she regained a measure of her legendary beauty. A little twit at a local salon wove long blonde tresses into Angelica's gray bob, then colored her natural hair to match. It felt glorious, powerful, and shimmered honey-gold in the lantern light. The esthetician and makeup artist turned out to be less of a twit, performing some serious cosmetic magic. As Angelica watched, her youthful, perfect face reemerged. Tonight, she looked damn good, and she knew it.

Ascending the stone steps with the grace of a queen, she suddenly longed for her slender, black cigarette holder. It had been a dramatic showstopper, and she thought perhaps it might have triggered an old memory in Korah. "I know you," she purred. "The noose is tightening, and when that happens, you seek solace here."

She gestured around and shrugged. "I was right, as usual."

"I have the situation under control," he said with haughty arrogance.

Angelica rolled her eyes and scoffed, "Of course you do."

He flared his nose, watching her.

She strolled around the chamber, fingering the artifacts, pretending to examine them. "I watched a riveting interview yesterday, along with half the kingdom. Terrible publicity, Korah, to have those two parents bawling on camera, blaming you for kidnapping their innocent babies."

She made a tsking sound of regret and mocked Zanah ben Joseph's accent. "All these months, I thought my daughter, Davianna, was dead." Angelica pretended to swoon with her hand over her heart. "These are our girls today. Tomorrow it could be your girls."

She put down the ceremonial knife with a thunk. "I hear they are printing t-shirts with that last little phrase. It's a rallying cry—against you."

Korah glared at her but remained silent.

"I also read you had Peter killed so you could steal his fiancée." Angelica circled him, the hem of her gown billowing like a malevolent red cloud.

"Another mysterious royal disappearance, another tragic death in your family?" The implications of her words hung in the air. Angelica knew the truth, all of it.

"Please tell me you did not kill Peter, at least not before I had one last shot at him." She stood before him, toe-to-toe. "He reminds me so much of you at that age." To emphasize her point, she ran her hand down the front of his silk trousers.

"He is nothing like me." Korah's eyes bore into hers, but he did not move away, allowing her to touch him.

"If he were, he would have married Keyseelough, not you." Her mouth lifted in a salacious grin as she felt his body stir. "Is she here? Perhaps a little *ménage à trois* can be arranged?"

Korah turned away. "She is back in Cairo."

"I think Lucifer did some permanent damage, such a waste." She cackled, "Ironic that I fucked your bride, and you have not."

Korah narrowed his brows, but his expression lacked the thunderous anger she expected, so she continued to jab. "You must admit, exercising *jus primae noctis* was devilish." She pressed a long red talon to her lips, pretending to consider the situation. "I suppose he originated the practice, so it comes as no surprise he took your wife to bed on her wedding night."

"I gather you have come to gloat?" Korah asked, averting his eyes away from the stone slab.

"Not at all," Angelica said with false sincerity. "I am merely here to support to an old friend."

"We are not friends." Korah laughed without humor. "The last time I saw you, you threatened to destroy me."

She stepped in front of him, and their eyes met, old heat and fire igniting. "I changed my mind."

"I cleaned up your mess in Thyatira." His haughty, regal expression did not waiver.

"Thyatira?" Angelica feigned a look of confusion. "I haven't heard that name in a very long time."

"Do not be obtuse." Korah grabbed her wrist and squeezed. "That debacle could have been no one other than you."

She flashed him a wicked smile. "I believe our mutual interests were served."

"As you say." Korah released her and stepped back.

Angelica finally got to the point of her little foray into Korah's dungeon by asking, "How has the Dark Master fared since Lucifer's release?"

Korah narrowed his hazel eyes, calculating. "He is gone, has been for weeks, banished, from what I can determine."

Angelica felt a thrill run down her legs. Adopting a droll tone, she said, "So, you are on your own?"

Korah glanced at the stone slab, his expression unreadable. When he turned, he looked at her, truly looked at her for the first time that evening. "Am I?"

She flicked her hair over her shoulder and said, "I should leave you to rot after everything you have done to me."

"Oh?" He came closer and traced a manicured finger over her bottom lip, a smile hovering in the corner of his mouth. "But you are here for a reason. I suppose you have crafted a plan?"

"Perhaps," she purred, feeling a kindling of delight, thrilled to be back in the game.

"Tell me," he whispered, giving her a smoldering look full of heat and promise, "Bella."

A shiver raced up her spine. "I am not that easy, Korah."

He laughed. "No one in their right mind would ever dream of calling you easy; diabolical, intelligent, cunning… beautiful, yes. You are all those things and much more."

"Flattery?" She rolled her eyes, pretending to be unmoved.

But they had known one another a long time, and her icy tone did not fool him. "We did have some amazing years together. Think of all we accomplished." His hand moved around her waist, drawing her close. "Come."

Angelica moistened her lips, staring up at his handsome face, and it felt as if the years had melted away. It had been more than a decade since she took Korah to her bed. For that matter, he was the last man she slept with, since her natural predilections leaned toward her own sex. She thought her affections had permanently shifted, but the idea of screwing him appealed to her. "Lead the way, Chukka."

Korah threw back his head and laughed. "No one has called me that in a very long time." He cupped her elbow, moving her toward his private entrance. "Those were interesting days, Bella. Shall we recreate a bit of magic?"

Part 5 - Workers

January 15, 1000 ME

In the Meantime - Esmeralda and Ian

Esmeralda stared at the computer screen in her office, fuming. She dialed Ian's number, and after a cursory greeting, told him to open his email.

He whistled as he read the forwarded message. "Ouch."

"Ian, I do not know what to do about this," Esmeralda hissed, keeping her voice low, lest anyone at the Center overhear.

Ian sighed. "I'm sorry, Esmeralda. I will address it."

"Well, I hope so! Malandra called after she read it. According to her, Judith has been sending this sort of garbage for years." Esmeralda moved around the side of her desk and closed the door. "You would not believe the nasty emails she sent Malandra when they were opening the Center in New Orleans."

Ian groaned. "It is the single largest conflict me and Joanna have, literally."

Esmeralda chuckled at his backhanded insult. "I am just thankful I don't have to deal with her every day. If I did, I'd have quit to become one of those mothers in the park with their strollers and baggies of snacks." She did not reveal how close she was to joining them.

"Aye, this email is over the top, isn't it?"

"I would say so. She does not call me out by name, but the inference is clear. Ian, she refers to me as an incompetent imbecile, which I am not. Seriously, who sends a message like this?"

"Judith." Ian's derision traveled through the line.

"Why does Joanna allow her to do these things?"

"Oh, she doesn't. They'll have it out. Joanna will lay down the law, and then Judith will pout and stomp around the office, not speaking to anyone for days. Meanwhile, she will do the work of three people, and next week she'll bring in homemade soup and hand-knit scarves for all the kids." Ian laughed in frustration. "Then, we will get 'Good Judith' for a while. She'll be helpful, she'll be knowledgeable, and she'll do something amazing that makes us all think maybe she isn't so bad."

"Until the next time." Esmeralda closed the email because it made her blood boil.

"True," Ian agreed. "The crux of the matter is that Joanna and Judith have been together for a long time, and Joanna feels responsible for her."

"Why?" Esmeralda could not comprehend how the formidable Lady Joanna ben Luke tolerated Judith ben Dan's behavior.

"Joanna is the daughter of an Earl, Esmeralda. Their world is different. She learned at an early age that her family's wealth and position came with great responsibility, to their subjects, but also for the people who worked for them." Ian coughed and cleared his throat.

"Her mother's butler, Corman, has worked at Hope House for decades. You have never met a more surly character. He is rude, condescending, and as old as Methuselah, but he, and most of the staff, stayed when Korah placed the Earl and the Countess under house arrest. To you and I, that may seem odd, but to them it was not. It is a microcosm of the aristocracy, one of the structures of authority ordained by the Iron King himself. By design, servants and masters have an interdependent relationship. They serve each other. And after I met Corman, I understood why Joanna kept Judith around. She is from a different world, and it's the way they do things."

"Rude and surly? That describes Judith." She sighed out her frustration. "Fine. I will not answer this. I'll let Joanna deal with her."

"She will, though I suspect it will take a toll. It always does. Judith does not come from Joanna's world, so she does not play by the same rules. Unfortunately, Joanna cannot see it, but that is part of her charm, what makes her who she is. She is loyal, and she trusts her employees."

Esmeralda cringed, feeling the sting of Ian's words. Since the accountant's visit, she waited and wondered if the people she loved and trusted were thieves. The uncertainty was maddening. "I like what you said about people having interdependent relationships. I've never thought about that before."

"Aye, it's true. But for it to function properly, honor and loyalty must govern both parties. From the family, to the church, to government and businesses, leaders and subordinates bear equal responsibility to ensure their relationships foster progress and harmony. If there is a breakdown, like we see with Judith, no one benefits."

"We experienced that in Rephidim," Esmeralda said thoughtfully. "The Barons of Thyatira were hot-heads and wastrels who abdicated their responsibilities so much that Prince Adam redrew the boundaries and dissolved the Barony. But we fell into a disputed area, and neither Easton nor Bethlehem intervened when the Witch of Endor began her campaign against us."

"They were likely afraid of her," Ian said.

Esmeralda scoffed, "With good reason, I suppose."

"Joanna actually told me an old rumor about her."

"The witch?" Esmeralda whispered, her eyes narrowing. "Tell me."

"Well, you know Joanna does not like to gossip, but apparently there is some sort of connection between Angelica and the Philadelphia Duchy."

"What sort of connection?" Esmeralda asked.

"Joanna does not know. But young Angelica traveled in some elevated circles, and the Dowager Duchess provided her letters of introduction."

"I see," Esmeralda said.

"Apparently, the Dowager helped her get a clerkship with one of the Supreme Court Justices."

"Interesting. I always wondered how she rose to the Alanthian Supreme Court."

"She left a disastrous legacy that carries on to this day."

"I haven't studied her legal career. I suppose Thaddeus has."

"Probably," Ian agreed.

"Well, if the rumors are true, and there is a connection between her and the Philadelphia Duchy, that explains why the Duke never intervened in Thyatira. Do you think Angelica is using them to hide?"

"I don't think so. The Dowager died over twenty years ago, and I served with the Duke's sons in the war. Philadelphia was an outspoken critic of Korah, one of the few who openly opposed him during the technology debates and negotiated the peace on behalf of the Noble Army. He has been on house arrest since. I doubt very much he is harboring Angelica."

"You are probably right. I'll relay the information to Thaddeus, though he probably already knows. He never tells me much about the investigation."

"He's just trying to protect you."

She blew out a long sigh. "I suppose you are right. I do the same for him. We never discuss Beau Landry." Adopting a casual tone, she asked, "Have you spoken to him?"

"Beau? Not for a couple of weeks. His grandfather was in town, and even if he hadn't mentioned it, we can always tell by the flurry of requests for stats and reports. Lenox keeps a close eye on his investments, even when it is charity."

"Oh, I guess that is to be expected."

"Is everything all right?"

"Yes, of course." She winced and changed the subject. "Well, not really. I've been out of sorts, having bad dreams and the like. How about you?"

"A bit more than dreams. That wedding turned out to be something else."

"I heard the rumors, and Camy showed me several websites she follows. Ian, did Satan really manifest out of a tornado at the reception?"

"Joanna and I left before that happened, which apparently was a tremendous breach of protocol to leave before the bride and groom, but I got us out of there."

"We had some family stuff come up that day. I was not in a party mood, and the whole spirit of that wedding felt sinister. For once, Joanna did not argue with me about proper etiquette."

"I am glad you did not see it."

"Yeah, me, too."

"Do you remember the day we hiked in the Redwoods?" she asked.

"When Jelena met us?"

"Yes. She was not the only one I spoke with."

Ian grew quiet over the line, then said, "I didn't think so. Jelena doesn't turn hair white, does she?"

"No, she doesn't." Esmeralda pulled the curl down and studied it. "Yeshua told me he was always there, even when the darkness surrounded me. But, Ian, with Satan free, we are headed for a fight that will make Thyatira pale by comparison."

"Aye, you might be right."

She paused, resting her head in her hand, then blurted, "I don't want to fight. I don't! I just want to love my husband and my daughter. I want to work here and help the kids. I don't want to go up against the Witch of Endor again, much less Satan!"

"Hey, it's all right, lass. Don't be getting yourself worked up over nothing."

Esmeralda smiled on the other end of the phone, enjoying the trace of his Irish lilt that came out occasionally.

"Perhaps you will not be called to fight," Ian continued, but his voice lacked conviction, and they both knew the likelihood of that. "But even if you are, it's not today."

"That's just it. I keep waiting for some calamity to befall us, but there is nothing going on."

"Stay in prayer, Esmeralda. It's all you can do. That, and trust that the Iron King has everything under control. If He calls us to fight, we fight. In the meantime, we live."

He snorted in self-deprecation. "It took me years to figure that out. I kept waiting for my next assignment, my next destination, and I did not live." He fingered his gold wedding band, new and precious.

"Yeah, I guess I understand that."

"And listen, when you were called to fight, you did. Right now, you've been given a respite, if you don't count an occasional nasty email from Judith."

Esmeralda snorted. "Well, there's that."

"My point is, you have to live, despite whatever scary thing is lurking around the corner. Because they can't get you unless the Iron King allows it. It doesn't keep us safe to hunker down or stop living while we wait for it to happen."

"You're saying I should let my mother throw me a wedding," Esmeralda groaned.

Ian chuckled. He knew that had been weighing on her for months. "The wedding, a trip to the ice cream parlor, a drive up to the mountains for a long weekend, whatever it is. Don't let fear keep you from living because I think that grieves Him. He does not want us to miss out on the blessings He has for us because we are worried."

Ian paced his office. "I'll admit, we are likely headed into hard times, but we should not manufacture them or fail to enjoy the good times out of some misplaced notion that we are not serving Him when things are okay, and we are at rest. Don't fret. He's got everything under control."

"I love you." Esmeralda smiled into the phone. "I truly do, Ian ben Kole."

"Of course you do. I am lovable."

January 17, 1000 ME

A Side Trip - New City - Ian and Joanna

"Princess, it's late and I'm hungry. Let's go home," Ian said, leaning on the door jam of Joanna's office.

Joanna ben Luke did not turn, studying a report on her desk.

"What's wrong?"

She shook her head.

Ian moved beside her and glanced at the papers. "Bad news?"

Joanna sniffed. "Not directly."

Ian laid a hand on her stiff shoulder.

"Malandra says they have had a rash of missing kids in New Orleans. Thankfully, none are from our place, but still."

"I know," he murmured, rubbing her back. "But New Orleans is a transient place. It won't surprise me if most of those kids don't turn up safe and sound."

"You're right." She hefted her thirty-pound purse with practiced ease and rose. "Let's get you some food."

"Are we dining in or carrying out?"

"Do you want Indian? I am dying for some saag paneer and garlic nan."

"We had that last week." He liked Indian food; Joanna loved it.

"Yes, but the buffet is divine. Besides, Saffron is near the park, and I want to drive through tonight."

"The park, why?" Ian asked, turning off the lights as they went.

Joanna was still digging in the depths of her bottomless purse when Ian pulled his set of keys from his jacket pocket and locked the door.

"Elijah is convinced there is a predator in the park. He swears that's who took Cynthia and Samantha," she said, referring to two of their early residents. "I just want to drive through."

"Elijah mentioned that to me as well." Ian shut the car door with a firm thud.

"He took their disappearances hard. We all did. And I suppose there is some logic to his theory. Kids like the parks, especially new runaways."

Joanna gazed out the window at the silvery moon and continued, "I spent a lot of time in the parks doing research to get the funding for the Center, but I don't go anymore. I sit behind my desk and fill out grant applications, write reports, and do statistical analysis. Then, I put on my fancy dresses and fundraise."

"Well, let's get some food, then go find you some kids to save. How does that sound, Princess?"

"That sounds very nice." Joanna relaxed into the cloth seat of her old car, a gift from her father for her college graduation, a living symbol of her frugal nature.

After dinner, cruising through the dark side roads of Prince Eamonn's Park, Joanna spotted them, two girls hiding in the shadows, huddled against the restroom wall. "There, you see them?"

"Where?" Ian slowed, scanning the area.

"Just there. I am going to talk to them." Joanna hopped out before the vehicle came to a complete stop.

"Be careful," he called after her rapidly retreating footsteps. She needed this, which was why he drove her around in the middle of the night instead of going home to their warm bed. She had been out of sorts since her last blow up with Judith. The confrontation escalated into a shouting match and culminated in Joanna placing Judith on suspension.

Ten minutes later, Ian smiled when the two girls rose from their huddled position and followed Joanna to the car.

There was a quivering excitement in Joanna when she said, "Ian, I'd like you to meet our newest guests. Elisabeta ben Yoder and Jenny ben Rip from Bezetha, Pennsylvania."

Ian's eyes flew open at the names and the place, but he stifled an exclamation of shock and turned to the backseat. "Welcome, girls. We'll get you settled in. You have made an excellent decision tonight."

As the car pulled away, a deep-throated sound of frustration erupted from the shadows. Thundering footsteps echoed in the quiet park as Rapha returned to the House of Amah without his midnight snack.

January 18, 1000 ME

Some News Just Can't Wait Until Morning - Esmeralda

Thaddeus did not hear the phone ringing, deep in the dreamless slumber of a man who had not had a full night of uninterrupted sleep in over a year. Woken either by his shoulder or his baby daughter, he grumbled every morning that it was a conspiracy.

Esmeralda was in slightly better shape, having the vigor of youth and a less stressful job. So, she lifted his phone from the nightstand and croaked, "Director Thaddeus ben Todd's phone. This is his wife, Esmeralda. May I help you?"

"Esmie," Ian sounded jubilant, "sorry to wake you, but I had to call."

"What's wrong?" Esmeralda moved out of their bedroom, stumbling and bouncing off the walls like a drunk.

"Nothing's wrong. We've found your cousin and her friend. They are here at the Center."

"Elisabeta and Jenny?" Esmeralda asked, coming instantly awake. "Are they all right?"

"They both seem fine, a little ragged, scared, but otherwise okay. Joanna found them in a park nearby."

"My aunt will be overjoyed. She never gave up hope." Esmeralda sagged in relief. "You did not tell her we were looking for her, did you?"

"No, you know how skittish new arrivals can be." Ian smiled at Joanna, who beamed across the kitchen table. "They are both legal adults and thus too old to become residents of the Center, but we did not go into that tonight. Joanna wanted to get them off the streets."

Esmeralda knew the protocols for the Centers. The oldest kids they accepted as permanent residents were sixteen. Elisabeta and Jenny were both twenty. "Thank you both," she said through a sudden tightening in her throat. "That's really great."

"Goodnight, Esmeralda. Sleep well."

Esmeralda disconnected the phone and buried her face in her hands, crying with relief and remorse. Tomorrow, she would call her aunt and right after that, Beau. This had gone on long enough.

Start Date - La Petit Pishon - Beau and Sarah

After Andrew ben Lenox left Louisiana, Beau decided he should have taken up a correspondence with his grandfather during his years of night prowling because the man never slept. He woke every morning to a loaded inbox, and his phone beeped with text messages at all hours. They spoke at 7:45 am and 4:15 pm every day. Beau mentally referred to them as his first and second shift conference calls.

Only Andrew's personal assistant, Fiona, knew what Beau and Andrew were doing. Neither was certain Beau was ready to run one of the largest corporate empires on Earth. Beau thought he was, but a part of him still woke at night expecting the madness, and he struggled against a niggling anxiety that he was not yet free. Something kept him tethered to his house on La Petit Pishon, waiting.

But they were both willing to start.

Cognizant of the potential backlash from stockholders, executives, partners, and bankers, Andrew planned to ease Beau into the role. His grandson was unknown, and his history might be used against him. If Beau was not up to speed, prepared, or capable, that made for bad business, so they agreed Beau would begin surreptitiously.

However, that did not mean Andrew planned to go lightly or slowly. Beau's immersion into Lenox started with a bang. Andrew inundated Beau with documents to analyze. Profit and loss statements, market forecasts, financial statements, projections, annual reports, budgets, and dozens of other documents littered his desk and filled his inbox. Beau worked sixteen hours a day... and loved every minute of it.

The only title he claimed was President of the Lenox Foundation, which allowed him to familiarize himself with some of the key players in the broader organization. Involved with the foundation for years, even in the dark times, he knew the donors, and some of the inner workings, so he and Andrew agreed the position offered a good launching pad. The foundation supported hundreds of charities across the globe, though one dominated his thoughts these days. By rote, he checked his messages, looking for the forensic accounting report.

A vehicle pulled up, though he was not expecting anyone, and the interruption annoyed him.

"Good Morning, *Maman*," Beau said, opening the door to Sarah Landry, who stood on his back stoop with her arms crossed and her brow furrowed.

"You are not taking my calls. That never bodes well," she said, sweeping past him. Her eyes scanned the kitchen, taking in the state of the place. It was clean and organized, but a spoon laid on the counter near an empty cup of coffee, with the half-and-half, still in its store-bought container, beside it.

She marched over to his refrigerator and jerked open the door.

"You hungry?" He crossed his arms.

"Just checking." Everything appeared normal, with no maniacal organization inside the cold storage. "When you stop answering the phone—"

"I'm fine," Beau growled, resenting the intrusion, but realizing there were precedents for her concern.

Sarah cut her eyes to the bedroom. "Are you shacking up with someone?"

"If I was, what damn business would it be of yours?"

"Watch your mouth." Her eyes flashed, and she suppressed a cutting retort that she would have preferred finding some slut in his bed over discovering Beau out of his mind.

"Now that you are satisfied I do not have a woman here, and that I am not *couillon,* I got work to do, *Maman.*"

That stopped her. "What work?"

"A little Foundation business."

Sarah narrowed her eyes. "We just closed out the year, and the big fundraising season does not begin until May. We reviewed everything two weeks ago, and the accounting reports are not back yet, so what work are you doing?"

"This and that, nothing for you to be concerned with." He stretched his arms over his head with a sigh and moved to the coffee pot. "Do you want a cup?"

"You are stalling, and you are hedging." She settled on a bar stool with her hands in her lap. "Tell me what is really going on."

Part 6 - Revolutionaries

January 15, 1000 ME

Decoy - Vegas - Kayah and Reuben

In a Vegas hotel room, five days after their epic showdown with Erica, Reuben ben Judah shrugged on his coat and said, "I am going to deliver the decoy phones. Are you sure you are okay, Yakira?"

Kayah ben Samuel rubbed her bruised wrists and answered in a dull monotone, "I'm okay."

Reuben lifted her chin, examining her face. Both her eyes were blackened and livid purple, the right still swollen shut. She bore numerous claw marks, the deep scratches raised and red. An unmistakable band of blue bruises circled her neck, the sight making him furious. "I will have a word with Prince Peter. Do not think I will not. He should have never sent you to do it—never."

"This was not his fault." A shiver passed over Kayah, and she pushed his hands away, carefully laying down. "I am certain he did not know, and I wanted the job. You know I did. After Gus' journals… I had to."

"He sent you to kill a man possessed by an evil spirit," Reuben growled.

"No one knew Guan ben Sheldon was possessed. I don't think he even knew. Who ever heard of such a thing? From what you've said, they are locked away, gone for a thousand years." Kayah reached for a glass of water with a shaky hand. "It is a miracle Davianna and Astrid escaped the camp alive if he was after them."

"Well, he will not hurt any more girls," Reuben said, kissing the back of her fingers. "But I do not like to see you hurt, Yakira. I do not. No more, you understand? No more."

Kayah was inclined to agree with him. In her long career, this was the first job that ever went terribly wrong, and she was reeling. "He was so strong, Reuben. I have never seen anything like it." She turned away, trying to forget, wishing it never happened. "But what that thing said—"

"Yakira," Reuben whispered, "do not give credence to the doctrines of demons."

Kayah pursed her swollen lips, hating the tears and tightness in her chest. The cracked ribs made it hard to breathe, which made her panicky, remembering the demon's hands around her throat. "I'm sorry, I should not cry." She slapped at him. "I never cried until I met you."

He cradled her precious face. "Because now you feel."

"I feel all over," she groaned.

"You should have stayed in the bunker and let Genevieve take care of you."

"And miss a trip to Vegas? No way. Besides, I never stick around after I've done a job, bad protocol."

"Vegas," Reuben snorted, "a hellish place, yet they look at me like I beat you. Did you see the receptionist's face when we checked in? Wicked Jew, woman beater, it is what she thought."

She did not deny it. Kayah had never given anti-Semitism a second thought until she fell in love with Reuben. Now she experienced it daily. "I'll heal. I just got the shit kicked out of me. It could have been worse."

"Worse," his voice cracked, "to have lost you, my Yakira."

As evening fell over the Vegas strip, a pale winter sun illuminated the open sky, painting it shades of dusty yellow. Outside, the frigid air pulsed with energy; palpable excitement, desperation, and greed fed in the dark. An infectious mania raced through casinos and hid around corners as night people slithered out of the shadows, peddling sex and drugs. And those dreaming of a jackpot flocked to the gaming tables and slot machines, seduced by the lure of easy money.

Through a haze of restless sleep, Kayah heard footsteps outside her room. She reached under the pillow and fingered her pistol, certain her visitor was Reuben, prepared if it was not.

The door opened with a key.

She cracked a swollen eyelid and croaked, "You brought me flowers?"

Reuben peered out from behind a bouquet of daisies and yellow roses and said, "It is traditional for someone who is ailing, is it not?"

"I love daisies," she whispered.

"They will cheer you, no?"

She nodded, blinking up at him, absurdly glad he was back, touched by his thoughtful gesture.

He put the vase on the bedside table and kissed her forehead. "You rested?"

Kayah eased herself up on the pillows, stifling a groan. "Yes, for all the good it did me. I swear I feel worse."

Reuben poured her a fresh glass of water and dug in his pocket for a bottle of pills. "Take one or two every six hours, compliments of Doctor Einar ben Yane."

"You did not fill a prescription!"

"Your head is addled. No, I did not. Our resourceful friend is traveling with his own pharmacy." Reuben passed her the medicine. "Prince Peter had a fully stocked medical clinic when they escaped. They took the medicine with them."

"What is it?" Kayah asked, popping two pills.

"A muscle relaxer with an anti-inflammatory. He said it will help."

She eased back into the pillows, her face pale under the spectacular bruises. "Good."

"I have something else." He took the laptop from his canvas satchel, inserted a small data card, and said, "Look."

Kayah rolled to her side, studying the photograph of the two Princes, a compelling study of light and shadow. Peter wore an expression of confident intensity that belied his affable Prince d'Or persona. He looked spectacular, but Kayah doubted he had ever taken a bad picture. There was something magnetic about him that drew people into his orbit. The cocky set of his shoulders and the gleam in his emerald eyes amused and charmed her. She smiled, knowing she had always had a soft spot for him.

But the radiance of his golden cousin did not overshadow Josiah, the lesser known of the two. The picture captured his handsome face in three quarter profile, black beard stubble giving him a rugged, edgy look. His strong arms were clearly defined beneath the sleeves of a battered leather jacket, and his whiskey-colored eyes burned with intensity. He possessed the brooding aura of a serious warrior. The tilt of his head and his quiet, commanding presence branded him as royalty.

Together, the two Princes exuded an undefinable charisma that carried an edge of force and power that put the world, and Korah, on notice. The photo proclaimed, 'We are coming, and we do not intend to lose.'

Reuben chuckled and hung up his coat. "It is extraordinary, yes? I think even Filippo would approve. It is the next Serendipity."

"I would call it, Intentions," Kayah whispered, unable to stop staring at the image. "Who took it?"

"Astrid. She did not like the pictures I was taking." The corner of his lip twitched. "She called me a troglodyte with a camera."

Kayah covered her mouth to keep from laughing. It hurt to laugh. "Where is the camera?"

"I left it with her since she seemed to enjoy it. I thought it would be a nice gift, after what she went through." His face softened. He had secretly guarded Astrid and Davianna for months as they trekked across Europe. And while he was a stranger to them, they were not to him. He knew their walks, their body language, their voices, and, of course, the way they laughed when they thought no one was listening. Kayah also had a strange affinity with them. If she had not approached them in Italy, she would have never met Reuben. "How did the girls seem?"

"Resilient, those two. They looked good." Reuben shrugged his shoulders forward. "Astrid and Peter are lovers."

Kayah rolled her eyes. "Why does that not surprise me? I knew he'd get one of them in bed. Though, I thought it would be Davianna. Astrid looks like his mother, and I know for a fact he does not like redheads."

"Peter would not touch Davianna, Yakira."

The undertone in Reuben's voice caused Kayah to look up from the photograph. "Why do you say that?"

"Because it is apparent to anyone with two eyes," he pointed his fingers in a V, gesturing to his dark eyes, "that Josiah is in love with Davianna. He has been for months, especially since London, but he brims with it now, though he fights it."

Kayah's quick mind ran through the implications of a match between those two and said, "That will cause complications."

Reuben frowned. "He knows that, but the heart does not care, does it, Yakira?"

Her hazel-green eyes softened. "No."

"You are right though, Prince Yehonathan will not like it." It remained unspoken that Yehonathan did not approve of Reuben's relationship with Kayah either. "Her common birth brings no allies, and Josiah needs to form alliances, but more than that, the scandal of her mother will haunt them."

Kayah looked at him, puzzled, not following his logic. "That video of their parents has gone viral."

"It is different. A video about two missing girls and a corrupt king is one thing. To have a Princess whose mother was the lover of a gangster is another." Reuben sat down heavily on the bed. "You heard what Filippo said. Marco ben Massimo made Zanah ben Joseph a whore."

He pulled off his boots and stretched his sore calf. "I met her when we were searching. She was a shiksa, even before Massimo, I suspect. She cared not a whit for her daughter. Her kind is only interested in money, and they use their beauty to get what they want. She will cause them trouble. I know this, trust me."

"Does Davianna know?" Kayah asked in a small voice, feeling empathy for the girl. She knew what it felt like to be abandoned and secretly suspected her own mother may have been a prostitute who left her unwanted baby at the orphanage.

"How could she know? I would not tell her."

"No, I suppose you wouldn't."

He stretched out beside her. Yellow roses perfumed the air, and the noise of the Vegas strip provided a pleasant hum, soothing in its constancy. With his mission complete and his lover safe, he relaxed. Kayah looked better, her face less swollen. "I had strong words with Prince Peter, but I made sure the girls did not hear, nor did I tell Josiah." Reuben shrugged. "He will one day rule and does not need to know."

"But he gave you medicine. What did you tell him?" Kayah asked through a yawn.

"Car accident. He did not question it."

"I feel like I was run over by a truck."

Reuben grunted. "Well, we have our next assignment, less dangerous than the last."

Kayah snuggled into his side, rubbing her cheek on the soft cotton of his shirt. "Does it involve a beach?"

"No, a mountain cabin." Reuben draped an arm around Kayah, cradling her body. "Once we take the digital photo to Himari, they want us to find Astrid's father and Davianna's mother and take them into hiding. Prince Peter feels certain Korah will target them for that video. He is probably correct."

"We should get Filippo involved. He knows them both." She yawned again, stretching her stiff joints.

"Himari would like it if we pulled him out of Massimo's."

"I think that's a good idea. I've got a bad feeling about Filippo staying undercover for so long. He's not made for it." Kayah closed her eyes as the medicine kicked in. "He's not a spy like us."

Reuben stroked Kayah's forearm. "And even we get into trouble sometimes, no?"

"Flesh and blood I can handle… it's wicked computers and evil spirits that tend to be unpredictable," Kayah mumbled, dozing. "We must remember that, no?"

January 16, 1000 ME

Pulling Leonardo – New City

Thaddeus was working late when his cell phone rang. He gave a curt nod to the agent he was conferring with and retreated to his office. "T, here."

"I need you to pull Leonardo," Mack said without preamble.

Thaddeus blew out a long, slow breath. "They will not like it."

"I don't give a shit," Mack drawled. "He's been under for two months. That's long enough. And from what I hear, the target has gone as crazy as a sprayed cockroach. That ain't no place for Leonardo. Get him out, T."

Thaddeus rotated his shoulder, trying to relieve a sudden pinch. Yesterday's briefing on the Massimo investigation corroborated Mack's assessment. By all accounts, the mobster was unhinged. "If we do, Leonardo will have to lie low. We are not ready to move."

"That won't be a problem. We got hidey-holes coming out the wazoo." Mack lowered his voice and added, "I need Sunflower at the top of her game, and right now she's distracted, worried. There's more at stake here than some two-bit gangster."

"He's more than a two-bit gangster."

"All the more reason to get Leonardo out of there."

"This might play out better if you pull him, less red tape. He's a private citizen. He can walk away."

Mack understood. "Good. We'll take care of it," Mack said, sounding relieved. Before ringing off, he asked, "How's everybody?"

"We're good. And you?"

Mack grinned. "Peachy. Now that Erica is out of commission, Mrs. Euler's on leave, at least for a little while."

Thaddeus frowned. Everything was temporary. "Watch your back. Tell me when it's done."

"10-4."

Mack pocketed the phone and met the expectant faces of his bunker mates. Alaina tossed a fashion magazine onto the coffee table, stretching her impossibly long legs, waiting. Kayah leaned against the wall with her arms crossed, looking like a cage fighter after a losing bout. Reuben sat in the recliner, bobbing his head, rocking out to his horrible music, but at Mack's signal, he pulled the earbuds. Genevieve stopped cleaning, holding her feather duster like a scepter, having determined weeks ago nobody else was going to clean the bunker. Himari stood, and Mack thought her jeans might fall off and puddle at her ankles. She was not eating or sleeping, and, at the moment, not breathing.

"We're pulling him," Mack said to the room.

Himari deflated, sinking into her desk chair with a sigh of relief. Kayah and Reuben shared a glance, pleased. Genevieve smiled and murmured something about an antipasto. Alaina stood up and stretched, then returned to her computer.

"Official or unofficial?" Himari asked.

"Unofficial, less hassle," Mack replied succinctly. "We can extract him tonight if we come up with a plan."

"That's no problem," Himari said over the rapid clicking of her keyboard. "We're tapped into their systems: security, surveillance, everything. I've had an evacuation plan in place since he went back."

Mack raised an eyebrow at her.

"He wasn't going back under without me having eyes on him, not after what we went through in December. No way." Himari dared Mack to challenge her. "You'd do the same, Mack."

Kayah made a brief snort and laughed. "Lavinia, the undercover agent?"

The thought was absurd.

Alaina leaned around her monitor, grinning. "Not unless we encounter an evil math cadre bent on world domination."

"Then we send in Lavinia with Dr. Ira," Reuben joked, referring to one of the brilliant Mossad operatives who helped them defeat Erica. "But I think they would forget what they were there to do and just end up doing math, no?"

Mack got a clear mental image of the scene Reuben painted. The corners of his mouth twitched. "Himari, what exactly do you have going on in Massimo's house? The Feds will have a hissy-fit if they find out."

"They won't. Shadrach shared a few little programs with me." She looked over her shoulder at Reuben. "You Mossad boys have some sneaky tech."

"Of course." Reuben shrugged as if it were a given, got up, and looked at her screen. "What did Shammah give you?"

"He called it Number 13. It's spyware like nothing I've ever seen. I had Filippo install it last week." She turned back to Mack and said, "That's why I've been so worried. I've been able to see what is going on."

Kayah leaned in, studying the video feed. Massimo paced his office, gesticulating wildly. The convulsive, jerky movements of his body looked unnatural and were disconcerting to watch. "Do you have audio?"

"I had to stop listening; it was freaking me out. He holds it together when people are around, but behind closed doors, he is raving."

A troubled expression clouded Kayah's battered face as she watched the screen. "Turn it on, Himari."

"All right, but I am warning you…"

The bunker filled with the garbled noise of muttered curses and blasphemies as Marco ben Massimo's incoherent ramblings came through the speakers. Then, he looked into the camera, bared his teeth, and made a low, snarling growl.

Genevieve looked at Reuben. "That's odd. Why is he ranting in Greek?"

Kayah scrambled backward. "Shut it off!" They all fell silent as the normally unflappable Kayah paled, then ran to their weapons cabinet. "Mack, we've got to move. We've got to pull Filippo—right now!"

"Yakira?" Reuben said, crossing the room. "What is it?"

Kayah jammed a clip into a nine-millimeter pistol with an ominous click. "That was not Marco ben Massimo's voice. That was that damn demon talking."

The Under Butler

Located on the southern tip of the New City in the fashionable Saxony Hills neighborhood, the manicured grounds and well-appointed living quarters of Marco ben Massimo's mansion oozed genteel luxury, however, the innocent appearance was a facade. The compound was a fortress, patrolled around the clock by dozens of armed guards, almost every inch of the estate monitored by video surveillance.

On the third floor in a small staff bedroom, Filippo ben Vincente paced. He had been undercover for two months, playing the role of an under butler, where he served during meals, ushered guests to Massimo's study, and supervised the housekeeping staff, most of whom did not understand the Italian being spoken around them, a fact that made Massimo and his underlings careless. They spoke injudiciously, heedless of who was in earshot, and Filippo tried to be in earshot as much as possible.

He had only been back for five days, resuming his role when Massimo returned from Italy. Before his departure, the gangster teetered on the edge of ruin, out of favor with the Martinelli family in Italy, and broke. The missives poured in, the dons demanding progress as the noose tightened. But Marco ben Massimo was a slippery character and, through dumb luck, claimed a six-million-shekel reward for delivering Davianna ben David into Korah's hands. He flew to Italy to assure the family he had everything under control.

The criminal investigation, launched by the New York division of the FBI, was being conducted without the direct knowledge of the Palace. The FBI might have stopped the reward, but it would have blown months of work. They feared the Martinelli Family would simply replace Massimo, and they would be back at the beginning. In the end, they made a judgment call, and Massimo got the cash.

Thaddeus recruited Filippo through their mutual connection, Mack, however, neither knew Filippo's history or why the assignment held such appeal. Then again, not even his wife knew, not the whole truth.

Filippo divided his life into two distinct parts: Italian and Alanthian. Himari belonged to the life he lived now, as the affable and successful fashion photographer and artist. She knew nothing of the man he had been the first twenty-four years of his life or the family he was born into. She did not know the Italian.

And it was the Italian who went undercover. He understood Massimo's world, having prowled the edges in his youth, so he recognized the scent of power, felt its lure, and hated the men who aroused the darkest part of his soul. Swimming the murky waters of intrigue and violence, ignited a hunger that coursed through his veins, as if it were embedded in his DNA—vendetta.

As much as he hated the underground bunker, he dreaded returning to the estate. He recognized the danger, not only for the covert work, but for the primal response he experienced being among these men. Sometimes, he even found himself in one accord with them, which was ludicrous.

However, after masquerading at the New Year's Eve gala, being undercover, and fighting Erica, he had changed. And as he looked into the small mirror in his room, Filippo was not sure who looked back. His wife's unexpected call tonight felt like a proverbial lifeline.

He checked his watch. Time to go. Arming himself with a smuggled pistol and a lethal thirteen-inch stiletto, he left. As he passed through the gaudy sitting room and headed to the kitchen, he realized they might be liberating him from the devil's lair, but this was not over.

White Van

As Filippo moved through the house, Himari watched him on the monitors from a mobile unit parked three blocks away. She bristled with nervous energy, barking orders, and typing. "Miss Pink, are you ready?"

"We're a go, Sunflower," Alaina answered from her post in the bunker. "We are one click away from ticking off a bunch of rich people."

Reuben, Kayah, and Mack took their positions, ready to cover Filippo's escape, equipped with night vision goggles and enough weaponry to take down the entire complex. Himari hoped they could pull off the extraction without firing a shot, but Kayah's bombshell cast the likelihood of that at about fifty percent.

Himari's task tonight was to jam communications inside the mansion and override the backup power. When Alaina killed the electricity, their feeds from inside the house would be cut. If they were not rescuing Filippo, Himari would have been in the bunker. But she wanted to be close. If something happened, she needed to be here.

Still buzzing from their victory over Erica, Filippo blindsided her with the news he was resuming his undercover work. She thought he was done, that this was over. They argued about it long into the night, both saying things they did not mean. After hours of shouting and bitter tears, Himari relented, but only after Filippo agreed to install the Mossad spyware and plan an exit strategy.

The intervening five days had been the longest of her life. The moment he left, she felt uneasy. But it was more than the danger of an undercover assignment. She checked on Filippo every chance she got, and what she saw concerned her. "Do you detect anything strange about Filippo?" she asked Alaina, who, of course, knew she was spying on the house,

Alaina studied the screen, watching her oldest friend. After a time, she said, "He is moving differently. His mannerisms are not right."

"I know," Himari said. "He seemed so different when he got back."

"We've all been under a lot of stress, Himari. I'm sure things will be fine."

Himari nodded, but Alaina's reassurance gave her no comfort; and now she understood why.

The plan currently in motion came out of their negotiations the night he left, though neither anticipated his exit would come so quickly. Unlike New Year's Eve, their mission tonight was straightforward. Filippo would escape during the confusion of the power outage and make his way to one of three extraction points: the gardener's shed, where he hid Reuben and Kayah last month, the gazebo at the south gate, or the empty stable near the rear of the property.

"Lights out in three, two, one. Go!" Himari called over the secured lines, and for the second time in two weeks, the uber-rich section of the New City went dark.

Arrivederci

As Filippo marched toward the kitchen exit, a guard stepped in front of him. "Hey, where do you think you are going?"

They were the last words the man ever spoke.

Filippo opened his stiletto directly over the man's heart, killing him without sound or blood spray, assassin style. "Martinelli pig," he snarled as the guard dropped.

He wiped the knife on the man's coat and dragged him out of the doorway, leaving the body in a corner without a pang of conscience. Last week, the guard kicked a kitchen maid without provocation. He was a loud-mouth bully who spat when he talked. Those were his good qualities.

Behind him, the house erupted in angry curses and crashing glass. Massimo's shouting rose above the clamor, sounding like a demented wild animal. Filippo left the chaos, blending into the shadows and doing his best not to appear furtive, simply a man out for a stroll, escaping the oppressive atmosphere inside. Glancing over his shoulder for pursuit, he saw the flicker of candles and bobbing flashlights in the dark windows and picked up his pace. As he walked, he realized he still held the knife. Retracting the blade, he palmed the weapon.

"Psst." The quiet sound drew his attention. Mack motioned from behind the gazebo.

Filippo jogged the last two yards, ducking behind the structure, still scanning the grounds.

"F3 acquired. M5 out," Mack whispered into the radio.

"Affirmative. Begin extraction," Himari answered. "K2, you've got a single guard at 2 o'clock, suggest you head south. R4, you're clear."

Less than seven minutes after it began, Operation Lights Out concluded. Filippo was free, but now, more than oil paint stained his hands.

Strangers

Himari flew into Filippo's arms the second the van door opened. He hugged her, murmuring a greeting as he kissed the side of her neck.

"Move your ass, Romeo." Mack pushed in from behind.

Reuben slid into the driver's seat.

Seconds later, Kayah materialized, making a break for the passenger door. She jumped inside, slightly out of breath and rubbing her sore ribs, but positively beaming. She flashed Reuben a smile and yanked off her stocking cap, brown hair tumbling around her shoulders, electrified and wild. "That was fun!"

"And you did not have to show your ass this time, huh?" Reuben teased as he drove away.

"Or get my ass kicked!" Kayah leaned across the seat and kissed his cheek, then turned over her shoulder and said, "Welcome back."

"*Mama Mia*, what happened to your face?"

Kayah rolled her eyes. "Car accident."

"It was not a car accident," Himari countered, taking Filippo's elbow. "That is why we pulled you out. Something attacked Kayah, and we believe it was in Massimo's house."

Mack shot Himari a look. She was always reluctant to mention anything supernatural. As a veteran of several skirmishes with the unseen, he was not nearly as circumspect. "Dude's got a demon. We figured it would be prudent to get you the hell out of there."

Filippo drew his brows down over his Roman nose. "What you say, a demon?"

"Mm-hm." Mack dared Himari to contradict him. "We've got an asset in touch with the spirit world. I'll find out what she knows about how one of them got loose. Regardless, we've got to be on the lookout." He nodded at Filippo. "You especially, he's gonna be hot."

A shadow clouded Filippo's eyes as he said, "I killed a guard. He tried to stop me."

Reuben broke the silence that had descended on the van. "On New Year's Eve, I killed three of Korah's men. Kayah killed one. It is a poor career decision to work for the bad guys."

Mack smacked Filippo's knee and said, "This is war, Filippo. You did what you had to do."

They all thought it disturbed him. It did not.

As they drove out of Saxony Hills, Filippo refused to meet Himari's eyes. Dark energy pulsed off him, and she knew taking him back to the bunker would be a disaster. "Reuben, drop Filippo and me off at the Bay safe house. We need some time alone." She gave Mack a sidelong glare, daring him to argue,

He looked between them, obviously seeing what she saw, and gave an imperceptible nod.

Twenty minutes later, Himari did not say a word as she unlocked the door. As they stepped inside, she experienced a surge of longing for their Golden Gate condo, knowing it would bring them back to who they were before Gus' murder and the subsequent chaos that rocked their lives. She closed the door, mentally preparing to conduct her own version of an exorcism. "Come, there is wine."

Filippo removed a gun from his waistband and shook his head. "Stay here. I will check the house."

"We monitor this place. It's empty." She tried to keep the impatience from her voice but failed.

"Himari, I will look." He crept into the empty house, moving on silent feet, brandishing the weapon.

She bit back a retort and waited. She sensed his anger and recognized the source since they had fought about it for months.

His silhouette appeared at the end of the hallway, the taut lines of his trim, muscular frame outlined in shadow. "We are alone," he said, sounding like a stranger.

And when she turned on the lights, she read it all. He resented her hovering, interpreting it as emasculation, when it was nothing of the sort. She was terrified of losing him. He thought she doubted him, which she had at first, but he disabused her of that notion when he pulled that wicked stiletto and said, 'I was not always a painter, Himari.' She realized then, there was a side to him she did not know, one he kept hidden, locked away. Tonight, he wore it like a cloak, as if he were a medieval Florentine Prince, as calculating as a Medici.

But Himari Nakamura was no wilting sunflower. She dropped her purse and threw the house keys in a bowl, the metallic ring sounding like the opening bell in a fight. She strutted toward him, her slender hips swaying a seductive rhythm. Years ago, over bottles of wine and much hilarity, Alaina taught her the catwalk, and tonight she employed it with feline prowess, stalking her black leopard.

He watched her come, burning with anger and lingering battle lust. The set of her shoulders signaled her intentions; the sway of her hips choreographed her passion. Heat coursed through his body as he caught the scent of the spicy oriental perfume she favored. She stopped inches from him, her straight black hair falling over her shoulders in a cascade. He wanted to jerk her head back and ram his tongue down her throat, then take her up against the wall without mercy.

She looked up at him, and he stared into her exotic, almond-shaped eyes. They were dark and beautiful and marked her as mixed blood, yet the wisdom they held was ancient Japanese.

"*Yōkoso, aisuru otto.*" Welcome home, beloved husband.

She ran her delicate fingers down his torso. "*Watashi wa anata ni hōshi suru.*" I will serve you.

He needed no Japanese to understand her meaning and remained still as she unbuttoned his trousers. His body thickened.

Himari went to her knees, nuzzling the heat of him, reveling in the bulge pulsing under her hand. She freed him with tantalizing slowness, easing his zipper down one tooth at a time. She pressed her cheek against his cock, anticipating the taste of him, the feel of steely silk, and the delicious way he would groan when she began.

Filippo watched her, her lower lip full and luscious, the upper, heart-shaped and perfect. His wife. He strained forward, moving his hips, seeking her, needing her. His breath came in short pants and growls, desperate for her to put that incredible mouth on him, to take him inside her.

Himari ran her tongue down the length of his erection, cupping his buttocks, holding him prisoner, unmoving and in her control as she serviced his desire, teasing, tempting, then taking him fully.

"Bellissima!" Filippo's cry shattered the silence of the dark hallway as he came apart, exploding in ecstasy. His head fell back, his body convulsed, and for a moment, she swept away the blackness in his soul. His legs gave out, and he slid to the floor.

Himari moved beside him, a secret smile hovering in the corner of her magical mouth. "Better now?"

"You make me feel like a whole man. You know what I needed, eh?" he murmured, drowsy and sated.

"I always know what you need, Filippo." She blew her warm breath in his ear, running the tip of her tongue around the shell. Unbuttoning his shirt, she dug her fingers into the wealth of black curly hair on his chest, reveling in her hairy Italian. "Come, I will get you that wine I promised. There is some meat and cheese, perhaps then we will have an espresso and a little grappa. Then, I will take you back to bed and love you properly."

He closed his eyes and smiled.

January 17, 1000 ME

Necessary Equipment

Mack arrived at the safe house the following morning. He pulled up in a sleek black sports car, the decoy they used New Year's Eve, and the fastest vehicle in their fleet. From the foyer window, Himari decided he looked as comfortable getting out of the Viper as he did driving a tractor. Mack ben Robert was a complicated character. At times, he appeared nothing more than a benign vintner, tending his grapes, fussing over his wine, a simple man of the soil. Then in an instant, his intelligent eyes flashed, and he would move in a way that revealed the lethal warrior who lived beneath his good ole boy facade.

But it was neither vintner nor warrior who unloaded Filippo's easel, pochade box, and canvas carrying case, it was their commanding officer.

Himari opened the door before he knocked and stepped aside, letting him enter. "Good morning, Mack."

"Morning." He took a deep breath and said, "Espresso and wine, it smells like home in here."

"It ought to. We polished off the last of the Bulizio last night."

"All of it?" Mack dropped the equipment in the foyer and gave her a speculative look. "There were four bottles left."

Himari moistened her lips, a little dry, a little hungover. "It was a homecoming, eh?"

Mack chuckled at her imitation of Filippo and smiled. He never tired of hearing that friends enjoyed his wine. "How is he this morning?"

"Distracted." Himari nodded to the dock where Filippo stood alone, staring out at the cold, rough water. "I'm glad you brought the paints. He needs them."

"We all need a little R&R. I'm headed up to Peccioli today. You two wanna come? It'd be good for him." Mack gestured to the solitary figure.

"They are pruning the vines, and I want to supervise that." He rubbed his nose and looked down at his boots. "I have been away too long, Himari. I fear we won't have another '97 Bulizio. I tended that wine like a first-time mother."

He sighed. "Two years in a row, all hell broke loose in November. Between hiding out, rescuing the Princes, and fighting Erica, the '99 has gotten very little of my attention. The '98 might turn out all right, although I spent a lot of time in New York while it was fermenting. I reckon the wine critics are going to call me a one-year-wonder, saying I just got lucky."

"I don't think they will say that, but if they do, we know the truth."

He shrugged, and she could tell it gave him no comfort.

"I've been thinking about what this has cost us," she said, laying her hand on his arm. "We've all had to make sacrifices, you more than the rest of us, because you have been involved for years."

Mack cleared his throat. "I suppose."

"When Vinia first told me about you, I thought she misread the situation. She is terrible at interpreting social signals, and she never recognized when boys fell for her, even when it was blatant. I thought with you she saw what she wanted because, for once, she was the one in love." She looked up at him. "And when the baby came, and you didn't, I thought I was right. But I was not."

He adjusted his ball cap, pulling it low on his head.

"What Prince Peter said at your wedding, about how you guarded him for years and saved his life dozens of times. I realized why you hadn't come, that you put your life on the line and sacrificed your own happiness. You are doing it again."

She squeezed his arm and added, "So, it does not matter what some wine critic writes about you. Mack ben Robert is no one-year- wonder."

"I appreciate that," he said, touched by the rarity of her praise. "You be sure to write some kind of program that counters all my bad reviews, will ya? I'd like to have a pot to piss in when this is all over with."

Himari laughed. "I don't think you have to worry about that. We've made a fortune selling the tech we've produced, and the last time I looked The Resistance investment portfolio was approaching twelve million."

"I've never taken a shekel," Mack said.

"Well, you ought to. That's what it's there for. We knew it would come down to this, that no one could work when we got in the thick of the fight. Who knows if I will even have a job when this is all over," she said. "The last thing any of us needs is to be worried about paying the mortgage. So don't be a pig-headed idiot."

Mack glanced away, a bit chagrined, but the corner of his mouth held a smile. "There's the Himari I've come to know and love."

"I just tell it like I see it. It does not always make me popular."

"Well, I never wonder where I stand with you," he said, checking his watch.

"I suppose that makes us two of a kind."

"True," he chuckled. "I suppose lately we have all been a bit short-tempered and ill."

"Everyone except Auntie," Himari said with a smile.

"I bet if she gets riled enough, we'll see some of that Italian temper."

"I am all too familiar with that," she said, throwing a dismissive gesture outside. But the sight of Filippo standing alone caused a pang in her stomach.

"The two of you should come with me."

"Do you think it is okay for me to be gone?" she asked, sounding wistful. She and Alaina had been underground since late December, and Peccioli sounded wonderful.

"The foursome left the Grand Canyon this morning, and they are headed to Albuquerque. Alaina and Genevieve are monitoring the transmissions, and Kayah and Reuben are there. Kayah is still low, even though she won't admit it." Mack shrugged. "Lavinia has equipment at the house, and we can be back here pretty quick if anything happens.

He looked off at the Bay, his expression serious. "The further afield the four of them get, the less we will be able to intervene directly. But they are well armed, and we've got assets along the way. If they run into trouble, there are contingency plans in place. I think the Resistance can survive a couple days without you." He pointed to Filippo who was heading back to the house. "And I think Filippo needs it. He seemed off last night."

"I expect killing a man might make anyone seem off."

"You got that right, Sunflower."

Mack left her side and went on the back porch, greeting Filippo. "Morning."

Filippo blinked, as if just seeing Mack. "Aye, *Buongiorno. Come va?*"

"Fair to middling. How 'bout you? Ready for a road trip?"

"To where?" Filippo tilted his head, his jaw dark and unshaven.

"Peccioli."

"And Himari, she can leave?"

"Yep, we just talked about it."

Filippo looked up at the gray sky and sighed. "I would not wish to put your family in danger, Mack. Massimo, he will probably be looking for me."

Mack shook his head. "Reuben and Genevieve have been tapped into the mansion, listening. They will let us know if they hear anything. But they don't seem too terribly concerned."

"Not yet," Filippo said darkly.

"True, and it's probably wise to get you out of here for a bit. I know Himari needs the break. Besides, Violet and Tony are up at the vineyard. I am sure she'll cook for you, and perhaps you can speak a little Italian that doesn't involve the mafia, eh?" Mack's eyes bore directly into Filippo's.

Filippo raised an eyebrow as the words hit their mark.

"We're pruning if you feel like getting your hands dirty. If not, you can paint. There's a decent art store in town if you're running low on anything. The valley is pretty this time of year, for those who can see it."

Filippo made a low grunt in the back of his throat. "I have painted almost every day for twelve years, even when I was married to Malibu. Those paintings are so bleak that I cannot even look at them now."

Filippo turned at the call of a winter sparrow, sitting on a naked tree branch. He dropped his head, studying his soft Italian loafers. "What does it say about me that I started not to miss it? That I began to enjoy what I was doing, and the art, the thing that makes me feel so alive, stopped mattering to me."

"It makes you human. Being undercover changes you." Mack clapped Filippo on the back. "The good news is, it ain't permanent. Trust me, I've been around this game for a long time. I know."

Filippo's mouth quivered. "Trust me, I know this is true?"

"Oh hell, man. We're all starting to sound like each other, piled up and packed in like sardines." Mack scoffed, "I even know what Reuben's farts smell like."

Filippo laughed. "*Mamma Mia*, you do need a vacation." Filippo motioned with his head to the door. "Peccioli is a good idea, Mack. And Reuben? He's a stinky bastard, eh?"

Mack hooted with laughter. "Yes, yes. This is true."

Blanks - Redding, California

Lavinia crunched down the gravel pathway, making noise, signaling her arrival to Filippo. She watched him out the living room window for over an hour while she and Himari chatted, and still, there was not a single dab of paint on the canvas. She stepped into his field of vision. The wind blew her hair into her eyes, she pushed it aside, and asked in Italian, "Blank canvas?"

He gave a rueful snort, answering in English, "It is terrible, eh? For months my hands ached to paint. Now I cannot do it."

"I understand that. After they raided the bunker when we were kids, Mamma and I moved up here." She gestured to the vineyard where Mack and the winter crew were pruning. "I did not do math for a year. Me, who does math in her sleep, who at this moment is calculating the tonnage of compost we will produce from the canes, the rate of decomposition, and the area it will cover, did nothing but cash register math for a year."

"What changed?" he asked.

"Gus. He sent me a problem. No note, no explanation, just math… from my friend."

"And you did the math, then everything was okay." Filippo looked past her. "Life is not that simple, Lavinia."

"That is not what I was going to say, but you are right, life is not that simple."

"Forgive me. I am a churlish."

Young Lavinia would have corrected his English, the wise woman standing before him let it go. "I did not do the problem because I saw what it was. He sent me a message in the math. It was not a difficult equation. I knew he could do it, so I put it in a drawer and did not answer. But it bothered me. I kept walking by my desk and knew it was in there, waiting."

Filippo stroked the handle of his fan brush, refusing to meet her eyes. "What was the message?"

"It was an equation for angular momentum and circular motion. In Gus' way, he was trying to tell me to stop spinning." Lavinia drummed her fingers on her thigh, holding back a sudden rush of grief.

"Spinning? That is one way to put it." The words left a bitter taste in his mouth.

"Do you remember our conversation on New Year's Eve, when you told me about your work?"

"Not really, it was an eventful night, eh?"

"It was, and I was scared. You said sometimes the blank canvas is hard, and you think you cannot do it. But you just begin. You put paint on the brush and something beautiful emerges, often unexpected and different."

He stared at the canvas but remained mute.

"You also said you do not paint over your earlier work, if you wish to paint the same subject, you do it as the artist you are now." Lavinia met his eyes and saw doubt swimming in their depths. She understood where he was. "Be the painter you are now, Filippo. Something beautiful will emerge." She blew him a kiss and went to find Mack.

Filippo watched her walk away, the wind whipped her peasant skirt around her ankles, a splash of Prussian blue against the blooming bismuth yellow planted between the rows. The foliage from last

Autumn's harvest glowed cadmium red, deep India gold, and burnt sienna. Mack was right, the vineyard was stunning this time of year.

The artist he was now?

Lavinia's words tumbled in his mind without an answer. Who was he now? Standing in the cold January wind, he could not fathom, but without a doubt, whoever he was, he no longer painted tranquil scenes of pastoral peace. If he put paint to canvas, nothing beautiful would emerge.

With a sound of disgust, he packed up and left the field.

He returned a quarter-hour later, wearing a pair of leather gloves and carrying pruning shears.

Mack did not say a word when he joined the crew, simply let him work.

January 18, 1000 ME

They Come By it Honestly - New City

Kayah threw down the photographs of Agnor ben Randall and Zanah ben Joseph with a grumble and rose from her chair, going to the sideboard where Genevieve had set up a coffee station. "Where the hell is that fat bastard?"

"Kayah, your language could use some improvement," Genevieve said, passing her the sugar and cardamom.

To Reuben's amusement, Kayah looked shamefaced.

"Sorry, Auntie. It is maddening, though. Where are they?"

"I don't know, honey. But I am certain we will find them."

Kayah brought the coffee back to her desk and sat down gingerly, rubbing her sore ribs. A stack of partial facial recognition hits came in overnight, but none were of the missing pair. "People seem to fall off the face of the Earth these days."

"The same can be said for you, Yakira. You disappeared on me for how many months last fall?"

"I enjoyed being Dorothy, and I liked my townhouse in Kensington," she said wistfully. Then she pointed a finger at him. "When this is all over, I am going to be Dorothy ben Quincy again."

"And I shall reprise my role as the banker, Isaac ben Joseph," he said, referencing the false identities they used in London.

"Oh yes, you looked very dapper in your bowler hat." She held out a pinky finger and took a delicate sip of her coffee. "We shall drink tea on the terrace and be perfectly respectable with my ridiculous cat." Hidden behind the sarcasm laid a concern for the stray she fed and had not seen since early December.

"We shall be very proper, indeed." Reuben enthused in his best British accent, trying to keep the mood light. She had been in a dark place since the incident with the evil spirit. Though she never talked about it, he saw how it troubled her, and caught her haunted expression when she thought no one was watching.

"Do you have a house in England, Kayah?" Genevieve asked.

"London. I bought it last summer when I had a vague notion of retiring." She waved a hand, dismissing the notion as if it was nothing.

"Retirement is not all it is cracked up to be," Genevieve said, recognizing the sentiment behind Kayah's blithe words. "I was bored. At first it was nice, but after a while?" She shrugged. "I was glad when Peter asked me to help. To support the cause, of course, but I enjoy having you young people here." Color crept up her cheeks. "Oh, that sounds pathetic."

Kayah folded her hands over her stomach and swiveled in her chair to face Genevieve. "Totally pathetic." The smile hovering at the corner of her mouth and a quick wink took the sting out of her words. "But did I hear you've rekindled a romance?"

Genevieve's face flamed. "That is Himari Nakamura making up tales."

"Not just Himari, Alaina seems to think so, too." Kayah pointed at the closed bedroom where Alaina slept after taking the night shift.

"Those girls have too much time on their hands. Alaina keeps trying to convince me to color my hair."

Kayah laughed and gestured to her brunette ponytail. "I could do it for you. There are several kits in the bathroom."

Genevieve rolled her eyes. "I am too old for such nonsense."

Kayah studied her, tapping her chin in thought. "Brunette number five, I think. It's not too dark, more of a chestnut. It would look good on you."

Genevieve made a great show of sorting through a stack of papers and changed the subject. "So, where are we on the hunt for Agnor and Zanah this morning, Reuben?"

Reuben took up a chair beside her. "They come by it honestly, no? These two, they are hiding like their girls."

"With Massimo and Korah after them, they better," Kayah said.

"That video has done more damage to Korah than anything we've concocted thus far. The public is outraged over it."

Reuben nodded. "And the surveillance of Massimo, he is raging about finding Zanah. It is not good."

Remote - Redding, California

Over dinner at Peccioli, Himari shocked everyone when she announced, "I am going back to the bunker tomorrow by myself."

Mack paused with a bite of bread halfway to his mouth. "You think so?"

"I know so. There is no reason for either of you to come." She gestured to Filippo and said, "You hate the bunker, it makes you stir crazy, and there is nothing for you to do there except pace around and complain." Himari turned, pointing her fork at Mack. "You are no better, and I've been thinking about what you said. The foursome is moving further afield every day. You can't physically intervene in any situation at this point, so it does not matter if you are here or there. The only difference is a three-hour ride to the airport, and if we have a true emergency, we can pick you up in the helicopter."

Lavinia stared down at her plate, moving the remaining pasta noodles around in the sauce. "Himari and I made some adjustments to the equipment here, Mack. Shammah gave her an ingenious little program that securely interfaces my office with the bunker. I was chatting with Kayah before dinner. It's working."

"Then why we got to be underground?" Filippo asked, not bothering to refute Himari's assertion that he hated the bunker.

Himari tilted her head and gave him an indulgent smile. "While we have secure communications with Lavinia's office, the servers still run through the bunker. I cannot do what I do remotely, not with the level of encryption we need. But Massimo might be looking for you in town, and Mack doesn't have to be in the bunker. He can direct operations from here, and you can paint."

Mack nodded. "I can sleep in my bed, hang out with my son, and make a little wine? That sounds like a winner to me, Himari."

Filippo placed his napkin beside his plate and rose, taking his glass of wine. "*Mi scusi,*" he said, an angry undertone to his voice. The plate-glass window shook as he slammed the terrace door.

Himari threw down her napkin and stormed after him.

Lavinia glanced at Mack, confusion clouding her face. "I thought he would be happy."

Mack took a long slow drink. "I expect it's more complicated than that, Valentine."

Shouting erupted from the back terrace.

Lavinia cut a quick look toward Richard's room. "I hope they don't wake Bino."

Mack chuckled. "If the Second Infantry marched through his room, I don't think he'd wake up tonight. He's tuckered out."

Lavinia took Mack's hand, rubbing the rough skin on the side of his thumb. "He has not left your side since you got home."

Mack pressed a kiss to her palm. "I haven't wanted him to, you either."

"If you are staying, I think it is safe to tell Mama and Papa they can go home, at least for a little while."

Violet and Tony were out to dinner with friends tonight, but Mack knew they wanted to get back to their bungalow by the beach. "That works all the way around. It will be nice to be home."

Lavinia cleared her plate and collected the empty pasta bowl. "Why is Filippo so angry? Himari was relieved when I said he could stay with us."

Mack scraped the dinner plates in the garbage can and stacked them in the sink. "He's readjusting. It's hard coming off an assignment, it takes time."

"What was that all about?" Himari demanded, storming outside, at her wit's end with his moodiness.

Filippo turned on her, incredulous. "You do not know?"

"No," she said impatiently.

He waved a dismissive hand and turned his back.

"You hate the bunker, you need a place to lie low, so I made both things happen. What is your problem?"

"You did not think for a minute, before you organize my life, that you have a conversation with me first?"

"What?" Himari looked at him agog. "It was not like that at all. Lavinia and I were in the office today, and it came to me. We installed the program, made the connection, and it worked. She said you were welcome to stay."

"But you did not think that I might have an opinion about where I stay, or if you go? You make a decision for us and announce it at a dinner with our friends and expect me, like your trained lap dog, to roll over?"

"That's bullshit! When have we ever acted like that in our marriage? We make decisions for each other all the time."

"About what the fuck we going to eat!" He advanced on her. "Not about important things, like whether you pull me out of an undercover investigation, or if I am going to hide, and where I live while you go back to the New City without me! Those are big decisions, not whether we have lasagna or sushi!" He shook his head, anger rolling off him in waves. "I think we got big problems, Himari."

The use of her name jolted her. He rarely called her Himari, and if he did, it was in love, always 'my Himari'. The fact he thought they had problems shook her to the core. Stunned, she protested again but with less volume. "That is not the way this happened at all."

He threw up his hands. "In what way has it happened?" His jaw worked, his face a shadow of fury. "Did we ever even have a conversation about you getting involved in all of this, or did you just do it?"

"I might have discussed it with you, but it happened before we got together. You were still married to that annoying brat!"

"And it seems that I am once again married to an annoying brat!" he shouted.

"Malibu? You are going to compare me to Malibu? That woman could not take a piss without asking you!"

"Unlike you, who never asks me a thing!"

Himari raised her chin. "I do not need your permission to do anything."

Filippo erupted. "Permission? You think you make a decision to become a revolutionary does not warrant a conversation? A decision that might send another one of my wives to jail, that affects my life and your life, you think those are permission?"

"That's not the way—"

"You think you always know the best, that my opinions do not matter, that you are the boss. That is disrespect." He pointed an accusing finger at her. "You disrespect me!"

Himari smacked his hand away and yelled, "Don't you point your finger at me! Don't you talk to me that way! You are being irrational."

"And you are a fucking bitch!"

"I am no different than I have ever been," she ground out. "One of us has changed, and it is not me." She spun on her heel and called over her shoulder, "You let me know when my artist comes home."

The door closed quietly, and Filippo stood alone, in the dark.

Several hours later, Filippo slipped into bed, bringing with him the warm smell of oak barrels from the cellar. He had taken refuge in the winery, prowling the empty corridors, exploring the quiet production facilities, thinking.

Himari curled on her side, pressed as far against the wall as she could get, motionless, but awake.

"I'm not staying here, Himari. We will drive back tomorrow, but I'm getting my car and going to New York. I have a big show in two weeks, and I was originally scheduled to be there. I spoke to Kayah. I cannot help her with her search. Zanah and Bubba will never trust me. I would make things worse. So, I am leaving, and I'm going to stay at her place while I am in New York."

He made a bitter sound in the back of his throat and continued, "With Massimo, you are right, I should not be in the New City. So, there is nothing for me to do here, and you said yourself, you do not need me."

"I never said I did not need you." Himari's voice was unsteady, strained.

"Not in so many words," he whispered, "but you do not."

Himari buried her face in her arm, crying.

"Bellissima," he breathed.

A keening sound escaped her. "You're leaving me."

Filippo reached out and touched her shoulder. "Shh, do not cry."

He did not deny it, and her heart shattered. "Please, don't go, please?"

"Come here." He pulled her into his arms.

She clung to him, weeping in earnest.

He cupped her cheek, his eyes tired and sad. "I'm a going to New York for a show, maybe hide from a gangster for a little while. You got important work to do. It's okay."

She covered her face and nodded, but they both knew there was more to it than that, a lot more.

January 19, 1000 ME

Golden Gate - New City

As Filippo exited the highway near their condo, Himari spoke for the first time in two hours. "Maybe you should take this car."

Filippo shook his head. "I want my own."

Himari closed her eyes, searching for patience, trying to say the right words. "Massimo still controls Facetec, Filippo. Even though you wore glasses undercover, we did not change your face. He may have loaded it into the system. If he does not know who you are already, he might soon, and driving our car puts you in further danger."

Filippo cast her a sidelong glance. She sat in the passenger's seat, her head bowed, staring at her lap, her straight black hair hiding her expression. He knew she was right, but he wanted to abandon everything that held the taint of The Resistance and reclaim his life. Despite what his wild emotions urged him to do, he did not have a death wish, so he conceded, "Well, it is a nice car, eh?"

Her shoulders relaxed, and she nodded slowly, her face still hidden. "I want to go home, at least for a little while," she paused, as her voice faltered, "before you leave."

"We sneak in?" he asked quietly.

She turned, her eyes swimming. "Yes."

"There are some things I want at the house. We will go."

Himari covered her mouth holding back a torrent of tears. She felt like she was drowning, swamped in an ocean of pain, capsized in an unsinkable vessel that hit a hidden reef.

It was risky going to their house, but short of Marco ben Massimo parked out front, nothing was going to stop her. She twisted around in her seat and brought up a large canvas bag that held their disguises. His work and clandestine activities, as much as her own, necessitated them. So, at least he could not lay the blame solely at her feet as he seemed to be doing with everything else. She pulled her hair into a quick knot and tugged a gray wig into place, adding dark sunglasses. They each had long wool overcoats. She packed a matching gray wig for Filippo and the cane he carried on New Year's Eve. It had a flashlight in the grip and a blade inside the shaft.

They planned their route in and out before they bought the property. Every Resistance safe house and members' permanent residence had around the clock electronic and video surveillance. So, while the visit was not without risks, they were mitigated.

Himari sent a text to Alaina. "Going home for a few. We need it, Al. Watch my back."

At a stoplight, four miles from their house, Filippo donned the wig and glasses. "The facial recognition, it is a little worrisome. We will change my face before I leave, okay?"

Himari hugged herself, glad he suggested it, glad she did not have to insist he do it. "Kayah has her kit at the bunker. I will ask her to make you up a few pieces before you go." She paused with her phone in her hand and added, "If that is okay with you?"

She could not read his eyes behind his dark glasses, but there was no laughter hovering on the set of his firm jaw, no teasing humor in his voice. "I think I am going to need my own kit but ask her to have ready for me the disguise I wore to the gala."

In a soft voice, full of tentative uncertainty, Himari said, "If you wait a day or two, we could plan a little better."

"No. I am going today. You are releasing the photo of the two Princes tomorrow and will be busy. I can manage to buy my own kit, Himari."

"Of course," she capitulated and sent the text to Kayah with shaking fingers.

He pulled into the underground garage, using the passkey from his wallet. The gate lifted, and they parked in a guest's slot near the entrance. "We take the steps? I got my key." He also had a gun.

The sound of the racking bullet in the pistol was as foreign to her as the man sitting beside her. She wanted to leap across the armrest and shake him, to demand he snap out of this, to scream at the top of her lungs, 'What have you done with my husband?' But Himari did none of those things, she simply nodded, and followed him upstairs, hoping to reach him.

They stepped inside and were hit with the smell of their own home, the indescribable scent of an abode, exclusive to the inhabitants who dwelt within its walls. It was not the house itself, for given any length of time, wherever they resided took on the character. Absent since November and unaware of its presence during the normal course of life, it greeted them as an olfactory reminder of who they were in this place, that what they created together was unique in the world—home.

Himari set her purse on the counter, looking around at the quiet house. Their lives had been interrupted. The evidence was everywhere. A laundry basket sat in the hall, a pair of shoes rested under the coffee table, and a pillow on the sofa lay askew. She moved to open the blinds and enjoy the stunning view of the Golden Gate, but Filippo's sharp command drew her up short.

"No, leave them closed. We are only here for a minute." He left the room to get his things.

Himari stood in the empty living room, surrounded by their life and his paintings. She felt like her soul was bleeding all over the rug.

Filippo found her staring at the Purple Rain picture, the one of her in a miniskirt, her hands covering her face, standing at the end of the alley of the Ramen Shop the last time she tried to see Ken. "That pain was nothing… compared to what I feel right now."

"I am sorry, Bellissima. It is not you. It is me." His voice cracked.

"I can be more submissive, I know how." She swallowed. "I did it for Ken, and I did not love him nearly as much as I love you."

"I am not Ken, and I would never do that to you." He turned her from the painting and directed her gaze to another. Himari in her red halter and jeans, posing in the doorway smiling at him, fragile but strong, regaining a measure of her power through his love. "This is who I say goodbye to today." He swept his arm around the room encompassing all the pictures, his wedding gift to her, Himari in all her moods and facets. "I love the whole woman, you no change for me. I will come back when I have my head straight back on."

She pointed to the erotic picture. "Don't leave without making love to me, in our own bed. Give me that, before you go."

"Like the first time? In the day, when you were in so much pain. You let me take it, you let me show you. I will come back." He cradled her face, put his forehead to hers, life imitating art; Filippo and Himari together.

By 5:00 pm, he was gone.

Part 7 - Priorities

January 16, 1000 ME

Give Me Your Hand - Grand Canyon - Josiah and Davianna

In a small cottage at the edge of the Grand Canyon, Davianna ben David was chopping vegetables when she dropped the knife and exclaimed, "Ow!"

"Are you okay?" Josiah asked, rising from his spot at the kitchen table.

Davianna nodded, bringing her finger to her mouth and wincing.

"Let me see."

"No," she said, scampering across the kitchen to the sink. "It's just a little cut." But the water ran pink, her finger obviously bleeding.

He gave her his doctor's look.

"Fine," she grumbled.

Josiah took her wrist, gently pressing the edges of the cut as the running water washed away the blood and gave him a visual of the damage. It was a superficial laceration but deep enough to require a bandage. He handed her a paper towel and said, "Keep pressure on it. I'll get my bag, and we'll get you sorted."

"All right," she sighed, turning off the stove and taking a seat. Her finger throbbed ominously, blood seeping through the paper towel.

Josiah returned with his doctor's bag, laid down a sterile cloth, ointments, and bandages. She watched him work, his black hair curling over his forehead, his dark brows set and serious. He approached the cut with the same care he would a severed limb, but that was the way he did everything, competent and exacting. She relaxed her hand as much as she could, but the cut stung, and she knew it would be sore tomorrow.

They had forged a tenuous truce after his rejection and her subsequent blow up in the cabin. However, the truce and his cool reserve were blown to smithereens after she had a nightmare in Vegas. They shared a moment of unguarded passion, and she knew he was not ambivalent toward her. Now tension simmered between them, bubbling just below the surface, and when she closed her eyes, she could still feel his hands on her body and taste his ardent kisses. It had been the most powerful experience of her life. She squirmed as he took her hand, and the sparks shooting up her arm had nothing to do with the cut and everything to do with the man.

"This might sting," Josiah said as he swabbed the wound.

"Ouch!" she hissed.

"Sorry."

She sighed, admiring the strength and gentleness of his hands. "What made you become a doctor?"

"I always wanted to be one. I suppose I have a natural inclination toward it."

He paused and looked up with a soft smile, his eyes far away. "We had a gathering at Gilead when I was young. I cannot recall the occasion, but there were a bunch of kids, which was unusual. I suppose that is why I remember it."

Returning to his work, he shined a light on the cut, checking for debris. "Anyway, the adults were doing their thing and sent the kids upstairs. The girls wanted to play house, but I told them we were playing hospital, so I could be the doctor."

"I knew a boy who wanted to play doctor with me," Davianna dead panned.

"I was about five, Davianna." His eyes sparkled with humor, though he did not like the idea of some randy kid trying to get in her underpants.

"As far back as that?"

"Yes, I think so, maybe even earlier, but that is my first real memory of it. I had planned to go to medical school after the RMA, thinking I might practice medicine until I took over the kingdom. I come by it honestly. My grandfather, on my mother's side, was a physician."

The corner of his mouth lifted, and he added, "He was also an Italian Duke and a notorious womanizer. My mother was his only legitimate offspring."

"So, he encouraged you to become a doctor?"

"I only met him once. My father and I traveled to the Golden Kingdom when I was seven or eight, and we stopped in Italy to visit him. I believe my mother was born when he was in his sixties, so he was quite old." Josiah looked up in remembrance. "He took me to visit his clinic. He still practiced, though you remember medicine was different then."

Davianna bowed her head. She did not have many memories of the world before the rebellion, the time before sickness, disease, and violence. She was born into it, but she was a toddler when Korah took the throne. "Everything was different then."

"Aye," he said ruefully. "I've had my time as a surgeon. Now I will simply shift my talents for healing to the Kingdom."

She curled her fingers into his palm. It was warm and solid. "Much blood will be shed, will it not, Josiah?"

"Perhaps, but sometimes it is necessary to cut, burn, and bleed. As brutal as it sounds, it is often the only path to healing. We live in a fallen world, Davianna."

She touched her left pocket, giving him a pointed look.

"The Civil War devastated Alanthia in more ways than people realize. I would like to avoid a recurrence if I can, which is why I consented to Peter's picture yesterday, and why we must get you safely to the Golden City."

He dabbed ointment onto her cut and continued, "If we destabilize Korah's government and establish my right to rule, perhaps we can avert another bloodbath."

"Korah is insane," Davianna whispered, "but there is a part of him that is so beguiling and charming, even kind."

Josiah pressed the bandage firmly in place, realizing this was the first time she had spoken Korah's name since the night of their escape. He suspected she might need to talk, so he did not shut her down. "Korah used that talent his whole life to disarm people, to fool them. Handsome, friendly, and harmless, he hoodwinked the entire kingdom, including my father, who trusted him to the very end. Peter and Alexa were the only people who saw through his charade. In hindsight, I suspect he was abusing them."

Davianna squeezed her eyes closed and shuddered. Korah turned on her several times, one moment loving and caring, and the next, violent and terrifying.

"Come here." Josiah rose and pulled her into a hug.

A dam inside her broke, and the trauma of her captivity spilled out. "I was so afraid. He never let me sleep. I could barely think."

He nodded, his amber eyes full of compassion.

"One day, I don't remember which, he insisted we go for a walk in the gardens, and we talked like we were friends. Josiah, he was nice." Davianna rested her cheek on the fleece of his blue sweatshirt, inhaling his scent, taking comfort in the strength of his body. "Then a few minutes later, he got this demented look in his eyes and punched me in the stomach so hard I thought I would never breathe again."

"Oh, Minx."

"But as I was lying there, I heard your voice and remembered that night in the park when I got the wind knocked out of me. You taught me how to breathe through it, so I did it, and it worked."

"Good girl," he said, closing his eyes against the fury, clearly picturing the scene.

"Then he picked me up, like I was a baby, and carried me to my room. He cried real tears and told me he was sorry. I believed him. Josiah, I swear he was telling the truth. Then he let me sleep."

She pulled away, walking back into the kitchen, her voice distant and monotone. "But an hour later it started again." She looked over her shoulder. "And that is when it got really bad."

Josiah's nose flared. He remembered that day. "He won't touch you again. I promise."

She gave him a look that suggested she wanted to believe him.

"He won't."

Davianna palmed her eyes and asked, "What happened to Astrid? I never saw her. Korah told me she was gone, which was obviously a lie. But she is not quite right, and she won't tell me anything."

Josiah glanced toward Peter and Astrid's closed bedroom door, cognizant of his duty to guard Astrid's privacy. "They kept her sedated."

"Well, she was sick when we left," Davianna said, turning the stove back on. "Peter knows what happened, but he won't say either."

"I surmise they've done something similar to him, which may explain why they have bonded the way they have. He is helping her through it."

Davianna looked over her shoulder. "So, he is not just bopping her brains out, he is taking care of her?"

Josiah snorted. "I suppose, in his way, yes. And while he and I disagree over his methods, you cannot deny she has responded positively."

A mischievous light flashed in her brown eyes. "True. I have heard her yelling, yes, yes, several times."

Josiah laughed, shaking his head. Their cabin mates were on a world record setting pace for the most sex by two people in the history of the world.

Growing serious, Davianna added, "You may be right. And now that she and I have cleared the air about Guan, perhaps she will confide in me. I am worried about her. Especially considering," she paused, searching for a way to put this delicately, "Peter's reputation. But he promised I had it wrong about the two of them, so I suppose I must take his word."

"Aye," Josiah agreed, leaning against the counter, watching her cook. "I don't think there is any room for distrust between the four of us. We won't make it otherwise."

"That's true," she said, scooping a handful of onions into a skillet.

"There has always been more to Peter than met the eye." Josiah passed her the salt and pepper shakers. "And he survived two decades living with that maniac. So, if anyone can help Astrid sort through what's happened, it's Peter. He said as much to me at the cabin."

"He talked to me that night I got so mad." She crinkled her nose in chagrin. "He helped me, too."

"Well, at least he did not try to take you to bed."

"Heavens, no," Davianna laughed. "As oversexed as he might be, he has been nothing but friendly toward me, and I'm glad he changed my nickname. Did you know he has officially dubbed me Davianna ben Fireball?"

"Officially?" Josiah chuckled. "I think I prefer Minx. Fireball is feisty."

"Feisty is an adjective that never applied to me before." Davianna tilted her head back, staring at the ceiling. "I was not feisty when Korah held me captive."

"Yes, you were. You did one of the bravest things I have ever seen."

"I did?" she asked, biting her bottom lip.

He nodded and tried to keep the horror of that moment off his face. "Yes, you did."

"Korah will never stop looking for me, Josiah." Her voice cracked, and it became clear she was remembering. "He wanted more from me than just this device."

The Real Priority

"It's cold out here, Fireball," Peter drawled, stepping onto the balcony.

"Fireballs have their own heat," Davianna answered, her frosted breath disappearing into the deep canyon below.

Peter chuckled and joined her at the railing, reaching into his breast pocket and coming up empty. "This not smoking sucks. I ordered Jarrod to stock our safe houses with my cigarettes. He did not."

Davianna looked up at him from beneath her long dark lashes. "Perhaps he forgot?"

"Jarrod forgets nothing," Peter scoffed. "He has been after me to quit. I suspect he knew I would not risk being captured for a pack of smokes." He gave her a dubious look. "He was right."

Davianna leaned her head against his shoulder, staring out at the craggy rocks illuminated by the silver moon, melancholy after her conversation with Josiah. "Why did you take it up?"

"It is relatively common to develop a placeholder addiction. Coffee and cigarettes are less damaging than heroin," Peter said, his face becoming a mask, akin to a granite statue, beautiful and austere.

Her eyes widened as she looked up at him.

"Korah and his goons have become adept at using it as a weapon. They turned me into an addict, and they attempted to do the same to Astrid."

Davianna gasped, unconsciously checking her left pocket. "They were giving her drugs?"

He nodded.

"And did they… I mean, is she?"

"An addict?" Peter provided helpfully.

Davianna nodded, feeling sick.

Peter shrugged. "I do not know, neither does she. I suppose time will tell."

"Tell what?" Davianna demanded.

"Whether she ever goes back to it."

Davianna covered her face, breathing into her hands. "That's terrible."

"Aye," Peter murmured.

She dropped her hands and looked at him, her eyes large and questioning. "And you? Are you okay?"

"I am today, Fireball."

"Oh, how awful. He is such a wicked man."

"Indeed," Peter agreed, absently flicking his lighter.

"But why wouldn't Astrid tell me? Why won't she talk to me about it?"

Peter cleared his throat. "She might never. I do not." He turned and looked her in the eyes. "But I think you understand that."

"I suppose I do." Davianna's whole body rose and fell with a great sigh. "Talking about things makes you remember, and that doesn't feel good."

"Give the girl a gold star," he said sarcastically.

Absently rubbing her sore finger, she whispered, "Were you there? Did you see what Korah was doing?"

Peter dropped his head, covering his eyes with one hand. "Yes. I am sorry. I got you out as fast as I could." He snorted with derision. "Well, no, that is not entirely true. I could have gotten you out earlier, but I would have had to leave Astrid and Josiah behind."

"What was he planning?" she asked, her voice just above a whisper, lost in the great canyon.

Peter moved in front of her and took her by the shoulders. "It does not matter because it will never happen. Josiah and I will never allow it. We will protect you and Astrid with our lives. I give you my solemn vow."

"I appreciate that," she whispered. "But it is not me who truly matters. It is not even this device," she added, tapping her pocket.

He gave her a curious look.

"Don't you see? The most important person here is Josiah." A gust of wind blew her hair away from her face, revealing a fierceness in her he had never seen before.

"He is who you must protect with your life. The fate of the entire kingdom hinges on him retaking the throne. If it comes down to a choice between any of us, you must choose him." Davianna gripped his hands and held his gaze. "That is the vow I would have from you, Prince. Promise me."

"Bloody Hell," he murmured, as the implications of her words registered. Heretofore, he would have made the vow without a second thought. To sacrifice his own life, yes, he risked that for years. Even Davianna, if given the choice between her and Josiah, he could do it. But Astrid? He had just found her. Could he sacrifice his own hope and happiness for the Kingdom? He prayed he would never face that choice because he did not think he could do it.

"Peter?" she prompted, leaning forward.

"The thing is, Fireball, Josiah would never countenance such a vow."

"Then we will not tell him." Davianna turned away and marched inside, assuming her new role as guardian of the throne.

January 17, 1000 ME

Left Turn at Albuquerque - New Mexican Desert

"Ándale! Arriba!" Davianna called from the backseat of the black SUV. "Play my song!"

Peter shot Astrid a look. "What is she on about?"

Astrid giggled. "When we were trapped in that dingy hotel in Baker's Corners, there was nothing to do but wait and worry. So, Davianna decided we should learn Spanish, and the way to do it," Astrid twisted around in her seat, laughing, "was to watch Speedy Gonzales cartoons."

"Not just Speedy," Davianna protested and felt her face grow pink. Josiah rolled his eyes, and she punched him in the arm. "They are funny. I love them."

He rubbed his arm, pretending it hurt. "You occupied your time watching thousand-year-old Looney Tunes cartoons?"

"Ha! How did you know Speedy was a Looney Tune?" Davianna wiggled her shoulders, scoring an invisible point for her side.

Josiah rolled his eyes again. "Reuben. He loves them, too. Between the cartoons and the wrestling, I thought my brain was going to turn to mush."

"Wrestling!" Davianna pointed at him playfully. "You can never make fun of me for watching cartoons, Carsten ben Hansen."

Josiah checked the front seat, and seeing neither Peter nor Astrid was watching, made his signature double-fisted flex, scowling at her with mock ferocity.

"I love it!" she squealed in delight. "By the way, who was that woman with you, the gorgeous blonde in the bikini?"

Josiah did not miss a beat. "Kayah, Reuben's girlfriend."

The vehicle swerved as Peter jerked his head around. "What?"

"It was a stunt, a way to draw Davianna out of hiding." Josiah shrugged.

"Kayah?" Peter corrected the wheel, his expression thunderous. "When? When was that stunt?"

Astrid turned in her seat, her danger alarm blaring. "Mid-December, why?"

Peter gripped the steering wheel so hard his knuckles turned white. "She knew where you were in mid-December and said nothing?"

Josiah leaned forward. "I cannot say if she knew where I was or not. I only saw her once."

"Once is enough," Peter ground out, simmering.

"Hang on, before you go off. Reuben and I discussed this at length. Initially, we planned to engage a Mossad agent to be my partner, but later determined the fewer people who knew, the better. It was a risky operation. And if I was exposed on television?" Josiah shuddered, not only at the danger, but it would have been disastrous for his future rule. "He wanted someone he could trust. If anything went wrong, I was supposed to go with her, not him. The assumption being, she would have brought me into The Resistance. Though she never came out and said that, but neither did he, for that matter."

Josiah continued in the patient lecturing tone he often employed. "I cannot publicly align with Mossad, but they are a powerful ally. And I spoke with him after we escaped, to find out where we stood, what they were doing, or planning to do. He went unofficial the night of the arrest, and he's still on leave."

"But she knew where you were," Peter growled through clenched teeth.

"Were you hunting me, Cousin?" Josiah's mild tone belied his fierce expression.

"You are damn right I was, but that is not the point."

"What is the point?" Josiah asked tersely. "You know damn well Reuben is on our side."

"You know that. I do not. But Reuben ben Judah is not the issue here; Kayah is!"

"I disagree." Josiah shook his head. "We walk a fine line with Mossad, diplomatically and otherwise. We would have had a major crisis on our hands if they arrested Reuben at Massimo's with me and the girls. She saved us from that complication when she pulled him out."

"She was at Massimo's?" Peter snarled, his eyes bulging.

Davianna and Astrid shared a look. Neither had seen Kayah or Reuben that night.

"Son of a bitch," Peter swore. "She called in the Code Black. In the chaos, I never put it together. How in the hell did she know where you were to pull him out?"

"I don't know," Josiah said, realizing he had just screwed up.

Peter vibrated with fury as the answer became clear. "Dammit! So, not only did she know where you were in mid-December and not say anything, but the night of the arrest, she must have known where all of you were!" Peter hit the steering wheel three times, hard.

Davianna flinched, seeing shades of Korah in Peter's temper. "Stop," she said.

But in his fury, Peter heard nothing. "She put not only your lives, but the lives of every single member of my team at risk. But above that, she risked the future of our kingdom. If she would have told us," Peter met Josiah's eyes in the rearview mirror, "those six days in the Palace would not have happened. We would have taken you all to safety."

"No," Astrid said, studying her folded hands in her lap. "I would have run, no matter who tried to help us." She swallowed hard. "I overheard one of the agents say Daddy's name and where he was. That's why we ran. You wouldn't have stopped me."

Davianna's voice sounded breathless as she added, "We would never have trusted Korah's son."

"And neither did I," Josiah said quietly.

Peter's emerald eyes flashed fire.

Davianna watched him draw into himself, saw his shield of offended royal dignity fall into place.

"Be that as it may, I will still have a word with Kayah about her conflicting loyalties."

"I do not see a conflict at all," Josiah countered, regretting the turn of the conversation, seeking to smooth this over. "Kayah and Reuben played a major role in our rescue. She was the guard posted outside Astrid's door. If not for her, the whole thing would have collapsed when Korah came down the hall while you were rescuing Astrid."

Peter skidded off the road and slammed the brakes in a cloud of dust and gravel. "What?"

Josiah nodded. "Reuben told me the story. She had incapacitated the guard posted in your mother's wing and was outside the door when Korah approached. She played it off, stepped out of the shadows, and challenged him. Kayah faced down your father, in his own house, while you and Astrid escaped."

"How in the hell did she do that?" Peter demanded.

"Reuben thought it was funny, but I think it demonstrates how unhinged he has become. He thought she was Grandmother Mary."

"Grandmother Mary?" Peter repeated. Then shook his head as a light came on in his brain. "I suspected he was seeing ghosts. A few days before we escaped, he passed me in the hall and called me Father."

Davianna let out a shuddering breath and said, "He hated them… his parents. He told me they did not love him. They never did, especially her. They only loved Eamonn." From behind a clenched fist, she whispered, "It hurt him."

The vehicle got very quiet. Outside, the bleak landscape stretched beyond the horizon, dusty and desolate. No cars passed. They were alone on the desert road.

Peter shook his head hard and turned back to the wheel. "I know a bit about being hated by a parent from the moment you are born. However, it did not turn me into a sadistic, homicidal lunatic." He met Davianna's eyes in the rearview mirror and said, "So do not waste a moment of pity on him, not one fucking minute."

Beyond Kingdoms - New Mexico - Peter and Astrid

After the explosive revelations, the ride to their next destination proceeded in relative silence. The foursome varied their travel time, some days driving for three or four hours, others twelve. The erratic distances threw off potential pursuers. Davianna suggested the strategy as one she and Astrid employed effectively on their run across Europe. Ironically, the short days proved to be the hardest. Today was a short day.

They stopped at a rustic New Mexican ranch that rented private bungalows. An hour after they checked in, Astrid pulled Peter up from the couch and gave him a friendly push toward the back bedroom. "Come on, Prince d'Or, you are grumpy." Halfway down the hall, she purred in a low, husky voice, "Let's go shoot something."

Deliberately misunderstanding her, he quipped, "Who do you want to shoot?"

"Whoever you are pissed off at."

He raised an eyebrow in wry amusement. "Capital idea, Red."

"All men like to blow stuff up." She moved to the corner of their room and picked up his favorite assault rifle, the one he used to kill the wolf a few weeks before. She struck a provocative pose, her cat blue eyes flashing. "They also like hot chicks with weapons."

He advanced on her. "Yes, we do."

Heat passed between them, full of promise.

"Later!" She thrust the weapon in his arms and sidled past him to her bag, pulling out her pistol. "We only have an hour of daylight left."

He gripped the weapon, enjoying the feel of the well-balanced rifle in his hands, but looked skeptical. "This will be conspicuous at the target range."

"You need to blow something away, bring the damn grenade launcher," she suggested, mischief hovering in the corner of her eye.

"Perhaps, I will."

"We'll have to sneak out the window. Doc will have a fit."

Peter laughed and whispered, "Lock the door."

Astrid tiptoed over and engaged the lock. "He'll think we are back here getting busy."

"We will be later." He flashed a roguish grin. "Put your hat on. Let's go."

They snuck out like two teenagers and made a mad dash to the target range at the back of the property. The ranch, a popular retreat forty years ago, fell on hard times when drought swept the region and the land reverted to desert. Their cabin was only one of two rented on a property of fifty.

On the run, Davianna and Astrid enjoyed anonymity, whether they stayed in luxury or penury. Since everyone thought Josiah was dead, in exile, he did the same. Conversely, Peter was safer staying on the seedy side, where no one expected to find him. Even if someone recognized him, the incongruity of Prince d'Or at a place like the Dry Creek Dude Ranch would be dismissed as a mistaken identity.

To that end, he learned to embrace Astrid's daily disguises. Each morning he got to be someone else. Today, she streaked his blond hair with brown. He hid his green eyes behind sunglasses and wore western gear and boots. From a distance, he appeared nothing more than a young man at a gun range. And for the first time in his life, he felt truly free.

Peter hefted the battered rifle case onto the wooden table in front of the targets and unsnapped the latches with a practiced hand. "I have had this weapon since I was fourteen. James gave it to me when

I was going off to the RMA. It was his in the war. I smuggled it in with my things, though in retrospect they would not have told me I could not have it."

She studied the weapon with renewed interest. "I expect very few people have ever told you no, or for that matter, told you that you couldn't have something."

He shrugged. "I have said it before. I am rotten."

"To the core." She raised on her tiptoes and kissed his cheek. "Now, let's see some of that fancy Royal Military Academy shooting." She put in her earplugs, thoroughly enjoying the view of Prince Peter with a weapon.

"Shooting was one of the few things I excelled at in school. By the time I graduated, I earned the rank of a marksman instructor." He aimed the weapon, his long fingers gripping the barrel toward the end. "This is a target grip, primarily used in speed competitions for its high degree of accuracy. In a fight, people use it in short skirmishes, or if you are shooting at somebody who is not shooting back because you present a larger profile." He demonstrated and let loose a volley of rounds.

"This is a combat grip, used in close quarters, side-by-side fighting, or during a longer engagement. You make a smaller target, and you can pack more men in the line. With your elbows tucked in, you can move easier through doors." He moved his hand back to the stock grip and fired. "You lose a measure of accuracy, though."

He turned his charming grin on her and continued his lesson. "Now, this is my favorite, and one you will not see many people use." He settled the rifle with his thumb wrapped around the barrel and his index finger flush along the underside of the weapon. His elbow rested against his rib cage and supported the rifle's weight. "It combines the best of both grips, delivering accuracy and aim. You are still a small target, but my bone structure supports the weight of the rifle, not my muscles. I can fight like this for hours." He obliterated the furthest target.

Astrid's mouth hung slightly ajar, thoroughly impressed. "Wow."

"It is a difficult grip to master and feels unnatural when you first begin, but James insisted I learn it. He can hit a target two hundred yards out, riding a galloping horse." He smiled with genuine affection and shrugged. "I am ambidextrous with a rifle, though I am a bit better with my left hand. I suppose it kept them from throwing me out of the RMA. My grades were not the best."

"I hated school," Astrid confided.

"Me, too." Peter shook his head. School was never his favorite topic of conversation.

She squeezed his upper arm.

He felt a rush of affection, appreciating that she never picked at his wounds. "All right, Red, let me see some of that Texas shooting you were bragging about at the cabin."

"I'm better with my knife, and this is only the second time I've done this, so no making fun of me, Dead Eye."

"I will not." Though the teasing gleam in his eyes suggested otherwise.

She paused, considering him. "You don't use contractions when you speak, ever. Most people would have said I won't. Not Prince d'Or, you say," she adopted a haughty royal accent, "I will not."

"It is a long story." He nodded to the targets. "Shoot."

"Snob."

"Wench."

Astrid giggled, then aimed her weapon, and fired. Several rounds went wild, completely missing the target. "You are distracting me." She turned with her hand on her hip. "I was much better the first time."

"Uh-huh. What is it you Texans say, all hat and no cattle?"

"Shut up." She removed her empty clip and handed it to him, flirting. "Reload for me, please."

He threw his hands up in mock bemusement. "Princes do not load. We have servants for that."

Astrid looked around, then studied her fingernails. "I don't see any servants. Besides, I'll break a nail. They are just now growing back, and I like being a girl again."

"You are definitely a girl." Peter loaded the clip.

Astrid fingered the old weapon case of his rifle. "And you are definitely a boy. Now hurry up and give me back my gun."

"You are a scrappy little thing."

She made a tiny laugh through her nose and accepted the weapon. "Yes, I am."

Peter wrapped his arms around her, adjusting her grip and stance. "There, try now."

"This feels weird, like my butt is sticking out."

Peter stepped back, admiring the view. "I know."

"You did that on purpose." She gave him a mock scowl.

His chest shook. "Not really, it gives you more stability. Your body will absorb the recoil of the gun better. Try it."

Astrid shook her bottom at him and resettled. This time she hit the target center mass. "Hey, the butt out position actually worked."

"I told you I was an instructor."

"I thought you were bluffing." Though she knew he wasn't, she'd seen him kill that wolf. "Go ahead and get a few more rounds off, it's getting dark."

Peter reloaded and shot three more clips.

As they walked back to the cabin, he took her elbow. "Watch your step. The old dude at the front desk mentioned they were having a problem with snakes."

"Don't tell Davianna. She hates them. They freak her out."

"I am not fond of them either," Peter said, scanning the ground.

"Should we sneak back in the window?" Astrid lowered her voice as they drew closer to the bungalow.

"Sure. Why not?" Peter lowered the rifle case through the open window and helped her through. He took a quick scan of the open sky and ducked under the sash. "That was an excellent idea, Red."

Astrid stowed her weapon and tiptoed over to the door. It was quiet on the other side, but Josiah and Davianna both read in the evening. She hoped they were each engrossed in a book and none the wiser to their little adventure. "I'm glad you had fun. You were mad today."

Peter sat down heavily on the bed. "I was furious today. I still am."

Astrid shrugged. "I've been thinking about that, specifically about Reuben, the Mossad agent."

Peter narrowed his eyes. "What about him?"

"He's Josiah's friend, right?"

Peter nodded. "I do not know him. Kayah brought him in the night they arrested you. For security reasons, I only had face-to-face contact with my head of operations once afterward, and the subject of Reuben did not come up. Mack's been with me for years, and he trusts him. But I thought I could trust Kayah, so…"

Astrid took a seat beside him. "Well, there are a couple of things I think you should know. When Josiah first approached Davianna with his plan, it involved Mossad escorting us back to the Golden City. However, I was adamant that we would not accept anyone's help. But she insisted we could trust Josiah. Believe me, we fought about it."

She took his hands and continued, "When we left the camp, we knew we were being followed. And when you see the same faces in multiple places, you learn to recognize and identify them. It's a matter of survival. There were several people tracking us, bad characters, but then there was Josiah. We hid from him, but neither of us feared him. I know that makes no sense, but it's true."

"I understand. When you live in a dangerous situation, you become attuned to threats."

Astrid nodded, pleased he understood. "Exactly, you can tell when someone is out to do you harm."

"I have a highly developed sense of that," Peter pulled off his shoes and threw them in the corner, "for obvious reasons."

"I suppose people have been trying to kill you longer than me." Astrid bit her thumbnail, disconcerted by the thought. "Anyway, Davianna and Josiah met when we were in London. I was sick with a headache, and she went out to do reconnaissance on her own. He gave her some headache pills for me, which I promptly threw in the trash. We were not certain of his identity. Now that I think about it, I suspect she knew who he was but did not say. I thought he was Mossad.

"And when we were arguing about going with him, she told me that when she and Josiah met in London, he suspected Mossad had been guarding us all the way across Europe. Davianna is convinced they are incorruptible. I am not as trusting."

She held his eyes. "The night we went to the Mossad safe house I recognized Reuben. I'd seen him a half a dozen times. He was like Josiah, one of the men following us, but he was not hunting us."

"What is your point here, Red?" Peter ran his fingers through his hair in a gesture she recognized as frustration.

"If Mossad was guarding us, they were doing it in secret, and we lost them in London. Nobody knew where we were when we were hiding in the New City. We did not leave that old hotel room. Davianna let Josiah find us. She sent him a message and went to meet him in response to that wrestling video. But our one caveat was that it was just him, alone. He agreed."

Peter narrowed his eyes, still not following her line of thinking.

"How do you think that went over with Josiah's Mossad buddies?"

"Ah," he said as the truth dawned. "They would not have liked it."

"Exactly, and what would you have done? You know how bossy he can be. He would have insisted they honor his promise." Astrid shook her head, a piece of the puzzle falling into place for her as well. "I thought he failed to live up to his side of the bargain when they discovered us so quickly, but now that I know him, I expect that is not the case. He is a man of his word."

"So, you think Reuben stood down but set Kayah on your tail as a precaution and extra protection."

"That seems reasonable to me." Astrid cupped his cheek, feeling his rough beard stubble under her palm. "They are lovers, like you and I, and there is a bond in that, a loyalty there that goes beyond politics. It supersedes other connections, does it not?" Her voice grew quiet, their eyes held.

"It does." He lowered his lips in a soft caress of a kiss. "Loyalty beyond kingdoms."

Page Turner - New Mexico - Josiah and Davianna

"Does he honestly think I would not go investigate gunfire?" Josiah sat down in a huff.

"So, they snuck out the window?" Davianna laughed.

"Unless Astrid has an invisibility cloak in her bag, and they walked by us unnoticed. Yes, they snuck out the window." Josiah picked up his book with a sigh.

"Invisibility cloak? Now that would come in handy."

He held up his book. "Harry makes good use of it."

Davianna drew in her breath. "Is that a Harry Potter book?"

"It is. I found it in my nightstand last night. I could not sleep so I started it. It's pretty good."

"Which one is it? Is it the first? Have you ever read them?" Davianna nearly jumped out of her skin.

He handed it to her. "It's the first. Have you read it?"

Davianna took the book with two hands, her eyes shining with excitement. "I started it right before we left on pilgrimage. It was in our local library, but I did not get to finish it. Daddy would not let me buy it or read it. He said it was a book about witchcraft, and I was not allowed to have it." Davianna hugged it to her chest. "But I loved it. I argued with him, but he could be so stubborn when he set his mind on something. I could not get him to relent." She held the book out, tracing the title with her finger. "I completely forgot about it."

Josiah smiled at her obvious pleasure. "Take it."

"Oh, no. I couldn't do that to you. I hate stopping in the middle of a book." Davianna handed it back to him.

He would not accept the novel. "Well, it obviously means more to you than it does me, go ahead."

Sudden inspiration struck. "How far along are you?"

"Christmas, Harry is sitting in front of a mirror and Dumbledore just walked in."

"Christmas seems so magical, doesn't it?" Davianna sighed wistfully. "I loved that part, and I wasn't much past that when I had to quit. Why don't we read it together?"

Josiah pictured her curled in his lap reading a book. The idea was appealingly innocent and highly erotic. "How do you propose we do that?"

"You read a chapter, I'll read a chapter. Daddy and I used to do that all the time."

The heat settling between his legs was not fatherly, but the idea took root. "We can try. I will warn you, though, I fall asleep when somebody reads to me. I had a study partner in medical school, though he was not as cute as you. We tried it, but I'd zonk out every time."

Davianna settled on the couch. "I'd say Harry Potter is more entertaining than advanced anatomy."

Josiah flushed, awash with the sudden memory of her advanced anatomy in the palm of his hand. He remembered the feel of her soft breast, the way she molded against him. He cleared his throat, even to his own ears he sounded hoarse. "Perhaps. Read."

"Well, come over and get comfortable if you are going to fall asleep. There's room on the couch. You lay at that end, and I'll lay on the other."

It was a temptation beyond what he could withstand. He kicked off his shoes and settled opposite her. She snuggled her feet under his back and began the story. As she read, he heard the soft cadence of her Southern roots emerge, like they did when she was angry or tired. He loved that about her.

A dozen pages into the tale, sleep crept up on him and he rested, utterly content with a little Minx by his side.

Part 8 - Photograph

January 20, 1000 ME

Bubbles Burst - New York - Esmeralda and Thaddeus

Thaddeus pulled the door to Claire's nursery shut, relieved the baby cooperated with bedtime tonight. Since she started crawling, she became much easier to put down. Bath, only one story, and she conked out, which was good, because he was exhausted. Some days he struggled just to breathe, and today had been one of those days.

Heading into the living room, he heard Esmeralda crashing around, cleaning up. "The baby is down. What's wrong with you?"

She turned, her hair wild, her eyes flashing with anger. "My stupid cousin."

"You talked to her?"

"Yes." She punctuated the word with a point of her finger. "She is impossible."

Thaddeus suppressed a smile, knowing she would not appreciate it if he laughed at her when she was mad. Esmeralda rarely said a negative word about anyone, but since her cousin's reappearance, she made an exception. He moved to the couch as she stormed around their apartment, picking up after Hurricane Claire. Their living room looked like a baby factory exploded.

"She and Jenny got themselves in a mess out in the New City and ended up homeless. But to hear her tell it, they lived some sort of grand adventure. She makes ridiculous choices, then acts like she is perfectly together, and I am the unstable one. She always has." Esmeralda waved a pink burp cloth and threw it in the dirty laundry pile.

"She told me she had this great job, which she lost, by the way, but said if I send her some money, she will be fine. I wanted to scream."

"Money?" Thaddeus suspected that was coming. "How much does she want?"

"It does not matter." Esmeralda went to the DVD player and ejected the movie, shelving, and sorting with librarian efficiency. "Because she would just waste it. We are not sending her a shekel. Let Uncle Yoder take care of her."

An imperceptible shiver passed over Esmeralda at the mention of her uncle's name, of which Thaddeus made a mental note.

"She is such a liar. She claims she was working for the head of the Ministry of Technology, of all things. Can you imagine? Elisabeta, a girl always more concerned with what color lipstick she was wearing than cracking a book, somehow lands a job as the assistant to an upper-level government minister?" Esmeralda scoffed, "His name even sounded made up, ridiculous."

Thaddeus stilled. "Who was it?"

"McSmoochey or something absurd like that." She picked up a set of rings, Claire's favorite toy, and threw them into a big wicker basket. "She was probably waiting tables and couldn't remember a simple drink order, so they fired her."

Esmeralda moved to the diaper bag, pulling out empty bottles and sorting through changes of clothes, separating the clean from the dirty. Thaddeus watched her building up steam. The madder she got, the faster she worked, and she was not quiet about it. He cringed and glanced down the hall towards Claire's room, while Esmeralda chucked bottles into the stainless-steel sink like a Vegas poker dealer.

"She was always a selfish, vain little brat. And if she would have gotten her lazy butt out of bed and helped when everyone got sick, I might have gotten some rest. Maybe then they would not have been able to take me!"

"Ah, there is a bit of truth," Thaddeus observed with a cock of his eyebrow. "That little nugget was buried, wasn't it?"

Esmeralda froze. "I suppose it was." Then, bracing her hands against the counter, she took a deep breath. "That explains why the sound of her voice makes me want to snatch her bald-headed."

Thaddeus burst out laughing. "Where did you pick that up?"

Esmeralda broke into a reluctant smile. "Malandra. That's what she says about Judith." She sniffed and wiped her nose, the firestorm abating. "She is right. Judith actually used baby-talk on the phone with me yesterday. I swear to you, that woman is insane."

Thaddeus made a wry laugh. "Your two favorite subjects, your cousin and Judith. Come sit down. There is a chance Elisabeta is telling the truth."

Esmeralda deflated and mumbled, "That would be a first." Plopping down beside him, she turned. "I'm sorry."

He took her hand and pressed a kiss to her palm. "No worries."

"Why do you think she is telling the truth?"

"Was the minister's name McSwilley, Stephen ben McSwilley, the Minister of Technology and Security?"

"Maybe." Esmeralda hugged her knees to her chest and regarded him with sulky indignation. "Is he real?"

"He is, but he's disappeared." Much of the investigation was in the public arena, so he said, "Stephen ben McSwilley was a driving force behind the Alanthian technology explosion. He and his team are responsible for a lot of what we take for granted every day. Anyway, in mid-December, he started calling in sick. He did so for about a week. Then the calls stopped. When he didn't check-in for two days, his office became concerned. With him being a government official, the case fell to us. We went to his house, but he was gone. The place was clean, and nobody has seen him since."

"So, it is possible Elisabeta was telling the truth?"

"Could be. It will be easy enough to check her story. They've appointed an interim head, but there has been a lot of turnover in that division. I understand the new minister fired about half the staff when he took over." Thaddeus shrugged. "I'll find out tomorrow. What about Jenny? What was her story?"

Esmeralda lifted her lip in scorn. "I did not speak to her, but Elisabeta claimed she was making big money at some tech start-up but quit a couple of days before terrorists attack the place."

Thaddeus paled. "Was she at Facetec?"

Esmeralda pressed her wide mouth into a pouty line. "Yes, heaven help me. Was she telling the truth about that, too?"

He laughed and leaned in for a kiss. "You do not pay any attention to the news at all, do you, Vixen?"

"You know I don't. Half the time it's lies. Look how they reported Thyatira. After that, I gave up. Even when they get it right, it's just bad news, and I sense that all by myself. I don't need Sondra ben Pierson jumping in my living room every night with her doom and gloom."

"Speaking of Sondra, I think she's on." He picked up the remote and clicked on the TV. "They've been teasing some big story all afternoon. Mack sent me a text and told me to watch."

"Good Evening, I'm Sondra ben Pierson…"

Twenty minutes later, Esmeralda turned to Thaddeus with her mouth slack. "Did you know Prince Josiah was alive?"

"Mack told me a couple weeks ago," Thaddeus nodded slowly, realizing he was about to burst a big bubble. "Have you seen the video of Agnor and Zanah, the parents of the two girls Korah had arrested?"

Shocked to discover Prince Eamonn's son was not dead, she tilted her head in confusion and asked, "What's that got to do with Prince Josiah and Prince Peter?"

"It does. Trust me. Have you seen it?"

"Camy was watching something the other day when I was walking through the office. She was up in arms about it. You know how she is," Esmeralda said, referring to her co-worker who followed every conspiracy website on the internet. "I stopped for a minute, but the mother was nauseating. There was putrid yellow all around her, the color of insincerity and lies. The man was just as bad, obviously a con artist, slimy green. I couldn't watch. Camy didn't catch any of it, and I wasn't going to say anything. Why?"

"The Princes and the girls are together, on the run from Korah, and whoever or whatever else is chasing them."

Esmeralda grew still. "You want me to look at something, don't you?"

"Yes." Getting up with a groan, he stood for a second, letting a wave of dizziness abate before retrieving his laptop.

"Are you okay?"

He nodded, then typed in a few commands and brought up the images. "This is Astrid."

Esmeralda leaned in, staring at the young woman, then clutched the left side of her head. "She has migraines."

"All right," he said.

"I've seen her before." Esmeralda touched the screen. "That day in the library with Ian, I had a vision of her during an earthquake, jumping on top of her friend to shield her from falling rocks."

Thaddeus blew out a long breath. "Anything else?"

Esmeralda studied the photo. "She's familiar, but in a way I cannot place. Who does she look like?"

"To me, she looks like Princess Alexa." Thaddeus' nose flared. "But that could just be me projecting, touchy subject."

"No! You are right." Esmeralda squinted. "What about the other one? Does she look like Princess Margaret?"

"That would be spooky, wouldn't it? No, I don't think so. Here's the second girl, Davianna."

Esmeralda turned away. "Oh, Lord, it's her."

"Who?" Thaddeus began to doubt the wisdom of this exercise. It was easy to forget how intuitive she was. A lesser man would have her looking at mugshots all day.

"The girl from Greece, the father's treasure, the one the giant was trying to kill." Esmeralda's white curls stood on end as she dug her hands into her hair. "Do you remember that night? I saw the giant die and his spirit rise as a demon."

"Davianna ben *David*," Thaddeus said in awe, "I never put it together with the Camp Eiran massacre last year."

"What?" Esmeralda cried. "The demon led a massacre?"

Thaddeus laid a hand on her shoulder. "I'm sorry, Esmie. I should not have brought this up."

"Tell me." She turned to him, resolute.

"I kept it from you. Ian and I both did. You started having contractions, and the doctor put you on bed rest again. Remember the day we were supposed to start work?"

Esmeralda covered her mouth, unable to speak, only nod.

"That night, they murdered about a hundred pilgrims in Greece."

"The demon is looking for that girl. Her father saved her." Esmeralda closed her eyes. "There were angels, and they drove the demon away. He must have figured out a way to get back."

"There is more than a demon hunting that girl," Thaddeus said gravely.

"If Korah had her arrested, he wants her, too. Prince Peter is with them? Mack is helping them? Where is Lavinia? Is she safe?"

"Lavinia's fine. She and Mack are home in Peccioli."

Esmeralda's eyes grew enormous as she shot off the couch. "They will send astrals after them."

"If they can find them, they will," Thaddeus conceded with a shudder.

"Do they know? Did Mack tell them? Thaddeus, no one knows how to fight astrals but us." Esmeralda paced, muttering. "We need to pray a strong hedge of protection around them." She stopped and stared at the skyline, her voice shaking. "There are five of us that know what to do, and three of us nearly died."

"But we did not." Thaddeus' deep voice penetrated her rising panic.

"The Witch will come out now. If she is alive, she will come!" She whirled on him. "I don't want to do this, I don't. I want to be left alone. I want to raise my daughter and work at the Center. I want to be your wife. I don't want to fight them!"

Thaddeus rose and gathered her in his arms, trying to calm her. "You don't have to. That's why I kept this from you. It is my job to protect you. You've been through enough."

Esmeralda rested her head against his chest. "Then why do I feel like I've just been called up to active duty?"

Out of the Loop - Redding, California - Persa and James

At Pepperwood, Persa dropped the magazine she was reading with a page-splaying flutter and turned to James as the News1 story ended. "You knew, didn't you?"

James nodded.

"How could you know something like that and not tell me?"

James had the good sense to appear sheepish. "Well, Peter only mentioned it once, and he had been raving for a week."

"So, he told you in '97?" Persa stared at him, aghast. "You've known Prince Josiah was alive for three years and failed to mention it?"

"We had a lot going on, and I wasn't sure." James lifted his shoulders, adopting an innocent expression. "He kept calling me Jarrod. Do you remember?"

Persa covered her eyes and sighed, "Yes, it was terrible."

"It was." James watched her carefully. In hindsight, he realized Peter's ordeal triggered Persa's agoraphobia, so he was loath to dig too deeply into that.

"What exactly did he tell you?"

James thought back to the morning he found Peter working with the horses, the first day he got up and around. "Not much. We were talking, and I told him he could stay with us as long as he wanted, but eventually, he would be King, whether he liked it or not. That's when he told me Prince Josiah was still alive. When I questioned him, he said that he and his mother helped him escape after Prince Eamonn's death."

"Jupiter's Moon!" Persa grimaced. "Think about how young he would have been. Josiah disappeared a couple of weeks after we won the Championship and first met Peter. He was seven." Visions of the little blond prince flashed through her mind, impish and daring—utterly charming.

James blew out a breath. "I think he's been planning whatever it is he and Josiah are doing since, without a doubt, he got serious after they drugged him."

"We should be helping." Persa leaned forward to catch James' eyes.

James met her gaze and held it. "I've thought the same thing. A couple of weeks after he left in '97, I rode over to Peccioli."

Persa's chin sharpened as she pressed her lips in a grim line. "What happened?"

He and Mack had a strained relationship. They were friendly enough as neighbors, but James blamed Mack for failing to protect Peter, and they never moved past that point of contention. "I confronted him," James answered simply. "We got into it, again."

"You didn't tell me this either!" Persa flopped back on the cushions with her arms crossed.

"Well, about that time, I started noticing something was wrong with you." Becoming defensive, he added, "And Mack said nothing, so there was little to tell. It's Peter's place to ask for our help if he wants it."

"You are right. And what could we have done here on the ranch?"

"I suspect that is why he never involved us. He wants us here. Pepperwood is his refuge. You said that the other night, and you're right."

Persa picked her discarded magazine off the floor and said, "That picture is going to give Korah an apoplexy."

"Good. Maybe the old bastard will drop dead."

"He is still Peter's father, James."

"Korah gave up that right when he shot that kid full of drugs, beat him while he was tied to a bed, and nearly starved him to death." James hit the flat of his palm on the couch. "Peter almost died lying on this sofa."

"I know." She absently stroked the cushion. "I'm sorry."

He wrinkled his brow in confusion. "About what?"

"I don't know… for being peeved with you earlier."

But it remained unspoken that Peter's decision to take Mack into his confidence and not James had hurt him. "It's all right," he said. "I suppose there may come a time when he asks for our help, and when he does, we will be there. Until then, we can't do much."

"He looked good in that picture." Persa smiled, love glowing in her hazel eyes.

"Yeah, he did… different."

"I thought so, too."

James scoffed. "Normally, he's got that dumb look on his face."

Persa tried to smother a giggle with her fingers. "Prince d'Or."

"His father forced him into that role. We never see that eejit's expression when he's here."

"Aye, you're right. He looked like our Peter." She tapped her nose, thinking. "Perhaps he has found another sanctuary."

James cut her a sideways glance. "You think he's with a woman?"

"Well, he's certainly not with a man," Persa deadpanned.

James laughed. "He was half-dead and still flirting with you, the little shit."

Persa waved him away. "Banter. That's just his way. He's like my brother or my kid or something. I don't know. He and I have always been that way."

"I know." James got a rueful expression on his face. "He stole my date…"

Persa glanced up at the mantle where the silver cup held a place of honor, a relic of times past, before Prince Eamonn died and the world changed. "I think they are trying to bring back something that has been lost for a long time."

James looked down. He had fought against Korah in the war and seen many good men die on the field of battle. The Noble Army had lost, but for the first time since, he felt a glimmer of hope.

He walked to the window and said, "I'm riding over to Peccioli tomorrow. Johnson saw Mack in town yesterday. They're back. But the timing of their supposed cruise does not add up, not with the harvest and the press in full swing. Mack is in on whatever Peter is up to. You mark my words."

"I'll go with you," Persa said quietly.

He turned and gave her a smile, relieved she could finally leave the ranch. "I'd like that, Fey."

Something From Me - Dallas - Peter and Astrid

"How does it feel to be back in Texas, Red?" Peter asked, flopping down in a low backed armchair. The penthouse suite of the Grand Royal was more to his liking than the hovel they stayed in last night.

Astrid peered out the peephole, checking the hallway. "It would feel a lot better if you picked a safer place. I do not like being high up." She clicked her knife in nervous agitation, prowling the room. "I am sure Davianna and Josiah are not in a penthouse."

"That is their misfortune. Relax, this disguise was brilliant." He made an effeminate gesture and affected a slight lisp. "No one recognized Steve and Joseph." Then he flashed his famous smile and added, "You know gay men love me."

She shot him a look of utter exasperation and activated the signal jamming device from her bag. "Fantastic, leggy blondes and gay men? The entire world wants to sleep with Prince d'Or."

Peter threw back his head and laughed. "I said that to Alaina once." He held up a hand at her thunderous expression. "Do not worry, she does not. Perhaps one of the few." He winked at her, teasing.

"Tonight, of all nights, we should be in a cheap motel. That picture of you and Josiah is rocking the planet, so you are on everyone's mind. We should be lying low. Instead, you dragged me into that bar downstairs, then started cooing about how handsome Josiah is. That was just reckless."

She tapped her foot, angry but a bit perplexed. "What got into you? This morning, when we argued over who was carrying the decoy phone, you were ready to jump out of your skin. But tonight, you go strolling into a bar, big as shit, and draw attention to yourself. If anyone actually looked at you, it would have been obvious who you are."

Peter laced his fingers behind his head and leaned back, his legs spread wide, all traces of the effeminate gone. "No one did. People do not see you, Red. In all your months of running, you failed to discover that?"

He studied her, watching the play of emotions on her face as the truth of his words penetrated her anger. "Do you know when they look at you? When they want something from you. When they want to take something from you."

"It was still dangerous," she said, turning her back on him.

"No one wants anything from Steve." He moistened his lips.

She scoffed, clearly peeved.

Peter's voice took on a hard edge. "And no one is getting another piece of me from here on out. Today was the final shot, my last public act."

Astrid looked over her shoulder. "What are you talking about?"

He unfolded from the chair and moved behind her. "It has been the plan all along, to place Josiah on the throne, and for me to disappear."

She made an inarticulate sound as he traced a finger over her jawline and circled her with his arms. "I am not coming back. From this day forward, Prince d'Or is dead." He kissed the side of her neck, his breath warm, his body molding against her back. "Although, I might have misspoken earlier. There may be one person who gets something of me." Heat passed between them as he murmured, "Are you interested, Astrid, in just Peter the man?"

Her head fell back, she reached behind and pulled him tight. "He is the only one I have ever been interested in."

Peter growled in deep satisfaction and bit her neck. "I know."

Truth in Fiction - Corinthian, Texas - Davianna and Josiah

Davianna and Josiah passed the day in virtual silence, with the bleak Texas landscape providing a backdrop for their shared misery. Josiah never imagined it was possible to watch someone's heart break, yet he witnessed it today when he explained to Davianna why he could never pursue a relationship with her. As he spoke about honor, he saw the color drain from her cheeks. When he explained there were alliances he must make, a bride he would take, he watched the glimmer of happiness die in her brown eyes. He shattered her hope with the truth and knew the devastation on her face would haunt him for the rest of his life.

Leaving behind the anarchist's van and dressing in new disguises, they drove away in a rattling pickup truck. The noisy engine discouraged any small talk they might have made to pass the time, but neither could think of anything to say. He had said everything back at the abandoned store.

Even after News1 declared to the world he was alive, they did not talk, just put in another hundred miles, and checked into a small motel.

He had dutifully gone to his room—alone. He turned on the television to watch the coverage, but it did not take long for the wild speculations to begin, becoming so absurd he had to shut it off. In the silence, his thoughts took a familiar turn, toward the dark broodings of exile.

For fifteen years, anger sustained him; vengeance consumed him. Day and night, he reviewed strategies, calculated contingencies, and formulated his attack. He compiled lists of potential allies and known enemies, mentally reviewing how he would deal with each. He rehearsed his speeches, planned his reforms, and sometimes imagined cheering crowds as he retook the Alanthian throne. Hundreds of times a day, his mind raced down those familiar roads until the thoughts became so ingrained he was no longer conscious of them. Yet they drove him, molding him into the single-minded, determined, Prince he had become.

He knew exactly who he was and what he was going to do until the Iron King gave him a ludicrous mission to find a young girl and escort her to safety. Instead of weeks, the chase turned into months, and when he finally caught up with her and looked into her dark-brown eyes, she turned his world upside down. Nothing since had gone according to plan. With his goal closer than ever, he should feel elated, revved up, and energized, but he was not. He was lonely, and he wanted the one person he could not have.

He left his room, knowing he should not, knowing he could not keep toying with her, pushing her away, then pulling her back. It was not fair to either of them. Yet, his heart cared nothing for the obstacles in their way. It hungered for her sweet smile, ached to feel her gentle touch, and craved the peace he only experienced in her company.

Standing outside her door, he felt like a cad but could not leave. His hand refused to knock, yet she opened the door.

"Is everything okay?" She peered past him, looking for trouble.

"Yes," he said, his voice sounding strained, embattled.

Davianna did not move from the doorway, did not step forward or back, just looked up at him. "What are you doing, Josiah?"

"I brought you something." *Me,* he wanted to say. *I bring you myself.* But he did not speak the words; he never would. Reaching inside his jacket pocket, he produced a book and said, "It's the second one."

The corner of her mouth lifted. "You fell asleep last night as I finished the first one."

"I heard it."

A teasing light came into her eyes, doubtful. "You did?"

"Yes, it was love that protected Harry, something the enemy does not understand. He cannot conceive that someone would sacrifice themselves to protect the ones they love, to keep them from harm, so he failed to comprehend the power. I heard, Davianna."

She covered his hand that held the book and stared into his eyes. "And now these three remain; faith, hope, and love, but the greatest of these is love." Giving his fingers a squeeze, she stepped backward into her room. "Come in, Dark Prince. We'll read the next book."

Part 9 - History

January 20, 1000 ME

Higher Ground - New City - Kayah and Genevieve

"Genevieve, we are leaving!" the unflappable Jarrod ben Adriel shouted into the phone. "After seeing the picture of the two Princes, the King flew into a rage and fired a weapon at a footman."

Genevieve gasped, covering her heart. "Get out of there!"

"I am! Nathan ben Henry is guarding my door. The rest of the Prince's security team is evacuating the staff. We will move to Gilead as planned."

The line went dead.

"Jarrod! Jarrod!" Genevieve yelled.

Kayah went to her side, taking the phone. "Jarrod?" She shook her head, indicating he was gone. Reading her distress, she braced her hands on Genevieve's shoulders and asked, "What happened?"

"They are evacuating," Genevieve gasped, growing pale.

"Hey," Kayah ordered, "breathe."

Genevieve nodded, looking around the room. Alaina, Himari, and Reuben were all on their feet, waiting. She turned back to Kayah, who looked like she was ready to take on the entire world if Genevieve asked.

"That was Jarrod. They are evacuating the Palace. Korah fired a weapon at a footman."

Kayah spoke, slow and deliberate, "Is he okay, Auntie?"

"Yes, he said, Jason or Nathan—I don't remember—one of Peter's team was guarding his door. They are going to Gilead like we planned."

"Peter's head of security, Nathan ben Henry, is an excellent agent, Auntie." Kayah held Genevieve's gaze, unblinking and calm. "Jarrod will be fine."

Genevieve's lip quivered. "You don't know what Korah is capable of, Kayah. I do." Tears spilled down her cheeks. "Jarrod means nothing to him. He would shoot him and not lose a moment's sleep. And I have seen what he has done to the people he claimed to love! He killed Marguerite; I know it. And Eamonn, oh Kayah, he was such a lovely man. You cannot know what we lost when he died. And Alexa? She was a good wife to him, and she loved him."

"It will be fine," Kayah soothed.

But old ghosts rose from their graves and swirled around Genevieve. "And even if Korah doesn't kill him, that does not mean he is safe. There are plenty of Korah's victims who did not die. You cannot imagine what he put Peter through.

"When he was about ten, he got a bad report card. Korah beat him… It was awful." Genevieve shook her head convulsively, and her voice broke off in a sob. "You should have seen him, lying there, covered in blood. Korah hurt him so badly, but Peter tried to pretend everything was okay. He knew I wouldn't stand for it, that I would be furious, and get into trouble. So, he cracked a joke and tried to get me to smile. Kayah, his arm was broken!"

Her face flushed in remembered outrage. "I took him to the hospital, which was against protocol. The doctors come to them, you know? But I would not let some Palace doctor gloss over it. I wanted evidence. I wanted witnesses. But it did not matter. In the end, Korah covered it up and dismissed me." She covered her face and wept.

At a loss for anything better to say, Kayah ventured, "Oh, Genevieve, I am so sorry."

Genevieve blinked up at her, desolate in remembrance. "He hurt both my little Princes. I was there the day they were born. I took care of them. I dressed them. I read them bedtime stories. I love them. They were MY boys. And Korah, that *ventosa di cazzo diabolica*, ran Josiah into exile. Then he exiled me… from Peter. What happened to him after I left?" Genevieve asked, breaking down.

Alaina covered her eyes, rubbing her temples. No one knew just how bad it got, but Alaina had an idea. Within The Resistance, she was the only one who knew about the drug abuse that sent him into rehab last December. To get a glimpse into his childhood broke her heart.

Kayah stood with her hands braced on Genevieve's shoulders, at a loss over what to do. She panicked and whipped her head around, seeking Reuben. He read it, placed an arm around each of them. and pulled Kayah into Genevieve's arms. Then he stepped away, letting them hug.

Himari looked away, unable to bear the sight. She understood the significance of Kayah bonding with Genevieve. Her lifelong friend, who had neither mother nor grandmother to love her, gave and received comfort under the most unlikely of circumstances. But to hear Italian spoken in anger ripped her heart out. She could not hold it together and fled.

"Thank you, Kayah." Genevieve sniffed. "I'm sorry I got so upset."

"It's all right. Everything will be okay, Auntie."

Sliding over to Reuben, Alaina whispered, "What did she just call Korah?"

From behind his hand, Reuben laughed, "An evil cocksucker."

Sometimes You Have to See for Yourself

Kayah and Genevieve sat alone in the upstairs kitchen, a rarity. But it provided a place of warmth and normalcy, away from buzzing computers and the intense surveillance they launched at the Palace. Kayah reasoned if the evacuation went wrong, they needed the freedom to act without upsetting Genevieve further, so she marched her upstairs and did the only thing she could think to do, made her a cup of tea.

"Go change. I'll drive you to Gilead." Kayah motioned down the hall, toward Genevieve's bedroom. "You'll not rest until you see for yourself that Jarrod is all right." Shrugging a shoulder, she added, "And I could use a break from the underground tomb, anyway."

"Oh, I could not." Genevieve touched her hair self-consciously. "He will be busy getting everyone settled in. It would be an imposition."

Kayah raised an eyebrow in wry speculation. "Not buying it."

"Not buying what?" Genevieve took a sip of tea and averted her eyes.

"The whole 'imposition' excuse." Kayah raised an eyebrow. "And your hair looks fine, besides it's just Jarrod."

"Do you know him?" Genevieve glanced up, her interest piqued.

"Our paths have crossed."

"When?"

Kayah waved her away. "You are stalling."

"No, I'm not." Genevieve drummed her fingers on the old table. "Besides, if you want me to go traipsing out in the middle of the night, on some folly, you will tell me."

Kayah rolled her eyes. "What does one have to do with the other?"

Genevieve smiled. "Nothing, I just want to know."

"You old busybody."

"Seems to me you are well on your way to becoming one yourself, trying to instigate a midnight assignation between old flames."

"Ha! I knew it."

"You know nothing," Genevieve answered with smug satisfaction. "And I won't tell, unless you do."

"That is not fair," Kayah protested, enjoying the little repartee.

"Oh, I never play fair. I was a nanny for years." Genevieve's eyes sparkled. "I can pry secrets out of the best of them."

"Then we'll put you in charge of enhanced interrogation in Josiah's new government," Kayah suggested.

"I will begin with Korah."

Kayah leaned back in her chair, mindful of a sore spot on her ribs, and said, "I think you might have to wait in line."

"Indeed. I would start by asking him what really happened to Margaret and move on from there." Genevieve waved away the dark speculation. "Never mind. You tell me how you met Jarrod. If you do, I will tell you how I met him," she raised a coy brow, "while you drive me to Gilead."

"Oh, that is blackmail. A juicy story and a chance to get out of here?" Kayah pretended to be annoyed. "Fine, he was Sir Preston's butler, or 'man', as Sir Preston referred to him, which I always thought odd. I mean, of course he is a man, but whatever. That is how I met him. Now go change."

"Not so fast, Kayah," Genevieve cackled. "What in the world were you doing in that old spider's lair?"

"Sir Preston?" At Genevieve's nod, Kayah shrugged. "He was my lawyer."

Genevieve narrowed her eyes. "How did you end up with Sir Preston as your lawyer?"

Kayah glanced away, always uncomfortable talking about that subject. "I don't know, fate, I guess."

"Fate?" she chuckled cynically. "I highly doubt that."

"Weren't we talking about Jarrod?" Kayah studied a stuffed goose above Genevieve's cupboard. "What's your deal with geese, anyway?"

"No changing the subject. You met Jarrod when he was with Sir Preston, but most of his clients would not have been to his house to meet his man, so how did you find yourself there?"

Kayah threw up a dismissive hand and attempted to gloss over her level of involvement with Sir Preston. "I was a pro-bono job. They assigned him to my case when the tech laws were repealed. We met. He took an interest in me. Now, go change."

Genevieve rested her chin on her fist and studied Kayah closer. "That man does not take an interest in anyone unless he has an ulterior motive."

Kayah took a sip of tea. She liked Genevieve and did not want to lie to her, so she hedged. "We came to a mutually beneficial arrangement."

"I'll bet," Genevieve scoffed. "Probably one where you did the dirty work while he sat in his comfortable office with plausible deniability."

The corner of Kayah's lip raised in a half smile, impressed by how succinctly she summed up her complex relationship with Sir Preston.

"I'm right, aren't I?"

"I did okay," Kayah shrugged. "And his house was nicer than a prison cell."

"He brought you to live with him?" Genevieve's eyes widened.

Kayah blinked. As an adult, she realized that was indeed unusual, but at the time she was so grateful to be free and had nowhere else to go, so it did not seem odd. "Yes."

"That snake," Genevieve muttered. "How old were you?"

Kayah took a sip of tea, hiding her inward discomfort. "I had just turned twenty-three. But he did nothing untoward, and had he not intervened, I would likely still be in prison." The thought made her sick. "I met with him recently, and he told me I had a role to play, which was why he helped me."

"I lived among the power players long enough to recognize a plot when I stumble on one. Did he tell you what that role was?"

Kayah stared into her teacup and confided, "Not in so many words, but he wanted me to lend my talents to ensure Prince Josiah retook the throne." She did not divulge that if they were successful Sir Preston promised to tell her who her parents were. No one, not even Reuben, knew that.

"Steer clear of him, Kayah. He's been chewing up and devouring young girls like you longer than both of us have been alive."

"Oh, I have no illusions about him."

Genevieve gave Kayah a knowing look and said, "Margaret distrusted him. She said he was a meddler, pulling strings behind the scenes, and cautioned Eamonn against him. Alexa, on the other hand, loved him." Genevieve shook her head. "Margaret was a better judge of character."

"I've heard him mention Alexa. I was with him the day she died. He took it hard."

Genevieve made a deep-throated sound of disgust. "I expect he did. Sir Preston's machinations arranged that marriage. Korah never wanted to marry Alexa, and she paid for it."

She sighed heavily and rose. "All right, Kayah, you lived up to your end of the bargain. I will go change, then tell you the tale of Jarrod and Genevieve."

Interesting Twist - New City - Angelica

Angelica ben Omri stepped onto the balcony of her rented house across the Bay in Sausalito. She was not foolish enough to reside in the New City proper, too well known, too many cameras, too many memories. The news tonight came as a shock, and the picture clearly signaled that Peter and Josiah were making a move, and it did not bode well for Korah.

Angelica understood the fickle nature of public opinion, having fallen from grace under a scandal, and she suspected Korah might not survive this one. The jackals were at the gates, looking for blood. With the Dark Master exiled, Korah found himself adrift. He garnered no favor with Lucifer. His alliance with Egypt backfired, and every dissident group in the kingdom seized upon his weakness, making Davianna and Astrid poster girls for their cause. The nobility were ready to pounce. After being sidelined for thirteen years, they were quietly resuming power, some covertly supporting the more radical factions intent on overthrowing the monarchy. Now, the rightful heir to the Alanthian throne rose from the dead and aligned with his wildly popular and charismatic cousin.

The way Angelica saw it, she had two choices. She could proceed with her plan and stand by Korah when everyone else deserted him, or she could go back to her villa by the sea. Fiji was looking more attractive by the minute.

January 22, 1000 ME

Better Living Through Chemistry - Kayah and Himari

"Egad, you look like a wraith," Kayah said, coming into Himari's bedroom in the bunker, uninvited.

Himari turned over in her bed with a snarl. "Go away."

"What is wrong with you?"

"Go away," Himari repeated. "I am sick of everyone asking me. I am fine. Leave me alone."

Kayah rolled her eyes. "You're curled up like a dried shrimp. They have nominated me to at least get you to bathe."

Himari pulled a blanket over her head and grunted. A bath took energy, and she did not have any to spare, devoting all her strength to keeping it together. She feared if she did not, she would scream at the top of her lungs, get in a car, and chase after Filippo. Bathing was the least of her concerns. "Why is everyone obsessing about my bathing habits?"

"Because you are musty. Besides, I know you. When you get depressed, you shut down. Alaina says you did the same thing when you separated from Ken. Is that what's going on?"

"He just went to New York," Himari said aloud the words she repeated in her mind a dozen times a minute. "No big deal."

"Lavinia told me you two got in a big fight," Kayah pressed.

Himari sat up in a huff. "Well, she should not be running her mouth. I don't talk about her."

Kayah raised a cynical brow. "Seriously?"

"Go away."

"Tell me what's going on."

"Genevieve's right. You are becoming a busybody." She waved a hand, shooing Kayah away. "Go bang Reuben or something. Leave me alone."

"Charming." Not dissuaded, Kayah sat on the edge of the bed.

Himari groaned. Kayah could be a bulldog when she set her mind to something, and Himari was not up to rehashing her last days with Filippo. To speak of it made it real, and it could not be real.

Kayah tilted her head, waiting.

"What?" Even Himari heard the whine in her voice.

"Do you want to go get drunk?"

Himari covered her eyes with her elbow. Alternately wishing Kayah would go away and fearing she would leave. "No. I'm a weepy drunk. You know that."

"Okay," Kayah snorted. "How about a Quaalude?"

Himari dropped her elbow and stared at Kayah incredulously. "That would be lovely. Can you imagine if we had an emergency, and I was bombed out of my mind?"

"All right, total inebriation is off the table. Fine. I've got just the thing." Kayah reached into her sweatshirt pocket and produced a rolled joint.

Himari sat straight up in bed, her mouth hanging open. "Kayah ben Samuel, where did you get that?"

Kayah shrugged in a gesture that looked remarkably like one of Reuben's. "Life sucks sometimes. I find a little chemical assistance is not out of the question."

"You are a bad influence." Himari scanned the room, absurdly feeling like she was back in high school, afraid her mother was about to bust them. She chuckled, despite her miserable mood. "You are going to get us in trouble."

"Shut up, Sunflower. Let's sneak out and smoke a joint."

Himari suspected Kayah would not give up and getting high sounded better than wallowing in misery. "All right, lead the way."

"Good. Get dressed. It's cold outside."

Kayah strolled through the living room, where Alaina, Genevieve, and Reuben manned the monitors. Giving them all a pointed look, she said, "Himari and I are going up top to have a smoke." She made a show of pulling a pack of cigarettes from her purse, feeling like a kid sneaking off under Genevieve's watchful eye. Genevieve snorted but refrained from giving Kayah another lecture on the evils of cigarettes. Kayah pointed a finger at her, silently conveying she did not want to hear it.

Alaina looked toward the door, her face registering intense worry. Filippo's departure was personal for Alaina. While not as distraught as Himari, she came close. "Well, that's a start."

Himari slunk out without a word, bundled up in what looked suspiciously like a bathrobe.

"You get her to bathe, yes?" Reuben frowned after the fleeing figure.

"One step at a time," Kayah said. Taking her leather jacket off the coat tree, she muttered under her breath, "I am becoming a freaking relationship counselor."

She stepped into the hodgepodge strewed basement and pulled the hidden door shut, which silenced the whir of computers and blocked the artificial light. Auntie lived here three years, but the place looked like a dumping ground for a lifetime of debris and junk. Kayah made a snarky comment about it a few weeks ago, but Genevieve informed her, in no uncertain terms, that the mess was by design, intended to throw off anyone who might come down here to investigate. She kept the upstairs neat and tidy, though the fussy old woman's style was not to Kayah's taste. There were freaking doilies under the lamps.

Tromping up the steps, she focused on the mission, to get Himari out of her room and back to the land of the living.

Lavinia called the moment Himari and Filippo left Peccioli. "Kai, it's bad." Lavinia poured out the whole tale, ending with, "She is as fragile as one of Dernangle's string theories. I am worried about her. And Filippo, I have never seen him like that. He is furious with her." Lavinia felt responsible because her offer to let Filippo stay sparked the fight.

"You did nothing wrong, Vinia. Readjusting after an undercover assignment takes time," Kayah assured her.

"That's what Mack said."

Kayah snorted, "Well, he's right... for once."

"You adore Mack, so you can play your games somewhere else. I've known you too long to fall for any of it."

Indeed, they had known each other for a lifetime. The Alcatraz 3... They were the only ones left. Stephen... Gus... both lost their lives in the war they waged against Korah. As Kayah walked through the kitchen, she determined they would be the last casualties.

She found Himari on the back porch, huddled in her bathrobe. Auntie G's old patio furniture needed a good scrubbing, so neither sat. Pulling the joint from her jacket pocket, Kayah handed it to Himari. "Fire it up, Sunflower."

Himari lit the joint, inhaled, then coughed her lungs out.

"You do that every time. Give me that." Kayah snatched the joint from her loose fingers and took a deep, satisfying drag. The smoke burned going down, but it felt good.

Himari recovered with a giggle and managed not to hack her lungs out on her second hit. "The last time I smoked this stuff was with you."

"I'm a bad influence. What can I say?" Kayah said through a massive cloud of smoke.

"Huh, my mother was right."

"Your mother wasn't right about anything." Kayah French inhaled and passed the joint back to Himari. "I'm done."

Himari studied the burning end in fascination, the dancing gray smoke, beautiful and seductive. She took one last drag and extinguished the half joint. "What do I do with this?"

Kayah shrugged and pulled the plastic off her cigarette pack. "You keep it. You might need it later." She lit up a cigarette and offered one to Himari.

Himari's eyes squinted to slits, but she was game for anything, so she took the cigarette. The air was crystal clear, though cold. Shadows seemed to beckon adventure, not danger. Himari exhaled and watched their mixed cigarette smoke swirl in the faint light coming from the kitchen window. "It's nice to be outside."

"Mmm-hmm." Kayah relaxed against the house, mindful of their surroundings. Genevieve's house was isolated, but there were a few neighbors.

"I'm high," Himari said, sounding mystified.

Kayah snorted, "That was the point."

Himari found that uproariously funny, and the two old friends shared a laugh.

"Lavinia was no fun to get high with."

Kayah grimaced. "Heavens, no."

Himari giggled, "She'd go off into some deep math never-never land."

Kayah felt the warm glow of nostalgia in her belly as she thought back to those innocent, exciting years. "Do you remember that time we got her high before we went down in the bunker, and she and Gus…"

Himari held up her hand, hissing a laugh. "Gus followed right along. He did not have a clue she was blitzed."

"I think they solved some incomprehensible problem that day," Kayah licked her dry lips and added, "which was my evil plan."

"They did! We had a functioning code compiler for the Alcatraz language after that."

Kayah waved her away. "I still don't know what that means."

"Stephen was so ticked off. He came down and found you and me hysterical, eating all Lavinia's licorice, with those two writing on the walls."

Kayah rubbed the bridge of her nose. "Stephen… what a waste."

Himari snuggled into her fuzzy bathrobe and said, "I don't want to talk about Stephen. I don't want to talk about anything that will make me sad."

"Fair enough." Kayah agreed. "Let's go raid the kitchen. I'm hungry."

Himari smacked her lips. "I'm thirsty."

They tiptoed back inside, giggling. Instead of facing the censorious glances of their 'not high' bunker mates, they decided to raid Auntie G's secret stash.

"What's she got?" Himari whispered, peeking over Kayah's shoulder into the refrigerator.

Kayah stared inside with mounting disappointment. "Not much. I thought she had mystical food up here. She's always coming downstairs with something amazing, but all she's got in here are ingredients to food. There's no actual food."

Himari smothered a giggle. "Where do you think food comes from, Kai? The food fairy?"

Kayah's voice cracked. "I think she's downstairs."

They collapsed together in the open refrigerator, laughing, imagining Genevieve in a fairy costume.

"I love her," Kayah said. "She's so sweet, and she brings me treats."

Himari laid a hand on Kayah's face. "And she patched up your boo-boo's."

Kayah made a disgusted grunt. "I don't want to talk about that."

Himari nodded resolutely. "That's fair, nothing sad, nothing scary."

"I guess that just leaves sex." Kayah looked down the steps. "I like Reuben."

"I hope so." Himari picked up Kayah's left hand, admiring the pearl and platinum engagement ring. "This is pretty. He did good."

Kayah preened, feeling a rush of tenderness. "Thank you. It belonged to one of his relatives. She was a doctor."

"Hmm, like our next monarch," Himari declared, looking absurdly pleased with herself for making that connection.

Stoned and waxing philosophic, Kayah said, "He's an interesting fellow, don't you think?"

"I can't say. I don't know him." Himari's glassy eyes looked off in deep contemplation. "That's the intriguing thing about this group.

We assembled under Peter, who we all know and trust. I suppose that speaks to his force of personality because, basically on his word, we are all risking our lives to put Josiah on the throne."

"It's more than Peter's word." Kayah abandoned the hope of the refrigerator and went to investigate the cabinets. "You know I have always been pretty pragmatic about things."

Himari nodded and made them each a glass of water.

"But that day, when we were fighting Erica," Kayah paused and looked down at her feet, "I felt something, something bigger than us, *someone* bigger than us."

"You, too?"

Kayah nodded and pulled down a jar of dry roasted peanuts. "Yes. Maybe it was Shadrach, Meshach, and Abednego dancing around and singing. I don't know. But I realized this was far more than who sits on the Alanthian throne. If we don't succeed, evil a thousand times worse than Erica will take over. That's what we are fighting for, Himari. Not for your computer code that Korah stole, or for the right to have a freaking cell phone or not. It is about who we are as a people. If Alanthia is going to make the right choices, we need the right leader. Korah is fully aligned with that evil, so if he stays on the throne, we are doomed."

"Damn. Where did that come from?"

Kayah popped a handful of peanuts and shrugged. "I have no idea. Perhaps it's from being around Reuben. He thinks and talks about stuff like that. And you cannot imagine how much hatred he endures simply for being a Jew and aligning with the Iron King, but he does not waver, ever. We have to be that strong; we have to stand up and say to hell with anyone who wants to drag us down. I've been in the pit, and that's no place to be."

She swallowed hard and said, "I have looked into the eyes of wicked men, but that's all they were, merely men. But the eyes of that demon… Himari, that was evil beyond this world."

"I'm sorry you got hurt, Kai." Himari blinked back a sudden rush of tears. "I'm sorry we both got hurt."

Kayah closed her eyes and said, "Everyone will be hurt if we don't win."

"Prince Josiah… Peter swears he is the right man to stop it. Yet we do not know him at all."

Kayah passed the jar of peanuts over to Himari. "I've met him twice. He seems like an honorable man. Reuben loves him, and he is an excellent judge of character. They have known each other for more than a decade. Reuben is devoted to him, thinks of him like a brother." She draped her arm around Himari's slender shoulders. "Like I think of you."

Himari wrapped her arms around Kayah, resting her cheek against her shoulder. After a moment, she said, "Thanks, Kai. I'm going to go take a shower now."

Kayah smiled into her hair with her eyes closed. "That's good, Himari."

Part 10 - Alphas

January 21, 1000 ME

Nouvelles Du Jour - Beau and Esmeralda

At the New York Center for Street Kids of Alanthia, Camy's voice buzzed over Esmeralda's intercom. "Call from Lenox coming through."

Esmeralda looked up from the stack of supply requisitions and stared at the ringing phone, regarding it as if it were a rattlesnake. Taking a deep breath, she steeled her nerves and answered in her most professional voice, "This is Esmeralda ben Claude. May I help you?"

"Morning, *chèr*."

"Good morning, Beau."

"*Êtes-vous prêt pour la bonne nouvelle du jour?*" Are you ready for the good news of the day?

His words were a balm to her frayed nerves, and she answered emphatically, "*Oui!*"

"The forensic accounting report came in. Ian and Joanna are in the clear."

She let out a long breath. "Oh, praise God."

"Amen." Beau sounded as relieved as she. "You were the first person I called. I know this has weighed on you."

"You cannot imagine. I did not even tell Thaddeus. I knew it wasn't true."

"Ah, yeah, but the suspicion, *c'est terrible*," Beau empathized.

"It was," Esmeralda groaned, regretting every wild thought of the past few weeks. "Who was it?"

"We are keeping that confidential at the moment, understand?"

"Yes. I am just relieved it was not Ian and Joanna. What happens now?"

"I'll take care of this."

"Okay." Esmeralda heard a phone ringing in the background and the faint roar of chatter. "Where are you at?"

"That's not how you say it, Esmeralda," Beau replied, and she could hear the smile in his voice.

"That's not what I meant." She chuckled and corrected the syntax of her sentence. "I meant, where are you?"

"My new office." Beau made a low, rueful sound. "They're trying to civilize me. I'll talk to you soon."

Esmeralda closed her eyes. The Beau Landry they wheeled out on a stretcher a year and a half ago was not fit for an office.

Camy's voice broke through her revery. "I think Lenox is back on the line."

"Send them through," she said. "Beau, did you forget something?"

"Pardon me?"

Flustered, Esmeralda fumbled for an apology, "Oh, sorry. I thought you were my last caller ringing back. This is Esmeralda ben Claude. May I help you?"

"So, you were speaking to my son?"

Esmeralda felt her face flush. "Mrs. Landry?"

"Hello, Esmeralda." Sarah Landry tapped her pen against the ever-present pad of paper on her imposing oak desk. "I trust you are well?"

"Yes, and you?" Esmeralda sat up straighter.

"Fine, thank you," Sarah replied. Never one to mince words, she got right to the point. "Esmeralda, do you recall our conversation over lunch last year?"

"Yes, ma'am."

"I must give you credit, young lady. You were correct in your assessment of the situation down here. There are indeed supernatural forces at the root of the trouble we have been having."

"Yes, ma'am. That became very clear to me during my visit."

"I shared our conversation with my husband and our family. After much prayer and consideration, we put a plan into action. For the last year and a half, we, along with the members of our local church, have engaged in a campaign of spiritual warfare."

"I see."

"It took a bit of study. The more sedate among the congregation were not initially on board, but they have come around. We have marshaled quite an army of prayer warriors, with at least two people praying around the clock, seven days a week. And the Lord is answering our prayers. We believe our efforts have curtailed a growing threat to our region, namely, a decrease in the number of violent crimes and mental health cases."

Across the lines, both women smiled.

"I expect that does not surprise you if you have spoken to my son," Sarah continued. "He is much improved, wouldn't you agree?"

Esmeralda took a sip of water. "Yes, ma'am."

"Good. I want to thank you. You were the impetus for this movement. I attribute Beau's recovery to your guidance and the Lord's intervention." Sarah picked a dried leaf off the prodigious spider plant sitting on the corner of her desk and flicked it in the wastebasket. "A few of the ladies in our group are specifically talented, people like you, who see and feel more than the rest of us. All of them agree, there is something brewing down here."

Esmeralda watched the hairs rise on her arms. "What do you mean, Mrs. Landry?"

"Nothing specific, but there is a feeling of urgency, perhaps precipitated by a noticeable rise in voodoo. We see it everywhere, and it's more than just fortune tellers hanging out on Bourbon Street."

"Astrals," Esmeralda whispered, "they are hunting."

Sarah sighed. "You are the third person to say something like that to me in two days."

"So, they have concentrated down there?" Esmeralda reached for the bible resting on the corner of her desk.

"Perhaps." Sarah cleared her throat and continued, "Beau is better, Esmeralda. Confidentially, he is taking over Lenox by the end of the year, so it is imperative we cover him in prayer. If they take Beau down, they take down Lenox, and you and I have discussed what that means."

"Yes, ma'am," Esmeralda said, clearly recalling their conversation.

"I think we are headed into a fight. Something is looming, we just don't know what. I cannot ask our congregation to focus on one person, so I am asking for a favor. I need someone to fight specifically for Beau, to pray a hedge around his home and around him. If they go after him again, he needs to survive and come out whole. Can you do that for me?"

A peaceful certainty fell on Esmeralda, the kind she used to walk in as a child. "Yes, ma'am. I've already started."

Sarah smiled at the other end of the line. "You are a fine young lady. We'll talk soon."

Esmeralda closed her eyes as the image of Beau Landry's pretty lake house came into focus. She remembered the terror she experienced there but also the victory. Stepping into the gap, she prayed.

Neighbors - Redding California

James and Persa rode to Peccioli along the back of their property through the old-growth forest that separated the ranch from the vineyard. Above, the pale winter sun did not penetrate the dense canopy, which made the ride seem colder, their mission more somber. James pulled his muffler high, suppressing a shiver. An ill wind blew through Alanthia, and he could no longer sit on the sidelines. "How are you holding up?" he asked, mindful Persa grew skittish whenever she left Pepperwood.

Persa patted Lightning's neck and gave James a reassuring smile. "Fine. We always enjoy a walk through the woods. Don't we, old girl?"

James winked at her, pleased to see the relaxed set of her shoulders. It felt good to be out. Persa's illness kept him tethered to Pepperwood almost as much as it had her. "After we finish, do you want to ride over to Rivergate and see your dad?"

"Curious, how you always suggest we go see Dad on meatloaf day."

"Do I?"

"Yes," she chuckled.

He shrugged. "Cook makes good meatloaf."

"That he does, and Lavinia makes lovely espresso. I think I will visit her while you speak with Mack. He might be more forthcoming if I'm not around but promise me you will watch your temper."

James made a disgruntled sound in the back of his throat. "I don't have a temper. It's that bumpkin vintner who's got a temper, that's what I say."

"There you go." Persa frowned at him.

He waved her away. "He just irritates me."

Persa widened her eyes at him in profound aggravation. "Your brother thinks highly of him, as does Peter."

James set his jaw, his posture taciturn and defensive.

"Oh, I can see this is going to be a roaring success. We may as well turn around and get your meatloaf." Persa nudged Lightning forward to come alongside James and his horse, Joey.

"I'll be polite."

Persa scoffed because she could feel him simmering. And while James rarely showed his temper, he did indeed have one.

They cleared the forest, and the one hundred fifty-eight acres of Peccioli came into view. The production facilities, barns, and warehouses were constructed over the decades from a hodgepodge of materials and designs, but somehow harmonized and blended with their surroundings. From their vantage point atop the crest, Persa spotted the remodeled visitor's center and tasting room that boasted a new Italian inspired fountain and gardens. Since the success of the Bulizio, visitor traffic at the vineyard increased.

Mack and Lavinia's private residence, with its low roofline, covered front porch, and splendid terrace occupied a corner of the property, away from the production facilities but still part of the working family vineyard. A stately oak tree had a new swing hanging from its bough, and children's toys were scattered around the backyard. Looking over the vineyard, Persa realized she had not visited in years.

"Be nice," she warned. "You two have got on fairly well since he started sending wine to Pepperwood. The clients like it, and it is a nice way to seal the deal with our new buyers. Remember that. It was a kind gesture and his peace offering."

"You're right." James nudged Joey forward, his face resolute.

Lavinia squinted out her kitchen window and called, "Mack, we've got company."

Richard ran to the terrace door and pressed his face to the glass. At nearly four, recent tests confirmed what everyone suspected, Richard had inherited Lavinia's intelligence. Precocious and funny, he often sounded like an adult, though he still struggled to pronounce r's, which came out as w's. He had adopted Mack's southern drawl, which made Richard ben Mack absolutely adorable. "Horses! Mr. Jay has pretty horses, doesn't he?"

"Yes, he does. They are fast, too. Do you remember last summer when we went to their ranch for a cookout? One of their horses won a very important race." Lavinia tousled his unruly curls and watched her neighbors make their way down the slope.

"I remember. Mr. Jay took me to see 'em, but I had to be very quiet." He lowered his voice to a theatrical whisper. "Horses don't like yelling."

Turning back to the glass, he said, "Daddy rides horses good too, even better than him, I think."

Lavinia suppressed a smile. According to Richard, Mack did everything better than any other man on the planet. "Well, Mr. Jay is a famous horseman, so is Mrs. Fey. I showed you the silver trophy. They won a World Championship once."

Richard crossed his arms. "Well, Daddy lived in the Palace and is best friends with Prince Peter. He talked to him today. I heard."

"Richard, you must not say that!"

"Sorry," Richard whispered, bowing his head. "I won't do it again. Please don't send me to San Diego."

"We won't," Lavinia squatted down, meeting his eyes. "But you know the rules, and we have to be careful. We fight the bad guys, but we do it in secret."

Richard folded his hands and nodded. "I keep secrets. I promise."

Mack came down the hall barefoot, distracted, and disheveled. "We've got company?"

Lavinia pointed out the window. "James and Persa."

"Damn, we've got a lot going on." Mack looked around the living room, searching. "Where are my shoes?"

"Go check your pile," Lavinia called after him. "I'll invite them in. Bino, you say hello, then I want you to go play in your room."

Richard appeared as if he was about to argue, then thought better of it, and ran to the back door to watch their visitors tie off their horses at the barn. "Momma, is Mrs. Fey a kid?"

Lavinia wiped down the kitchen counter, suddenly aware the house was not company ready. "No, why?"

"She's little," Richard said with the truthfulness of a child.

Lavinia hid a smile. "I expect it made her a very good acrobat."

Richard pressed his face against the glass. "She's a bat? Like the kind that live in Daddy's barn?"

Lavinia heard Mack laugh from their bedroom.

"Not a bat, an acrobat. It's someone who can do tricks like flips and handsprings, but Mrs. Fey did it on the back of a horse."

"I wanna see!" Richard ran outside. "Mrs. Fey do a flip on the horse! Momma says you can."

"Hello, Richard. My, you have grown since I saw you last summer." She shook his little hand, feeling a familiar pang. Children always did that to her.

"Can you do a trick?" he urged, with a sparkle of excitement in his big brown eyes.

"I have not vaulted in a very long time," she said, glancing at James. "And you use a special saddle that I did not bring with me today. Perhaps you can come over to Pepperwood, and I will show you a few tricks."

"Can we go now?" Richard asked, batting his beguilingly long eyelashes.

"I'm afraid not." Persa chuckled and laid a hand on James' arm. "Mr. Jay was my partner. He used to stand on the back of the horse and hold me above his head while I did a handstand."

"I'll bet that was something, Persa." Mack joined the trio on the terrace. "James, good to see you."

James nodded a greeting but addressed his comment to Richard. "Persa was the greatest vaulter Alanthia's ever seen. She could backflip from a handstand, land in a ground jump, then rebound onto the horse in a standing position and curtsy. No one, before or since, has ever done that."

Long out of the spotlight and unaccustomed to public accolades, Persa flushed with embarrassment. "I didn't do that trick by myself, Jay."

"My daddy can do that," Richard said, fully expecting to hear that Mack could, and probably even better. "Can't you?"

"No, buddy, not in a million years." He picked up Richard and gestured to the back door. "Y'all come on in. It's cold out here."

They sat around the kitchen table, making small talk and drinking Lavinia's excellent espresso, which Persa proclaimed divine, and informed James that the proceeds from their next sale needed to go toward their own machine. "Peter will adore it." she asserted with a quirk of a strawberry blonde eyebrow.

With that simple statement, the energy in the room focused.

"Bino, go play." Lavinia gave Richard a little pat on his bottom, shooing him out.

Mack rose from the table and grabbed his coat. "One of my old mares is not looking so good. I wondered if you might have a look-see?" He directed his comment to James.

Everyone recognized the ruse. James nodded, shrugged on his coat, and followed Mack out the back door.

"You have a phone on you?" Mack asked. James pulled a sturdy functional one from his pocket and palmed it. "Leave it inside and any other electronics, watch or whatever."

James gave him a curious look but did not argue. Stepping back inside, he handed the phone to Persa.

Instead of the stable, Mack led him out to the dormant vineyard. When they were about a hundred yards from the house, he produced a signal jamming device from his pocket and flipped it on. "Never know who might be aiming a microphone at us."

James knew that whatever Peter was up to, Mack was knee-deep in it. "Is he all right?"

Mack met James' eyes. There was no need to clarify who he was speaking about. On New Year's Day, Peter asked Mack to tell Persa and James he was safe. In the ensuing chaos, their battle with Erica, exchange of decoy phones, the rescue of Filippo, retrieval of their son from hiding, and managing a covert revolution while simultaneously running a vineyard, Mack had not found an opportunity. "At the moment, he's fine."

The two men were much the same, of similar height and build, personality, and character. Both were veteran warriors and fierce protectors, leaders of men, and thus, could not stand each other.

James let out a long breath and nodded. Then, raising a sardonic eyebrow asked, "And how was your cruise?"

Mack scowled. "Eventful. Trust all has been peaceful here?"

The dig hit its mark. James moistened his lips and said in a mild tone, "I want to talk to him, to assure myself you haven't sent him off on some hairbrained folly."

"What the hell is that supposed to mean?" Mack growled.

James set his jaw. "It means you've got a personal vendetta against Korah over what befell Peter on your watch. When you add to that the incident with your friend last year in Thyatira, a debacle that nearly got my brother killed, you cannot fault me for seeking assurances that you have not manipulated the situation to suit your own goals and petty need for revenge."

"You self-righteous, arrogant, son of a bitch," Mack said in a conversational tone. "I am out here risking my ass every day while you hang out with your horses and drink my wine."

"Well, boyo, you can take your wine and shove it where the sun don't shine. I want to talk to him!"

They stood chest to chest, glaring at each other, poised and ready, this confrontation years in the making.

"Mack! James!" Their wives shouted in unison from the back terrace.

Neither man flinched.

"You take a swing at me, and I will drop you. We ain't on horse-back." Mack's ruddy complexion flushed with adrenaline. He hoped James would. It had been a while since he beat the shit out of any-body, and at the moment, it seemed like a mighty fine idea.

James laughed without humor. "You've been wanting to do that since I called you out for getting Lavinia pregnant, then abandoning her, alone, in shame."

James was ready for the blow, saw the flash of fury in Mack's face and moved backward to avoid the full thrust of the gut punch. He countered with a cross that grazed Mack's jaw and caught him hard in his bad shoulder. Mack brought up a nasty uppercut that snapped James' head back with a tooth clattering crack.

The two men broke apart for a second. James lowered his head, ready to charge. Mack stood poised and ready, a human lethal weapon.

"Stop!" Persa yelled and jumped on James' back like a monkey.

Lavinia recognized the fury in her husband. "Mack," she coaxed in her breathy voice.

The two men stared fire at one another.

"Get off my land!" Mack shouted.

"Gladly." James shrugged Persa off and stormed away.

Persa and Lavinia exchanged pained murmurs of mutual apology.

Persa stalked after James, fuming. She knew he provoked the confrontation, simmering all the way here. James did not stop or acknowledge her angry calls, simply mounted Joey and thundered off. She saw his expression as he rode away and let him go.

"Persa?" Mack said from behind her.

She drew in a deep breath and turned. "I'm sorry, Mack. He has not been himself. We're both worried about Peter, and... and there's been some other things."

Mack did not need Esmeralda's second sight to read Persa's energy and self-protective body language. "You wanna take a walk?"

Her ponytail swung around her head as anger flashed in her clear hazel eyes. "That would be grand because if I go after him now, I guarantee the scene will not be pretty."

"I've got the same excuse." He smiled sickly and waved to Lavinia, who stood on the back terrace with her arms crossed. "Except I'm the one who'll be getting my ass chewed."

Persa dug her hands deep in her pockets and nodded. "I cannot say that I blame you. I saw her get angry at a drunk at the bistro once. She beamed him in the eye with a ripe lemon and cursed him out in six languages."

Mack chuckled and took Persa's elbow. "It's that fiery Italian temper. They throw things. She smashed a big ole glass bowl during an argument with me a couple weeks ago." He adjusted his ball cap and lowered his voice. "Come to think of it, the origins of that argument were identical to what your husband, and I just fought about."

Persa tilted her chin up, studying him. "I don't follow."

"It's about keeping the people you love out of harm's way, and worrying about them when they are in the thick of it."

"Oh, I understand that," Persa whispered in a voice as small as she was. "Is Peter okay?"

Mack nodded.

"We saw him on New Year's Eve."

Mack's attention sharpened. "You did?"

Persa looked up at the low-hanging clouds. "He called to say goodbye, but we were in town, and I insisted on seeing him." She turned, her gaze probing and intense. "There was a finality to that parting that has haunted me."

"None of us knows what the future holds, Persa."

She sighed. "He has been planning this a long time, even before '97, hasn't he?"

"I suppose," Mack said noncommittally. "I have a couple of questions for you, if you don't mind?"

The hair on the back of Persa's neck prickled. She looked into Mack's eyes and realized he had not asked her out here for an ordinary stroll. "What questions?"

"Oh, just a few details that require some clarification."

She glanced around, suddenly very uneasy. "Okay."

Mack cleared his throat and said, "Did you know I was with the strike force that eradicated the jihadists accused of killing Princess Alexa?"

"No," she replied, unsure why he would bring that up.

"I was. My unit supplemented the Royal Guard, so we were assigned to security detail for State Dinners and such." His words hung in the air. "Like on 9/11…"

Persa stopped.

"Several times, during those years, I was in the Palace." He tilted his head, studying her. "But so were you, Persa."

She sucked in a breath and held it.

"I had forgotten, but then I heard a name that jogged my memory." He nodded slowly and narrowed his eyes. "It was the name of the man who sent my unit into a terrorist's trap, who got my best friend killed, and me shot." Small flickers of emotion flashed across Persa's face. Mack held her gaze. "Coincidentally, he was the same man you were always with… Secretary Tristin."

Persa turned away with a gasp.

"You some kind of witch, Persa? You and James, over there living at Pepperwood, pretending to be Peter's friends, coming here, trying to find out what's going on with him? Is that why he's never told you anything?" He closed in on her. "He's got sense and damn good instincts. Is that why he's kept you out, because deep down, he doesn't trust you two?"

"No!" Persa protested as her face flushed.

"I remember you. I don't forget a face, and I've gone up against a witch." Mack's voice sounded low and menacing. "She did not win."

"I'm not a witch," Persa growled, balling her fists, thinking she should have let James pummel him.

"Is that right?" Mack lowered his head, coming eye to eye with her. "To hear you two tell it, you've been sweethearts your whole lives, Jay and Fey," he mocked. "But if that's the case, how is it I remember you keeping company with the devil incarnate?"

"You don't understand the first thing about it!" Persa shook her head, backing away, intending to leave.

Mack advanced on her. "You are damn right I don't. But you are going to explain it to me because we are up against some nasty shit, and I aim to find out everything about who and what we are fighting."

He was no longer recognizable as her kind neighbor, the honey-voiced gospel singer, or the stalwart protector of Princes. Mack ben Robert morphed into a ruthless commander, an interrogator of enemy spies. Persa realized she was the perceived enemy.

"You can quiver your pretty little chin at me all you want, sweetheart, but you will tell me what I want to know."

Persa's cheeks flamed crimson. "I don't have to tell you anything!"

She made a move to leave, but he took her arm. "Yes, you do!"

In the end, she told him, not for herself, not for Mack, but for Peter because she needed to ensure the man Peter trusted with his life wasted no time or energy pursuing red herrings. Despite his strong-arm tactics, Mack was correct. They were fighting a powerful, unseen enemy. So she relayed her abduction and imprisonment, telling the story as clinically and dispassionately as she could. However, as she spoke, the horror of her ordeal swam to the surface.

When she finished, Mack reached out, as if to comfort her. She pushed him away and snapped, "How dare you?"

"Persa—"

"Sod off, Mack." Without another word or backward glance, she spun on her heel and stalked away.

The thundering hoofbeats of her horse a minute later were an ee-rie echo of her husband's exit a half hour before. He had the truth; of that he did not doubt. No one would make up a story like that, and he could tell when someone was lying. She hadn't been. For a year and a half, the evil entity that lived in the Palace held her captive, an inconceivable horror. Having fought it for seven years, he could not imagine what it did to that little woman.

Wandering the rows of barren vines, he realized he had just suc-cessfully angered and alienated not only his neighbors, but Prince Peter ben Korah's closest friends and allies. Worse, he half expected James ben Kole to ride back over here and try to shoot him. He hoped he would not. He'd hate to kill the man.

January 22, 1000 ME

But for the Grace of God - New York City - Thaddeus

Navigating the sidewalk on his way to the office, Thaddeus stepped over a spilled milkshake, then avoided another splattered mess that was far more dubious. The man huddling in a doorway of a closed nightclub was the likely culprit. It occurred to him that without Esmeralda and Rephidim, he might have ended up in a sim-ilar spot. When she discovered him in Thyatira, he was well on his way. So, he decided to stop.

As he squatted down, the ripe tang of body odor and booze as-sailed his nostrils. "Hey, here's some money. Do you need anything?"

A red-rimmed eye opened, peering out from behind shaggy bangs. The grizzled beard obscured most of the stranger's face, and he took the cash with a trembling hand. "Nah, man, thanks though."

"Okay then, take care." Thaddeus rose without patronizing, offering advice, or giving directions to the nearest shelter. The man knew where to find those services and help—if he wanted them. But a few shekels might buy him a sandwich, or if he chose, a bottle of oblivion. What business was that of his? When he was in that state, the busybody do-gooders annoyed the hell out of him. Back then, he wanted everyone to leave him alone. However, he remembered what it felt like, so he anonymously supported several soup kitchens and shelters and had since he sobered up at Grandma Eve's.

Homeless kids were a different story; they needed intervention and protection. Life on the streets offered nothing but drugs, gangs, and prostitution. Esmeralda worked to prevent catastrophes. Thaddeus cleaned them up, or at least he tried.

In his role as a Director at the FBI, his division investigated everything from organized crime to terrorist groups. But he had a special place in his heart for the unit that investigated missing and murdered children. Given his history, he might have distanced himself and focused on fraud or white-collar crime, but working on children's cases kept him connected to his sons, Jacob and Matthew. He never wanted to lose his boys to time and fading memories.

He did his best to give the families closure, knowing from experience that unanswered questions were like walking through life with a stone in your shoe, always there, a constant source of pain. Thaddeus would never be normal again, not in the traditional sense of the word. The human soul never completely recovered from such an epic blow. So, he channeled that feeling into his work and tried to keep others from suffering as he had.

Even today, he did not know all the circumstances or motivations that brought those animals to his house that fateful day. He suspected the perpetrators who slaughtered his family did it as an act of revenge, in retaliation for his campaign against the jihadists' leaders, who organized riots and violence after the tech laws were repealed, but he could not be certain. During the raid to arrest the suspects, they fired on the police, and the officers responded with deadly force. One survived a few days, but he never regained consciousness, never told his story. So, two weeks after his family's murders, his superiors at the Ministry of Justice closed the case.

That was what sent him on the bender, not just Olivia, Jacob, and Matthew's deaths, but the unanswered questions. Had the perpetrators acted on their own, or had someone else planned the attack? Were men with his family's blood on their hands still walking around free?

For years that anger bubbled just below the surface. But he found peace in the Golden City. Standing in the temple, he laid down the burden and tried not to pick it up again. He largely succeeded, but not always.

However, the Lord let him see his family. They were whole and happy. The vision gave him the assurance he needed to move on. Yeshua, in his infinite wisdom, timed it perfectly. He started his life with Esmeralda free, a gift he did not take for granted.

As he pushed through the doors of his office building, he shook off the familiar burning in his gut, setting aside the unanswered questions, and focused on the day ahead.

As much as Esmeralda railed against it, he planned to help her cousin and her friend. His wife simply did not understand the significance of the connections Elisabeta and Jenny made in the New City, and after mulling it over, he made a decision.

Further Considerations - Redding, California - Mack

The sun had barely broken the horizon when the phone on Mack's nightstand vibrated. Seeing it was Thaddeus, he slipped out of bed and took the call. After conducting a quick, quiet conversation, Mack promised to consider Thaddeus' proposal. It had merit, and the timing could not have been more fortuitous.

Mack spent most of a restless night reviewing his conversations with James and Persa. James figured out that he and Lavinia's absence coincided with Peter's escape, and if he put it together others might too, including Korah. The minute Peter escaped the Palace, the agreement he negotiated with Korah to leave Mack alone ended, so there was a distinct possibility government troops might show up at Peccioli with guns blazing. Mack was not the sort to tuck his tail and run, but neither was he a fool, plus he had Lavinia and Richard to consider. The more he pondered the situation, the more he warmed to the idea of getting the hell out of here for a while.

He wandered past Richard's room and peeked inside. Early dawn cast the room in misty blue. Toys overflowed a big grapevine basket, and Richard lay on his side in the new big-boy bed. Under his rosy cheek, he snuggled with his nanky, a tattered yellow blanket that sported a red juice stain that defied laundering. Its silk binding frayed at the edges, and the embroidered duck in one corner curled tightly into itself, no longer recognizable, but Mack knew what it had been. He smiled at Richard's peaceful expression. In repose, Mack could still see the baby he had been. A surge of love roared up his spine, and he squelched the urge to pick his son up and hug him. Richard was safe, but to remain at Peccioli put him in unnecessary danger.

Closing the door, Mack cringed as the hinges made a loud creak. He kept forgetting to oil the damn thing. Outside, he paused, but other than a sleepy grunt, all remained quiet. Breathing a sigh of relief, Mack walked down the hall, thankful he would not have to deal with the little chatterbox before sunrise. Richard opened his eyes and his mouth at the same time, and Mack did not relish having a lengthy discussion about which jelly Richard wanted on his toast. Yesterday, he decided strawberry was his favorite, but that was subject to change. And while Richard considered his fruit spread choices, he treated Mack to a dissertation on the merits and drawbacks of every type, accompanied by a thousand questions like, why didn't they make banana jelly? Mack chuckled, remembering the conversation. Living with two geniuses was challenging at times.

He got a drink of water and slipped back into bed, his thoughts returning to Thaddeus' proposal that he and Lavinia escort two runaways back to New York. Mack remembered Elisabeta ben Yoder, Stephen ben McSwilley's last assistant. The Resistance had back doors into the government's system and their own network of informants, but she might be worth interviewing. Gus mentioned Jenny ben Rip in his journals, the girl raped at Facetec. And while they were not focused on Marco ben Massimo, she might have seen or heard something useful to the FBI.

Thaddeus wanted to question both girls unofficially. To that end, he paid for their flights to New York, and asked Mack to join them under the auspices of a family friend seeing them safely home. The ulterior motive being that Mack would ensure they did not cash in their tickets and slip away before Thaddeus spoke to them.

Snuggling next to his lovely wife, Mack decided to go along with the plan. Peter, Josiah, Davianna, and Astrid were headed to New York, and the Iron King willing, would be there in two weeks. The second half of their plan required Mack to be in New York, so he may as well leave early and take the family. He kissed Lavinia's ear and whispered, "Valentine, what do you think about taking a trip to visit Esmeralda and Thaddeus?"

Long Lunches - New York City - Thaddeus and Esmeralda

At a street corner vendor's cart, Thaddeus spread mustard on a hot dog and passed it to Esmeralda. Loading his with onions and ketchup, he asked, "So you convinced her?"

Esmeralda wiped a spot of mustard from the corner of her lip and rolled her eyes. "Yes, I did. It took some persuasion, but as soon as she heard Jeremiah was back in Bezetha she was ready to flap her arms and fly home."

Thaddeus closed his eyes in bliss, enjoying the satisfying snap of the hot dog as he bit into it. "And Jenny, she's also coming?"

"Yes. I finally got to talk to her. Up to this point, I've only spoken to Elisabeta. I remember her vaguely. Honestly, I paid little attention to her back then, but I do recall she was pale pink."

She paused, then explained for his edification, "It's a soft color. There was nothing dynamic about her. She was timid, a follower, who did whatever Elisabeta told her." Shrugging, she added in a dismissive tone, "I suspect she ran away because Elisabeta convinced her, and she will come back for the same reason."

"Likely."

"She asked me if we had any open positions at the Center. She was apparently impressed with what she saw out in the New City and said she did not want to go back to Bezetha." Esmeralda stared at her half-eaten hot dog and handed it to him.

Thaddeus raised a questioning eyebrow but accepted without protest. He was still hungry.

"The way she said Bezetha made my skin crawl. Ernst told me many of the Bezethans became followers of the Witch. We know Dr. Nephel was one of hers, and a dozen of the bodies they recovered in Endor were from there, including Jenny's uncle. I think she's seen some things. I wouldn't be surprised. They were not subtle."

Thaddeus made a mental note. "How did you explain Mack as an escort?"

Esmeralda flashed him a broad grin. "I told the little brat that I did not trust her, and I was not giving her cash. So, if she wanted to stay off a park bench and see Jeremiah again, those were my terms."

Thaddeus grinned. "You've toughened up, Vixen."

"I work with street kids every day, Thaddeus. They would eat me alive if I didn't toughen up."

But more than street kids toughened her up, and they both knew it. A cool wind blew through the park, lifting her hair and reddening her cheeks. She no longer tamed her glorious, white curls into a tight braid, and they danced in the breeze, giving her a wild, dangerous appeal. The scar on her face came into sharp relief against her flushed cheeks, but instead of detracting from her beauty, the mark made her more interesting. After Thyatira, Esmeralda abandoned her drab librarian clothes, and now dressed primarily in jewel tones. She favored funky designs and patterns and developed a style all her own. Large hoops dangled from her ears, and she wore three gold bangles Lavinia sent after Claire was born. The gray eyeshadow she favored made her eyes look like tempered blue steel. His wife was the sexiest thing he had ever seen.

He draped a loose arm around her shoulders, walking with her in the peaceful park, enjoying a rare respite away from the office. "We should meet for lunch more often. This is nice." Esmeralda snuggled against him, and he realized she was cold. Pulling her tighter, he caught a faint whiff of the anniversary perfume he bought her last November.

With a wistful sigh, she said, "It is nice, just you and me. I'm so tired after work. We both collapse after getting Claire down to bed."

"Bed…" He looked at her with sultry, lidded eyes. "What do you say, I give you another kind of wiener for lunch?"

Esmeralda actually snorted as she laughed, which Thaddeus did not find funny.

But in the end, he didn't really mind.

No one on his staff said a word about his three-hour lunch.

January 23, 1000 ME

Burnished - New York - Thaddeus and Esmeralda

In their New York apartment, Thaddeus and Esmeralda were changing for dinner. Surrounded by pillows, Baby Claire sat on their bed watching them. Esmeralda discarded her third outfit with a grunt and stormed back into the closet.

Thaddeus turned to Claire and said with a wry grin, "Your mother is not looking forward to dinner tonight."

"No, I am not," Esmeralda called from the closet. "Aunt Jean is sweet, and I love her, but…"

Thaddeus looked up from tying his shoe. "But what?"

"Uncle Yoder is not a nice man, and Elisabeta?" Esmeralda snorted with disgust. "Did you hear the way she spoke to me today? Ungrateful brat. You bought her ticket and sent Mack across the kingdom to make sure she got home. We are paying for their hotel room tonight, and I am certain you will pick up the bill for dinner. After all that, Elisabeta barely had a word of thanks."

Thaddeus straightened his tie, hearing her building up steam.

"Ian is letting Jenny stay at his apartment, so she does not have to go back to Bezetha, and we are giving her a job. But Elisabeta acts like all this is nothing, like the world owes it to her. What the world owes her is a park bench!"

Esmeralda stuck her head out of the closet, stripped to her bra and panties, her fourth outfit discarded. "Though Jenny seemed grateful, poor thing. I never understood why she was friends with Elisabeta."

She disappeared back into the chaos of her wardrobe and continued her tirade. "Aunt Jean drove all the way from Bezetha in that rickety wagon pulled by that ancient horse to pick Elisabeta up and take her home. For a year and a half, she has worried herself to death, and two seconds after saying hello, Elisabeta starts complaining she did not bring Jeremiah."

"What color is she?" Thaddeus asked, a teasing light in his eyes. Esmeralda's vehement dislike of her cousin amused him.

"Overcooked broccoli, baby-turd green, the color of envy and vanity."

Thaddeus suppressed a smile and picked up the baby who was crawling precariously close to the edge of the bed. "They will be gone tomorrow."

Esmeralda slipped a red sweater over her head in jerky little movements. "I would much rather spend the evening with Lavinia and Mack, instead of going out to dinner with my cousin."

Thaddeus rubbed noses with Claire who squealed in delight. "Little Miss Claire gets to spend time with them, doesn't she? Are you going to play with your new friend, Richard?"

Claire puckered her lips and pressed a slobbery kiss on Thaddeus' cheek.

"None of that, young lady. No kissing boys until you are thirty." He called into the closet over the racket. "The primary reason for this dinner is for me to scope out your uncle. You don't like him, and I caught a weird vibe from Jenny when Elisabeta mentioned him." He shifted Claire to his left side with a grunt. "He let those thugs take you out of his house, after you delivered his son and wiped his ass when he was sick." Thaddeus smiled into Claire's eyes and said in a sing-song voice, "Your daddy wants to have a word with that son of a bitch. Yes, he does, yes, he does."

Esmeralda reappeared, her face shining with satisfaction, wearing one of the stunning outfits he bought her in New Orleans. "I think I might enjoy dinner after all."

Thaddeus wolf-whistled in appreciation. "Wow, you look fabulous."

She twirled for him with a smile. Her dress brushed her slender ankles and there was a gleam in her eye. Her curls hung loose and free, and for just a moment, Thaddeus saw the little imp he met by the river.

"I am overdressed, but I do not care." She examined her reflection in the mirror and pressed her post-pregnancy pooch with a scowl. The long-sleeved rust-colored dress fit every curve to perfection. She added her gold bangles, hoop earrings, and a chunky necklace. Glancing over her shoulder, she laughed, deep and throaty. "It's armor."

"Look at your mom. She is beautiful, just like you." Thaddeus kissed the top of his daughter's head and smiled. "Your aunt and uncle won't know what hit them."

"That's the point." She strolled in the bathroom, feeling powerful, her high heels clicking on the tile floor. A final dab of lip gloss and a spritz of perfume, and she was ready. But as she turned to go, she caught a glimpse in the mirror, not her reflection, something else. Esmeralda turned back slowly.

For the first time in her life, she saw it on herself, an aura, glowing burnished copper. Her hearing became acute, and she picked up Thaddeus talking in the living room, Lavinia cooing over Claire, Mack's deep-throated drawl telling Richard to pipe down. Esmeralda's heart pounded. Moving her hand to her hair, the copper glow followed her movement and cast a sparkling hue over the white curls. She brought it in front of her face, but she could not see it. In the mirror, it was visible.

Copper was used as a conductor, primarily for electrical power. She thought that might be fitting.

"Pray, Esmeralda. Pray for those in the bayou," The Voice spoke in her spirit.

"Yes, Lord," Esmeralda answered.

Several minutes later, Thaddeus found her standing in front of the mirror, still and quiet. "Esmie, are you coming?"

Esmeralda returned from a deep prayer, blinking. Tears hovered in the corner of her eyes, and she exhaled. "I'm so sorry. Yes, of course." She reached for a tissue, gathering the bits of herself scattered in the ether.

"What does Ian call that, 'getting prayed up?'" Thaddeus asked with a wry lift of his brows.

Esmeralda nodded, still not quite back.

"You okay?" he asked.

Esmeralda patted her hair, noting the copper glow was no longer visible. "I'm fine, just a little active duty, I think."

"Ah," Thaddeus nodded with understanding, "gotcha. We need to go. They'll be waiting."

"Well, we wouldn't want to keep Elisabeta waiting, now would we?" She rolled her eyes and sashayed out of the bedroom.

"Whoo wee!" Mack exclaimed when he saw Esmeralda. "Look at you. Thaddeus, I can't figure how two ugly mugs like us got so lucky, but I swear we have the prettiest wives in Alanthia."

Esmeralda flushed. "Thank you, Mack."

"You see these two, Son? They are the sort of woman you want to marry, smart and pretty."

Richard considered Esmeralda with serious brown eyes. "You do math, too?"

"Not like your mother."

Richard seemed satisfied with her answer. "That's okay, nobody does math like her. Don't feel bad."

Esmeralda suppressed a smile and met his earnest gaze. "Thank you, I won't."

Mack dropped his work-roughened hand to the top of Richard's curly hair, and Esmeralda noticed the deep rich umber he emanated. She remembered his valor in Thyatira, how he saved their lives, and stayed by them in the aftermath. She leaned in and kissed his cheek, overwhelmed with gratitude anew.

Riding the elevator down to the lobby, Thaddeus shimmered quicksilver as he backed her against the wall and growled, "You look amazing. When we get home tonight, I plan to peel that dress off you with my teeth."

Esmeralda draped her arms around his shoulders, a private smile on her wide lips. "I look forward to it, Tin Man."

When they exited their building, Esmeralda saw two angels unsheathe their swords and flank either side, walking with them all the way to the restaurant.

Yoder for Dinner - New York - Thaddeus

At the end of dinner, the ladies excused themselves and went to the powder room together. Thaddeus took a sip of chianti and examined the color in the amber light of the Italian restaurant.

Yoder stifled a belch and patted his belly, stuffed so full of bread, manicotti, and tiramisu the buttons of his best white shirt gaped open.

Thaddeus eyed him like a great cat, stalking his prey. "Tell me, Yoder, how are things in Bezetha these days?"

"We get along fine, thank thee for asking." Yoder nodded, causing the slack, pallid skin of his neck to fold over the tight collar. A naturally thin man, he wore his long illness like a dirty gray blanket.

"Good to hear." Thaddeus employed a low and soothing tone, cultivated to put suspects at ease. "Did you know I spent several years in Rephidim?"

Yoder wiped his thin lips with his napkin, though desert had been over for ten minutes, their plates cleared away. "Jean mentioned that, yes."

"Fine area, the Thyatira Woods, good people," Thaddeus raised a glass and narrowed his eyes, "in Rephidim."

Yoder cleared his throat, his mouth opening and closing like a landed fish. "Um, well, yes. Our esteemed brethren in Rephidim are behind the times, quaint, but devoted."

"Oh, indeed. Like your Endorite brethren?"

"Well, um… what?" Yoder shifted in his chair, glancing toward the ladies' room. "Bad business over in Endor. And what befell thee," he made low gurgling noises of discomfort, "was unfortunate. Bad, bad business."

"Several of your friends were involved, Yoder. My friends and I," Thaddeus paused for the space of two heart beats, "we killed them. They died."

Yoder's face lost all color as he squirmed.

Thaddeus reached out, gripped Yoder by the upper arm, and squeezed. "I've looked into you… and your lodge brothers."

"Ah, well, ah," Yoder stammered, trying to shrug off Thaddeus' grip without success. "What lodge? I hail from no lodge."

Thaddeus released his arm. "I understand. Within these types of organizations, you are not free to discuss."

Yoder's eyes darted.

Thaddeus smiled without humor. "But I am curious. What happened? Everything seemed to be going so well. Your life was on the upswing. After ten years as a mason at Bezetha Stone, you finally got a big promotion." Thaddeus took another sip of wine. "You bought a new house, fine clothes, and became a deacon at your church. You and your wife had a baby on the way. Everything was going splendidly, wasn't it? But then you got into a little gambling debt, and there was that girl."

Yoder held up a hand. Beads of sweat shimmered on his scalp, illuminated by the overhead light. "Now, see here—"

"They had you then, didn't they? They owned you."

"They did no such thing." Blood rushed up Yoder's neck as he realized his mistake.

"What did they want? Because they beat the shit out of you before Esmeralda got there." Thaddeus pitched his voice into a low vicious whisper, "What did you trade? What did they give you in exchange for handing over my wife?"

Yoder looked like he might faint.

The ladies exited the powder room.

"You remember this. I could bring you and your slimy lodge brothers down in an instant." He snapped his fingers. "I gave you back your daughter, and you owe my wife a huge debt. One day, Yoder, I will collect."

Thaddeus rose from the table, resting a hand on Yoder's shoulder, squeezing a nerve he knew would cause maximum pain. "It's been a pleasure."

Eureka! - New City - Alaina and Reuben

"We've got a hit!" Alaina declared, jumping up from her chair and pointing at the screen.

Reuben stuck his head out of the bathroom, half his face covered in shaving cream. "It is Zanah or Agnor?"

"Both!" Alaina made a low, satisfied growl. "Gotcha!"

Reuben came over to investigate, wearing nothing but a towel wrapped low around his hips. "Where are they?"

Alaina's fingers started flying. "Eureka, California. This picture is time-stamped a half hour ago."

"How far is this Eureka?" Reuben leaned in, studying the photo. It was them, disguised, but them.

"About five hours. Mack is closer, Redding is about two-and-a-half hours, but he can't do it. They are already on their way down here." Alaina hit her palm against her desk. "*Merde!*"

"Is not so far by helicopter, is it?" Reuben asked, a smile growing on his half-shaven face.

Alaina turned. "You dirty dog. You have been looking for an excuse to take that helicopter since I told you about it, haven't you?"

He shrugged, adopting a boyish innocence. "What, what? This helicopter, it is for us to use, no? The Prince wants the girls' parents safe. We get them safe. It is good." He swaggered off to finish shaving.

Alaina called after him, "You just want to show off for Kayah and prove you can fly a helicopter."

He stopped and turned over his shoulder, his strong nose in profile, the bulge of his muscles on full display. "I am Mossad, is sexy, no?" He winked and then disappeared into the bathroom.

Alaina let out an unsteady breath. Heat crept up her neck, and she fanned her face, murmuring, "Yes, you are, and that woman would kill me for even noticing."

Part 11 – Moiety

January 22, 1000 ME

Food Snob - Texas/Louisiana Border - Peter and Astrid

"Here, take it. It's a burrito," Astrid coaxed, trying to hand Peter a cellophane-wrapped package.

He scrunched his face, casting her a dubious glance as he pulled away from the gas pumps. "It smells like dog food."

She laughed and set it beside him. "It does not. It's bean and beef, Texas food."

"They had nothing more palatable?" he asked, staring down at the offending burrito with distaste.

"They were fresh out of caviar at Jimmy's Snack & Fuel Stop." Astrid said, taking another bite. "I figured we needed some protein."

"Cheese?"

"They had something labeled cheese food in there, no brie or Stilton."

"Stilton is vile." Peter ignored the burrito and took a tentative sip of stale coffee, whose temperature rivaled molten lava.

"Celery is vile."

Peter turned to her, curious. "Celery?"

Astrid shuddered. "All those creepy strings, like coconut. Yuck."

"You do not like coconut, either?"

"No, It reminds me of chewing toenail clippings."

Peter recoiled at the mental image. "Oh, that is terrible," he chuckled. "I have never thought about that before. I shall never be able to eat coconut again."

Astrid made a small squeak of triumph. "See, I am right."

"I suppose you are." He smiled at her and looked at the burrito again. "Open it for me. I will try it."

"You might like it, even if it is common." She unwrapped it and handed it to him, so he could eat it while he drove. "I am common, and you seem to like me just fine."

"I like you, a little." He flashed her a dimpled grin.

"I like you a little, too, even if you are an insufferable food snob." She tucked her knees under her bottom and turned to face him. "Come to think of it, you are much snobbier than your cousin, at least when it comes to food. He eats anything."

Peter took a bite of the burrito to prove her wrong, but after tasting it, set it aside. "I expect that is because he has been in the army."

"Well, you were in military school," she countered.

Peter looked ahead at the flat Texas road and said, "I had a cook."

Astrid burst out laughing. "You had a cook in military school? I bet that made you popular."

"Poison." Peter shrugged. "It was a precaution. Mack insisted."

Astrid flushed. It was easy to cast him in the role of spoiled Prince, but the realities of the role often shocked her. "You've mentioned him before. Who is Mack?"

He turned and studied her. To tell her meant he trusted her, not only with his life but the entire organization. Everything hinged on Mack. Only he and Peter knew all the assets, human and otherwise. If they captured her, the whole thing could come apart. And while he did not plan to allow her to ever be taken captive, he still had to protect the rest of his people, so he hedged. "He was my PPG while I was growing up." At her confused expression, he clarified, "It stands for Personal Protective Guard, basically my Head of Security."

She narrowed a cat blue eye at him. "Well, he did not keep you very safe."

Peter glanced over at her in surprise. "Oh, that is not true. The years he was with me were the safest of my life. Korah never touched me when Mack was around."

"But he is no longer with you. What happened?".

Peter rubbed his nose. "About three years ago, I sent him overseas to find Josiah. While he was gone, Korah did to me what he did to you." He cleared his throat, shaking his head in disgust. "When Mack returned, he smuggled me out of the Palace and took me to Pepperwood. After that, it was no longer safe for him to continue in my service."

"Oh," Astrid said into the silence. "And your new PP whatever, is he any good?"

"PPG," Peter corrected. "Yes, he is, actually. Mack trained him, and he and his team played a role the night of our escape. You will meet him when we get to New York."

"Is that safe?" she asked, deeply suspicious of everyone, for good reason.

"We cannot do this on our own, Red. There are a dozen people supporting us, putting their lives on the line to ensure our safety."

She sighed and looked out the window. "It was simpler when it was just me and Davi."

He gave her a quick look, reading the sentiment behind her words. "Simpler, but not safer. You are going to have to trust me."

"I do," she said. "It is all these other people that I do not know, that I have never met. How do you expect me to trust them?"

The glib answer that sprang to his mind faded when he considered how he might feel in her circumstances. "I suppose you are right, so I will not ask it of you. And I promise, if you ever feel uneasy, I will heed the warning."

"You will?" she whispered.

"Yes," he said, bringing her hand to his lips. "I trust you, Astrid ben Agnor."

An array of emotions flickered across her face. She blinked at him and turned to look out the window.

They rode in silence for a time, neither suspecting his promise was about to be put to the test.

Fifty miles from the gas station, Peter noticed Astrid was growing agitated, fidgeting in her seat, looking behind them. "Is everything okay?"

Astrid pressed her fingers against her temples, rubbing in slow, hard circles. "Something is wrong."

"Are you getting a headache?" he asked.

"Not really."

"Then what?"

"I can't describe it. It's like the hair on the back of my neck stands up, and I feel it."

He scanned their surroundings, assessing the terrain. They were driving back roads, and the flat scrubby plains of Texas changed over to the twisting rich forests of Louisiana an hour ago.

"Peter," she said, her blue eyes growing huge, "something is hunting us. Get us out of here, now."

Accustomed to situations that required split-second safety decisions, Peter did not hesitate. Flooring the accelerator, the SUV's engine roared, and they shot down the road.

I Can Be One - Josiah and Davianna

Since separating from Peter and Astrid two days before, Josiah and Davianna took a meandering northern route to New Orleans, traveling through Texas, Louisiana, and Mississippi. They did so in relative quiet.

Davianna struggled to keep her barriers up, not an easy task with Josiah sitting next to her. She found it simpler not to talk and filled the quiet hours contemplating how she could help him, dissecting the obstacles he would face, and wondering if the Alanthian public would rally to his side. There was a possibility they were facing a bloody civil war. As support for the Iron King waned, people were becoming more callous, violent, and corrupt. She and Astrid witnessed the decline across Europe, and the hours of news coverage they watched while hiding demonstrated that things were much worse in Alanthia.

She wondered if Peter's plan to expose Korah's corruption would work, and if it did, would people even care? What would happen if they did not reach the Golden Kingdom? Would the Iron King still give Josiah his support and his army, and if so, would the Ruling Princes come to Josiah's aid?

The Alanthian nobility might, but Korah's unrelenting campaign against the aristocrats had weakened them to their lowest point ever. Did they still have enough power and influence to make a difference, and if they did, would they rally behind a Prince rumored to be unstable?

Businesses were making a lot of money exporting technology, so they might not be too keen on disrupting their enormous cash flows, and if they supported Korah, so would the media companies they owned.

The only thing that seemed clear to her was that Josiah had to retake the Alanthian throne. She witnessed Korah's corruption first-hand, and that evil had infected the very soul of the kingdom. If things did not change, if Josiah and their mission failed, the judgment Alanthia faced would make what the Iron King did to Egypt and Greece pale by comparison. The faithful knew… the clock was ticking.

Josiah spent the silent ride also thinking, though not about matters of state or his future rule. Instead, he wrestled with the first identity crisis of his life, imagining life as an ordinary man with Davianna ben David by his side.

"What is the first thing you plan to do when you take the throne?" she asked.

Her question startled him out of a daydream about a beach. He pictured her wearing a swimsuit, sitting beside two brown haired children, a boy and a girl, while Benny barked and dug holes in the sand, spoiling their picnic lunch. It was a powerful fantasy, one of a laughing, happy family. "Pardon?"

"I said…" She repeated her question.

"Restore fellowship with the Iron King and end the rebellion," he answered without hesitating. "Everything else falls in place after that."

"That simple?"

He glanced over at her. "No, it will not be simple."

She cleared her throat and fidgeted.

He sensed her discomfort and hoped she had not discerned the turn of his thoughts because in his fantasy, bikini-clad Davianna had just put their two brown-eyed children to bed.

"You will need people around you that you can trust when you retake the throne, and I suspect you do not have many after living as an exile for so many years. Even the people you served with, like Reuben, are Mossad, which will pose difficulty for you."

He raised a brow, looking over at her. She was right.

Davianna stared ahead, a look of determination on her face, as if after breaking the silence, she needed to speak her mind. "Many of your father's loyal supporters were jailed, killed, or have since died. Those who survived might hesitate to put themselves at risk, especially at first. They will probably hold back, to see if you are worthy, before pledging their support.

"We all know Korah will not leave without a fight. Even if the Iron King smites him, his allies will bedevil you. And the younger generation," she paused, biting her lip and squeezing her eyes tight, "might rally to put Peter on the throne. They know him. They do not know you."

Josiah relaxed an arm along the back of the bench seat, replacing the beach blanket fantasy with one of her sitting in the Palace, giving him advice. Dangerous, because it was paradoxically more and less attainable than the seaside family. "You speak the truth."

"I've thought about this quite a bit. The thing is, you don't have many people you can trust, but I wanted to say," she turned, her big brown eyes shining with sincerity, "you can count on me."

Josiah stared at her, touched beyond words. If he loved her before, he fell hopelessly, permanently in love with her at that moment. He studied her lovely face, the curls at the nape of her neck, the delicate arch of her eyebrows. He memorized the moment, scarcely able to breathe.

At his silence, she became flustered, digging her hand in her hair. "I mean, I realize I am not anybody important. But I thought, you know, as a friend?" He read her panic and before he could reassure her, she blurted, "Because sometimes we need friends, you know, people we can trust, and if you ever did—"

"Minx?" His voice was low, husky with emotion. The words he longed to say strangled in his throat, but he gave her what he could. "I am honored. Your friendship and loyalty are precious to me, of great consequence, as are you."

Davianna closed her eyes and smiled. He watched the relief wash over her and was glad he did not have to hurt her again.

She gave him a sidelong glance from beneath her long, dark lashes and rested her cheek against her hand. "If you ever want to just call me when you need to laugh, or if you want to talk about books, or whatever, you can.

"In the grand scheme of things, I know I am not important. The only thing that makes me important right now is this," she said, touching her left pocket. "Once this is over, no one will even remember my name. I will go back to being regular Davianna ben David, and you will be the ruler of this great kingdom. But, Josiah, I just wanted you to know. We are friends, and you can trust me."

Josiah controlled his breathing, feeling like she thrust her delicate little fingers into his chest, removed his heart, and held it in her palm. He would have to leave her in the Golden Kingdom when they reached safety, for he could not have her nearby and not be with her. He envisioned himself as righteous David, who in a moment of weakness, sinned before the Lord and took Bathsheba as his lover. Not today, maybe not tomorrow, but he would. He was dying of it now and knew time would not quench his desire, his need for her. If he accepted her offer of counsel and friendship, if he kept her close, he would falter eventually. But he would not hurt her by telling her that.

He reached out to touch her, to feel her, flesh and blood Davianna. Fixing the moment in his mind, he hid it away so he would have it in the long, lonely years ahead. "Trust is a rare commodity in this world, is it not?"

"Oh, yes," she sighed, sounding world weary. "We learned that when we were running. Astrid and I only trusted ourselves. That's why I wanted to tell you." She stared at her lap and whispered, "I understand what that feels like, to be alone."

"Ah, but thou art not alone, Davianna ben David."

She took his hand and pressed a kiss to his palm. "I have not felt alone since I met you, Prince Josiah ben Eamonn. Perhaps that street runs two ways."

Josiah curled his hand, holding her kiss. She was right.

Coven - Louisiana Bayou - Charlotte

Deep in the Louisiana Bayou lay a moldering antebellum mansion, surrounded by water, and built on a narrow peninsula. It was accessible by boat through a forbidding swamp or by car for those with eyes to decipher the markers and signs. Hidden from the naked eye and aerial surveillance, Mademoiselle Charlotte veiled Loa Hall with spells and enchantments. Her son, Emite, set deadly snares and traps through the bogs, trails, and hidden paths that periodically caught an unwary visitor, much to his delight.

Charlotte's grandfather, Pierre Durant, built Loa Hall at the turn of the last century. Pierre, a French Baron, fled the kingdom of his birth one step ahead of the hangman's noose. His family's money and influence saved him from extradition. He settled in Louisiana, a region rich in ancient traditions, among people who overlooked his darker predilections. In a brothel, run by a famous voodoo madam, Pierre and three of his equally reprobate cronies conceived a plan to resurrect New Orleans from its watery grave.

The massive undertaking destroyed the lives and fortunes of countless investors, becoming known as the Bayou Folly, an ill-fated endeavor mired in corruption, scandal, and all manner of corporate and governmental malfeasance. Pierre declared bankruptcy twice before the project finally succeeded, but the gamble paid off. The fortune set up the Durant family for generations.

However, the windfall came at a cost.

The Iron King destroyed New Orleans in the Great Judgment. So, to dig beneath the swamp and unearth the condemned place from its murky grave constituted an act of defiance on par with rebuilding Sodom and Gomorrah.

Pierre's family was cursed. Alcoholism, violence, and madness infected them all. His first wife, a girl of fourteen, drank a lethal cocktail of absinthe and arsenic after discovering Pierre in bed with her eight-year-old sister. Pierre secretly married the sister, but five years later she died in childbirth, leaving behind twins, a boy and a girl. Born clinging to each other, they never stopped, and conceived Charlotte Durant out of a passionate, incestuous relationship.

When Charlotte was thirteen, a madman broke into Loa Hall and murdered the family in their beds, all ten of them. Charlotte survived the massacre because her mother had locked her in a closet as punishment for spilling a drop of water on her pink silk gown at dinner. Trapped for two days without food or water, she was near death when a local voodoo priestess named Mambo rescued her.

Mambo ordered the bodies buried, Loa Hall cleaned, and took Charlotte to her village to nurse her back to health. Unwilling to return to the manor house alone, Charlotte stayed with Mambo for five years. There she received her indoctrination and education, learning the power and ceremony of voodoo. However, the tragedy, her ordeal, and the dark rituals she learned at Mambo's side warped young Charlotte's psyche beyond repair.

She returned to Loa Hall at eighteen and began her reign of terror. Paranoid beyond reason, she saw plots where there were none, imagined slights that had not been given, and flew into murderous rages at the slightest breach of protocol. Madness poisoned every part of her soul, making her impossible to predict. Mercurial in what pleased her, no one ever anticipated what would make her happy. Fanatical about procedures and rituals, she beat a young protégé to death for offering a gift with her left hand.

A fearsome witch of unparalleled talent, she rose to the highest rank in the occult secret society of the New Way. Those chosen to attend her marital rites with Lucifer stood in awe of her daring and fortitude. However, Charlotte feared what would become of her at the hands of Satan if she did not deliver what he desired. She returned to Loa Hall wounded, but determined, and launched an audacious plan.

Loa Hall became the epicenter of occult and magical mysticism in Alanthia. Warlocks and witches from across the kingdom arrived, called forth by their Ba'alat Ob. They came without hesitation because to ignore such a summons invited death, and they knew it. The grand manor transformed into an evil factory, pumping out spells, charms, and curses hidden in music, drugs, books, and games. Their evil wares flooded an unsuspecting Alanthia.

Charlotte transformed the grand ballroom into a base dedicated to astral projection. Around the clock, witches and warlocks sent their spirits forth, causing all manner of mischief as they searched for Davianna ben David and the Black Key.

However, they did not conduct their nefarious business unopposed. They encountered and battled the Hosts of Heaven frequently. Harried and harassed, some nights they failed to even clear the bayou to search for their quarry. Even Emite, who focused his efforts and unrivaled talents on the task at hand, could not break through the phalanx of golden, sword-wielding warriors.

Thus, when one of Charlotte's favorites, Ghislaine Girad, returned from a projection and announced she located Prince Peter ben Korah and Astrid ben Agnor within their territory, a celebration erupted. Ghislaine explained she followed them to within twenty miles of New Orleans before the enemy turned her back. However, she saw the SUV enter the city. Mademoiselle Charlotte controlled New Orleans.

"Stop celebrating," Charlotte shouted, "and find them!"

What I Will Not Miss - New Orleans - Peter and Astrid

Later that evening, Peter flashed Astrid a lecherous grin and said, "You look very exotic in that black wig."

Astrid turned, giving his leather-clad form an inspection. "Too bad the anarchists don't like you; you make a very sexy one."

"The anarchists hate everyone, humorless creatures," he said, stretching his neck and examining the fake tattoos. "Nice touch with the artwork. I rather like the flaming skull."

"You would," she teased. "There is a dark side to you. I suspect if you had not been born royalty, you would be in jail."

"I doubt it. I am entirely too diabolical to get caught."

Astrid rolled her eyes. "Along those lines, are you sure you want to go out?"

"I have never been to New Orleans, which I realize, given my dark side, may come as a shock, but they manufacture very little down here, so I have made no official visits." He lifted a shoulder in a casual shrug. "They are also not too fond of Korah, which I suppose applies to me by extension."

"Does anyone actually like Korah?" Astrid hip-checked him out of the way to finish her makeup. "It's a wonder you ever got invited anywhere."

Peter drew himself up with royal effrontery. "I am not without charm."

"You are hideous." She wiggled her bottom at him as she applied her lipstick.

He laughed.

She blew a kiss in the mirror and said, "We are here a day early, so that gives us an extra night to explore. Did you call Sunflower?"

"I did." He did not tell her about the sighting of her father, choosing to wait until they had definitive news. "She scolded me for veering off plan. But you got your wish. This is the seediest place we have stayed in thus far." He gestured around the dank hotel room.

"I like it." The corners of her purple lips quivered. "I find it charming. Besides, that creepy feeling did not stop until we were almost here. Did you tell her that?"

"I did and assured her tomorrow we will be back on plan. Jarrod personally arranged the flat off Royal Street."

"Royal?" Astrid snorted as she applied heavy black eyeliner.

"Indeed."

"Do I detect Jarrod, the Wonder Servant, disapproves of you living in sleazy hotels?" she asked, accentuating her eyes' feline shape with an outward flick of the liner pen.

Peter leaned against the wall, watching her apply the final touches to her makeup. He enjoyed watching her transformations, enjoyed watching her in general. But when she pulled out the mascara, he groaned. "How many coats?"

Astrid paused with the wand held aloft. "Shut up."

"New Orleans will be asleep by the time you finish putting on your mascara," he complained.

"New Orleans does not sleep, besides mascara is crucial. I did not get to wear it for almost a year when I was masquerading as a boy." Astrid emphasized her point by batting her eyelashes at him.

He grinned and gave a start at his reflection. For a second, he had not recognized himself. Astrid darkened his hair, beard stubble, and eyebrows, then applied fake tattoos to his neck and hands. Dressed as an anarchist, he wore black leather pants, boots, and a vest with a long sleeve t-shirt underneath, though they drew the line at multiple piercings. "There is freedom wearing disguises, is there not? Perhaps we shall employ them even after we are safe and living in anonymity." He smiled, enjoying the dream. "Utter bliss and debauchery."

Astrid tilted her head back. The long black wig brushed her back as she moaned, "Freedom."

Peter came up behind her, cupping her breasts and biting her ear with a growl. "Freedom," he whispered. "No one will know who we are, and I will never stand in another receiving line again."

She giggled, "Receiving lines?"

Peter rolled his eyes in exaggerated pain. "Torturous."

"What else?" she coaxed, grinding into him. "What else will Prince d'Or leave behind and never look back?"

"State Dinners," he pulled her backwards to the bed and sat her on his lap, "with their court speech, thees, thous, and thines. I cannot abide it, not to mention, I am abominable at it."

"Sounds horrific."

He nibbled her ear and murmured, "Would you like to know a secret?"

She made a low hum of pleasure. "Yes."

"That is why I never use contractions when I speak. I could not master court language, so my mother encouraged me to always utilize proper English to cover my shortcomings. Perhaps I shall adopt contractions in my new life."

"Oh, you rebel." She settled in his arms, smiling. "What else?"

Peter embraced the game, pleased she did not question him about his failure to grasp court speech. He gave her hints and clues, but she never dissected them, or if she did, she never turned them into an issue. He loved that about her. She simply accepted him. "I shall never open another factory, cut a ribbon, or use a golden spade... ever again."

"Sounds particularly trying. How did you ever manage?" She tapped his lower lip. He tried to bite her, but she pulled her finger away, shaking it at him with mock severity.

"You have no idea how tiresome being on public display is. In my new life, I shall burp, fart, and scratch in public."

Astrid collapsed into him, laughing.

"It is terrible," he protested, laughter ringing through his words. "I learned at an early age to never mount a stage if I had to wee. You cannot leave once you are up there. They surround you with security, and if you leave the dais, you make the news. Heaven forbid you scratch an itch, it makes the front page of the tabloids." He threw up his hands, making big quotes. "'Does Prince d'Or Have Crabs?'"

"I certainly hope not!"

"Because you would have them too," he beamed.

"So, you really won't miss it?" Astrid rested her forehead against his.

Peter closed his eyes, inhaling the warm, clean scent of her skin. "No, I truly will not."

She felt a queer flutter in her stomach, and speaking words that sprang out of the deepest hope in her heart, she asked, "How do you know? You have never known any other life."

"Pepperwood," he breathed the word. "I have known another life, Red. I have been part of a genuine family. The ranch is the only place where I am just Peter. James and Persa were the only people who knew that man, but now… there is you."

"Now there is me." Astrid looked into his eyes and said, "Oh yes, now there is me."

He held her gaze, enchanted by her, desperate for her. "Will you come with me, Red?"

Astrid cradled his face, holding him gently in the palms of her hands, her heart open and vulnerable. "I'll come, Peter. I will come."

January 23, 1000 ME

Out of Left Field - New Orleans - Peter and Astrid

Inside a stylish flat off Royal Street, Peter waited for Astrid to finish getting ready. Mardi Gras was in full swing, and the foursome planned to venture out for a bit of fun and dancing.

Affixing a platinum blonde wig, Astrid styled it into a poofy bob, and gave him a kiss in the mirror. She slipped into a spunky, bright green mini-dress and pulled on a pair of high-heeled pink boots.

"That is sexy," Peter said with a smile.

She giggled and twirled for him. "Well, I'm glad you approve. And I must say, you look fabulous in that European jet-setter kind of way. I like this skinny necktie."

Peter let her pull him in for a kiss, then wandered over to the open balcony door. "I have no idea why I have never been to New Orleans. I like it. Perhaps we will hide out here for a while, and when this is all over, we can sneak back and live incognito. Half the population is blasted. They will never notice us."

"That will have to wait until you are old. You are entirely too beautiful not to be noticed," Astrid purred, running her hands up his back.

He chuckled and leaned back into her. "In that case, disguise me, turn me into a troll."

She unsnapped his trousers and laid the flat of her palm over his warmth. "Ah, that is one way to keep the female population from swarming you. I will make you ugly by day, then undress you every night, taking secret delight, reserving you for my pleasure alone."

Peter's breath caught, both at her touch and the picture she created. "I can dress in waders and camouflage, like a wild river boatman with a long beard."

Astrid unzipped his trousers, taking liberties with his body, as familiar to her now as her own. She laughed, low and sensual as he sprang to life under her hand. "And this will be your wooden leg."

He turned on her, blazing with passion, knocking over a table in his haste. They ignored the clatter, intent on one another. Peter dropped her to the bed, spread her legs, and ran his hand over her lace panties. She was moist, waiting for him, ready. "You are so hot, and this," he stroked her, "is so mine."

Astrid moved under his hand, her arms stiff behind her, arching to meet his touch, holding his emerald eyes with her cat blue ones. "Is that yours?" she panted.

"Uh-huh." He rubbed her with the flat of his two fingers.

"Then take it." Astrid licked her lips in a seductive invitation.

Standing at the edge of the bed, Peter pulled the sexy strip of lace to the side, grabbed her hips, and drove himself deep. Feeling heat envelop him, she infused him with her energy, her indomitable spirit, and zest for life. She was wild, passionate, endearing. He drank in her courage and humor. She let him inside her body, and in return, she filled his soul. Astrid wanted him, not his kingdom, or his power, or his money... him.

Lost beyond rational thought, shudders wracked his body, washing away everything he had ever been. He was no longer the Prince or the player. She touched his wounded heart, comforted the lost boy, and pulled the junkie out of him, declaring, "I am succor, escape, and shelter. I am all you need."

She cried out, joining him in the pure joy of it.

Shattering into her, Peter, the man, made love to a woman—his woman.

He collapsed atop her, gasping and fully clothed. They lay entangled on the edge of the bed, spent.

Josiah's sharp rap at the door interrupted the surreal moment. "Hey, rabbits, I'm taking my girl out to dinner. See you all later."

Peter lifted his sweaty head from the comforter, dazed. "Did he just call us rabbits?"

Astrid's chest shook with a giddy laugh. "Did he just call Davianna his girl?"

Peter rolled over with a grunt. "If he did, he is in for a load of trouble."

Astrid wiggled beside him, getting comfortable. "Why? I think they are cute together."

"Cute is one thing." Peter rested his hand behind his head with a deep sigh, then gave her a lazy smile. "Never mind. Maybe they will have some fun. Heaven knows, Prince Grouchy needs it."

Astrid rolled on top of him with a snicker. "Prince Grouchy?"

"Shall we call him that henceforth?"

Astrid nibbled his ear. "In retaliation for rabbits?"

"All is fair in love and war. Is that not what they say?" He wrapped his arms around her, enjoying the feel of her weight resting on him.

"Who says that?" Astrid snuggled into his embrace.

"My tutor. He was full of all sorts of archaic platitudes. I believe we attribute the quote to John Lyly's *Euphues,* whose work gave rise to the word euphemism."

"My, my, so that royal education did impact you," Astrid said, completely charmed.

Peter stroked her delicate ear and said with a sardonic sparkle in his eyes, "Not necessarily. Assorted bits and pieces took hold, but I was an abysmal student. I am sorry to inform you, but Prince d'Or is not very smart. Deuced handsome, yes. Smart, no."

Astrid raised her head and frowned. "That is not a very nice thing to say about yourself. Besides, Prince d'Or is gone." She kissed him, light and playful, declaring, "Peter is smart."

He puckered up. "Is he?"

"Oh, yes." She wiggled her hips against his, finding a slow rhythm. "He has a wooden leg, too. I feel it."

Peter flashed her his famous smile and took her lovely little derriere in his palms. "I suppose we are not going dancing tonight, are we?"

Her eyes grew hooded, and she bit the lobe of his ear. "We have plenty of time, my beautiful man, and we are dancing."

After cleaning up, Peter and Astrid ventured onto their private, second-story balcony to people watch and throw beads to the revelers. They were in the French Quarter during Mardi Gras with the biggest party in Alanthia outside their window. Fully intending to join the fray, they reserved the right to disappear back into the bedroom. Below, a group of jazz musicians played a soulful tune, and they swayed in each other's arms. The Royal Street balcony held the best of both worlds.

"I adore you," Peter whispered.

She rubbed her cheek against his, holding him close, feeling cherished and safe. "Of course you do. I am adorable."

"I particularly like… the blonde wig."

"I rather enjoy being blonde. Perhaps I will become one."

"No." He shook his head, staring into her lovely face. "You are my feisty redhead, and I would have you no other way."

"Good." She moistened her lips, tasting the strawberry flavor of the shiny gloss. "Because I am who I am."

"I know," he murmured. "Conversely, I think I am becoming who I am."

Astrid reached up and smoothed his straight, perfectly formed eyebrow. "For the first time in your life, you have the freedom to do so, and I must admit, I adore Peter, the man."

He laced his fingers in hers and said, "I shall buy you a yacht and fill it with the things you love. Then I will command the waves to be calm as we sail around the Mediterranean. I will keep you by my side and seduce you every day."

"Just once a day?"

Peter rested his forehead against hers and chuckled. "As many times as you want."

A loud noise on the street drew their attention to the raucous party below. Astrid thought she spotted Davianna and Josiah among the crowd, then realized she was mistaken. She grabbed Peter's arm with both hands and exclaimed, "Look!"

He followed her gaze. Walking down Royal Street, sporting huge golden crowns, two young men, one blond and one dark, looked remarkably like Peter and Josiah. "Bloody hell."

"Over there!" She turned his chin toward a half a dozen women dressed and bewigged in their own versions of Davianna and Astrid costumes.

"What in the world?" Peter murmured, studying the crowd. Then he threw back his head and laughed. "That is priceless, Red. We picked the right place to hide. I have utilized body doubles on a number of occasions but never an entire city of them."

A sudden flash of pain hit Astrid in her left temple. Her hand flew to her eye, and she swayed.

"Are you all right?"

Blinking up at him, she said, "Will you get me a glass of water, please?"

He leaned down and studied her. She could see his warm breath in the chilled night air, concern written across his face.

"I'm okay, just a little dehydrated I think."

He nodded and gave her a quick peck on the cheek, wondering in abstract contemplation whether he had ever brought anyone, other than her, a glass of water.

Astrid caught herself against the balcony as her vision blurred into wavy lines. "Oh, no."

The beast was coming on, hard and fast—migraine.

The wig squeezed her head as the proverbial ice pick struck. She sobbed, as her sense of smell jolted into overdrive. Cajun spiced jambalaya wafted out of a cafe across the street and seemed to ooze out of the sweating bodies below. The humid air carried a miasma of cigarette smoke, urine, and the muddy Mississippi, but above it all, the pervasive stench of alcohol surrounded her. It drifted out of open containers and puddles spilled on the street, sickly sweet and gag-inducing. She closed her eyes, fighting nausea.

Below, she heard a chorus of drunken slurs and shouting, the coy laughter of a girl flirting with a boy. An argument broke out in the distance, two men, ready to fight. Feeling along the railing, she needed to get inside, but she was afraid to move, trying to keep the monster at bay. So she stood alone, blind, nauseated, and trapped in the cold.

When someone vomited below the balcony, she lost it. The sound, the smell, and the sympathetic nervous response caused her to heave over the railing. Below, the crowd scattered, shouting protests, but no one paid her particular attention. This was New Orleans.

Peter returned and found Astrid crumpled on the concrete, clutching her head, and crying. He sprang into action, hearing Mack's voice, 'Get down. Get out. Get safe.' In a move that would have made his former Royal Guard proud, Peter threw the glass aside, crouched low, and gathered Astrid around her waist, pulling her inside. From start to finish, the maneuver took less than three seconds.

Astrid cried out, writhing in agony as he jolted her. "Stop!"

"Are you hit?" he shouted.

She grabbed her head. "Get the wig off."

He examined her, frantically looking for a bullet wound and blood, while the other part of his mind calculated their situation. His weapon lay on the dresser, an arsenal in the living room. His tablet was near the door, the keys to the car in the duffle—time to go.

"Headache," she whimpered. "I need water… dehydrated."

"Bloody hell!" Adrenaline thundered through his body as he sat back on his heels. "Just a headache, are you sure?"

One red eye cracked open, and she snarled, "I'm sure."

He sagged with relief, resting his forehead on her hip. "Okay, give me a second. I thought someone shot you."

"That would probably hurt less," Astrid moaned without moving her lips.

He nodded. "Wig or water first?"

She swallowed, wincing in pain. "Water."

He closed the balcony door and sprinted from the room to retrieve another glass of water. His knees felt like jelly, and he could hear the blood pumping through his ears.

He returned a moment later, and helped her sit up, holding the water to her lips. She took a slow sip, though her body cried out for her to gulp it. From experience, she knew she would not keep it down. "We've done this before, haven't we?"

"Hmm." Peter made a noncommittal sound, loath for either of them to relive her ordeal in the ambulance.

"The wig has spirit gum around the band. Loosen it with your finger." Tears leaked out of her left eye and coursed down her cheek, her mascara melting in a river of pain. She held absolutely still, her only movement the shallow rise and fall of her chest.

Peter watched her face as he removed the wig. Her lips trembled as the skin pulled away from the band, but she remained stoic. A slight relaxing of her shoulders told him the relief she felt. "Can you stand up? I will get you out of that dress and into bed."

"Turn out the lights." She sounded pitiful.

"Of course." He extinguished the bedside lamp, leaving the streetlights to fill the suite in deep gold shadows.

"Boots first, my legs are numb." Her every word sounded like an effort.

He unzipped the sexy pink boots and pulled them free. She winced at even the slightest movement, but it could not be helped. He lifted her to her feet. She swayed and threw her arms out, reeling as the room spun into a sickening swirl of vertigo. He caught her around the waist, whispering, "Hold on. It is almost over."

"Gimme a second," she said, weaving in his arms.

Her dress had a side zipper and fit tight over every curve. He lifted it over her head, and she let out an involuntary moan. The pale light from the streetlamps cast her fair skin in a ghostly glow. Her peach bra and panties were beautiful and delicate, some of Jarrod's handiwork. With her eyes closed and her body trembling, Astrid looked utterly defenseless. He had never seen her like this. She was always tough, in control. Even in the throes of drug withdrawals, she fought, raging against what they did to her. But standing before him now, bare and vulnerable, tenderness welled inside him. "Come now, Love. Rest your head. I will take care of you."

She covered her left eye with her palm and pressed, shaking with pain.

He led her to the bed, then eased her down and tucked her in, leaving her left foot free. "Now what?"

"Cold washcloth, ice," she said.

Her breathing became shallow and rapid. He recognized the signs, snatched up the trash bin, and held it under her chin while she retched.

She cried then, in shame and humiliation. "So sorry... hate this. Hate, I am like this."

"Shh," he soothed, then set the bin outside. "Do you want me to find Josiah or search his medical bag?"

In the way of migraine, vomiting relieved the pain, and she could speak. "You will never find him out there, and the pills he gave Davi in London did not have a name I recognized. The writing was in Hebrew. When they come back, maybe I will take something, but I am not a fan of drugs, for obvious reasons." She attempted a brave smile. "For now, just an ice pack. If that does not work, then my tea, but that will keep me awake. If I can sleep, it might go away."

Peter brought her a makeshift ice pack, fabricated with a hand towel and ice cubes. He helped her alternate between her temple and her neck, which seemed to bring her a measure of relief. A little color returned to her face. He could tell by her breathing that she was not in the grip. "Do you know what triggered it?"

Astrid hovered on the edge of sleep, exhausted by the battle. Fading away, she whispered, "They are hunting us, Peter. One of them hit me." Then she slept.

*   *   *

In the grand ballroom at Loa Hall, chaos reigned. Witches and warlocks returned to their bodies with reported sightings. People disguised as the Alanthian Princes and runaway pilgrim girls overran Mardi Gras. However, Charlotte sensed the Black Key within her grasp, she just had to figure out where. "Emite," she screeched, "come with me, it is time. You and I will find them."

With those words, the fearsome mother and son disappeared into their innermost sanctum, to hunt.

*   *   *

Through the long night, Peter held vigil, watching Astrid. Stroking her temple, he soothed away the pain and coaxed her back to sleep. He heard Josiah and Davianna return after midnight. But Astrid rested peacefully, cradled in his arms, and he did not move. The words she spoke, right before she drifted off, haunted him. He understood far better than they did what hunted them. As he had done more nights than he cared to remember, he stayed awake and alert, dreading the smell of sulfur.

Part 12 - Flight

January 24, 1000 ME

The Night Shift - New City - Himari and Genevieve

Himari sat alone, listening to the soft whine of the servers and cycling fans that cooled the bank of processors in her underground lair, which was her secret name for the bunker. A crowd lived here during their fight with Erica. Now only she, Auntie, and Alaina remained. Kayah and Reuben were in Northern California, searching for Zanah and Bubba. The elusive pair blew away with the wind. But worse, so had Filippo.

He would arrive in New York today, his solitary journey across the country complete, five long days, five interminable nights. Every evening, he checked into a hotel and called, but with each mile and each conversation he grew more distant. Sometimes she forgot, getting lost in her work and managing a brief respite. But she lived with a sick, all-consuming fear. Filippo had left her. No matter what he said, her heart knew the truth. He was gone. Whether it was forever or for a time, it mattered little, measured only by degrees of agony.

Himari spoke of it to no one, even Alaina, who had been with them since the beginning. To voice her fears made the situation real, and she could not bear for it to become real. Genevieve sensed but did not press. Instead, she lovingly and artfully presented Himari with Ujicha tea and Japanese tea cakes every afternoon. The thoughtful gesture made Himari want to throw herself in the older woman's arms and weep, but she did not. Instead, they spent quiet time together. She taught Genevieve the intricate protocols of the Japanese tea ceremony, and in so doing, felt a grounding in herself, a return of a part of her that had been missing since she left Ken and her family behind. To reclaim it now, when she was swimming in a sea of turmoil, comforted her in a way she could not convey, but Genevieve understood, which was why she did it.

Filippo's show opened next week, and that worried her. He had not made a public appearance since November. While they no longer had access to the Facetec servers, they continued surveillance of Massimo's mansion. Himari lived in constant fear the mobster would discover his former underbutler's identity, but other than a cursory interest, his disappearance raised little concern.

As much as Himari wanted to focus on Massimo, for Filippo's safety, The Resistance had a higher mission, and the fugitives were in New Orleans, so she monitored police activities and dispatches in and around the city. Every time they accessed the street cameras outside the flat on Royal Street, Alaina became giddy, waxing nostalgic about her time in Louisiana. She opened up, becoming talkative about Beau Landry. For a decade, she held her tongue and locked away her pain, adhering to Filippo's 'Broken Heart's Club Rules' for survival. But they breached a dam last autumn when Beau broke his silence, and Alaina blossomed in the hope of rediscovery. For Himari, coping with her own heartbreak, listening to her friend without wincing became an exercise of extraordinary will. She let Alaina dream, encouraged her to try, and refused to rail against love and men in general. Ironically, the longest-serving charter member of the Broken Hearts Club put in her notice, while the other two founding members might be rejoining. Sadly, this time, Himari and Filippo would do so alone.

Police dispatches entertained Himari through the long night. She copied the most outlandish ones, planning to share them with Alaina when she woke and wondered how many naked people were running around New Orleans. Judging by the police reports, it sounded like half the city. She particularly liked, "Inebriated man, naked, atop the statue in Jackson Square. Proclaims he is Prince Josiah. Demanding all bow down to him." Despite her morose disposition, Himari laughed at the visual and the absurdity. The last person on Earth to strip naked and climb a statue in a public square was Prince Josiah ben Eamonn.

As if the thought of him brought the computers to life, she started getting hits on his name and his face, setting off alarms. Himari cursed in English and Japanese. Alaina burst through her bedroom door, sleep tousled and incredibly beautiful, which Himari thought with abstract bemusement was unfair. She heard Genevieve's careful steps descending the stairs as the shrill alarms continued blasting.

"Himari, what do we have?" Alaina dashed to the monitors.

"Video!" Himari yelled over the alarms, her fingers flying. "Dammit, it's going viral. I can't grab it."

Genevieve killed the alarm, watching a video of a masked Josiah singing and kissing Davianna.

It exploded across the internet with commentary and amateur facial mapping, but worse, a pinpointed location—New Orleans.

Genevieve braced her arms against a desk, scanning the flashing text. "We've got multiple police units dispatched to Royal Street; the closest unit is five minutes away. Pull them out!"

Himari punched the panic button. "You've got four minutes, Falcon. Get out!"

In a full-on emergency evacuation, they each knew their roles. "I'm in the traffic cameras," Alaina said. "*Merde*, a bunch of them are down, but Auntie's right, there are multiple units en route. Some streets are still closed for pedestrian traffic. Route their evacuation."

"Mapping it now," Himari confirmed.

"What assets do we have in the area?" Genevieve asked. "They won't have time to reach the next safe house."

"I know one," Alaina shouted. "Himari, take them south to Delacroix!"

With no time to think or consider the dangers of engaging an asset, they exchanged looks, in one accord.

The bunker rehearsed the New Year's Eve evacuation a dozen times, so they fell back on that plan. "Alaina, get into the traffic lights and control systems. I've got the traffic cameras. Himari, jam those radio transmissions. Alaina, we may need you to cut the power to the police station if you can." Praying, Genevieve opened communication to Peter's tablet, waiting for confirmation they were out of the flat.

Peter's voice echoed off the bunker walls. "Who have they got?"

Genevieve swung her screen around and nodded. Alaina and Himari both saw the black vehicle they were traveling in pull out of the underground garage.

Himari could barely speak, so intent was she on her task. "Doc and Sparrow, get 'em down."

The video of Josiah and Davianna continued to play, the share and view count climbing by the second.

"Give me eyes, Sunflower!" Peter shouted.

"Right on St. Peter's. You need to go, Falcon. They are shutting down the Quarter!" Genevieve called before Himari could answer.

"I got traffic, Sunflower. Get the lights!"

Alaina was one step ahead of him. "On it!"

"Falcon," Genevieve tried to keep her voice calm, "confirmed, second locale in play."

"Right on Dauphine, they blocked St. Peter's!" Himari shouted, her rising panic traveling over the line as they watched the police closing in. "Right on St. Louis and right on Basin. Falcon, you've got one shot at this."

Alaina, Himari, and Genevieve held their breaths as a police car, lights flashing, came up behind the escaping vehicle, but in the next instant, the getaway sedan disappeared. Genevieve shouted with praise. Himari threw herself backward, her chair rolling away from the desk. Alaina just stared at the screen, her eyes as big as soccer balls. It happened again. One moment the car was there, and the next it was gone.

Overjoyed, Genevieve said, "You're off the grid again, Falcon. Your angel is in play."

Himari watched in awe as the police cruiser diverted.

Alaina's voice cracked, choked with emotion, "I have no eyes on you, but we have an asset in place, sending you the coordinates. Go there." With fingers that shook like an old woman's, Alaina sent the address of the Landrys' old boat dock in Delacroix. She heard the text message blip over the speakers and sprinted from the room to call Beau.

Himari could hardly speak. "Falcon, we will send revised instructions ASAP."

Peter growled, sounding dangerous. "Trigger?"

Genevieve stared at the video screen, her expression inscrutable. In the quiet, the deep timbre of Josiah's singing came over the speakers. "Mary just about wept this morning."

Davianna and Josiah's matching groans were audible over the speaker. Astrid sounded furious. "What in the hell did y'all do?"

"Thirteen million views and counting," Genevieve said with a touch of humor. "Quite a finale, Doc. You are still dark, Falcon. Praise the Iron King. Signing off."

Himari watched in slack jawed wonder as police cars descended on the Royal Street flat. "They disappeared again."

Genevieve did not hear her, transfixed by the video, watching with intense concentration. Focusing on one part, she backed it up and played it again.

Himari rubbed her eyes, trying to see what Genevieve found so compelling. "What is it?"

Genevieve sat stunned, her expression dreamy and faraway. "I have never seen it before. It must be the mask. He looks so much like his father it is hard to see past it." She squeezed her eyes tight and sniffed. "He is manifesting his mother. That is my Margaret on screen with her lively, playful spirit. Do you see it?"

Himari drew closer and played the video, watching the man they were risking their lives to put on the throne.

Remembrance flickered across Genevieve's lined face. "Himari, she was extraordinary, so lovely and full of life." She covered her mouth, stifling a sob. "And she could sing, oh, the voice of an angel." Shaking her head in profound, old grief, she said, "I did not realize Josiah inherited it. I never heard him sing… because with her gone, Himari, no one ever let him."

Then Genevieve fell apart.

She mourned her friend, Princess Marguerite ben Alfonso, her beautiful life cut short. She wept for Josiah, who never knew his mother, and for the loss of her influence in his life. Genevieve cried out in fear, because the man who extinguished the light and love of her precious friend was just as determined to murder her only son.

Another Day of Spreadsheets, Not - Louisiana - Beau

Beau sat in his office with a view of the azure waters of La Petit Pishon. The winter sun hit the waves, making them sparkle like sapphires. It was a good day for fishing, a day to be on the lake. However, he was inside, reviewing a sheaf of reports six inches high with spreadsheets open on three monitors. Oil. He was delving into oil today. Lenox Energy was the largest and most lucrative of all the divisions, the one that brought the Landry and the Lenox families together, the final company his grandfather sent for analysis.

Buried in forecasts, geological reports, and production numbers, at first, he did not hear the phone. The unfamiliar ring failed to penetrate his brain. He snapped back to the present and scanned his desk, realizing the noise came from the secure phone Alaina sent him two months ago. He answered with a sense of trepidation. They never spoke on this line, and if she was calling, something dreadful happened.

As the phone rang, Alaina paced her room in the bunker, tunneling through the bedding strewn across the floor. Filippo's last painting hung on the wall, of her and Himari fighting Erica, their heads together at a computer monitor with Genevieve's maternal presence hovering in the background. She kicked a stray shoe in her distraction, and a thousand-shekel Bitanni boot hit the wall. Becoming frantic at the number of rings, she prayed Beau would pick up. When he did, she shouted into the phone, "Pishon! Falcon in the wind. Pick up four packages, now! Just sent coordinates."

She heard the text chime on his phone.

"Miss Pink, I've got it. Are you okay? *Dis-moi la* **vérité**."

She loved it when he spoke French. "Scared, Pishon. They are pursued."

"I will not fail you, Jolie Catin. Not this time." He sounded resolute.

His misguided sentiment took her aback. Amid the crisis, with no filters, she spoke the truth. "You did not fail last time. You saved me. You saved us both."

A pregnant silence followed, then he spoke the words she had not heard him utter in a decade. "I love you."

Her long legs turned to jelly, and she fell against the door. "As I you, every day since we met." She was sending him into danger, but they had no choice. "Be careful."

"Nay, *chèr*. I've been careful long enough. I'll call you in a bit."

She clutched the phone to her chest, felt her heart thundering, and caught sight of her flushed face in the mirror, realizing at the moment she looked every bit her code name. Miss Pink went back into battle.

Beau realized the coordinates Alaina sent were for their old boathouse in Delacroix. He looked at the lake with a smile. He was getting out on the water, after all.

Shutting down his computer, he locked his office and changed his clothes. As he walked onto the dock, his phone rang. He saw the number and considered letting it go to voicemail, however, his *maman* became relentless if he did not answer. Whatever he was getting into, the last thing he needed was a surprise refrigerator inspection. "Morning, *Maman*. I am getting ready to go out. *Tout va bien?*"

Sarah huffed into the phone. "I do not know if everything is all right. That is precisely the reason for my call."

"*Mon Dieu!*" Beau's patience reached its end. "*Tu m'étouffes!* Quit smothering me. I am fine, two hundred and forty-three days of red check marks. *Sérieusement,* I think I was just low that day back in May when I put a black x." He set his jaw and ground out, "So stop calling me and asking if I'm okay. Stop dropping by and checking my refrigerator, *arrêtez Maman, arrêtez!*"

"I don't think you understand." She sounded stern, but her voice rang with a note of maternal hurt.

"I do. But it ends right now, today. I will call you next week. In the interim, do not come by, do not call, and do not send anyone over here to do it for you. Goodbye, *Maman*." Beau hung up with a grimace, knowing it had to be done.

He boarded the boat and took off to pick up the VIPs. Pulling away from the dock, Beau Landry finally broke free.

Back at her house, Sarah turned to her husband Jorge and said, "He just told me to bugger off."

Jorge turned away, hiding a smile. He saw this coming for months. "*Doudou*, he is a grown man, and he is better. Leave him be."

"I know he is better. No one knows that more than me. I do not hover for the sake of hovering." She pointed to herself and exclaimed, "I am the one who called Father. I am the one who said Beau was ready to begin taking over the company. Does anyone actually believe I don't want that?"

She stomped her foot and put a hand on her hip. "There is something else going on, Jorge. I feel it. Something is brewing, and I am not the only one who thinks so."

She pressed her fingers to her temples, brimming with frustration. "I sat straight up in bed this morning with an urge to pray."

"Then pray, *chèr*. There's nothing stopping you. That's pleasing to the King. He knows you love your children, and the Word commands us to pray without ceasing. But it does not say you got to be checking up on your prayers all the time, like you supervising to make sure the Lord is doing His job. 'Cause that's what you doing. You praying, but you not trusting."

Sarah shot him a belligerent look.

He crossed his arms and waited.

"I hate it when you are right."

Jorge wrapped an arm around her shoulders and pulled her tight. "I'll join you in prayer, *Doudou*. I feel it, too."

Nowhere to Hide - Louisiana Bayou - Charlotte and Emite

Charlotte and Emite rejoined their bodies at the same moment. They looked at one another, horrified and out of breath. In the early morning hours, they located their quarry. Assured of their victory, their prey seconds from capture, Charlotte cried out in the spirit to Lucifer, "Beloved, I have found the Black Key. Come to Loa Hall. I will present it to you as a token of my worship and esteem."

The moment she finished her summons, the enemy attacked. The entire sky filled with the Hosts of Heaven in the largest show of force they had seen to date. Charlotte and Emite fled for their lives.

Emite constructed a series of hiding places after their first encounter with the Host of Heaven eighteen months ago when they failed to kill Beau Landry and the White Woman. Since, he prowled the depths of the swamp, creating enchantments of protection and concealment. Those hiding places saved their lives. But to what end? Lucifer was on his way, and they did not have the Black Key.

"He will kill me," Charlotte panted, clutching Emite by his shirt. "Lucifer does not accept excuses. I am doomed."

Emite did not doubt she spoke the truth. She was close to death fourteen days ago and still bore the marks on her body. "What would you have me do, *Maman*?"

Charlotte panicked. "Hide me."

Emite growled at her suspiciously. "And leave me to face him alone?"

"Tell him I perished in the fight." Her fingernails dug into his chest, desperate and clinging. "His rage will slacken, then he will reward you for bringing him the news. Tell him the Black Key is within our district."

Emite paused, considering her words, calculating the consequences. "And when you resurface, Lucifer will brand me a liar and punish me," he bleated like a newborn calf.

"I will stay hidden. No one will know I survived, including Lucifer. You will be Master here, just as I trained you. You are ready." A dark shadow covered the sun, and she screeched, "Do this for your *Maman*, Emite!"

He narrowed his hellfire eyes at her. "If I do, you will never put me in the cage again?"

Charlotte nodded.

He read her panic, though she tried to hide it. They both felt Satan. He was coming.

"Never. I will never put you in the cage again."

"And the whip? The chains? Will you allow me access to my treats?"

"Yes," she cried, hanging off his shirt, coming unglued.

"Very well." He moved to his workbench and prepared a sleeping draught. "Drink. He will not detect your spirit."

With shaking hands, Charlotte drank the vile potion and collapsed into her son's arms. He laid her in the closet of their secret room, cast a concealment enchantment over the door, and watched it disappear.

With his great heart crashing in his chest and tears coursing down his cheeks, he left her. Walking down the steps, he set his mind to the task, to lie to his coven, but most fearsome of all, to deceive Satan.

Standing in the ballroom, with all eyes upon him, he announced his mother's death and commanded everyone to prepare for their master's arrival. By the end of the day, the global order of the New Way heard the news; High Priestess Mademoiselle Charlotte Durant, Ba'alat Ob, was dead, and the Nephilim, Emite ben Marduk, was now in charge.

Best Father in the World - New York - Mack and Richard

Richard ben Mack refused to play with the other kids. He refused to slide down the sliding board, refused to do anything other than sit by himself and wait for a miracle because that sunny afternoon in Central Park, he discovered his father was not the best at everything. Mr. Thaddeus ben Todd showed him that, and Richard decided he did not like the tall man. He did not like him at all. So, when Daddy missed a rebound and the basketball rolled over to where Richard sat, instead of throwing it back like Mr. ben Todd asked, Richard kicked it across the playground.

"Boy," Mack shouted, "go get that ball!"

Richard turned an accusing eye toward his father, sulky and defiant. He crossed his arms over his chest and held his ground.

Thaddeus looked up, struggling to keep from laughing. The stubborn expression Richard wore was Mack to-the-life, a miniature version, giving his father what for.

Mack was having none of it. He stormed across the court like a charging bull, whose son dared wave a red cape of defiance in the face of his paternal authority. "Go get that ball, now!"

Richard, having determined his father was not God, tested his luck. He planted his little legs, put his hands on his hips, raised his chin, and said, "No."

"What did you say to me?" Mack did not wait for an answer. He grabbed his son by the arm and spanked his behind, four hard pops delivered with lightning speed.

Richard burst into tears, his butt stinging, his pride hurt, embarrassed in front of everyone.

"Now, go get that ball," Mack ordered, cutting a warning look at Lavinia.

She and Esmeralda witnessed the exchange from their bench on the other side of the court. Maternal instinct caused her to jump to her feet, but she sat down, understanding that Mack had been correct. They parented in mutual accord.

Richard left the court in defeat, trying to ignore the kids on the playground who stopped to point and laugh. Snot clogged his nose, and he sniffed at it hard. Hot, humiliated tears ran down his cheeks, but he wiped them away and picked up the basketball. It felt awkward, and he had to carry it with both hands. He could not even see his feet, which made his long walk of shame even worse. When he finally made it back, he tried to hand the ball to his daddy.

"No, Son, you go give that ball to Mr. ben Todd and tell him you are sorry."

Richard's lip quivered. He almost cried again, but the look Daddy gave him warned he better do as he was told. "Mr. ben Todd, here is your bassetball. I sorry." He held it out but did not look up.

Thaddeus took pity on his brother's namesake and asked, "Richard, would you like to dunk the ball?"

Richard looked up in wonder. Mr. ben Todd was the tallest man he had ever seen. "I'm too little."

"Not if I hold you up." Mr. ben Todd grinned down at him like a friendly giant.

The expression on the little boy's face melted Thaddeus' heart. He scooped him up, ignoring the twinge in his bad shoulder, bringing Richard eye level with the hoop. "Stuff it!"

Mack jogged over and grabbed the rebound. "Good shot, buddy. Do it again." He gently placed the large basketball in his son's pudgy hands.

Richard's eyes sparkled, all memory of his mortification forgotten. "Watch me dunk, Daddy!"

The dunk fest continued, masculine bonding, two friends enjoying physical exercise and competition, but they included the boy. Richard settled in, comfortable with his place in the world, secure under the care and protection of his father. His daddy loved him enough to correct him when he did wrong and was wise enough to teach him how to make it right. Richard learned what it meant to be sorry and take his punishment, then to be forgiven, loved, and restored.

Mack might not be God, but that was who he emulated to his son that day, and there was no higher or better role model. Richard ben Mack did indeed have the greatest Father in the world.

The One in Charge - New York - Esmeralda

After seeing her aura last night, Esmeralda had been distracted. Lavinia teased her that she was lost in her own version of the labyrinth. Esmeralda apologized for being preoccupied but did not explain her urge to pray or her growing sense of unease. Something was happening; she could feel it. So the instant Mack's phone rang, she knew the news would not be good.

His aura flamed crimson as he listened to the caller. His ruddy face grew redder, and his body tensed. Lavinia started gathering their belongings before he hung up. "We've got an emergency," he said. "I've got to get back to your apartment so I can deal with it."

Thaddeus turned away, coughing. Esmeralda watched him, looking for any telltale signs of chest pains or dizziness. Wheeling Clair over in her stroller, she took his hand and murmured, "Are you all right?"

He nodded and drew a hand through his sweaty hair.

Together, they hurried out of the park.

Mack walked with angry, determined steps, roiling red turmoil. Lavinia shimmered and pulsed pale yellow. Baby Claire seemed fascinated by them, cooing in delight, and protesting loudly if she lost sight of them. No one spoke until they were alone in the elevator.

"Is everyone alive?" Lavinia whispered in her low and husky voice.

"For the moment, yes. But we've hit a major snag." Mack frowned, watching the numbers of the elevator climb.

"Do I need to involve my office?" Thaddeus asked under his breath.

Claire's face lit up, and she kicked in excitement as Thaddeus glowed with silver intensity.

"Find out what they know. See if this is federal or not," Mack replied in the same covert manner.

The doors opened, and they rushed down the hall.

"Do a sweep. No one say a word!" Mack ordered and pulled a signal jamming device from his pocket and set it on the counter. The low hum broke the silence. "Richard, go low."

Richard nodded and fell to his knees, crawling on the ground, searching underneath tables and chairs for listening devices. He was an accomplished bug-finder.

Mack ran to his briefcase and scribbled a note: "Thad - check the FBI dispatches in New Orleans. V - get me a secure video connection to the bunker. Esmeralda - pray!" He pulled out a wand-shaped device and started sweeping the room.

Esmeralda stared at the hurried scrawl, *New Orleans*. Moving with robotic slowness, she unbuckled Claire and released her into the fray. Even amid the crisis, she smiled as Claire took off after her new friend Richard.

Ten minutes later, Mack emerged from the back bedroom and pronounced, "All clear."

Thaddeus sat back in his chair, the laptop open in front of him. Lavinia did the same. Esmeralda opened her eyes, feeling blue, stormy knowledge. "They came under attack this morning, didn't they?"

Mack pulled his ball cap low and gestured to Richard. "Son, why don't you take Claire back to her room and see if there are any toys for you two to play with?"

Richard stuck his head out from behind the sofa. "Those are baby toys, Daddy."

The warning look Mack gave his son cut off further protests, so Richard sighed. "Come on, Claire. They want to talk about the bad guys." As he led Claire away, his little voice floated down the hall. "I hate those damn bad guys."

Esmeralda's hand flew to her mouth, stifling a laugh.

"What'd you find, Thad?" Mack asked.

Thaddeus closed his laptop and said, "Not a thing, official or otherwise. I sent Paul a text since he's down there."

"We might have to involve him, though I hate to do it. We've already got an asset in play." He pulled off his ball cap and ran his fingers through his hair, then resettled it firmly, clearly agitated.

"What happened?" Lavinia breathed.

Mack relayed the details of the evacuation. When he got to the part about them disappearing from surveillance, Esmeralda covered her face.

Thaddeus listened with dispassionate intent, his investigator's mind fully engaged. "This was a local action then. It did not come through the Palace, not officially."

Mack exhaled with relief. "Well, we can be thankful for that, but they are boxed in." He sat down at Lavinia's computer and brought up a map of New Orleans. "It will be too dangerous to bring them out by car with the locals on the hunt. They are down here." He pointed to Delacroix, the last-named town on the map, deep in the Louisiana Bayou.

Thaddeus swore like a New York construction worker. Lavinia and Mack looked at each other, glad Richard had not heard that particularly creative use of the English language. Esmeralda stared at the map, knowing exactly who the fugitives were with.

"You tell me now," Thaddeus intoned, "that the future leader of this kingdom is not, and I repeat, is not with those crazy-ass Landrys."

The blood drained from Mack's face as his aura grew dark red, and his protective instincts went into overdrive.

Esmeralda whirled on Thaddeus. "That is not fair. Sarah Landry is not crazy. None of them are. I work with them every day. You just don't like Beau." She turned to Mack. "Is that where they are?"

Mack's nose flared. "Yes. They are with Beau Landry."

"How in the hell did you let that happen, Mack?" Thaddeus exploded from his chair. "The man is a menace. You pull them out. Now!"

Esmeralda smacked the flat of her hand on the table with a crack. "Stop it! Right this instant. Do you hear me? Beau Landry saved my life. He is not a menace, and he is not crazy!"

She jerked her head around to Mack. "Astral spirits attacked us a year and a half ago, just like in Thyatira." She glared at Thaddeus and said in a low, angry voice, "Except with Beau, it was much worse. It was personal. They know him."

"Worse?" Thaddeus rounded on her, outraged. "What Beau Landry went through after he kidnapped you was worse than what happened to me in Thyatira Woods?"

Baby Claire began to cry. Lavinia left to attend the children, having no dog in this fight.

"It's not the same thing." Esmeralda leaned over the table and lit into Thaddeus. "And don't you dare twist my words. Don't you dare use that investigator-lawyer word manipulation crap on me, Thaddeus ben Todd. Not about this. No!"

Pointing at him, she shouted, "You do not understand what it is like to have someone attack your mind. You got a glimpse in Thyatira, and you saw how difficult it is to battle the invisible. But that poor man has endured it for years and never understood what was happening to him. You had me by your side, with Ian and Mack. You knew what we were up against because I told YOU! Beau didn't. He never has, and he's better!"

She stalked over, coming chest to chest with him. "Do you know how?"

"I heard." He lifted a lip in scorn. "The last looney bin did him a bit of good."

"You hard-headed, carnal, stubborn man! It was prayer!" She clenched her fists, shaking with fury. "Prayers of protection against the astrals that plagued him, those saved his life. As soon as his mom and others prayed for that, he got better."

Esmeralda pointed to the map, glaring at Mack. "Do you think that car disappeared from the satellite feed by accident? Do you think the Iron King would send His angels to protect those people, then send them straight into the arms of a madman?"

Esmeralda whirled away in frustration. "They are in the safest place on Earth right now. And do you know why?" She looked between the two men, daring either to interrupt her. "Because the Iron King sent them there. But before He did it, He prompted me and a hundred others to pray a hedge of protection around that area, specifically around Beau Landry's house. And that labyrinth Lavinia has been teasing me about all day? This is what it has been about! That is where I've been, what I've been praying! So, you can come at this situation with maps, and you can come at this with logic, and you can dissect it six ways to the eleventh power of a trillion, but it won't matter, because not a single one of you is actually in charge! Now, if you will excuse me, I am going to have some private time with the one who is!"

They watched her stalk away, heard the slam of the bedroom door, and baby Claire's renewed howling.

Mack made a tsking sound and said, "I need to learn how to do that."

Thaddeus drew back, put out and thoroughly chastised by his wife and not a bit pleased by it. "What?"

"How to have a complete come apart and not use a single cuss word. That takes talent."

Thaddeus stared at Mack in utter disbelief.

Mack tilted his ball cap back on his head and laughed. "Go get your kid, Thad. I need to figure out how to charter a boat to get those four out of the Bayou. Regardless of what Esmeralda says, they are still trapped down there."

Battlefronts

Later that evening, Esmeralda triple bolted the apartment door and leaned against it, exhausted. A gentle hand rested against her back, and she heard the soft clink of gold bangles as the quiet, subtle strength of Lavinia surrounded her. "I'm sorry," she said with a ragged sigh. "I have been a terrible hostess."

"Nonsense, come sit down. It has been a long day, and you need to relax while the men are out picking up food."

"You have been a lifesaver, again." Esmeralda hugged Lavinia, who had entertained the children, fed and bathed them, and put them to bed with two stories. Richard loved sleeping on the trundle in Claire's room, calling it his super-secret spy bed and promising to keep Claire safe from the bad guys.

Esmeralda collapsed onto the sofa and accepted a glass of red wine with thanks. They sat in companionable silence, the city noise of New York a quiet hum forty-two stories below. Lavinia swirled her wine with the expertise of a connoisseur and said, "I heard you mention Beau Landry today. I am curious about him."

Esmeralda tilted her head, surprised by the comment since Lavinia rarely discussed other people. "You are?"

"Yes, because the Princes are with him, but also on a personal level. I have known Alaina ben Thomas 3331 days, and we recently spent quite a bit of time together. I am fond of her."

"Three thousand days?" Esmeralda smiled.

"Nine years," Lavinia said with a shrug. "She is nothing like you might imagine."

"Oh, I think I can imagine," Esmeralda said cryptically. They had never officially met, but she had two supernatural encounters that involved the famous supermodel, one of which included seeing Alaina's face staring out of a mirror. "How did you meet?"

"When Himari and her first husband, Ken, broke up, I went to the New City to spend New Year's Eve with her. I didn't want her to be alone, but she wouldn't have been. She had become friends with her neighbor, Filippo, who is her current husband, and Alaina, his roommate. Filippo took us dancing. We had fun, but we all drank too much. On the ride home, Alaina kissed her engagement ring and whispered, 'Beau Landry, I love you. I promise I'll wait. Get better, *mon Loup*.' She looked like a lost kid, and I never forgot the heartbreak in her voice."

Lavinia paused and took a sip of wine. "She still wears his ring, though she never talks about him. So, I've often wondered what sort of man engendered that kind of loyalty in a woman like Alaina."

"Well," Esmeralda chuckled, "he is charming, gorgeous, and fabulously wealthy, but don't tell Thaddeus I said that."

"I won't," Lavinia smiled.

Esmeralda tapped her thumb against her chin, choosing her next words with care. "I do not know him very well, though we bonded, in the way you do when you share a traumatic experience with someone."

"I understand that. When we were fighting Erica, all of us bonded."

"Who is Erica?"

"An artificial intelligence resurrected from the Last Age, a truly wicked beast."

Esmeralda stared at her, taken aback by the intense energy shimmering off her normally mild-mannered friend. "And this artificial intelligence was named Erica?" When she said the name, she felt something sinister.

"Yes. Is something wrong?" Lavinia sat her glass on the side table and leaned forward.

"Erica… Erica… why does that name seem familiar?"

Lavinia paled as she crossed and uncrossed her legs. "I don't know, but she was the most fearsome thing I ever encountered."

"Why?" Esmeralda asked, feeling dread settle in her stomach.

"She was no mere computer program, which executes commands entered and controlled by humans. Erica became a learning, adaptive entity, who overrode systems, gathered information, and changed programming. Had we not stopped her, she would have infected every aspect of technology, which would have given her visibility and control of everything."

Esmeralda stared at Lavinia aghast and pointed at Thaddeus' extensive film collection. "That sounds like a horror movie."

"Worse, because it was real. She had a personality, which sounds ridiculous, since she was a computer, but I swear she exhibited human characteristics." Lavinia rubbed the back of her neck and added, "She hated me."

"You?" Esmeralda gulped her wine and rose, going to the sideboard for a refill. "Why?"

Lavinia grinned. "Because I took the vicious bitch down."

Esmeralda laughed. "Oh, that sounds delightful. My nemesis is still on the loose." She carried the bottle over to Lavinia and poured their refills. "Though, oddly, that brings us back to your original question about Beau Landry."

"How so?" Lavinia brought her knees up on the couch and settled in. "Beau was not in Thyatira."

"No, but the same sort of thing happened while I was visiting New Orleans." Esmeralda took a seat and recounted her bayou adventure with Beau Landry.

Lavinia sat quietly, drinking her wine, and digesting the tale. When Esmeralda finished, she said, "Funny, if I did not know better, I'd say there was an astral spirit inside Erica."

Esmeralda paused, thinking, then exclaimed, "Oh, my heavens, that's it!"

"What?"

"I think I know what she was, or rather who she was."

"Who?" Lavinia's question was barely audible.

"Professor Erica Slater, of Silicon Valley California."

Lavinia stiffened. "She was a real person, a computer person?"

Esmeralda nodded convulsively. "She went insane and planned to upload her brain into a computer."

Lavinia swallowed hard, calculating. "That would be fatal."

"Dr. Erica Slater did not care. She was in agony, tormented day and night after being stung by one of Abaddon's locusts."

"Abaddon?" Lavinia recalled the scripture. "He, along with all the other fallen angels, are trapped in bondage, which is why everyone is chasing poor little Davianna ben David."

Esmeralda nodded, feeling a heaviness in her spirit. "I believe a couple have escaped, as well as Satan."

Lavinia glanced down the hall to where the children slept. "That is a horrifying thought."

"It's true. I have encountered one face to face, twice now. He is a fearsome thing." As if summoned, a swirling darkness covered the sky, eclipsing the full moon.

Esmeralda gasped, swept away in a vision of utter terror and desolation. "Oh, my Lord, the enemy has found them. Lavinia, Satan is in the bayou! We have to pray. We have to intervene."

Red wine spilled on the white sofa. Both women began praying in earnest, pleading, and crying out to the Iron King.

The Holy Spirit swept the Earth.

A dozen devout souls in a little church in Louisiana fell on their faces. At Landry's, all conversation over dinner tables stopped, and they began to pray.

Mack and Thaddeus were riding up the elevator. They turned to one another and groaned, "Something is happening!"

In the Golden Kingdom, the Iron King's chosen cried out in one accord, praying.

Standing in line at an Indian buffet near their house, Joanna and Ian exchanged glances and left the restaurant without a word, running to their car, praying with every footfall.

James and Persa were eating spaghetti when Persa jumped to her feet. "Jay, Peter is in trouble!"

With the Pacific Ocean flying by at eighty miles an hour, Reuben turned to Kayah and said, "Josiah is under attack."

The prayers of the righteous went before the throne room of the Iron King, like sweet incense, pleasing and acceptable. With a nod, the Most High released the Host of Heaven. Those who had fallen to their knees, heard the Iron King's voice for the first time in their lives.

"How you have fallen from heaven, morning star, son of the dawn! I have cast you down to the earth, you who once laid low the nations!"

Later at Loa Hall, Emite tended Lucifer's wounds and promised never to speak of it to anyone. As they left his laboratory, he wondered if he could ever wake his *maman*, or if she would stay locked in her closet forever because Lucifer decided to take up residence.

Part 13 – More To It

January 24, 1000 ME

Character – New City - Bunker

After a tumultuous day, Himari flew across the room and took Alaina by the arms. "What? What's happened, Al? Where are they?"

Alaina looked up at her, stupefied.

Himari gave her a little shake. "What did Beau say? Where is Peter?"

Alaina blinked. "He said the Devil came and there were snakes, then angels came and took them away. They are gone."

"They are gone?"

Alaina nodded. "Everyone except Beau."

"Oh, I cannot handle this! I cannot. I am done. I am packing my stuff and going to New York to find Filippo. I am out."

"He's coming," Alaina breathed. "Himari, Beau is leaving right now. He said we had unfinished business, and it was time."

Himari banged her fists against the sides of her head. "Now? All these years, he leaves you waiting and wondering, lets you sway in the wind—alone, and now he decides to come?" Her legs gave out, and she fell cross-legged on the floor, rocking back and forth. She wanted to leave; she wanted out. But if she left, Alaina would be trapped, unable to see Beau, and she had waited a decade.

Genevieve appeared in the doorway, looking between a stupefied Alaina and a tantrum throwing Himari. "Did you and Alaina go outside and smoke that joint Kayah left? I know that's what you girls were doing upstairs the other night."

Himari looked up, startled. "No, Alaina and I did not. But now that you mention it, that is a damn good idea." She scrambled to her feet and stalked off.

"Himari Nakamura, what has gotten into you?"

"The Devil made me do it, Auntie," she called from her room.

Genevieve turned to Alaina, who looked like a mannequin in a department store window. "Alaina, honey, what's happened?"

"Beau is coming." She blinked with exaggerated slowness. "I've waited to hear those words for… a lifetime." She cradled her left hand, staring at her ring, tears running down her cheeks. "Auntie, he is coming."

"Well, don't forget to mention the Devil. He came tonight, too!" Himari yelled, slamming drawers, trying to remember where she hid the joint. "Oh, and more angels, who carried everybody off to who knows where!"

Genevieve turned to Alaina for confirmation.

But Himari continued to rant. "This was supposed to be a computer hacker's job. That's all. Revenge against Korah for throwing Kayah in jail, stealing my research, and being an all-around despotic shit head!" She found the joint and took a deep drag, coughing her lungs out.

"Are you smoking marijuana in the bunker?" Genevieve cried in disbelief.

Grinning, Himari appeared in a cloud of smoke. "Yes. Would you like some?"

Genevieve raised a disapproving eyebrow, then with a resigned sigh said, "Sure."

Himari threw back her head and laughed. "Oh, this night cannot get any crazier. Here you go." She passed the joint to Genevieve, who took a drag like a pro.

Genevieve handed it back and shrugged. "What? I use it occasionally for medicinal purposes."

"I've never done it." Alaina emerged from her trance and held out two fingers for her turn. "I've never done a lot of things."

They passed the joint around until it was gone, and the bunker smelled like a teenager's basement.

"What are we going to do now?" Alaina asked, glassy-eyed and dreamy.

"I suppose we will just wait until they call us and tell us where they are? Do they have phones in Heaven? Because apparently, they don't have phones in New York. Filippo has not called me all day."

Genevieve sighed. "If they had phones in Heaven, there are a lot of people I would like to talk to."

"Nope," Himari interjected, "that's against house rules. Nothing sad when we are high. Kayah says."

"Oh, if Kayah says, then we have to do it." Alaina pointed at each of them. "She can be scary, and Reuben is hot. That is a terrible combination."

Himari laughed through her nose, her arms flailing. "It is a good thing Beau Landry is on his way. Kayah would kill you."

"I know!" Alaina fanned herself. "Reuben walked out wearing a towel the other morning. I thought I was going to swallow my tongue."

Genevieve turned away, trying to hide a smile.

"It was awful!" Alaina laughed. "I went to my room and had phone sex with Beau, which is the only kind I have ever had."

Himari drew back. "Seriously?"

Alaina covered her eyes, her face flaming. "I cannot believe I just said that. Remind me never to smoke that stuff again."

"You've never taken a lover?" Himari asked, astounded. "All these years, I thought you were just being discreet because of your public image."

"Well, that played a part. I did not want my love life splashed all over the tabloids. Even doing nothing, they still wrote things about me. You remember that big case?"

Himari nodded. Alaina engaged in a protracted legal battle with a tabloid for years after they claimed she was on drugs and sleeping with Filippo.

"I did not want Beau reading about me with another man." She flicked a fleck of debris from under a manicured nail. "I never wanted another man."

"That is honorable, Alaina," Genevieve said with a gentle smile. "You are an extraordinary young woman. Very few in your generation have chosen to live in holiness and chastity."

Alaina flushed crimson. "There are a lot of preachers out there who disagree with you. I have done lingerie and swimsuit modeling for years. To hear them tell it, I am Jezebel incarnate."

Genevieve shook her head. "Do not listen to them. They are judging outward appearances. You are beautiful, God's own creation. Besides, I've met Jezebel, and you are nothing like her."

Himari sat up, rubbing her hands. "Oh, this sounds good, the Devil, angels, now Jezebel. Go on, Auntie, who was she?"

"You are incorrigible, Himari." Genevieve tried to look serious, but the tick under her eye gave her away.

Alaina stretched out on the sofa. "I want to know, too. Who was she?"

"Angelica ben Omri." Genevieve shook her head.

"The former Chief Justice?" Himari asked in disbelief.

"Yes, the most wicked woman you could ever meet, and a true testament that you should never judge anyone by their outward appearances. When we were young, she looked like an angel, with a heart as black as tar."

"What did she do?" Alaina asked and tucked her arm under her head.

Genevieve turned to Himari with a wry smile. "Are we barred from scary, as well as sad?" At Himari's confused expression, she clarified. "Kayah's rules?"

"Kayah did not want to talk about anything scary, but I don't care."

"As long as I don't have to tell scary stories, I don't care either," Alaina chimed in.

"Well, I suppose I can tell you." Genevieve downed a glass of water, cleared her throat, and said, "Angelica was Korah's lover for years."

"No, shit?" Himari absently picked up her phone, looking in vain for a missed call.

"Yes. I think he cast her aside, but she was always skulking around. And I never liked the way she looked at Peter, like he was a bonbon she wanted to devour."

"Eww!" Himari grimaced.

Alaina shivered. "I think she got to him."

"Heavens, I hope not. I saw what she did to Korah."

"Whatever it was, Korah deserved it," Himari grumbled.

Genevieve grew very still. "I don't know, Himari. I don't wish eternal damnation on anyone, even Korah."

"I was the one who brought her down," Alaina said quietly.

Genevieve leaned forward. "You did?"

Alaina nodded. "That picture of her and Keyseelough, I broke the story."

Himari scowled at the mention of Keyseelough, who had thrown her across a dance floor last month with the strength of a full-grown man. Something was terribly wrong with that woman.

Alaina snickered. "I thought Peter was going to die laughing when I showed him the story. He called Angelica a horrible name and said he hated her, but there was a certain mania about him when he said it."

"Well, if Peter was manic, he gets that from his father."

"How long did you live with them?" Alaina asked.

"I came to Alanthia with Margaret when she married Eamonn. I was her companion." Genevieve stared at her lap and added, "That's the second time she has come to my mind today."

"So, that was quite a long time ago," Himari said, doing the calculations.

"I stayed at Gilead after Margaret died. Josiah was ten months old. I suppose that is how I became a nanny, though I was not trained for it. I had been one of Margaret's ladies-in-waiting."

Himari's mouth fell open. "That's a big deal."

"Oh, I don't know. We were friends, and Eamonn was not the Ruling Prince at the time, so I stood beside her at parties." Genevieve dismissed it all with a wave. "I enjoyed taking care of my babies much more."

Alaina turned to Genevieve and said, "I knew you were Peter's nanny, but I guess I did not realize you were Josiah's too. Himari and I have been talking, and we are curious about him. What can you tell us?"

"About Josiah?"

They both nodded.

Genevieve looked up at the ceiling, thinking. "He was a very serious child, not like Peter, who was always a bit of a scamp. Josiah was different, likely because he knew he would be the Ruling Prince. That made him thoughtful, deliberate in his manner and speech."

"But what of the man?" Himari asked.

"Well, obviously, I have not seen him for many years, but in my experience, people don't fundamentally change who they are. I remember a lot of things about him, but perhaps a story might illustrate my point best?"

Alaina snuggled up with a pillow and grinned. "Do tell."

"Well," Genevieve began, "this happened when he was quite young. We lived at Gilead, which was not only the royal residence, but also a large farming community. Josiah loved the animals and became especially fond of dogs. They had guard dogs on the Castle grounds, on the farms, and for the livestock, but Josiah wanted a puppy of his own. For over a year, he begged his father for one. Princess Mary was adamantly against it. She was quite a stickler, but Eamonn saw how much it meant to Josiah.

"They discussed it, and Eamonn laid out the conditions. Josiah had to take care of the dog himself. He had to clean up after it, and above all, he had to keep it from destroying anything in the Castle. Josiah agreed. So, for his sixth birthday Eamonn gave him a beautiful Belgian Tervuren pup named Rex." Genevieve smiled in remembrance.

"They were quite a pair, inseparable, and so cute. Josiah did a good job, living up to his promises. But when the puppy was a few months old, he got into Princess Mary's drawing room and chewed a rug. It was not bad, just a few marks and a missing tassel. Mary discovered Josiah trying to repair the two hundred year old rug, and she was furious. I think he made a bigger mess of it than Rex, but he never told her it was the dog.

"When I asked him about it later, he said, 'Auntie, Rex is my responsibility. If I had been watching him, he could not have chewed the rug. He is a baby, and he did not know better. So, I took the punishment because it was my fault.'"

Genevieve looked from Himari to Alaina. "Think about the character of that little boy. I could tell you a dozen or more stories like that. I was a nanny for decades, and I never met another child, or another person, for that matter, with such ingrained honor and integrity."

Himari looked over at Alaina, and they shared a smile.

"The last thing he said to me the night he escaped into exile was, 'I know my duty. On my honor, I will return.' So, when Peter told me he found Josiah, I fell to my knees and praised the Iron King. For all those years, I thought he was dead. I do not know what delayed him, but I rejoice knowing he will one day assume the throne."

She held up a finger. "Do not misunderstand me, I love Peter. We have always been close, likely because his home life was so volatile, even before Alexa died. So, he needed me more than Josiah did, and we developed a special bond. But I am not blind to his faults. Peter is more like Korah than either would ever care to admit." Genevieve paused, letting that statement sink in, half ashamed to have spoken the words aloud, even if they were true.

"So, given the choice, I would always pick Josiah. He is the heir, the rightful ruler, and I believe the Iron King designed it that way."

"Well, that settles it for me." Himari toasted with a glass of water.

"Thank you, Auntie," Alaina said through a yawn.

"You are most welcome, my dear."

"Peter never wanted to be the Ruling Prince, anyway," Alaina said. "He's told me that a number of times."

Genevieve chuckled. "He was four the first time he told me that. I don't think he has ever changed his mind."

"That says something about Peter when you think about it. How many people would honestly pass that up?" Himari asked.

"True," Alaina nodded. "And he has certainly risked his life to bring us all together, finance this revolution, and restore Josiah to the throne, when it could have easily been his."

Genevieve smiled. "I raised them well."

Himari went to the sideboard stocked with drinks and snacks. After selecting a chocolate granola bar, she turned and asked, "So, which of you is going to call Mack and tell him we've lost Alanthia's greatest hope?"

Alaina nodded to Genevieve. "He's less likely to hit the roof if you call."

"What exactly do you propose I say?"

Alaina gave a caricature of her toothy smile, discomfort, and chagrin written all over her face. "Say, the Devil dropped by, and everybody decided to leave?"

"Oh, can you hear him?" Himari groaned.

Genevieve puffed out her chest and said in an exaggerated southern accent, "What the bleepedy bleeping bleep bleep do you mean, you bleepedy bleeping lost them?"

Himari and Alaina howled.

Genevieve winked.

Alaina's cell rang, her personal line. "That might be Beau." She scrambled from the couch. "Hello?"

"Good evening, Miss Pink."

"Falcon!" she said, sighing in relief. Himari and Genevieve ran to her side, so she put the phone on speaker. "Are y'all okay?"

"Yes, we are together, unharmed, with our package intact. We landed at my Penthouse in New York."

"New York?" Himari asked, stunned.

"Indeed," Peter said.

"What happened?" Genevieve asked.

"I will fill you in on the details in the morning." He laughed, sounding tired. "In the interim, do have someone book my next trip via Angel's Express. I found them exceedingly prompt. The customer service was excellent, and the transit time extraordinary, four stars from Prince d'Or. Goodnight, ladies."

January 25, 1000 ME

Can't Sleep - New York - Esmeralda and Thaddeus

At 1:07 am, Thaddeus rolled over in search of a snuggle, annoyed to discover his wife missing. He glanced at the baby monitor, no bouncing lights, no sound. A dim light shone under the bedroom door, so he surmised she must be getting a glass of water and fell back to sleep.

An hour later, her side of the bed was still cold. Esmeralda only prowled the apartment if something was brewing, and after the extraordinary events of the day, he should not be surprised. With a grumble and a groan, he threw back the covers and stumbled into the living room. He found her curled up on the couch, reading. "What are you doing? It's the middle of the night."

Esmeralda rested the open book on her chest and gave him a guilty smile. "I couldn't sleep."

Thaddeus rubbed his eyes and said, "Come back to bed. I don't sleep well without you. I keep rolling over, looking for you."

Esmeralda marked her page and sighed, "All right."

He gave her a sleepy smile and held out his hand.

She shrugged off her robe and snuggled in beside him, wide awake. "Extraordinary night, don't you think?"

"Mm-hmm," he agreed.

"I have decided to go see Dr. Moreh tomorrow."

Thaddeus yawned. "The man you worked with at the library?"

"Yes," she said, sounding uneasy. "I want to look at some old journals I was working on before I left."

"Rub my shoulder, will you?" Thaddeus mumbled. "What journals?"

She rolled onto her side and began a well-practiced massage. "I may have mentioned them to you. Remember the computer scientist bitten by the locusts?"

"Vaguely." Thaddeus rotated his shoulder joint and put her hand on a particularly sore spot.

"It might be a coincidence, but her name was Erica Slater. Lavinia mentioned the computer entity they were fighting went by that name, and I got spooked. It was probably just the heat of the moment, you know how I am, but I'd like to look at the writings." Esmeralda found a tight section of muscles and worked on them.

Thaddeus jumped involuntarily as her hand hit a nerve. "Always follow through on coincidences. That is a good rule in any investigation."

"Well, I am no investigator, but I was not a bad researcher." Esmeralda pressed the hot spot.

"Yes, right there. Damn, that hurts." He moved his shoulder, wincing. "Research is investigation, and you are an amazing researcher, Esmie."

"Thanks. I'll see if Lavinia wants to go with me. There was a lot of technical jargon she might understand, that is, if Dr. Moreh will give us access. I did not leave on the best of terms."

"Let me know if you need a warrant." Thaddeus grunted in relief when the pinching pain eased.

"For a set of thousand-year-old journals?" she asked, amused. "Though, if they are what I think they are, there could be grounds."

Going Public - New York – Mack

"You're sure about this?" Mack asked into the phone, staring at Peter's building in the distance.

"Yes, Josiah and I discussed this at length. We will not conceal the fact we are here." Peter nodded to Josiah, who was pacing the Penthouse floor. "And we will not run from the local police again. That was absurd. The Princes of Alanthia are not common criminals."

"I don't think they were after you two," Mack said, shaking his head.

"Perhaps you are correct. However, we will continue to keep the girls' location secret."

"Korah knows you are together. I think you should still lie low."

"It has been the plan all along. Once we reached New York, we were going public." He quirked an eyebrow at his cousin in wry amusement. "We simply arrived ahead of schedule, which is convenient, since it is the perfect place to audition background singers for Josiah's big solo at his coronation."

Mack blew out a long breath and ignored the joke. "All right, I'll activate the second part of the plan at your word."

"It seems fortuitous that you are already in New York, does it not?"

"Almost like it was planned," Mack deadpanned.

"Indeed," Peter replied. "Alert everyone. I have called Jarrod and arranged for my guards to come. By this evening, Prince d'Or will officially be back in residence."

"As you wish, my Esteemed. See you tonight." Mack disconnected the line.

Behind him, the balcony door opened, and Esmeralda came outside. In the bright winter sun, her hair glowed and the scar on her cheek became more pronounced. "You are pulsing with intensity, Mack."

He thought the same of her. To date, he had not employed her unique talents, but given the events of the last twenty-four hours, he would be a fool not to engage her. "What exactly do you see, Esmeralda?"

She twirled a white curl and let it spring back over her eye. "Auras, visions, and occasionally, supernatural beings. Periodically, I see beyond the veil and perceive colors in a way most do not. I can interpret their meaning and understand what they signify. When I was seven, I met Yeshua and befriended a bossy Gune, who comes to visit me when there is something the Lord wants me to do."

Mack blinked, surprised by her frank recitation. To date, she always hedged when he questioned her, skirted her abilities, and seemed uncomfortable talking about what she saw.

She laid a gentle hand on his upper arm. "I have shocked you."

"Just a tad," he confirmed.

"There is a reason I have been given these gifts, Mack." Esmeralda smiled, her slate-blue eyes kind and understanding. "We fight an enemy in two realms, the natural and the supernatural. You understand that, and there are very few who do, which makes you unique. It is why you were chosen for this role, and why you experienced the things you have. The Lord put you where you were supposed to be and gave you the skills to carry this through. I am simply one of your soldiers, officially reporting for duty."

Mack covered her hand, touched by her words. "So, is Esmeralda ben Claude ready to fight?"

Esmeralda smiled in wry amusement and pointed across the skyline. "Is that where the Princes are?"

Mack followed her direction, looking at the gleaming steel and silver glass building on the edge of the Hudson. "Yes, on the top floor, in the Penthouse."

Esmeralda moistened her lips and nodded. "I thought so."

"Why?" Mack narrowed his eyes, scanning the surroundings, looking for threats, but saw nothing.

"There are three angels positioned on the roof and a golden hedge of protection covers the building." She turned with an ironic smile, saluted, and went back inside.

Scholar of Renown - New York - Lavinia and Esmeralda

Over espresso and bagels, Esmeralda relayed what she could remember about Erica Slater's journals to Lavinia. However, the computer lingo meant nothing to her during the transcription, and she could recall nothing about it. Lavinia felt confident she could interpret that portion, being familiar with Last Age computer text, having deciphered plenty when she was sixteen.

The possibility that Professor Erica Slater uploaded her cognitive functioning brain into a computer was a discovery of stunning academic potential. However, in the wrong hands, the journals could become a manual for someone to attempt it again, and if that was the case, they needed to secure them. The last thing Lavinia wanted was another Erica to contend with.

Mack suggested they simply show up as opposed to calling ahead. "It's harder to choke a cat if he's looking you in the eye. The curator is more likely to let you examine the journals if you are standing in front of him. Besides, if there is something to them, we don't want to tip anyone off and have them disappear."

So, after breakfast, they dropped the children at the babysitter's and set off to see if Esmeralda inadvertently discovered the true origins of Erica. Marching down the sidewalk, Lavinia looked over at Esmeralda. "I admit to a macabre excitement about our outing today. If your hypothesis proves correct, it will be fascinating to delve into the journals."

Esmeralda made a noncommittal nod, and Lavinia sensed her unease. Before becoming a wife and a mother, she would have been oblivious. Now she was not. "What is wrong? Do you sense something?"

Esmeralda's face clouded. "I've not been back to the library since I resigned."

Lavinia tilted her head, not understanding the significance. "You think he might throw us out?"

She looked down, toeing a soggy matchbook lying on the sidewalk. "I was not completely well when I worked there. I don't relish reliving it."

"I understand that. My friend Gus recreated our original computer lab before he died. When I stepped inside," she paused, "I remembered who I was, and it was not entirely comfortable."

Esmeralda's pinched expression relaxed. "Oh, that is exactly what is going on. I do not like remembering those days."

Lavinia ran a complex algorithm in her head, then answered, "But those days were necessary." When Esmeralda's brows narrowed in confusion, she elaborated. "It is like an equation, steps in the process you must complete to reach the final solution."

Esmeralda lifted her chin and recited, "My steps are ordered, my paths are guarded, and my purpose is to serve the King."

"Then lead the way, and we shall see where the King takes us."

Doctor Moreh ben Sephar glanced up from his desk, surrounded by research stacked a foot high, with the irritated air of an avid researcher interrupted in the midst of a groundbreaking discovery. "May I help you?"

Esmeralda stepped into his office, her face a mix of emotions. "Hello, Doctor Moreh, it's Esmeralda ben Claude."

"Esmeralda?" Moreh squinted, stretching his neck forward like an ancient tortoise, and switching from reading glasses to corrective lenses. "Your hair is different. I did not recognize you."

"I've brought a friend, Doctor Moreh. This is Lavinia ben Anthony."

Moreh shot out of his chair with an exclamation, "Lavinia ben Anthony, the mathematician?"

Lavinia knew instantly how she was going to play this; Kayah would have been so proud. She glided into the room and used her seductive, breathy voice, the one that earned her roughly 42.7% higher gratuity from male patrons than if she spoke in her normal voice.

"Doctor Moreh, I am so pleased to meet you."

Moreh stared at her with his mouth agape. "You cannot be."

She extended her hand, with its graceful long fingers, slender wrist, and sparkling bangles. "I cannot be what?"

"This beautiful," he breathed, "with such a mind."

"Are you familiar with my work?" Lavinia smiled.

"Oh yes," he enthused. "Though I am a novice. Research is my passion, of course, but a few of my fellows and I dabble." He moved around the desk, digging through his piles. "Last month we were discussing your paper on Brocho-Peshneic models for partial actions of Q, extraordinary, absolutely stunning, elegant work, Mrs. ben Anthony."

"Thank you. It was an interesting little project, one that I—"

"Doctor Moreh, Lavinia will only be here for a short time, but perhaps she could speak with you and your fellows?" Esmeralda suggested.

Moreh never took his eyes off Lavinia. "Oh, would you?"

"If I can. I would be honored." Lavinia tilted her chin, quelling the urge to discuss her paper.

"Oh, the gentlemen would be so pleased."

"Actually, my current project brings me to your facility today. Would it be possible to examine a few of your journals?" Lavinia batted her eyelashes. "I am doing a paper on advanced computer technology in the Last Age, and Esmeralda mentioned you have an extensive collection of ancient manuscripts."

"Of course, Miss ben Anthony, anything for a scholar of your renown." Moreh ushered Lavinia out of his office, brushing past Esmeralda without a second glance. "Please allow me to escort you to our research room. Just this week, we received several new texts that might interest you."

Esmeralda watched them walk away, thinking she could have been a paperweight for all the attention anyone paid her, not that she minded because it allowed her to move through the library unobserved. She paused at the top of the basement entrance, bracing herself.

The third step still creaked, the wallpaper still peeled, and the air still smelled of old paper and wood. She was transported back in time, remembering the confused young woman who hid down here twelve hours a day, lost in journals from a thousand years ago, battling memories and visions, that seemed evidence of her continued madness. Living utterly alone in New York City, she isolated herself from everyone and everything. However, she enjoyed the work, odd because the subject matter was often gruesome as if reading about a world mired in chaos made her own seem less frightening. But she was no longer that girl and refused to give her enemies the power to drag her under—ever again.

So, she stepped into her old workspace with confidence born in fire, sure of who she was, and intent on her purpose. She pulled on a pair of cotton gloves, and without asking for permission, retrieved what they had come to see.

Doctor Moreh scuttled around the space, retrieving the journals Lavinia requested, laying them before her like an offering, and adding several more he thought might be of interest. He obviously wanted to continue hovering, but for all his sycophantic fawning, he remained a consummate professional and withdrew, excusing himself with promises to cater to Lavinia's every desire. She must only ask.

As Esmeralda took her seat, she met Moreh's eyes for the first time. He had to look away. And in that moment, she knew.

They were on hostile ground.

Lavinia seemed oblivious, and Esmeralda decided not to enlighten her, not yet. As the door at the top of the stairs closed, she said, "I did not realize you were famous."

Lavinia looked up, distracted. "I have garnered a bit of renown. Four papers I've published in recent years have been well received."

"I see that." Esmeralda gestured up the steps.

Lavinia's eyes glazed over, clearly not interested in discussing her selective fame in mathematical circles. It was a fact of life, one she accepted as her due, and did not find particularly riveting. Conversely, the journals before her were.

Esmeralda acquiesced with an inviting sweep of her gloved hand, and they got to work.

Ten minutes into their study, Lavinia looked up. "Esmeralda, these are not programming notes. We could send them to Himari for a second opinion, but I can say with high probability this is not computer code."

Esmeralda came around the desk to examine the text. "It looks that way to me."

"I understand how it would, but the instructions are random, nonsensical. Take this for example," Lavinia said, pointing to a line of text. "It is a looping command. If executed, the program would accomplish nothing, simply repeat back on itself ad infinitum."

The hair on the back of Esmeralda's neck prickled. "So, it is code, just not computer code?"

"Either that or the scribblings of a madwoman. You were correct in your assessment of her mental state. And while I am not a psychologist, I estimate she is deteriorating at a factor of roughly .45x every sixty days."

Esmeralda pulled the journal closer and studied the odd script with renewed interest. "I worked on these for over a year, not exclusively, there were others I was transcribing, but if you asked, I feel certain your admirer upstairs will give you copies of what I've already done. That will allow us to focus on the text I did not review before I left."

"It's the key code we need. Without it, we cannot interpret this," Lavinia said, studying the page. "Alaina may be the one to take this apart. She has an eye for patterns and is remarkably astute in analyzing and spotting anomalies in code."

Esmeralda pressed her thumb against her chin, thinking. "If she is unable, there is always Thaddeus' team at the FBI. I am certain they have code breakers."

They shared a dubious glance, both understanding that would be a last resort, so they put their heads down and got back to work.

An hour later, Esmeralda's stomach growled, and she looked up to find Lavinia shaking her head, a distressed set to her delicate jaw. "What's wrong?"

"How did they not see this?" Lavinia murmured. "How did they live through this time, which was clearly foretold in the Scriptures, and still shake their fist at heaven and spit in the eye of the Iron King?"

"I don't know," Esmeralda said.

"He is on every page, yet she curses him with each breath and blames him for her suffering. It is illogical." She looked up, a deep crease between her eyes after hours of holding an expression of disbelief. "We are doing the same, in this time."

Esmeralda closed the journal with care and removed her gloves, having had her fill of Professor Erica Slater for one day. "My friend Ernst says the same thing. He told me we've made a grave error assuming all prophecies occurred in the past, and we are doomed to repeat the mistakes of those caught in the Great Judgment."

"What sort of world will our children grow up in?" Lavinia tapped her gloved finger against the journal. "Will Richard endure war, plague, and famine?"

"That is why we are here." Esmeralda lowered her voice to a whisper. "We must ensure Prince Josiah takes the throne. If he does not, we will experience judgment just as they did. I feel it. The Iron King's patience with Alanthia is nearing its end. We don't have much time left."

Dead Phones and Worried Wives - New City - Bunker

After a brief call with Mack, Himari got to work on the second phase of their plan. They were not scheduled for weeks and had a thousand things to do. Already frazzled, the additional stress caused Himari to morph into a tyrant, issuing orders faster than Genevieve or Alaina could execute them.

An hour later, Alaina threw down her pen and snapped. "Stop! We know what to do, and we do not need you shouting at us every thirty seconds to do it faster!"

"Alaina, will you give us a minute, please?" Genevieve folded her hands serenely, but the steel in her voice invited no argument.

"Gladly, Auntie. I am going to take a shower." Alaina stressed the word "I", an obvious dig at Himari who had been wearing the same clothes for two days.

"Let's sit down, Himari," Genevieve suggested gently.

Himari deflated and moved into the living room without protest. Sitting on the sofa, she pulled a soft blanket into her lap and wished she could disappear.

"What's wrong, *shōjo*?" Genevieve asked, calling her little girl in Japanese, an endearment they both loved.

Himari covered one eye, resting her forehead, exhausted. "I'm sorry. I have not slept, and I have not heard from Filippo for two days. He should have called last night when he got to Kayah's, but he didn't."

Genevieve squeezed Himari's knee. "I am sure everything is fine."

"I swore I wouldn't call him, that I would give him time to think, that I would not be pathetic." A sob caught in her throat as she pressed her knuckles over her mouth. "But Auntie, I'm worried. Not just about us, which is bad enough, but what if Massimo's men found him? What if he's hurt or worse?"

"No, do not do that to yourself. Filippo loves you. I'm sure his secure phone ran out of battery, and he probably fell asleep before it charged. You will hear from him soon.

"As far as the other, Massimo's men finding him, they have not uttered a single word about Filippo since the morning after he left. They are not looking for him, so don't make up stories. We have plenty of real obstacles in front of us without you creating imaginary ones."

Himari desperately wanted to believe Genevieve. "You are right."

Genevieve nodded sagely. "Of course I am. Now, go get some rest. Your mind is playing tricks on you."

Himari wiped away a tear and did as she was told.

Genevieve sat alone as the fear she did not dare let Himari see wrapped around her like a boa constrictor. She rose, feeling every day of her sixty-seven years, and called Mack. "Honey, I know you have a lot going on, but can you go by the townhouse to check on Leonardo? He has not called in a couple days."

"I am up to my eyeballs around here."

"I know, but it would mean a lot to Sunflower if you could do this for her. She's worried, and truthfully, I am too."

Mack remembered the stormy look in his friend's eyes when he left Peccioli and relented. "All right, I'll get over there."

"If he's not there, don't tell Sunflower. Call me."

Mack muttered a colorful curse. "Perhaps I'll send T. If Leonardo's not there, this might just turn into a matter for him."

"That's what I am afraid of," Genevieve whispered.

Your Old Job Back - New York City - Mack and Peter

After weeks on the run, Peter declared the foursome had been entirely too serious and needed some fun. So, he, along with Jarrod the Wonder Servant, cobbled together an impromptu celebration in honor of Josiah and Davianna's engagement. An exclusive, and extremely discrete, catering company delivered a feast fit for the occasion, that did not feature anything even closely resembling a gas station burrito. After dinner, Peter plugged in the ancient pink iPod, and they all began to dance.

A light on the security system indicated they had a visitor. Peter gave Astrid a quick peck on the cheek and pressed the intercom. Music blared in the background.

"Some things never change," Mack drawled. "Even on the run, you are partying."

Peter chuckled. "I will buzz you in."

Moments later, Mack entered the Penthouse. Peter flashed his famous smile and extended his hand, an unusual gesture since royals did not shake hands. "Thank you for coming, Mack."

"My Esteemed, of course. I gave you my word that we would see this thing through to the end."

The music lowered, and three pairs of eyes turned toward him. He was the first member of The Resistance they met.

"Folks, may I introduce you to the man who led the rescue and saved our lives on New Year's Eve? This is Agent Mack ben Robert."

"My Esteemed, I cannot take all the credit. That was a joint operation."

Josiah stepped forward. "Agent, I know we have spoken briefly on the phone, but I am pleased to express my sincere gratitude in person. Thank you very much for your service and your aid. We are in your debt."

Mack bowed, studying the Prince. He was larger than Mack expected, broader, too. His resemblance to his father was uncanny. There could be no doubt who he was. "My Esteemed, it is an honor."

Josiah turned to the brunette at his side. "Agent, may I present my betrothed, Miss Davianna ben David?"

"I am very pleased to meet you, sir," the young lady said, and Mack detected just a hint of southern accent in the way she said sir.

"Miss Davianna, it is a pleasure to meet you as well." He looked between the pair. "So, this is a celebration?"

"It is," Josiah replied. "Davianna has done me the honor of accepting my proposal."

Davianna looked up at him with adoring eyes.

Mack had to admire her pluck. It was quite an accomplishment to land Alanthia's most eligible bachelor while simultaneously guarding a dangerous artifact and outfoxing half the world's bounty hunters. Up to this point, Davianna had been a mystery, but a footnote in the grand scheme of things. However, if she married the Prince, she would play a crucial role in the kingdom's future. She was a pretty little thing with big brown eyes that flashed mischief and good humor, but she carried an aura of awed innocence about her, the sort of sweetness the world relished crushing. Mack hoped she would keep that spirit after she married Josiah, but he knew royal life was no picnic.

Peter draped his arm loosely around the last of the foursome and brought her forward. "Mack, this is Astrid ben Agnor. Astrid, this is

Mack, who I have told you about."

Mack turned away from Davianna and met a pair of wary blue eyes. He drew back in shock, feeling as if he were looking at a ghost. Her resemblance to Princess Alexa was startling. But he schooled his features and extended a hand, saying, "It is a pleasure to meet you, ma'am."

"Agent ben Robert, it is nice to meet you." She shook his hand with a firm grip, holding his eyes. "You were Peter's Head of Security for seven years, correct?"

Mack nodded. "Yes, ma'am. That is correct."

"But not for the last three, you're retired?"

"Semi," he replied, sizing her up.

"And what do you do now?"

"I'm a vintner. My wife and I run a small vineyard and winery in California," he replied, amused at her interrogation. She reminded him of a banty rooster his grandmother had when he was a kid.

Peter chuckled and kissed her cheek. "Although we give the official honor to Mack's lovely bride, Lavinia, Mack was the first member of The Resistance. He saved my life on a number of occasions."

The slight tilt of Astrid's head telegraphed exactly how little stock she put in past actions. Mack realized he would have to do more than simply stroll into the Penthouse to earn her trust, a whole lot more.

January 26, 1000 ME

A Bit of Personal Business - New City - Beau

"Good morning, *Grandpere*."

"Where have ye been?" Andrew ben Lenox grunted.

"You sound like *Maman*. Would you believe I am pulling up to the gates of one of your houses?"

"Which one?"

"Grande Dame by the Bay." Beau lowered his sunglasses and smiled at the attendant. "*Grandpere*, please tell the guard to let me inside? I do not believe he recognizes me."

"Considering ye have not left *yer* house in ten years, are ye surprised? Put the bugger on the line."

Beau watched the young guard's befuddled expression as Andrew ben Lenox personally told him to let his grandson onto the property. The man's hand shook as he bobbed and handed Beau back the phone, calling up to the main house to alert the staff that the heir was in residence.

"Don't be mistaking me," Andrew wheezed, "I'm pleased *tae* hear you've left Louisiana. But what are ye doing in the New City, lad?"

"Foundation business. I am here to deliver the forensic accounting report on the Center for Street Kids. Ian and Joanna deserve to hear the news from me. Then I plan to take care of some personal business," Beau said, pulling up the drive to the Spanish style mansion at the southern tip of the Bay.

Andrew grunted with disapproval. "The model?"

"She's more than that. You'll like her." Beau stopped the car and allowed the attendant to open his door. "Now, if you will excuse me, *Grandpere*. I am going to get cleaned up and drive over to the Center. Tonight, I have a date with Alaina, so I will tell you like I told *Maman*, I'll call you next week."

Andrew handed the phone to his nurse, who replaced it with his oxygen mask. He closed his eyes, gratified Beau had finally broken free. While not fond of his grandson's choice in women, he lacked the energy to focus on Beau's love life. He had an empire to turn over and not much time left to do it.

The Key to Invincibility - New City - Rapha

The House of Amah retained three servants, men once employed by the old Baron, who were now too old and too terrified to leave. One blind, one deaf, and one mute, they tended the grounds, received the supplies left at the gate, cleaned, and prepared Rapha's meals. They lived in the guest cottage and never interfered with Rapha, fearing for their miserable lives, with good reason. They had not come into his service maimed.

Through their long association, Rapha studied them, discovering the vast differences between humans and his kind. Size, strength, intelligence, and abilities were a given, but he observed subtle differences too, sleep, for example. Nephilim required very little, a mere three hours a night. Consequently, Rapha could devote about twenty hours a day pursuing things that interested him. He absorbed information without effort and grasped complex subjects with ease. With the diligent application of his mind, he could master anything in short order and channel that knowledge into action.

He read every book in the manor house by the time he was five, and just as he finished, a computer arrived. Technology opened a new world. Rapha discovered the alternate internet of the Last Age, mining the treasure trove of ancient texts, black writings, and most tantalizing of all, pornography. He feasted on images of sexual depravity and violence, particularly films and photos featuring children. Drawn to their smooth perfect bodies, their fear and suffering thrilled him. However, he limited his consumption, recognizing the material made him restless, awakening a lustful hunger to hunt, which he did so sparingly. Unlike his brothers, Rapha disciplined his appetites and his mind.

He discovered the art of astral projection on the dark web and mastered it as a child, but he limited the practice because he disliked leaving his body vulnerable while his spirit traveled. However, as his confinement grew to a close, he decided to hone his skills and familiarize himself with the world beyond the walls of his estate.

After Lucifer's disappointing visit and callous abandonment, Rapha determined that astral projection might prove to be an untapped weapon in his arsenal. His unique genetic makeup, half-human, half-elohim, might give him an advantage over both races. If he could learn to project while retaining control over his body, he would become invincible, able to exist in two places at once.

He began field-testing a few nights after Lucifer departed, making a brief foray into Prince Eamonn Park, his favorite hunting ground. As his spirit traversed the familiar landscape, he ordered his body to type a message on the computer. But the exercise proved painful, as if he was being cleaved in two. The experiment failed.

He ignored the discomfort and tried again, but the second time he thought he heard his dead brother scream and returned to the House of Amah, shaken. To his disappointment, he found the screen blank.

Undeterred, he continued, discovering with practice he could move further afield, though the task he set before his body remained unaccomplished. Heady with his increased range, his nightly forays ceased being aimless sorties or incursions into the homes of the New City humans; Rapha acquired a target, Persa ben Yereq.

In the ether, he tried to detect her spirit, focusing on the part of her encoded into every strand of his DNA. A week into his testing, he concluded she did not reside in or around the New City because he found no trace of her.

Frustrated with his lack of progress, he shifted his focus. On the evening of January 15th, he flew to Korah's Palace to ascertain if his father remained in Alanthia. Deep in the underground cavern, a place he had seen in the Witch of Endor's memories, Rapha made a startling discovery. The hag had returned and was rekindling her relationship with King Korah. Watching two old people have sex amused him, but more than the voyeuristic thrill, he eavesdropped on their whispered plans, and when he returned to his body, one word flashed on the screen—Endor.

January 28, 1000 ME

A Lifetime of Service - New York - Mack and Josiah

At Peter's Penthouse, Mack sat across the table from the two Princes, discussing the next phase of their campaign. The opening volley involved a series of videos featuring Davianna and Astrid, followed by the strategic release of several photographs of the two Princes working together. As expected, the videos and images garnered worldwide attention. The Alanthian public clamored for more, and a headline-hungry media covered the story around the clock.

The long exiled and hamstrung nobility took notice, sending secret missives between manor houses and strategizing. Dissidents and critics became more vocal and organized. Public cries for Korah's abdication gained momentum, as a growing group of protesters gathered outside the Palace. Nightly flash polls showed his popularity plummeting. The second phase of their campaign exceeded The Resistance's most optimistic expectations.

Considering their success, the change the two Princes proposed stunned Mack. "You are certain?"

They exchanged glances, then Josiah spoke. Throughout their discussions, Josiah took the lead as Peter faded into the background. "The lawyers arrive tomorrow, and the legal proceedings against Korah in the courts will commence. Prince Yehonathan is working on our behalf, and we expect to have clearance to land in London before the week is out. Once there, Prince Yehonathan will grant us asylum in the embassy and call for an emergency meeting of the Ruling Princes' Council, which I will attend.

"To date, members of The Resistance have remained secret, but as the plan moves forward anyone associated with us becomes a traitor to Korah's government. If we are unsuccessful," he paused and held

Mack's eyes, "he will not only kill you, but he will kill your family, and make you watch while he does it."

Mack's nose flared, but he did not interrupt.

"Right now, you are a loyal and trusted former Royal Guard, nothing more. But if you accompany us, or align yourself with us publicly, you become a conspirator. There is no compelling reason to endanger yourself or your family when Mossad will assume a protective role.

"When we are successful, I will call upon you to serve again. According to Peter, you were an unsurpassed talent in the Royal Guard and have led The Resistance admirably." His brown eyes crinkled at the corners as he smiled. "I also hear you make an excellent Cabernet Sauvignon."

"Thank you, my Esteemed."

"Agent Nathan ben Henry reports the Royal Guard is in shambles on the west coast. We must secure this critical agency from the outset if we are to survive long enough to govern. Given your history and experience, I ask that you prayerfully consider taking the position as Head of the Royal Guard."

"I am honored, my Esteemed." Mack bowed his head in respect. "But before I agree, may I have a private word?"

Peter raised an eyebrow, looked between them with a curious tilt of his head, then rose in silent acquiescence, and departed.

"Agent, what is on your mind?"

Mack met Prince Josiah's direct gaze. For two days, he took the measure of the man, finding him intelligent and thoughtful. Josiah appeared to be gracious, well-spoken, and benevolent, but to the world, so did Korah. The proposed change in plans made practical sense, but Mack needed reassurance before stepping aside. "My Esteemed, with your permission I will be frank."

Josiah nodded. "Please, do so."

"Thank you." Mack folded his hands on the table, measuring his words. "I wish to share a bit of my background with you, so you might see this situation from my point of view."

"Perspective is always welcome. Please proceed."

Mack looked up and began, "I joined the military when I was eighteen. Shortly after basic training, I was assigned to a unit that accompanied Princess Alexa across the Kingdom on a goodwill tour."

"I seem to recall that tour," Josiah remarked.

"I suppose you might. Although it was unusual, Peter accompanied her. He was about four, the same age as my son." Mack paused, remembering the blond imp who loved the horses and charmed everyone he met.

"Princess Alexa was a gracious and fine lady, a loving mother. She ensured the troops were well provisioned and always had a kind word. We all fell in love with her, especially my best friend Richard." Mack blew out a long, hollow breath of old grief. "The tour took about six or seven months. We got back to the New City a few days before your Bar Mitzvah, which we attended as supplemental security.

"Over the next few years, we deployed to various outposts but spent a good bit of time in and around the Palace. After Princess Alexa was murdered, they sent my unit to terminate the terrorist responsible. The mission was personal for us, and it went badly. I was wounded in action and left the service just prior to the Civil War.

"I went home and served as the sheriff for our local Baron. But four years later, Princess Alexa's godfather, Sir Preston ben Worley, came to my office and showed me a photograph of the Princess, beaten to death. He said we all had a duty to prevent that from happening again—to her son." Mack paused. "I answered that call, and I kept him alive."

Josiah frowned. "Not a straightforward assignment in Korah's Palace, I assume?"

"No, it was not. I have never seen a man hate his own son the way Korah hates Peter. He hides it in public, but the staff sees the truth. And that is what this conversation is about, the truth."

Mack took a drink of water, gathering his thoughts. "After Peter graduated from the RMA, he gave me an assignment, to find you."

Josiah's face registered his surprise.

"In October of '96, we received intelligence you were living in Turkey, and he sent me to investigate. I did not feel good about leaving, but he was adamant. He had to know if you were alive."

Josiah counted backward, reckoning where he had been in '96, his second year of surgical residency. He was in Greece, not Turkey.

Mack laid his palms flat on the table and leaned forward. "He knew if you had not survived, he would become the Ruling Prince." Mack's eyes bore into Josiah's. "Prince Peter ben Korah never wanted your throne, my Esteemed."

"I know that." Josiah nodded. "He made that perfectly clear when we were children and has repeated the sentiment several times recently."

"I suspect it is one reason Korah hates him so much." Mack shook his head, unable to comprehend it.

"Perhaps you are correct, though the logic of a madman defies reason."

"I will grant you, he is mad," Mack replied. "But Korah ben Adam is not insane. He is devious, persuasive, intelligent, and remains a formidable foe."

"Aye," Josiah said, shaking his head in disgust, his hand brushing his still injured ribs. "So, did you find me, Agent?"

"It took several months, but yes. You were working in a hospital."

"But you chose not to make yourself known, why?"

"Because we did not have a viable plan at the time and feared making premature contact would put your life in danger."

"Perhaps a wise decision, the Iron King had not yet set the time," Josiah said. "What happened when you returned?"

"All Hell had broken loose." Mack closed his eyes and rubbed his temples. "Korah would have never attempted it while I was around, but he saw his opportunity, sent my men away, and seized Peter."

Mack turned away, pinching the bridge of his nose, remembering the skeletal, beaten, drug-addicted mess chained to that hospital bed. "He was near death when we pulled him out. Korah held you for six days, my Esteemed. He starved and tortured Peter for over a month."

Silence filled the room. Mack read Josiah's shock and understood Peter well enough to know he would not have shared any of this.

He sniffed and his voice shook with raw emotion and anger. "You have no idea what he went through, nor do I suspect you comprehend the extent of the planning, danger, and personal sacrifice that young man has made to ensure you take the throne." He closed his eyes, trying to control his temper and his emotions.

"Since he was four years old, I have made Prince Peter ben Korah's safety my concern. I have thwarted a dozen attempts on his life, pulled him off the ceiling of his bedroom, and rescued him from a sterile torture chamber. My wife and I lost years together, and I missed the birth of my son because I was doing my duty. So, my Esteemed, I am not merely a former Royal Guard."

Mack swallowed. "And while I appreciate your concern for my safety, you can perhaps understand why I do not blithely stand down and turn his protection over to anyone else." He stared at Josiah, trying to penetrate his brain, seeking the answers he required. Without fear or apology, he added, "You royals kill each other."

Josiah held his eyes, absorbing it all. At length, he said, "If I would have had you at my side, Agent Mack ben Robert, I would have never fled into exile." He gestured to the door. "My cousin is blessed to have such a stalwart man guarding his back. I give you my solemn word of honor that Peter is not now, nor will he ever be, in danger from me."

Mack exhaled and felt the Spirit move, the words coming clear in his mind. *"Fear not, for Prince Josiah ben Eamonn is a righteous man, chosen from birth for the role I have for him. He is my faithful servant, and my hand is upon him."*

Without hesitation, Mack rose from the table and went down on one knee. Josiah rose to stand before him.

With his head bowed, Mack said, "From this day forward, the fealty I have sworn to Prince Peter ben Korah I extend unto you. I render my homage and loyalty, and will remain true in all ways, serving you faithfully. This I swear, by my sword and by my honor. I vow to support and protect you and all the members of your royal household. As the sovereign and true ruler of Alanthia, to you, my Esteemed Prince Josiah ben Eamonn, I pledge my troth."

Standing tall and regal, Josiah assumed the role of monarch as never before. The weight of the moment and the significance fell upon both men as the Spirit of the Almighty bound them together.

"Mack ben Robert, I humbly accept thy vow." Josiah closed his eyes and laid his hand on Mack's head. "May the Iron King pour out His blessings upon thee and thy house and rewardeth thee for thy faithful service. May He protecteth and prosper the work of thy hands, bestowing unto thee His supernatural favor and discernment in the execution of thy pledge this day.

"The Lord gave King David his mighty men of valor, who stood with him and beside him during his reign, to serve, protect, and counsel the wise and righteous King. May He do so for us, as He did unto them. I am honored to have thee at my side.

"And in recognition of thy courage and thy faithful service thou hast rendered unto the Kingdom of Alanthia, I bestow upon thee the title of Knight of the Realm. Henceforth, thou shalt be known as Sir Mack ben Robert, the Valiant."

A fierce resolution welled in Mack's spirit, as the Lord sealed their vows for eternity.

Mack rose with a formal bow. "Thank you, my Esteemed. May your reign be long, your decisions wise, and the Kingdom of Alanthia be blessed once again by your righteous leadership. The Lord willing, I shall remain by your side."

Prince Josiah ben Eamonn smiled; it was a good beginning.

"Sir Mack, we shall, of course, do that again publicly with much pomp and ceremony. I would like to have your wife and son present when I honor you before the Kingdom."

Mack returned the smile. "At your pleasure, my Esteemed, I am certain my son would cherish the memory. He is quite a little warrior himself." He gave a short laugh and added, "He is also an accomplished bug-finder."

"That he has grown up in a kingdom where he knows of such things is a testimony for why we must prevail."

"My Esteemed, shall I remain at the head of The Resistance?"

Josiah glanced at the closed door. "That is my wish, however we must consult Prince Peter. It would be presumptuous of me to make that decision without his counsel."

Mack smiled. It was indeed a good beginning.

Advance Team - California Mountains – Kayah and Reuben

Kayah looked at her phone in consternation, frowning.

"What is it, Yakira?" Reuben asked, navigating the winding mountain road, mindful of black ice.

Kayah flared her nose and exhaled. "Himari."

"What of her?"

"There is something she is not telling me." Kayah stowed her phone in her bag and gave Reuben a sidelong glance. "Now that we've got Bubba and Zanah stashed away, we're supposed to head to London, as the advance guard."

"Dorothy and Isaac back in residence?" He waggled his eyebrows at her.

Kayah hid a tiny smile and whispered, "And Mr. Mumps."

Part 14 - Nobles

January 30, 1000 ME

Litchfield

Six days after arriving in New York, Peter's phone lit up, his personal line, not the secure one. Since the news of Josiah's resurrection hit the press, it had not stopped ringing. The caller caused him to reach for the phone where he sent others to the full voicemail he had not bothered to check or clear out. "Litchfield," he said with a smile, greeting one of his few true friends.

"So, you're alive," drawled Tobias ben Cramer, the Baron of Litchfield, and eldest son and heir of Cramer ben Braxton, the Duke of Sedgefield.

"Indeed I am." Peter settled into a low-backed chair in his bedroom, listening to Astrid as she sang in the shower. "How are you?"

"Fair to middling," Tobias said in the slow, easy cadence of the deep south. "I'm at our beach cottage, taking in the salt air."

"That ought to be good for you. What do the doctors say?"

"I did not call to chat about my blasted lungs," Tobias replied with a faint wheeze. "You had me worried."

"No, I did not." Peter grinned. "You know me better than that."

"I do," Tobias scoffed, "which is precisely why I was worried. Are you honestly with your dead cousin?"

"No. That would be disgusting. He is not dead."

Tobias laughed, which set off a bout of coughing. "Damn you, don't make me laugh."

"I will do my best," Peter remarked drolly, concerned at the seal-like bark coming over the line. "You sound dreadful."

"It's actually better, believe it or not. But seriously, Prince Josiah is alive? The Duke could not stop smiling. He is over the moon."

"You have seen your father?" Peter asked, surprised.

"The illness, you know. I arrived in an ambulance," Tobias said drolly. "It was very dramatic."

Peter laughed. "You did not."

"It worked. They let me in." Tobias cleared his throat. "Even Korah's goons are not so callous as to keep a man's first-born son from visiting if he is on his deathbed."

"You always were a calculating bastard. Perhaps that is why we always got on."

"We did not always get on," Tobias jabbed in a lighthearted tease.

"True," Peter chuckled. "You and half the RMA were ready to string me up when I arrived."

"Learned hatred, my friend. We were simply following the leads of our parents."

"With good reason," Peter said, "though it did not make my plebeian year very pleasant."

"No, I suppose it did not," Tobias replied with his characteristic affability. "But you proved not to be the scoundrel we all thought you were."

"Says you," Peter laughed. "I am rotten to the core."

"As you would like everyone to believe, however, I know the truth."

Peter snorted. It was an old exchange, a beloved one. Had Tobias not befriended him, Peter might have spent his entire career at the RMA alienated from his peers.

"What can you tell me, Prince? They are all champing at the bit."

By 'they', Peter knew Tobias meant the nobles of the Sedgefield Duchy, a territory that encompassed Virginia, the Carolinas, Georgia, Alabama, and Florida. The Alanthian aristocracy comprised a Duke, two Earls, and ten Barons, a structure repeated across the ten Alanthian duchies. From the day Korah seized absolute power, he confined many noblemen to their estates, barring them from conducting and fulfilling their traditional duties.

"What would you like to know?" Peter asked, keenly aware they were not discussing this on a secure line.

"Don't play coy with me. There is too much at stake, and this is the first genuine hope we've had in over a decade. What is Prince Josiah's plan?"

"To take the throne."

"Korah's throne or Eamonn's, because there is a big fucking difference!" Tobias snapped. Only their long friendship gave Tobias leave to speak to Peter in such a manner, and he had a point.

"I know," Peter sighed. "But I cannot discuss this over an unsecured line."

Tobias made a dry, wracking cough. "Pardon me."

Peter waited, listening as his friend struggled for breath.

Tobias returned to the line. "Your father will not give up without a fight. What sort of protection do you have?"

Peter winced. "Other than public opinion?"

"When has that ever stopped him, particularly where you are concerned?"

Over a stolen bottle of vodka when they were sixteen, Peter confessed some of the abuse he endured at Korah's hands, making Tobias one of the few who knew, but even Tobias only knew a fraction.

"My Guards are here, as well as two hundred members of the press. He will not make a move."

"Korah would drop a nuclear bomb on New York to stay in power."

"If he had one, he might," Peter conceded. "But I have not ventured into this without resources or a plan."

"It had better be a good one."

"I never pick a fight I cannot win," Peter said.

"Liar," Tobias protested. "You are the most arrogant, over-confident, son of a bitch I've ever met."

"Bloody Hell, remind me again why we are still friends?" Peter asked, smiling into the phone.

"Because I call you out when you are being an idiot. Seriously though, what can I do?" Tobias asked gently.

"Josiah will need you and your father's support." Peter ran his fingers through his hair, thinking of the long road ahead.

"He is going to need a lot more than just our support. I don't need to tell you the shape we are in. The last fifteen years have been devastating, and time has not tempered Korah's campaign against us." Silence fell over the line before Tobias added, "One of my physicians suspects my illness may have been brought on by poison."

Peter's nose flared. The Sedgefields remained staunch and outspoken opponents of Korah before and after the Civil War. If Tobias had been poisoned, he would not be the first noble to suffer such a fate. "What type of poison?"

"They don't know, but they've sent tissue samples over to London for testing."

"Is anyone else in your household sick?" Peter asked.

"No, and I've gotten marginally better since relocating to the cottage. I left the rest of my staff at Crawford," he said, referring to his manor house near Charleston. "It's just me and Gene here at Pawleys. You remember my valet? He's been with me since I was twelve. I trust him."

Peter thought of Jarrod and nodded. "I am glad to hear you are getting better."

"Thank you." Tobias made a rueful chuckle. "You know it's funny, when I was growing up, I could think of nothing worse than becoming a Duke. I didn't want any part of it. Only when it was taken away, and I saw what happened in the vacuum, did I realize how important the role my father played was. I have spent the last year longing for something I never thought I'd want."

"I understand," Peter said, "being with my cousin, talking to him, planning—"

"Exactly," Tobias agreed. "I see it so clearly now. I've had a lot of time to think, to listen. They still write to me, you know, the older folks especially, who remember the way things used to be. I never read their letters before. If I'm honest, I didn't care. I couldn't do anything, so why bother?

"And thanks to my trusts and the inheritance from my mother's side, I had money, women, cars, houses, even a title Korah could not strip me of, since they never convicted my grandfather of treason. I was living the life. You were too. We were having fun. I never gave the people I was supposed to care for a second thought.

"But when I got sick, I got bored, or, I don't know, the Iron King put it on my heart, and I started paying attention. Their letters are heart wrenching. You would not believe the things they tell me. We have radicals moving in from everywhere, and the injustice, the corruption, the unfairness of the system is mind-boggling. People are suffering."

"I know," Peter said.

"No, I don't think you do, not the full extent of it. You are too far removed. But it was supposed to be that way. Princes, Dukes, Earls, Barons, and Knights we all had our roles and duties, to serve the Iron King, each other, and the people we protected. Local matters were never intended to reach the Palace.

"Twenty years ago, I would have already taken my seat in the Council of the Senate. As a Baron, I'd have appointed prosecutors, overseen the sheriffs, the courts, the county governments, and arbitrated disputes. I can tell you, I would have never permitted the sort of injustices that have befallen my people. Never."

Peter closed his eyes, thinking this story repeated a hundred times across the kingdom.

"You know the saddest part?" Tobias continued, a bitter edge to his raspy voice. "I would have been busy. My life would have had a purpose. My duties as the Baron of Litchfield would have prepared me for the role for which I was born. I'm to be the Duke of Sedgefield, one of the ten men charged with ensuring Alanthia stays faithful to the Iron King, because when you get right down to it, beyond the taxes, beyond the arbitration, beyond the administration, that is the core of our duty, and we have failed, all of us. We allowed Korah to do this. We let him dismantle one thousand years of tradition and governance. For what?"

"Technology," Peter said.

"No," Tobias objected. "That was the facade, the temptation. It was about money, good, old-fashioned greed. Korah played us. He went to every member of the Council, promising big money, and to his credit, he delivered. Everybody who sided with him got rich. Hell, since the Geneva Accords, everybody is getting richer. But only a few ever calculated the cost, men like my father, Stockton, and Philadelphia, and damn me, they have paid a heavy price.

"The rest of them sold out. As a class, we abdicated our responsibilities and became derelict in our duties. It is our people, not us, who have suffered, and they know it. The mood of the public is volatile, Prince. There will be bloodshed before this is over."

The First of Many

"My Esteemed," Royal Guard Nathan ben Henry said, entering the Penthouse, "Lord Hartford ben Bruce, the Earl of Concord," he paused, flipping through the calling cards, "Chief Alexi ben Christopher, the Baron of Hampton, and Sir Preston ben Worley, Knight of the Realm, Attorney at Law, are downstairs, requesting an audience."

Josiah raised an eyebrow, expecting the ancient solicitor, not the other two. He turned to Peter.

Peter sighed and said, "Send them up."

"As you wish, my Esteemed." Nathan nodded.

Josiah noticed the lines of strain around Nathan's mouth and asked, "Agent ben Henry, do you and your team need reinforcements?"

"If we maintain the status quo, the three of us can manage. I helped design security here, so barring a military strike, the Penthouse is secure." He paused, looked down at his feet, then met Josiah's eyes. "Please remember, my Esteemed, you must only speak the word, and we will accompany you on the rest of your journey."

After a decade in the army, Josiah learned to discern between men who said what their superiors wanted to hear and those who meant the words. Royal Guard Nathan ben Henry fell into the latter category. "I appreciate the offer, but it is far safer for you and your men if we proceed as planned. However, I realize you are working around the clock, so you must only speak up."

"We are rotating, sixteen on, eight off," Nathan said. "But I will let you know if it becomes too much. We will not permit any of you to be in danger."

As the door closed, Josiah shook his head. "You have chosen well, Prince. Every member of your team I have met thus far has been exemplary."

"They are," Peter remarked, watching the cameras in the lobby as the nobles waited to board the elevator.

"Do you know these men?"

"I have met Concord two or three times. He is a wild card, plays everything down the middle, and nobody is ever certain which side of any issue he falls on, including Korah. But he retained his Earldom and his lands when most did not. He will report this meeting back to the Palace. He will have to."

"Indeed. And the other?"

"I have never met Hampton, but I know his son, Tommy. He is a boozer and a pill-popper, ran over a kid riding his bike two summers ago. Hampton got him out of it."

Josiah's lip lifted in scorn.

"Hampton married one of Concord's daughters. I cannot remember her name, but she is a big fundraiser, focusing primarily on the arts."

"And why do you think Sir Preston has brought them here? It is dangerous, as well as premature, to begin meeting with the nobles."

"Everyone wants to talk to you," Peter said pragmatically. "I have a hundred messages from people seeking an audience. I feel like your bloody secretary, though I am not answering any of them." He nodded toward the screen. "This meeting will be the first of many. Concord and Hampton are influential, specifically in the courts. The old lawyer knows that."

"I'll warn the girls to keep a low profile," Josiah said.

Peter winced. "Astrid is going to love that."

"Did you work things out this morning?" he asked, referencing an argument the couple had after Davianna suggested they become handfast.

"I certainly hope so." The look in Peter's eyes suggested the underlying issues were far from settled.

"You need to fix this," Josiah warned.

Peter gave a dismissive flick of his hand. "We can discuss my love life later. Go put on a suit and wait in my office. I will assess the situation and debrief you before escorting them in."

Josiah grinned. "You always had a sense of the theatrical."

"It is protocol, Prince. If you were receiving them at the Palace, you would not be greeting them at the front door."

"True. I need to re-acclimate. I have been gone for quite some time."

"Indeed," Peter said in a droll, bored tone. "For now, I shall continue in my role as your secretary."

"That would be a bloody waste of your talent."

Peter scoffed and shooed him away.

Josiah watched Peter relax onto the sofa, arranging himself into an indolent pose. His quick intelligence disappeared behind a banal, simpleton's smile as he pulled his hair over his forehead, and let his eyes grow unfocused and blank. Josiah shook his head, amazed at the total transformation. "Play the role, Prince d'Or. I appreciate it."

"What role?" Peter asked, examining his nails. Then he laughed and added, "Go. You are ruining my concentration."

The visitors entered by rank. The Earl of Concord came first, a wiry, neat man in his late seventies, whose face hinted he had once been an adorable child. Sadly, his looks had not transitioned well into adulthood, and he now resembled an aging elf. The Baron of Hampton followed closely on his heels, a brown-haired man in his middle fifties, whose suit buttons pulled around his middle. Out of his soft, spongy face stared a pair of calculating colorless eyes. Sir Preston came last, looking dapper in his English suit, carrying a battered and bulging leather briefcase. He had the most extraordinary moustache and eyebrows Peter had ever seen. In profile, some of the brow hairs had to be two inches long. But behind the ancient façade and cracking old man's voice, his wily gray eyes missed nothing.

Peter rose, and after formal greetings, gestured to the sofas and said, "Gentlemen, please have a seat."

They exchanged surreptitious glances, doubtlessly wondering where Josiah was, but too well-bred to ask. They allowed Prince d'Or to direct the conversation, and as they spoke, Peter assessed their body language, their tones, listening to what they said, but more importantly, what they did not.

At length, and by what appeared to be mutual consent, Sir Preston ventured, "My Esteemed, may we beg an audience with Prince Josiah? We have some pressing matters to discuss."

Peter looked around, as if expecting Josiah to pop up from behind the sofa. "Yes, of course. Please allow me to determine if it is convenient."

Leaving his visitors behind, Peter entered the office and found Josiah pacing. "Let the games begin."

"What's your read?"

"They have the power to determine which court will hear Sir Preston's petitions. Apparently, one will be more favorable toward us, but they want something in return."

"Of course," Josiah said with an edge of impatience. "Were you able to determine what?"

"There is not a single member of the aristocracy who ever forgave Korah for disbanding the Councils. They want that back."

"As do I," Josiah said. "It is a founding principle of the Kingdom."

"Yes, but they do not know that, and you need to keep that as a bargaining chip."

"Aye," Josiah agreed, settling behind the desk. They spent hours discussing their multi-pronged strategies, with the fractured Alanthian nobility high on their priority list. They needed them on their side, before and after Josiah took the throne. "So other than the obvious, what can you tell me?"

"They are concerned about the growing influence of the radicals, from the Republicans at one end of the political spectrum to the Greenmen at the other, with the jihadists and the anarchists thrown in for good measure."

"Fair enough."

"Hampton's got an active cell of Greenmen disrupting a timber operation in the northern part of his land. I could not gauge what Concord wants, but if I had to guess, he has been steadily encroaching into York territory for a decade. I venture he aims to keep it."

"The Earl of York died suddenly, what, seven or eight years ago?"

Peter nodded. "He left behind four daughters, who remain at Allegany and are not too pleased with Concord's incursions. Three of York's daughters have married and petitioned Korah to name the new Earl."

"Which he has not," Josiah scoffed.

"No, he has not. Concord wants you to name his second son."

Josiah raised his brows. "Which, upon his death, consolidates the two Earldoms with one family."

"Giving the house of Concord power to rival the Duke of Philadelphia," Peter finished.

"Because Philadelphia has no male heirs," Josiah finished grimly.

"Correct. They both died in the Civil War," Peter said with a shake of his head. "And Philadelphia refuses to name his successor while he remains under house arrest."

Josiah grabbed the back of his neck and closed his eyes, inwardly cursing Korah for yet another dereliction of duty. "Show them in but do stay. I want you at my side, Prince."

An odd expression crossed Peter's face, a mixture of pride, hope, and reluctance. "For now," he said and left the room.

Inheritance

Sir Preston ben Worley cackled as the two aristocrats took their leave, affording Josiah a private word with his attorney. "Oh, I say, you handled that splendidly, my Esteemed."

Josiah raised an eyebrow but deigned to comment.

"Your grandfather in his prime could have done no better, and that is a compliment of the highest order."

Josiah regarded the ancient barrister with interest, having rarely heard anything positive about his Grandfather Adam. "Is that so?"

"Oh, indeed. Adam was a force of nature in his day. Tall, handsome, a phenomenal athlete, no matter the sport, and he had a brain. But more than that, he possessed charisma. People were drawn to him. His father, Simon, was the exact opposite, and the two never got on. Simon signed the Reform Act into law, which, if you know your history, was extremely unpopular with the people and gave birth to a fierce movement to abolish the monarchy. You can thank Adam there is even a throne to petition for, my Esteemed. It was in serious jeopardy at his coronation. But he was an adept politician and a master negotiator. He knew how to build coalitions and alliances, and he saved the monarchy, though it cost him dearly."

"In what way?" Josiah asked.

"His marriage to Mary was part of the bargain."

Josiah winced inwardly, glad, at least in that matter, he would not be following in his grandfather's footsteps. "I knew it was not a love match. I cannot recall a single kind word she ever spoke of him."

"I doubt she ever uttered one." Sir Preston shook his head. "But she doted on Eamonn and made several specific provisions for you in her will. Those will be the first order of business in our suit against Korah, to have him return the properties bequeathed to you personally."

"That is reasonable," Josiah said.

"Hampton and Concord will ensure Newberry hears our case. He will rule in our favor."

"Well, it would be difficult to deny that I am alive," Josiah remarked drolly.

"Aye, but we both know it is more complicated than that. I beg you to reconsider. We can petition the courts and restore your throne."

"I won't be swayed in that matter. Korah took the throne through the courts. I shall not do the same."

Making Due

While the visitors met with Peter and Josiah, Davianna and Astrid hid across the hall in the empty butler's apartment. For security, the six staff apartments on the top floor remained unoccupied, except for the one set aside for the Royal Guards.

After everyone departed, Davianna popped her head into Josiah's office and said, "I made lunch."

"You did? How?" Josiah asked, looking up from his book.

She shrugged. "There were a few staples in the apartment, so I pulled something together. It is nothing fancy, just a tuna noodle casserole."

He smiled. "Your industriousness astounds me."

"I can make a meal out of almost anything. My mother hated grocery shopping, so I learned to make do with what we had."

"That's a talent."

"Sadly, one that will not come in handy. I doubt the kitchen staff will take kindly to me whipping up a quick dinner."

"Perhaps not," Josiah said with a half-smile. "However, using the resources you have on hand will be infinitely useful."

She gave him a dubious look.

"No, it's true. I had a Lieutenant under my command, who regularly came to me with grand plans and ideas. The only drawback being we never had the supplies, nor did he ever consider a perspective other than his own. Conversely, the unit had a medic, Isaac ben Levi, who could improvise the most ingenious solutions in the field. He once brought in a soldier who sustained a spinal injury. Isaac used a jacket and a roll of tape to create a highly effective cervical collar. Had he not, the soldier would have sustained further, perhaps irreversible, damage during transport. Isaac drove his superiors crazy, bucking protocols, but the men knew who they wanted with their units, and so did I."

She looked up at him, considering his words.

"Davianna, all of us are going to have to get creative, and that won't come easily to men like Peter or the two noblemen I met with today because they are accustomed to having everything at their fingertips. But we cannot spend our way out of the mess we are in. It is going to take ingenuity, brains, and innovation. You have that."

"Shall I tell everyone to eat tuna noodle casserole?"

Josiah laughed. "In a manner, yes."

"I hope you are right."

"If I learned anything in exile, it was that when the time comes, He will tell us what to do."

Davianna sighed. "I cannot help but worry. This is a big task set before me, before us."

He pulled her into a hug, and they stood in silence.

At length, she pulled away and motioned to the book on his desk. "What are you reading?"

"*Maple's Comprehensive Guide to the Alanthian Peerage.*"

"It's rather large," she said, picking up the book. "Have you made these notations?"

"Some. This is Peter's copy. He's already started," he said, pointing to the section on the Lexington Duchy, a territory that encompassed

Michigan, Indiana, Ohio, and Kentucky. "I went to the RMA with Troy ben Hollister, the Duke of Lexington, good chap, we played rugby together."

"Are you going through the lists to see who you know?" she asked, flipping through the pages, drawn to the Sedgefield Duchy where she grew up. "This guy is a snake," she said, turning the book back to him.

Josiah grunted at the picture of the well-groomed, moderately handsome man. Something about the aristocrat's broad smile and bright eyes rang false. "Brandon ben Adam?"

"The Earl of Charlotte," she spat. "He ruined my father's life."

"How?" Josiah asked, closing the book.

"You know my daddy was a master woodworker, right?"

Josiah shook his head. "I don't believe you have ever mentioned that."

"Well, he was. He made the most beautiful furniture and opened a small store when I was about five. I don't know all the details, but the Earl commissioned a dozen pieces for his home near Asheville. He made a big publicity show out of supporting local business and craftsmen, but he took delivery, then never paid the bill."

Josiah scowled.

"It forced Daddy to close the business, which infuriated my mother, who just went on and on about it. I was too young to understand what was going on, but in retrospect, her constant nagging drove him crazy. He started making high-risk investments to recoup his losses, but they never paid out. We had to leave our house, and for a while he worked construction jobs. It…" She hung her head, remembering how exhausted her father would be when he came home and how terrible her mother treated him. "Well, never mind. The point is, if the Earl had paid him, none of it would have happened."

"Well then, we will place Charlotte in the 'Cannot be Trusted' category," Josiah said with a decisive nod. "And once I take the throne, I shall determine whether he is worthy of his earldom."

"You can do that?" she asked, embarrassed to have revealed how low her family had sunk, but feeling a glimmer of power heretofore unavailable.

"Under the current structure, absolutely. Korah took full control over the aristocracy, subverting the laws in place since our founding. But there is precedent for it, even before Korah. The Ruling Prince has oversight of the nobility and can, under certain circumstances, remove any aristocrat from power."

"What circumstances?"

"If they are found to be in serious violation of their oath of fealty and code of conduct, both of which come directly from the Iron King."

"Well, Charlotte certainly did, at least where my family was concerned."

Josiah nodded. "Unfortunately, that story is repeated far too often."

She picked up the book, feeling its weight. "Then the question remains, who is on our side?"

Part 15 – Rotten Call

January 31, 1000 ME

Make Myself Scarce - New York – Mack and Peter

Mack stepped into the Penthouse's entertainment room and found Peter preparing for a videoconference with the bunker. "I've checked on Nathan and the boys. They are holding up, so I am going to step out and grab lunch with my family."

"You are not staying? Himari said this meeting was important."

Mack nodded, his jaw working. "Himari will debrief me, and I've asked her to record it."

Peter straightened and clasped his hands behind his back, the very picture of a displeased royal. "May I know why?"

Mack shrugged one shoulder and looked away. "Persa and James are going to be on the call."

"And is that a problem?"

"I believe it carries the potential, yes," Mack said, but did not elaborate.

Peter cleared his throat, an impatient mannerism Mack was familiar with. "Why?"

Mack shifted, calculating what he might say, and feeling downright uncomfortable. "We had a dispute a couple of weeks ago."

"Did one of his horses nibble your vines?" Peter asked, his voice dripping sarcasm.

"No, my Esteemed." Mack still evaded.

"Then what was this dispute about?" Peter asked sharply.

Mack set his feet, angry and defensive, harried from all sides. "They came over to Peccioli looking for information about you, and it did not go well." He held up a hand, cutting off another question from Peter. "They aren't stupid. They put the timing of my absence and your disappearance together."

"That seems rather benign. Of course, they were concerned. I told you to tell them I was safe," Peter said in a clipped voice.

"Oh, forgive me, I have been a bit busy running this damned revolution, and I lost my temper, all right?"

Peter's nose flared.

"And now, Alaina is bringing them into the bunker, along with a host of others." He shook his head in frustration, transforming from Sir Mack ben Robert into the Head of the Resistance in a blinding flash. "She and I had some heated words on the subject, believe you me! It's dangerous, and it's reckless, and personally, I don't think it's necessary. But Alaina's got some damned fool notion that everybody's got pieces of a puzzle that will only come out if y'all get together! Her words, not mine,"

He threw up his hands, pacing. "I said, well shit fire and save the matches, let's just bring everybody in and have ourselves a proper staff meeting. We can phone the Palace and say, 'Hey, Korah, come on and get us. We're all together in a couple places, right convenient for you.'"

Peter raised a golden eyebrow, stifling a laugh. "I trust you put Auntie in charge of the snacks?"

Mack gave him a blank look, then rolled his eyes. "Antipasto for everyone."

"Do you feel better now that you have vented your spleen all over me this fine afternoon?"

Mack sighed. "Pardon me, my Esteemed. I simply believe it is ill-advised and puts our base of operations in unnecessary danger. It's stupid."

"Tell me what you really think, Sir Mack." Peter crossed his arms, wry amusement written all over his face.

Mack scowled, but when he looked at Peter, he saw shades of the boy he had been, and his temper abated. It had been years since he had seen that expression on Peter's face. "You rolled out of bed this morning prepared to give me a hard time, didn't you? I recognize that glint in your eye. It's the same one you had when you showed up at that State Dinner wearing a toga with a—"

"A crown of fig leaves?" Peter finished the sentence, laughing.

A dam inside Mack broke, relieving the tension building all day. "I had to pull you out of there." His chest shook, and he could not continue.

"Because Korah looked like he was ready to kill me in front of the European delegation?" Peter bent over, remembering the expression on his father's face.

"You came strolling in, audacious as shit," Mack held up his hands in helpless surrender, "wearing that get-up."

Peter fell backwards onto the sofa, clutching his stomach. "I abhor State Dinners."

"Well, that was one way to get out of it! But what the hell possessed you to do that?"

Peter wiped his eyes and gave Mack a diabolical smile. "Never let it be said that I failed to give him a warning."

"What?"

"I am surprised you failed to catch the significance. Your lovely wife would not have missed it. That State Dinner fell on the Ides of March."

Himari Gets a Grip - New City - Bunker

The video conference proved to be an unmitigated disaster. Himari felt a growing sense of panic as the revelations and ramifications reverberating in her brain. She left Genevieve sobbing on the couch and showed their visitors out of the bunker.

It took every ounce of her strength to hold it together. The world felt as if it were splitting apart at the seams. Hers certainly was. Filippo had left her. He was gone. One curt phone call and life as she knew it was over. He needed space. No one in a happy marriage needed space. The ensuing days of silence nearly killed her, but she had not told anyone, most of all Alaina.

It would be cruel to taint her long-awaited reunion with Beau. Trudging up the basement steps, she wanted to throw her arms around her friend and sob out her pain, taking comfort from the one person who had been with them since the beginning. Only Alaina would truly understand her heartache and loss. However, she sacrificed her own needs and refused to burden the friend she loved.

But the world cared nothing for Alaina's feelings and was no respecter of her reunion with Beau. Himari saw her face when Prince Josiah gave his account of the Greek massacres. Alaina froze when he called the culprit by name—Nephilim. And when he said it, Himari remembered Alaina's long-ago, drunken ravings about an orange-eyed monster that was going to devour her. She never doubted something terrible happened in the bayou. Alaina was traumatized by it. Beau Landry became catatonic afterward, but Himari never imagined the monster was real. The video conference radically altered her opinion, which freaked her out.

She wanted to laugh at the absolute absurdity of a half human, half fallen angel, but there was no denying the truth. She had seen too much, had witnessed too much. The truth was there, whether or not she chose to accept it. Her acceptance or denial did not change the fact that they were battling a supernatural enemy, something more powerful than bits and bytes. But that was where it began— with a phone—in a tomb. Himari knew where it came from, and who found it.

She kissed Alaina goodbye, returned to the bunker in a daze, pulled up Professor Erica Slater's journals, and started digging.

A Bad Idea that Just Got Worse - New York - Mack

Minutes after the conference ended, Mack received back-to-back calls, recounting the disaster. The first came from Genevieve, who could scarcely speak. "Mack, it was awful."

"What happened? Is everyone safe?"

Genevieve sniffed into the phone, still crying. "We are, but it was terrible. I am sending the video now. Watch it before you go over to the Penthouse. You need to understand what happened, so they don't have to recount it." She made convulsive, hiccupping sobs. "That poor child, that poor thing. My heart is just broken… and Persa, oh Mack."

Mack swore under his breath. "Let me talk to Himari." Despite Himari's personal challenges, he could always count on her to have her head together.

"She's seeing everyone out and locking up. I just couldn't do it, but I wanted to tell you. Mack, watch the video. We will call you later."

Mack let loose a blue string that caused Richard to perk up from across the room. Mack pointed a finger at him. "Not a word out of you, buddy."

He opened his laptop and saw the video downloading.

Esmeralda moved around the kitchen, packing Claire and Richard's lunches for the afternoon, and wisely remained silent.

Lavinia came down the hall, dressed and ready to continue her research at the library. She took one look at Mack and asked, "What's happened?"

"What's happened is, sometimes I really am the smartest guy in the room. I knew this was a bad idea! The video conference went sideways."

Lavinia put her hand over her heart. "How is Himari? She is pretending everything is fine, but she did not look good yesterday."

Mack sneered. "I did not talk to Himari. Apparently, she was showing our guests out. Meanwhile, I am supposed to watch this blasted video before I go to the Penthouse." He rolled his eyes. "So they don't have to relive it, whatever the hell that means."

Esmeralda cleared her throat. "Mack?"

He swung around, ready to bark, then caught sight of Esmeralda's pale face. "What?"

"There are at least a hundred angels over the Penthouse right now."

Before he could react, Thaddeus called. "Korah is making a move, but he's doing an end-around, not going after the Princes like we imagined. The AG has issued arrest warrants for all the guests in the bunker. The charge is treason. They must have intercepted that call."

Mack closed his eyes and tilted his head back. "I gotta call in the Code."

He hung up and redialed the bunker. Himari answered. "We are blown. Arrest warrants have gone out for our visitors."

"Hold on!" Himari shouted, and he heard her pick up another ringing phone. "Yep, confirmed. Our intelligence, too. Run, babe. Be safe."

She came back on the line, her voice shaking. "That was Miss Pink. They are running."

"Dammit, Sunflower, what happened?" Mack asked, trying to control his fury.

"G sent you the video. Watch it with Miss Euler, but include Curly and T. This is beyond the pale, Bobby. Afterward, I'll let you make the call, but we might need to bring in London. This needs their eyes, too. Miss Euler will understand. I'm shutting everything down, all but this secured line. I need to figure out how we got hacked."

Giant Fallout - New York - Josiah and Davianna

Josiah left the conference, carrying his sobbing wife, shockwaves traveling from her body to his. The revelation about her father's murder still rang in his ears as he kicked open their bedroom door. While heartbreaking and tragic, her father had been fortunate not to suffer as most of the monster's victims had. Ruination and depraved desecration were hallmarks of the beast's reign of terror. David ben Jesse had died by a javelin to the heart, but Josiah had seen worse—far worse.

"Shh," Josiah soothed, laying Davianna on their bed. "I'm sorry."

She gulped air as a tidal wave of grief hit her, drowning her in a sea of pain. She curled into a ball, devastated anew, and wept.

Josiah cringed, disturbed to see her in such pain. He laid down beside her and held her as she cried.

At length, the tumult subsided, and she clung to him, her voice tiny and heartbroken. "Who killed my daddy?"

He pulled her head to his chest as memories of cannibalized bodies flashed across his mind. "We never had a suspect. I was a resident when the massacres began. Reuben served on the front lines and knows more about this than me. If you want, we can call him later."

She nodded.

"Minx, when did your father die?"

"November 1st of '98." She closed her eyes and said, "We were about a week outside Camp Eiran. There are no towns to mark the place, but it's off the southern road. We planned to catch a boat because my mother didn't want to travel overland any longer, but it was a bad choice. The drought devastated the region, and we found ourselves out there all alone with no water. Mom and I almost did not make it after Daddy died." She moistened her lips. "Did I ever tell you that? It's why I cannot abide being thirsty."

Josiah empathized, and it broke his heart. "It is a desolate country."

She wiped her nose with the back of her hand and looked at him, helpless. He scrambled off the bed and got her a tissue. She mopped her eyes and blew her nose, gathering herself. "I hated Greece, always dust in your mouth, in your clothes, in your hair. It was dreadful, but Daddy and I tried to make the best of it, you know? There was nothing we could do except move forward. But my mother?" Davianna groaned. "She was a nightmare. Oh, Josiah, I fear I have given you quite a mother-in-law."

The corner of Josiah's mouth lifted. "Reuben called her a shiksa."

"A shishka? What the heck is a shishka?" Davianna laughed, sounding drunk, exhausted from spent emotion. "Like a kebab?"

Josiah chuckled. "A shiksa, not a shishka. It's Yiddish. It means a good-looking gentile woman who does not have the highest standards of conduct or moral character."

Davianna snorted. "That's a nice way to put it. I'm sorry. I have never even told Astrid how Daddy died, and I just lost it in front of all those people." She hung her head. "Princesses do not air their dirty secrets in public."

"Hey, look at me." Josiah lifted her chin with his knuckle. "We were there to talk about what we knew. You told the truth, so did Lady Joanna, and that call was not easy for anyone. These are extraordinary times, and we are fighting an extraordinary enemy. You did nothing wrong."

Davianna leaned into him, exhausted. "Okay, I just don't want to be a shishka."

Josiah's chest shook. "A shiksa… and you couldn't be, even if you tried."

Mind, Body, and Soul - New York - Peter and Astrid

From inside the master suite, Peter found Astrid weeping, huddled with a blanket in the back of his closet. She turned away when he opened the door and said through tears, "I hate Greece."

He held it together until he saw her, until he heard her crying. Then something terrible inside him broke. "Red?"

Astrid reached for him.

He fell to his knees as a cry tore through his heart. "Persa! Oh, God! Persa?"

"I'm sorry," Astrid said, hugging him tight.

"She is my dearest friend, my precious friend! And that monster kidnapped her, held her captive." He made no noise, shocked beyond sound.

"He is… unspeakable… and the things he can do. And you saw how little she is. She is tiny. And he, he… he bred her as if she were nothing more than a broodmare!"

Astrid jolted at his description but could not deny the accuracy.

Coughing, Peter scrambled to his knees and fled.

Astrid crawled after him.

In the bathroom, he convulsed as waves of nausea racked his body. When the attack passed, he collapsed onto the floor, writhing in agony.

"Peter?" she gasped, growing frightened.

He covered his face and rolled away. "Go… leave me alone."

"No!" Astrid fell to her knees. "What's wrong?"

His chest heaved, and he blinked up at her, his face a mask of unspeakable torment.

She grabbed the sides of his head and brought them nose to nose. "Whatever it is, it is over!" Gentling her touch and her voice, she soothed, "I'm here, and I won't let anything happen to you."

"You cannot stop them. Nowhere is safe. No one is safe." He closed his eyes, quaking with violent, silent sobs. "Even Pepperwood, they got Persa." He thrashed, going wild with grief, throwing her off. "I thought James and Persa were safe. I thought that was the one safe place on Earth. But the monster destroyed it!"

Astrid wrapped her arms around him, hanging on with every bit of her strength, riding with him as waves of pain crashed, washing away his sanctuary.

"It was a lie, nothing but a trick, a delusion." He pointed a trembling finger at her and said, "Like this man you think I am, nothing but a fantasy."

"Stop it! You are overwrought. Come lay down with me."

"No." He pushed her hand away, his pupils growing large as his eyes turned black.

"I love you," she declared, trying to reach him.

"You do not even know me!" He shook his head. "You do not know what I am capable of, what I have seen, what they made me do! Astrid, I am nothing but a junkie. If I had a boost right now, I would do it and not think twice!"

"Stop!"

"You think not?" He pulled his phone from his pocket, his hands shaking.

"What are you doing?" she hissed.

The look he gave her said it all.

"Give me that," she shouted, trying to take the phone.

He evaded her, holding it out of her reach. "Leave!"

"No! I won't let you."

"You cannot stop me, no more than you can stop…" his voice faltered, "no more than you can stop them."

"You stopped them from harming me. Peter, would you let me make that call? Would you let me put a needle in my arm? Because if you do, so will I."

"No!" he said, collapsing to the floor, burying his face. "Just go before you get hurt."

"You won't hurt me."

"You do not understand," he whispered, his voice slurred and defeated.

She took the phone and moved it out of his reach, then sat beside him. "Yes, I do."

"No," he shook his head. "You cannot, not the full extent of it."

"Come lay down. You've had a shock."

"It is not a shock, Red. This is the truth, the reality of me."

"It's not true!"

He looked at her, and despite her resolve not to, she shied away from the darkness reflected in his eyes. "It is true," he growled. "There is a dungeon beneath the Palace where they perform rituals. All the witches are there... the Hell Bitch... the Mistress... the fucking crazy one. They forced me to participate, to break me, to make me one of them."

His face collapsed in bewildered agony. "Three years ago, they tried to force me to marry the Hell Bitch. I would not, so they tortured me, turned me into an addict."

"Oh, baby."

"Even after I escaped, they came after me." Brimming with self-loathing, he turned away. "I started using, and I could not stop. I was not in the dungeon anymore, but I was still a prisoner. I fought so hard to get clean, and I did. I swear it."

"I know you did," she said, stroking his back, tears coursing down her cheeks.

"But you saw what just happened." He gestured to his phone, brimming with self-disgust. "Once a junkie, always a junkie, you know?"

"You did not make the call, Peter."

He shrugged. "The night is not over yet."

"Then you will have to put the needle in my arm first," she said, deadly serious.

He rested his head back against the wall and closed his eyes with a sigh.

"And you won't do that, will you?"

He looked at her with emerald eyes, a thousand years old. "No."

"I didn't think so," she whispered.

"Unfortunately, my enemies hold no such sentiments. They know very well how easily they can keep me enslaved."

"So, they have done it more than once?" she asked.

He nodded. "Yes. Last November, Alaina had news she needed to deliver to me in person. I threw a party here as a cover, but my guards had already seen her once, so I sent them away, which was idiotic. I should have known better.

"I had been clean for months, but they drugged me again. And when I woke up…" His voice caught, and he looked away. "The Hell Bitch had tied me to my bed. She was naked, and I was—I could not—" He scrambled to the commode, vomiting again.

Astrid drew a glass of water out of the sink and handed it to him. He swished the water and spit. She wiped his face, cleaning his nose and mouth. "I'm so sorry."

"I tried to kill myself."

She reached out a trembling hand. "No."

"I had the gun in my mouth, and you know I am a good shot."

"But you didn't."

He shook his head. "Yeshua stopped me. He said they could not touch me again."

"Then they cannot."

"I thought it was over, but they were not done with me. They did not give up. If they could not touch me, they still tried to break me. They planned to use you to do it." His face crumpled. "That is what Korah meant when he said you were a gift."

A cold chill hit her. Those diabolical words had haunted her.

"Because you resemble my mother. They were going to make me hurt you." He covered his mouth, unspeakable, old horror reflected in his eyes.

"Peter?"

A tentacle of ancient trauma reached out of the pit and wrapped around his leg, pulling him down. She watched him give in to it as he collapsed onto the cold bathroom tile.

"Look at me!" she shouted. "You did not hurt me. You took care of me."

"They killed my mother. They sacrificed my uncle. They got Persa." His eyes rolled back in his head as the horror sucked him down the vortex.

Astrid panicked and rolled on top of him. "James and Persa are okay. They will survive this. They will pull each other through. Like we have."

Tears fell from her eyes into his. "I survived what happened to me at the Palace because of you. I would still be trapped there in my mind, but you understood that." She sobbed. "You knew it was more than the drugs. You helped me through it in the ambulance, and you set me free in the cabin."

She curled into him, realizing the magnitude of what he had done, the sacrifices he made to reach her, and the incredible bravery of the beautiful, broken man in her arms. "You have fought too hard and come too far. Peter, don't give up."

His breathing slowed, as his eyelids grew heavy. "I do not think we can run far enough or fast enough to escape." Panic seized him anew. "What if the monster tries to take you like he did Persa?"

Astrid narrowed her blue eyes and looked deep into his soul. "Then you, Prince Peter ben Korah, will find me."

"I will protect you with my life." He grabbed her waist and thrust his hips against hers. "I vow it."

Heat shot through her body like a bullet. This was their love language, the way they touched the soul-deep wounds that words could not heal. With a quick motion, she pulled her shirt over her head and unsnapped her bra.

Her body seemed to glow with alabaster purity, beckoning him back to the light. She offered her breast, like a lifeline out of the abyss. He groaned as his lips touched her tender skin, silk under his tongue. He pulled her deep into his mouth, kneading her with an elemental, primal need. She rocked her hips, matching his rhythm.

"You were the first person I touched… afterward," he whispered. "I could not bear to let anyone touch me, even Jarrod. Please… make love to me."

She removed their clothes in a frenzied rush.

"Astrid," he moaned, "I need you."

She reached between their bodies and held him. "Peter."

He blinked his eyes open.

"This is us. This is now."

With those words, she took him into herself. He arched his back and thrust deep, suspended between heaven and hell, her soul pulsing around him. Instinctively, she knew what he needed, and he cried out as she took him without mercy. There were no soft caresses, no stinking oil, or coaxing hands. He needed her fierceness, needed the pain. Like the first night when he took her, there was an edge of violence to their passion. She pulled the darkness out of him, reveling in the power as he poured it into her body.

Astrid took it gladly, becoming a willing repository for the unspeakable evil that had befallen her beloved—mind, body, and soul.

No Popcorn for This Movie - New York

As the video played, Mack had a hard time watching. James and Persa were his neighbors. They attended his wedding, invited his family to their ranch for barbecues, sent birthday presents to his son, and worshipped with him at their local church. He had never felt more ashamed in his life.

Thaddeus sat dumbfounded, staring at the screen. He knew Esmeralda's visions were trustworthy, but to hear Davianna ben David recount the tale of her father's murder, shocked him to the core.

Esmeralda sat through the video in utter stillness, riveted. As it ended, she said, "Mack?" Thaddeus heard the tremble in her voice and reached out with his good arm to gather her close. "Davianna's telling the truth."

"I can corroborate that," Thaddeus said. "She recounted the events to me the night they occurred. Their stories line up. However, there is something else."

"What?" Mack asked with a strangled groan.

Esmeralda moistened her lips and closed her eyes. "When the nephilim fell, I saw its spirit rise. It did not die, Mack. It became a demon."

"A demon?" Mack blew out a long breath, finally understanding the origins of the thing that attacked Kayah.

Esmeralda pressed her thumb against her chin and nodded, then turned to Thaddeus and said, "I told you there was one in the bayou, the thing taking those kids, a giant, utterly insane, who lived with his mother. Do you remember?"

He nodded, regretting he had not given her account more credence.

"The name Beau called out, Mademoiselle Charlotte, does that mean anything to you?"

"No, it doesn't." Thaddeus buried his forehead in his hand. "But I will need to call Paul and have him look into it, and I'll alert the New

City division." He swallowed a lump in his throat. "That must be where the third beast lives, where we have our highest concentration of… of missing kids."

"I think we have another problem," Lavinia murmured. She sat through the video and subsequent discussion without speaking. She was often quiet, so Thaddeus had taken no particular notice, but her voice held an other-worldly, haunted quality that made his hair raise.

She backed up the video and said, "Listen to this section." The video, shot in split-screen, showed the underground bunker in the New City and the Penthouse five city blocks away.

Prince Peter cleared his throat. "We now know that Prince Eamonn was killed by Korah. He performed a ritual with the aid of some ancient tech, and in so doing, released a supernatural being. Korah calls him the Dark Master. His real name is Marduk."

Lavinia fast-forwarded through an interplay between Astrid and Persa about Marduk until Himari appeared on screen, pale and thin. "Peter, the old tech that Korah used, was it a cell phone like the Black Key?"

"I believe it was," Peter said. "I think Korah had it for a couple of years before he used it."

Himari grimaced. "They have used it as a model to track Davianna. Damn."

James ben Kole leaned forward. "And one of those things freed Marduk?"

Peter nodded.

Lavinia paused the video with James ben Kole's face, frozen in deadly fury, looking out at them.

Mack turned away, concentrating on his wife, shamed to the marrow of his bones. Persa and James clearly loved Peter. The video made it abundantly clear, and he felt like a bastard, but there was nothing he could do about it at the moment, so he asked, "What's significant about that section, Valentine? We've known they were using old tech to track the Black Key for months. We read about that in Gus' journals."

Lavinia turned to Thaddeus. "Are you an FBI agent right now?"

"Not unless you murdered someone."

"I did not," Lavinia said, her chest growing red and blotchy.

"When we signed on for this, I understood there would be times when I would need to look the other way. Is this one of those times?"

"Yes. But not how you might think. Perhaps it does not even matter anymore. I suppose it doesn't, but I've kept it secret."

She got the misty-eyed, faraway expression she wore when she was calculating, but instead of getting lost in her own mind, she said, "When we were fifteen, Kayah discovered an underground research lab and server farm. We did not realize it then, but it was one of the most secure facilities of the Last Age, likely top secret. I surmise it was buried at the end of the Great Judgment by an earthquake, but large sections remained intact. We named the most secure part of the facility Quadrant G. It lay behind a door we could not breach, though we tried for several years, on and off." She shrugged. "We had other projects going.

"There were five of us." She smiled in rueful resignation. "The world knows about four, but I was the fifth. My friends got in a lot of trouble for what we created down there, but I never did. I hid my part for years, but I was not the only one keeping secrets."

She glanced at Mack, her eyes holding a lifetime of regret. "While we were preparing to fight Erica, Kayah confessed she got into Quadrant G before us. It was a tomb. There was a skeleton inside with a suicide note that read, 'I killed it, leave it dead.'"

She blew out a shaky breath and continued, "Kayah stole an artifact out of the tomb and hid it. We were just kids, and she was an orphan, so she planned to sell it. Once we had a working system, she gave the artifact to our friend, Stephen ben McSwilley. He worked at the Palace and had access to Prince Korah. Kayah discovered he was covertly buying and funding technological research, which was illegal at the time, so Stephen was supposed to give it to Korah to gain his support for our project."

Lavinia pointed to the screen. "The artifact she found in Quadrant G was a phone like the Black Key, and according to Peter, Korah used it to free Marduk. Considering where it came from and what it did," Lavinia's husky voice caught, "knowing that was where Erica came from, and hypothesizing about who she was, I believe we were dealing with something more than just an artificial intelligence gone rogue." She reached out and took Mack's hand. "Do you remember Erica's last words?"

Mack's eyes widened as his lips parted in dismay. "'Where's my manger?'"

Esmeralda gasped, covering her mouth at the blatant blasphemy.

Lavinia's eyes glistened with unshed tears. "Mack, that tomb must have held something supernatural, and if so, then that means that Erica is not dead."

A New Calling - Mill House Beach - Joanna and Ian

That evening, Lady Joanna ben Luke rested her head against the sliding glass door of her bedroom, staring at the ocean. They were in hiding at Mill House Beach, wanted for questioning on charges of high treason, a situation that felt hauntingly familiar.

"Joanna?"

"Oh, I thought you were asleep."

"What's wrong?" Ian asked, through a yawn.

"It's nothing. I was just thinking about my mother," she glanced over her shoulder, "and my father."

Ian rubbed his chin, the dark stubble incongruent with his shock of white hair. He was normally fastidious about shaving and did so twice a day. It was an intimacy she discovered as a newlywed. His beard was the color his hair had once been, a deep, rich auburn.

"I expect that is natural, considering you find yourself wanted by the same government that imprisoned your father on identical charges."

Joanna's eyes clouded with worry. "Mark my words, if they brand me a traitor, they will go after my mother and what remains of our money. If they seize it again, we'll never get it back." She covered her face with her hands. "I learned to live without it, but Mother? She is still grieving my father. The return of her fortune, while it did not bring him back, at least restored a bit of her dignity."

Joanna slumped in misery. "Just going to her club, seeing her old friends, and playing bridge has meant the world to her. She has some of her old life back, and she's overseeing the family foundation. Last week, she sent over paperwork for a charity that helps children of Noble Army veterans killed in the Civil War attend college. She was so excited about it. Ian, it would be cruel to take that from her again."

She turned back to the window. "I'm sorry. Faced with everything that has happened today, that must sound petty. I should not have even mentioned it."

Ian rolled out of bed and came to her. "You never think anything that applies to you is worthy of consideration. You always put everyone else's needs and problems ahead of your own."

He brushed her bangs out of her eyes and smiled. "Your mother is elderly. She has been through a very difficult time, and this must feel reminiscent of your father's ordeal. They barred him from conducting his duties as Earl, stripped him of his authority and wealth, and held him on house arrest for the rest of his natural life. There is nothing petty about that."

"I wish he was still here," she whispered, her chin quivering. "He always suspected King Korah killed his brother. And to hear Prince Peter say it so matter of fact was as shocking to me as anything we heard today, which again, sounds silly, considering."

She dropped her head to his chest and let him hold her. "Prince Eamonn was a great man, and he was always kind to me. We were regular visitors at Gilead, then later at the New City Palace. So, seeing Prince Josiah on screen took me back. His resemblance to his father is uncanny, which should not surprise me. He always looked like him, even as a child." She chuckled. "We used to play together."

Ian stared down at her. "You never told me that."

Joanna shrugged, seeing nothing unusual about a childhood spent among royalty. "Father and Prince Eamonn were friends. I am two years older than Prince Josiah, so he probably does not remember me, and even if he does, he will remember a little fat girl who always wanted to play house." Her shoulders shook. "If I recall, he always wanted to play doctor."

"Doctor?" Ian laughed.

"Yes. I was one of his bariatric patients. His diagnosis," she laughed in self-deprecating humor, "was morbid obesity."

Ian laughed.

Joanna's eyes grew melancholy. "My father would have been overjoyed to discover Prince Josiah is alive. He mourned Prince Eamonn. My mother was friends with Princess Margaret. They were all friends, even with Prince Korah and Princess Alexa. We were a tight-knit group, so many wonderful families."

She smiled, remembering a time long past. "Some of my earliest memories are at Gilead, as far back as Princess Mary." Her eyes grew wide, and she shivered. "She was scary."

Ian drew her to the bed, amused by her expression. "Why?"

"Formidable is perhaps a better word," Joanna said, snuggling beside him. "She was very tall, or at least she seemed to be. In hindsight, I think she had presence. The press and some of the braver souls at court nicknamed her the Ice Princess, though no one dared utter that in her vicinity."

"She would not have found it amusing?" he asked, remembering the Princess' fearsome reputation.

"No," Joanna said with a shiver. "But I think she must have been beautiful in her youth. Even when I knew her, she was striking. But she had such a forbidding manner, as if she disapproved of everything and everyone. I remember wanting to disappear when she looked at me."

Ian grimaced. "Charming."

"She was not that, more of a personification of royal authority and power. She was a force, even as the Dowager. Everyone feared her, and the Palace under her rule was very sedate and strict. She demanded court speech, even though it had fallen out of fashion. We never used it at home or when we entertained, but Princess Mary insisted visitors observe royal protocols."

Ian stroked her hair, letting her talk. She never reminisced about her childhood, and he sensed she needed to tonight.

"We dressed formally at all times, even picnics." Joanna covered her eyes and groaned. "I spilled barbeque sauce down the front of my white pinafore when I was about six. I will never forget the humiliation. It was awful."

"Tragic," he said, the corner of his mouth lifting into a half smile.

"I cried all the way home," she said, matching his grin. "Probably because I missed the ice cream."

He rolled his eyes at his calorie conscious wife. "What else do you remember?"

"It was the height of offense to fail to use someone's proper address, which is likely why you will never hear me refer to any of the royals without their title. It is ingrained in me."

"I believe Prince Peter referred to his father as Korah on that call."

She shook her head. "I heard that, too. It is the height of disrespect and intended to demonstrate his antipathy toward his father, though I am likely the only one who caught the significance."

He obviously had, but he was not going to nitpick.

"I once saw Princess Mary unbraid Baroness St. Nathaniel for referring to her husband by his given name. They met at university and fell in love, but she had not come from our world, so she did not know better." Joanna shook her head. "Princess Mary reduced that poor girl to tears."

"That's rather unkind," Ian said.

"I suppose it appears that way, but it really was not."

"And how do you figure that?"

"I believe St. Nathaniel's given name was Christopher, which was very common. There might have been five or six men at that gathering who shared the name. And let's just say, for the sake of argument, the Baroness mentions Christopher plans to raise taxes to pay for some new project, but someone overhears and thinks she is talking about another man. That rumor might have made its way around the ballroom, morphing a dozen times, and before you know it, four Barons, an Earl, and a Duke are facing backlash at home over a rumor they plan to raise taxes."

Ian looked up at the ceiling and said, "So if the Baroness had said St. Nathaniel everyone would have known who she was talking about."

"Right, because there is only one. But that is not the only reason Princess Mary insisted on proper protocols. The formalities remind everyone of the responsibilities we held, that we were called to a higher purpose, and charged with upholding a moral standard and code of conduct. We were accountable to each other, but ultimately to the Iron King. Rules clarified our roles and governed our interactions, which kept the waters from being muddied. They guided people on what to do and how to behave, which prevented anyone from embarrassing themselves and others."

"Hmm," he said, hearing the wisdom in her words. "I don't think I ever considered that."

"It's true." She sighed, her eyes tired and troubled.

"Something else is bothering you, isn't it? You may as well say it all, lass." Ian's soft lilt came out in his exhaustion.

"You know me too well," she murmured, taking his hand. "I see trouble ahead now that Prince Josiah has married Davianna ben David."

"Why? I thought she was lovely."

Lady Joanna ben Luke shot him a look and adopted a stuffy upper-crust accent. "She is without family, connections, money, or consequences. In other words, she is exceedingly common and entirely unsuitable."

Once spoken, the truth of her words seemed to settle between them.

"Royalty marries within their social strata, Ian. It is the way things are done." Her face flamed as she added, "At one point, there was discussion between Prince Eamonn and my father about a betrothal."

"Between you and Prince Josiah?" Ian looked at her aghast.

"Yes, but I suspect Prince Eamonn did not wish to saddle his beloved son with a fat wife; I was quite a sight back then, so it amounted to nothing. Besides, my father was already an ally, so nothing could be gained from a match between us."

"Well, I suppose I should be thankful you were a fat girl." Humor danced in his pale blue eyes.

"True," she said, suddenly glad, too. "Had Prince Josiah not gone into exile, he likely would have married one of York's daughters, there are four of them, all of our age, or perhaps Ontario's daughter, Leticia. Canada has always been a bit contentious, and we haven't had a Canadian in the royal family for several generations. Now, more than ever, a match between them might have quieted some of the secessionist talk coming from up north."

"Ah, but he didn't. He married for love." Ian tapped Joanna on the tip of her turned-up nose. "Like we did."

She brushed a light kiss over his lips and whispered, "But you are the great grandson of the Duke of Sierra, Ian."

He pulled away, looking surprised. "Did my mother tell you that?"

"Yes." A blush crept into her cheeks. "But I already knew."

"Is that right?" he asked. "And how did you find that out?"

Joanna ran her tongue over her front teeth, looking uncomfortable. "I looked you up in Maples," she admitted, referring to the comprehensive guide on Alanthian nobility.

"Why? I never claimed a title."

She rolled her eyes and fell back on her pillow. "Because I wanted to make sure we were not related."

He laughed.

"It's not funny, Ian. You know there are strict rules governing marriage between the families of Dukes and Earls. So even though we are not related, at least that I could find, if you had been third generation and not fourth, we could not have married."

"Yes, we could have," he said, raising an eyebrow at her. "You just would have forfeited your honorific."

She stiffened. "It is more than that. Our descendants would have been barred from marrying into the nobility for three generations, and by that time, it would be too late."

"Too late for what?" he asked, not unkindly.

"To make a difference."

He nodded, understanding her perspective, duty toward the kingdom had been bred in her bones. "Well, if you want to go down that path, Prince Josiah made an excellent choice for a bride. If I recall my Alanthian history correctly, the Marriage Act of 330 ME encouraged all members of the nobility, no matter their rank, to marry commoners."

"True, but it is rarely done in the monarchy. So, at least in society's eyes, Prince Josiah married well beneath himself. And it will not affect him as much as it will her. Princess Davianna has her work cut out for her. Every society matron in Alanthia is sharpening their fangs, ready to take a bite out of her. She does not understand what she is in for." Their eyes met, and Joanna rested her hand over Ian's heart. "Society can be vicious, Ian."

"Then it falls to you to help her. No one understands the rules of that world better than you. You are connected to all the families and understand how to navigate the dragon's nest."

As he spoke, a sure knowledge fell upon him. "Perhaps that was the secondary reason we were on that call today, so you might begin to understand what you are being called to do."

Joanna paled as the truth of his words resonated. Even to Ian, she had not voiced the restlessness plaguing her these last few months. She had not shared the uneasiness she felt or the niggling feeling that her time at the Center might be coming to an end. She attributed it to burn out, her endless battles with Judith, the constant fundraising, and the heartache of working with troubled children. Beau's bombshell about Judith's embezzlement seemed like the final straw. She found it difficult to get out of bed, and for the first time in her career, she had to force herself to go to the Center. She loved the children, but after twelve grueling years, she was not sure she still loved the work. On the run, hiding at Mill House Beach, she was about to experience life away from the Center for the first time. Ian might have just given her a glimpse of what the future held, and it scared her. "We are a long way away from making that choice."

Ian nodded. Knowing how her mind worked, he did not press. "Turn out the light, Princess. It's been a long day."

As they lay together in the silence, he took her hand and pressed a kiss to the back of her fingers. "I looked you up in Maples, too."

Briefing - New York

Mack and Thaddeus entered Peter's building through the service entrance, dressed as electricians. They rode up the private elevator in silence, the events of the day weighing heavily on them. A bleary-eyed Nathan ben Henry waved them through with barely a word. It was late, close to midnight.

After the bombshell video conference, the atmosphere in the Penthouse felt somber. Prince Josiah let them in. Davianna and Astrid were presumably asleep, and Peter slumped in an armchair, his eyes blazing red, a highball glass in his hand.

Mack made the introduction. "My Esteemed, this is FBI Director Thaddeus ben Todd."

"My Esteemed." Thaddeus bowed.

"It is a pleasure to meet you, Director ben Todd."

Peter raised his glass, "Thaddeus, nice to see you again.

Mack turned to Josiah and said, "Director ben Todd oversees units responsible for investigating organized crime and subversive groups, as well as one that investigates murdered and missing children. He joined our organization a year and a half ago."

"We read him in after Korah and the Witch attempted to kill him and his wife." Peter rose and walked to the bar. "Would you two care for a drink?"

Thaddeus studied Peter, recognizing the look in his eyes, intense pain with nowhere to go. "I will, my Esteemed, thank you. Mack, Prince Josiah, shall we join Prince Peter? I think what we need to discuss might go down a little smoother."

Peter nodded and began pouring, embracing his role as bartender. He leaned against the cooler, letting each man take a few sips in silence. He felt raw and was well on his way to being drunk, a state he had not found himself in for ten months. But after today, he figured he would either have a drink or call his dealer, and he had been too damn close to calling his dealer.

He eyed Mack, mentally reviewing their conversation this morning, and said, "I take it you watched the video?"

Mack nodded and met Peter's eyes. He realized he was angry, and that anger was aimed squarely at him. "I did, my Esteemed."

"What did you fight with Persa and James about?" Peter asked in a deadly whisper.

The hair on Mack's arms rose. "It does not matter. I will make it right."

Peter's nose flared, and the look he shot Mack was an eerie reflection of Korah in its murderous intensity. "You do that," he hissed. "Nobody hurts Persa and James."

Mack nodded solemnly. "Understood."

Thaddeus was aware of Mack's general dislike of James ben Kole, but this appeared to be something deeper, though to his mind, not pertinent to the pressing matters at hand. "Gentlemen, it's late, so with your permission, I will begin."

"Indeed," Josiah said, sipping his rum and cola.

Thaddeus had taken a perfunctory sip of his whiskey, something he had not tasted in a dozen years. It warmed his belly, and he thought tonight that was not a bad thing. "Approximately twenty minutes after your video conference, Attorney General Nabal issued arrest warrants for the participants. They amended the warrant two hours ago to include Himari Nakamura and Genevieve ben Willard."

Peter covered his face and groaned.

Mack rubbed his forehead, then drained his glass of red wine. "We've cut off all but emergency communications. Himari and Genevieve are in full lockdown. Even if Korah's men discover the house, they won't find the bunker. Alaina and the others are at another safe house."

Peter looked at Josiah and said, "He is making his play, but he is not moving against us. He is coming against our people."

"The landing rights came through this evening." Josiah leaned down the bar and said to Mack, "We depart mid-morning."

"We are doing the same." Mack raised a glass in a toast, "We are taking our families into hiding, and I suppose we will come out when you come back."

They drank long into the night, discussing plans for a future Alanthia they all prayed would one day exist.

Part 16 - Wanted

February 1, 1000 ME

Lockdown – New City - Bunker

When Mack called to say the government had added Himari and Genevieve to the arrest warrants, the duo went into action. They ran upstairs to secure the house. Genevieve tidied up, made her bed, and packed her medicine, clothing, and toiletries. Himari emptied the refrigerator and took out the trash. With a shaking hand, Genevieve wrote a note, thanking a fictitious friend for stopping by to check on things while she was away visiting her ailing sister in Baton Rouge. She added a few comments about garbage day, which was Wednesday, and plant care. She mentioned the backdoor stuck and said she hid a key under a geranium pot on the porch in case the friend got locked out. Since her sister was quite ill, she was not sure when she would be back, but promised to check in next week. She signed it with a fake name, dated it yesterday, and left it on the kitchen table. With one last look around, they went downstairs, taking extra care to pull as much junk in front of the secret door as possible, then sealed themselves inside.

They ate a somber dinner, neither saying much. The bunker seemed eerily quiet without the constant whir of computers and servers, friendly banter, and chatter. Three weeks before, there had been eight of them living down here. Now only Himari and Genevieve remained.

Just before 10pm, Genevieve announced she was going to bed and encouraged Himari to do the same. But Himari knew she would not sleep until she discovered how they got hacked. So, she ignored Genevieve's urgings for her to rest and began the laborious process of system analysis. At first, she feared a remnant of Erica might be their culprit, however, she detected no evidence of that. There were no telltale signs of altered code, or the vicious little messengers Erica embedded in programs to relay information back to her. So, she concluded it had not been Erica or a remnant thereof, which meant they had another enemy.

With her eyes burning and her neck aching, Himari stood up and stretched. She wished Alaina was here, not only for the companionship, but for Alaina's unique ability to spot anomalies and patterns. But Alaina was in hiding, as were they all.

She picked up her secured phone, staring at the blank screen, willing it to ring, willing Filippo to call. But it was the middle of the night in New York, not that it mattered. More than time zones and distance separated them now. He did not even know she was wanted by Korah's government. Would he even care? She thought he might, but she wasn't sure, not really, and that made her knees give way. She sat on the floor by the empty bank of desks, looking up at the plugs, cables, and lines, thinking her life felt much the same, a tangled mess.

"Get it together, Sunflower," she said aloud. "You have work to do."

At 2:58 am, the police arrived.

From the hidden cameras mounted around the property, Himari saw their stealthy approach and woke Genevieve. They watched in terror as the black-faced SWAT unit moved into position. The cameras captured the invasion in real time, as dozens of men stormed the house.

Before the video call yesterday, they shielded the computer equipment and disguised the bunker, using painted screens as a backdrop. To anyone viewing stills from the video, it would appear they were in a house overlooking the Bay. Creating the screens occupied Filippo's time while he was in the bunker, and Himari could barely look at them without breaking down. The murals were extraordinarily realistic, not executed in his usual style of deep pigments and distinctive brushstrokes. As inspiration, he used a photograph from a magazine that featured the living room of an art dealer who swindled him when he was young. He claimed if they ever had to use them, investigators might harass the dealer, perhaps take him into custody, a thought that amused him. As the front door burst open and police poured into the house, Himari wished he was here. At the very least, she wanted to tell him the last thing he painted might save her life.

Genevieve and Himari could scarcely breathe when they heard thundering footsteps descend the basement steps. However, the piles of junk, discarded furniture, and old clothes did as they were intended, and after a cursory search, the men left without discovering the hidden door.

Upstairs, the lead investigator conferred with his men, read the note, and seemed satisfied the house was empty. Despite Genevieve's name being on the arrest warrant, the police had no record she ever lived here, and if they questioned her neighbors, they would learn that a widow named Agnes ben Pyle moved in about three years ago. The Resistance concealed ownership of all the safe houses behind trusts, shell companies, false names, and fake documents. Genevieve received no mail here, and anything containing her real name was safely hidden away in a lockbox in the server room.

As far as the police were concerned, they got a bad tip. It was clear from the pictures, which was all Nabal provided, that the conspirators were operating from a location near the Bay, and this old house was miles inland.

By 3:43 am, they were gone.

The diversion and the ruse worked.

She and Genevieve held on to one another and wept in relief. And while they may have escaped tonight, they both realized they would have to remain underground until Josiah returned. Three thousand miles from Filippo and her failing marriage, Himari Nakamura knew she was trapped.

If You Want Something Done Right – New City - Rapha

In the halls of the House of Amah, Rapha raged. He picked up a solid oak desk and hurled it across his study where it splintered into a hundred pieces. A chair followed. Defeat, snatched from the hand of victory, just when he had her trapped, at last.

He found Persa ben Yereq weeks ago, living three hours north, on a ranch called Pepperwood. He hated the vile name, hated the hedge that protected her from his seeking spirit. His methodical, constant surveillance yielded few clues as he stalked the perimeter of

Pepperwood, searching for a way in. The golden hedge proved to be the converse of his own, and his spirit felt as if he skirted the flames of Hell if he got too close. Nevertheless, he knew where she hid, though she rarely left the property.

On the two occasions he caught her outside, an enemy warrior accompanied her, a hideous female elohim dressed in gaudy gold armor. Her name came unbidden to his mind—Ilsidor. As he studied her, he experienced a fit of irrational jealousy, discerning at a molecular level that his father knew her. They were connected somehow; he sensed it.

While he traveled, his body remained in his computer lab, carrying out commands. He could now exist in two places at once. With the skill mastered, he learned to split his vision and maintain absolute control over his mind, body, and spirit. He was becoming invincible. When his confinement ended, he would move. Until then, he watched.

Yesterday, Persa presented herself like a proverbial lamb to the slaughter. Rapha followed at a discreet distance, undetected by her ever-present guard. He tracked her to a mansion in the New City, then tailed the vehicle to the outskirts of town, where her possible destinations were limited. Flying through the houses, staying ahead of her guard and out of sight, he almost dismissed the old woman's house, until he heard voices hidden deep underground. Pausing to listen, he detected the hum of a vast computer network and went to investigate.

Rapha found the bunker.

He hit the servers with his spirit, discerned their location, detected their capacity, and followed the wires that connected them—to everything. Undetected, he eavesdropped and learned they were preparing a video conference, which they planned to record. Ecstatic, he sent commands to his body to intercept and capture the transmission. Moments before Persa's party arrived, he escaped and rejoined his body. In an elated frenzy, he hacked into the lines and pulled up the live stream.

He screamed when the white-haired man prayed. The mere sight of him burned his eyes, and his words scorched his soul. He feared if it went on too long, he would be forced to disconnect, but the repugnant worm finally stopped, and Rapha settled in to watch.

They discussed the events that brought his father out of bondage, but he already knew the story after tapping into the hag's memories.

He discovered Lucifer had attempted to gain control of The Black Key and failed, which did not surprise him and cemented his low opinion of the fallen angel. Rapha chose wisely when he decided not to align with that loser.

He listened to their stories and laughed when he heard Marduk had bitten the little redhead. When the chubby woman with the big ass described the Coronation Ball, he leaned forward, riveted by the tale. It gave him deeper insight into how and when his father selected his breeding stock. Smiling through the story, he delighted in their fear and pain.

When the Would-be Prince of Alanthia recounted the antics of his brother in Greece, Rapha paid particular attention. He learned Zuzite had roamed a vast territory, and Rapha suspected he garnered that right by killing his mother. However, he failed to govern his baser instincts and paid the price. Rapha shook his head in regret when the sniveling brunette described what was surely his brother's last battle. Zuzite should have known better than to go up against a man named David. Rapha recognized Davianna ben David and knew what she carried. However, the Black Key was never his goal, his mother was.

And there she sat, even more of a sniveler than the rest of them, a pathetic, tiny woman. He despised her, revolted that he came from her, and hated that his father chose her as his mother. It explained why he failed to attain a stature greater than his brothers. She was no larger than a child. Throughout the discussion, she clung to her husband as if he could save her. Rapha burned with hatred, finally understanding why she abandoned him. She did it for a man. He planned to kill James ben Kole and make Persa ben Yereq watch him do it before he devoured her.

The moment the call concluded, he sent a copy to Korah and another to Attorney General Nabal ben Caleb, an adherent to the New Way and a high-ranking warlock. Rapha recognized him when he invaded the Witch of Endor's mind. He attended the ceremony when his father broke free. Nabal was there.

Along with the video message, Rapha even identified the humans with Persa, her friends. He supplied all the evidence Korah and Nabal needed to seize them. Then he went in pursuit. He was determined not to lose her again or allow her to escape behind that impenetrable hedge.

But the moment he left his body, a phalanx of enemy warriors swarmed him, wielding flashing swords and blood-curdling shouts to the Most High. One, in particular, Gabriel, nearly destroyed him. But Rapha escaped with his life back to the House of Amah. The hedge that kept him inside, kept them out, and for that, he praised his father.

Enraged, he went on a rampage, destroying everything in his path, including two of his servants, who happened to be at the wrong place at the wrong time. It mattered little, they would have been dead in a fortnight, anyway. He had not planned to leave any witnesses behind.

When he regained a measure of control, he returned to his computer lab and monitored the pursuit. He had little hope the humans would accomplish their objective, and they did not.

By morning, the siege ended. He could fly, but it was too late. Persa blew away in the wind. He did not know where, neither did Korah, who proved to be a great disappointment. His father imbued Korah with unlimited power, yet he failed to exercise it. He was as paltry and weak-minded as the rest of them, but Rapha had plans for him.

Bit of a Mess – Peter and Astrid

Twenty minutes after takeoff, Astrid reached across the armrest and took Peter's hand. "You didn't sleep much last night. Why don't we go lie down?"

He turned, his chin resting on his fist. "All right." He rose without a word, customary quip, or lecherous sparkle in his eyes.

Astrid led him to the private jet's sleeping quarters. She dimmed the cabin light and kicked off her shoes, part of the extensive wardrobe that arrived daily, courtesy of Jarrod, the Wonder Servant.

He sat on the edge of the bed, resting his elbows on his knees, his head drooping. "I am sorry, Red. I have been a mess for the last twenty-four hours."

She knelt and untied his running shoes, the same style and color as the ones she wore. He had a closet full of them. "You're exhausted, and you drank too much last night. Between the video conference and your father's call this morning, no one blames you for being out of sorts." She ducked her head, looking up between his arms. "But we made it out of there."

He closed his eyes and whispered, "I left behind a disaster. Everyone is in hiding, wanted for questioning. It was not supposed to be that way."

She pulled off his shoes and climbed into bed. "It'll be all right. Come on, Prince d'Or, rest your head." She settled him in her lap, running her fingers through his thick blond hair, massaging his scalp. With expert hands, she soothed his headache the way her mother had done for her many times.

"Prince d'Or," he murmured, "you need to find a better name for me. I am not particularly fond of that one."

"You aren't?" Astrid continued her comforting touch. "Who gave it to you?"

"My father," he answered, tired and monotone. "The press picked it up. They thought it was an endearment. It was not. He did it out of spite. Royals are not supposed to have nicknames." The hint of a smile teased the corner of his mouth. "We are not even supposed to shorten our given names, which is why you will never hear anyone refer to me as Pete."

She giggled and kissed his forehead. "You are not a Pete." His breathing came slow and steady, but she felt his heart thumping. "I do usually just call you Peter."

He tilted his head and looked up at her. "I love hearing you say my name. There are fewer than a dozen people who do. Ironically, everyone who has that privilege is being hunted by my father, everyone I love."

"We'll make it. Remember, 'Finish the journey well.'" She repeated the words the angel had spoken to him a few days before.

"But what does that look like, Astrid?" Peter sighed and closed his weary eyes. "It is shaping up differently than I thought."

It hung between them, growing since they arrived in New York, the realization that he could not simply walk away. The stakes were too high, and too many lives hinged on the success of Josiah's future rule. As much as he dreamed of a life devoid of royal responsibilities, duty was embedded in his DNA, as inescapable as his blond hair. Silent tears fell over her lashes. She could see no future role for her to play, no place for her in Prince Charming's real life. She wrapped her arms around him and held on tight, knowing she would continue to do so, for as long as he, and the world, let her.

Factions – Josiah and Davianna

In the main cabin of the jet, the roar of the engine droned deep and steady, making Davianna drowsy. She touched Josiah's forearm and said, "You are awfully quiet."

He glanced at her, his whiskey-colored eyes bloodshot and hooded. "Sorry. We had a long night, and I've been going over the intelligence briefing I received."

Davianna turned in her seat and checked the cabin, finding the steward well out of earshot. "From whom?"

"Sir Mack ben Robert and FBI Director Thaddeus ben Todd."

Davianna narrowed her brows. "And what is your read on them?"

Josiah shrugged imperceptibly and said, "Mack and I came to an understanding. He is an honorable man. He has led The Resistance admirably and will take over the Royal Guard when we return."

"Good," she said quietly.

"We are feeling each other out, though no one says it, other than Mack, who was quite forthcoming." Josiah smiled. "Honestly, that was refreshing."

"He is pretty straight forward, isn't he?" Davianna said with a smile.

"That is putting it bluntly."

"Well, tell me about this FBI Director." Davianna took his hand and gave it a squeeze.

"He's about seven feet tall."

"Seriously?"

"Not quite," Josiah chuckled. "I'm exaggerating. But he did say he played basketball in college. He's a lawyer and started with the Ministry of Justice before moving to the FBI. He has personal reasons for getting involved with The Resistance. Last year, a witch and her coven came after him and his new wife on their way to their wedding. He almost died, so did she. Mack was with them, as was Ian ben Kole, who was on the call yesterday."

Josiah rested his head in his hand. "They are all friends, all connected, everyone in The Resistance. That is how it was born. They have been careful who they brought in."

"That is logical, considering how dangerous the work they have been doing is." She got a gleam in her eyes and added, "But everyone we have met thus far, other than Mack, has been female. I suppose that comes as no surprise, considering Peter recruited them. But I nearly fell out of my chair when I recognized Alaina ben Thomas."

Josiah grinned. "It's a brilliant strategy. Men always underestimate beautiful, smart women."

"True," she said.

"I was tired, and he was drunk, but apparently Mack's wife, Lavinia, is a genius. She and Peter conceived the idea for The Resistance at their kitchen table after about a thousand shots of espresso." Josiah laughed. "I had to physically restrain Peter to stop him from waking you up to see if you knew how to make espresso."

Davianna giggled, envisioning the scene. "For the record, I do know how to make espresso."

"Good to know," Josiah said with a smile. "I lived on black coffee when I was a resident."

"I will keep you supplied in coffee, Prince."

He yawned. "I think I am going to need it."

"I think we all are," she sighed.

He turned to look out the window. "Sometimes I think we should just stay in the Golden Kingdom and let Peter rule Alanthia." He gave her a tired smile. "I've come to realize Alanthia is his kingdom more than it is mine now."

Davianna's mind seized on the possibility, enticed by the prospect of living away from the inevitable struggles and trials of royal life. However, Princess Davianna discarded the notion before it took root. "It may seem that way because you have been in exile, but it will come. And consider this, Alanthia is not clamoring for Peter, nor was it his line the Iron King chose to rule Alanthia. It is yours. It is you."

The soulful look in his eyes touched her heart, and she continued, "Like He chose me to carry this artifact and be your bride, neither of which I have the remotest idea how to accomplish, nor do I understand why, but the Iron King has His reasons, and His ways are higher than ours."

She took his hand. "It is a testimony to your integrity that you would even entertain allowing Peter to rule in your stead. That sort of humility and honor will become a hallmark of your reign."

Josiah wrapped a burly arm around her neck and kissed the top of her head. "Thou art not alone," he murmured. "He did indeed choose wisely for me. You are extraordinary."

"Thank you." Davianna shifted in her seat and squeaked, "Ouch, my hair is stuck in your watch."

"Hold still," he said, trying to free the antique links and taking several strands with him.

"Ow," she said, rubbing the spot. "That thing is dangerous."

"Sorry," Josiah chuckled and began extricating the hairs caught in the band. "It's old."

Davianna examined the watch closer, platinum, studded with diamonds and bold Roman numerals marking the quarter hours. "Was that part of the jewelry Jarrod sent over?"

Josiah pulled the last hair free with a surgeon's precision. "Yes."

She suspected discussing jewelry might be one of those off-limits 'royal things', but they were alone, so she asked, "Whose was it?"

"My Great Grandfather's on my mother's side, I think. All the jewelry Jarrod sent over came from her estate. Heaven knows how he got a hold of it." He smoothed the clasp back into place. "I am sure there is documentation on its origins somewhere, but I needed a watch this morning, so I grabbed it." He thought for a moment, then added, "Genevieve might know."

"Your Auntie G? I thought she was your nanny." Davianna scanned the cabin again, ensuring they were still speaking in private.

"She was, but before that, she was my mother's companion," Josiah said, breaking into a yawn.

"There are not many people who would go from the companion to a Princess to a nanny."

"I suppose. I never gave that much thought. She grew up in Italy, but she is an Alanthian citizen. Her father was a diplomat who married the daughter of an Italian count. She and my mother attended school together and became friends. So, when my parents got engaged, she came to Alanthia as her companion, which was helpful, especially at first, because my mother barely spoke English. From what I have been told, she tried her best, though my father spoke Italian. Her real name was Marguerite, but she changed it when she married my father as a goodwill gesture."

Intrigued by the description of her deceased mother-in-law, Davianna asked, "Did your auntie tell you stories about her?"

"A few, and I am ashamed to admit, I did not ask. I was a kid, and I suppose I thought there would be plenty of time. Plus, I sensed discussing her was painful for everyone. There was always," his voice trailed off, "always a hole where she should have been. It's strange, missing someone you never knew."

"I get that."

"My father did not talk about her much. They had an arranged marriage, but from all accounts, my grandmother chose wisely. I asked him why he never remarried, when I was seven or eight, and he said he had a great love, and that only happens once in a lifetime." He squeezed her hand. "I understand that now."

She tilted her face up for a kiss. He obliged.

"Well, we will have to ask Auntie G. about the jewelry and your mother. I would like to know more about her."

"That's sweet, Minx."

"Hmm, perhaps. I must admit to an ulterior motive."

He lifted his eyebrow in silent question.

"Peter makes that same expression. I can't do it." She tried and failed.

Josiah laughed. "You can't wink either."

"True, but I can whistle with my fingers." She put her fingers in her mouth with an impish sparkle in her eye.

"Oh… don't do that in here."

"I wasn't," she said. "But I could."

"I have no doubt. More of your hidden talents." He grinned. "But what is your ulterior motive for finding out about my mother?"

She lifted a shoulder and said, "I am interested to know how she settled in. Perhaps your auntie can give me some advice?"

"I am positive she would be delighted, but don't fret. I will make sure you have all the support you need."

"Thanks." Looking over her shoulder, she saw that Peter and Astrid were still in the bedroom. "I can't really discuss it with Astrid, that being a touchy subject. But I am concerned. I married the man, but I've got the Prince. I just need to figure out how to be a Princess."

"You will do fine. As you said, you were chosen for the role."

Davianna rested her head against his shoulder and yawned. "Why do Peter and Astrid always get the bed?"

Josiah snorted a laugh. "I think they simply beat us to it."

"Well, we need to fix that," she said, "or get a bigger jet."

"Spoiled already," he teased and moved his seat back as far as it would go. "This isn't bad. Move your seat back."

Davianna reclined and lay on her side, facing him. "So, was there anything pressing in the briefing last night?"

"Everything is pressing, Minx." He held the back of his neck. "The nobility is in shambles. I fear those who managed to retain power did so at Korah's whim, so they have failed to uphold their duties as they ought, and the people have suffered."

Davianna's face darkened. "Especially in the south. My father always said the Duke of Sedgefield was an honorable man, and Korah's treatment of him sent the entire region on the road to destruction."

"Unfortunately, it falls to me to restore things, though empowering them again does not come without significant risks."

"Such as?"

"They might turn on me."

She cut him a look, her expression guarded. "They might."

"Untangling the web is going to take years. We can't just flip a switch. That will throw the Kingdom into chaos. And there are plenty of Alanthians who wish to do away with the entire aristocracy and move toward a more democratic form of governance."

"Can you not blend the two?" she asked.

"It splits loyalties, besides going against our founding principals of governance." Josiah closed his eyes. "Korah knew exactly what he was doing when he hamstrung the nobility, because, for all their faults, they swear an oath to preserve faith in the Iron King, to rule under His authority, not their own. Civil authorities swear no such oath, pledging their allegiance and loyalty to the government."

Davianna tsked and said, "And in the process, they have become unbearably corrupt at all levels, verging on lawlessness in many places. In the end, it is why my family left."

"You and countless others. But I will make an appeal for the pilgrims to return. Alanthia needs the faithful, Davianna. I can only do so much, and I fear the descent may be too great. Factions have risen like toadstools, and each has their own brand of radicals. People are flocking to their causes."

Davianna squeezed his hand. "Such as?"

He sighed. "There are almost too many to name. They run the gamut from extreme left to extreme right, with anarchy lurking on both ends. There are the Republicans with the Libertines, the Greenmen with the Gaians. Even in the church, we see Jihadists on one side, Catholics on the other, with both groups willing to pull the sword in defense of what they call true religion. Sadly, neither remotely resembles what the Iron King ordained.

"They all seem to believe the structures that guided us for a thousand years were too simple, that true knowledge is found in the ancient, hidden philosophies of the past. They never stop to consider that the Iron King judged the nations for those practices, that their origins were satanic. I fear the Devil will find fertile ground, not only in Alanthia, but elsewhere. Their movements are gaining momentum across the globe."

Davianna winced. "That is bleak."

"Yes, unfortunately, it is. There is a spirit of lawlessness. FBI Director ben Todd reports the mafia has moved into the west coast, but they may have been operating underground for years. We simply do not know. In times past, the nobility would have dealt with this, beginning at the local level, but those checks and balances are gone.

"Korah kept the radicals under control through fear, intimidation, and imprisonment. However, this tactic prevented the more moderate members of these groups from airing genuine grievances and seeking legal redress. They are simmering. There is credible intelligence we will see violence in the coming days as Korah's government begins to collapse."

"Is there anything you can do?" she asked, biting her bottom lip.

"Not at the moment, but it makes me second guess my decision to tell Sir Preston to stand down, to wait for the Iron King to restore the throne."

"No," she said, shaking her head. "You were right. All the Alanthian Ruling Princes, from Robert Malcolm to your father, were granted the right to rule by the Iron King. Korah gained his throne through the courts. You cannot do that and expect to be blessed."

Josiah sighed. "I know. I just fear a lot of innocent blood is going to be shed."

"Can the FBI do anything? Do they know where the threat is coming from?"

"They have some intelligence, yes, but not the resources, not on the scale required, and only in Alanthia. Director ben Todd believes the first group to strike will be the anti-tech terrorists, who have been in an uproar since the Geneva Accords last summer.

"A dozen people died trying to get into a phone store in China last week, and the jihadists are using the incident, claiming technology kills people. They are determined to stop its spread, even if they must use violence to do it." He rolled his eyes at the incongruence.

"They are congregating, taking over abandoned towns, and setting up their own communities. Peter is close friends with Tobias ben Cramer, the Baron of Litchfield, and the Duke of Sedgefield's heir. He confirms jihadists have taken control of large swaths of the duchy. They are using these communities as training grounds and murdering residents who wish to remain but refuse to convert to their beliefs."

"That's just the devil," Davianna said, bringing her hand to her heart.

"Not according to them," Josiah remarked, pinching the bridge of his nose. "In their minds, they are the true servants of the Iron King."

Davianna dismissed them with a wave of her hand. "Astrid and I ran into a group of them while we were running. We thought they were pilgrims at first, but her danger radar started blaring the minute we sat down, so we got out of there."

"Smart choice. They are dangerous. There are rumors the jihadists have formed a loose confederation with the Libertine and Gaian anarchists. The Catholics know it, and they are ready to fight."

"And where does that leave all the normal people?" Davianna asked, thinking of Taylorsville, and wondering if anyone she grew up with had been hurt.

Josiah shook his head. "It's hard to say, and I pray it does not come to that."

"And you got this information from the FBI?"

"Not all of it. I spoke to Reuben this morning. He will be with the entourage meeting our plane." He traced the delicate shape of her brow with his finger, thinking how precious she was to him. "We'll be safe."

She gave him a look, so world-weary and cynical, it broke his heart.

"Trust me on this. I served with them for twelve years. They are the most formidable warriors on earth. An Israeli in battle is a fearsome thing to behold. No one can stand against them, which is why I put us under their protection for this last leg of the journey. It was a wise decision, especially since Korah made his move yesterday."

Davianna squeezed her eyes shut. "What did he do?"

"Somehow, they intercepted the video call. All the participants from the New City have arrest warrants on them. As far as we know they are safe, but they are in hiding."

"Oh, no wonder Peter is so upset."

"Aye."

"Is that all?" she asked.

Josiah cleared his throat, unwilling to share the most disturbing part of Thaddeus' briefing, that the beast who killed her father had transformed into a demon and might be hunting her. She was still reeling from her traumatic memories, so he did not want to tell her yet. But he would not have her ignorant, so he said, "Director ben Todd has opened a top-secret investigation into the occult societies, the elite Gaians. These are the people pulling the strings on all these radical groups, the actual power behind what is brewing. Their existence comes as no surprise, considering my esteemed uncle played a direct role in their establishment, and according to Peter, actively takes part in their nefarious activities."

"Peter witnessed this?"

Josiah looked over his shoulder, ensuring his cousin had not emerged. "You remember what he said the night we were at Beau Landry's place and his confession afterward? I think he has seen more than he will ever admit."

"Do you think it is important?" she whispered.

"Perhaps not at the moment, but there might come a time." He moistened his lips. "You asked me on our way to New Orleans what I was going to do when I took the throne. I can tell you now, my top priority will be eradicating these covens. There is no place in Alanthia for Luciferian worship. While the other groups may seek violence or political upheaval to enact change, the occultists pose a clear and present danger because they have supernatural power behind them. If we stand a chance in averting the Iron King's judgment, we must start there. He does not have fellowship with witches."

Downsizing? – New City – Angelica and Korah

"Quaint, this minimal staff, Chukka, but really? Don't you think you've taken it a bit far?" Angelica strolled into Korah's bedchamber, uninvited and unannounced. "I just walked through the Palace. There is barely a footman on duty."

Korah whirled on her and snarled, "How did you get in here?"

She flipped her blonde hair off her shoulder and grinned. "I have my ways. Pour me a brandy, will you? It's bloody cold outside."

He clearly did not appreciate the intrusion, but he poured her a glass, nonetheless. Handing it to her, he moved away and said, "There's a new video."

"Oh, what did we do? Releasing technology has been a double-edged sword for us, has it not? I take it by your tone, this one is not flattering?"

"Damning, to say the least, though only Nabal has seen it, and he is in this up to his neck, so there is no danger."

"Nabal is a fool," Angelica said, rolling her eyes.

Korah cut her a look. "You are the one who brought him in."

She shrugged. "He has proven useful in the past. But what of this video?"

"It seems my son's treachery knows no bounds. The video captured the machinations of his little revolutionary group." His words dripped with scorn. "I called the misbegotten brat today."

Angelica joined him at the glass doors that led out to the formal gardens. "Brazen. I like it. Do you have him under control?"

He raised a brow at her. "What do you think?"

She chuckled. "I suppose you reminded him of our little dungeon; he does so fear that."

The corner of Korah's lip lifted in an ugly smile. "In so many words."

"You should have let me break him," she said with a tsk.

He gave her a baleful look. "You almost killed him. I wanted him alive, at least I did at the time."

"You got squeamish," she countered.

"Perhaps," he sighed and ran his finger around the rim of the brandy snifter, making it sing. "The video proved enlightening. I was shocked to hear how much he has pieced together, more than I gave him credit for. Though by the end of the week, it won't matter."

"What have you planned?" Angelica purred.

Korah moistened his lips, setting his shoulders in a confident pose. For the first time since Satan crashed his wedding, he seemed the Korah of old, regal, diabolical, and in control. Angelica waited in near sexual arousal to hear his plans.

"The anarchists and the jihadists are rioting in multiple locations tomorrow, beginning in London. Josiah will not make it to the Iron King's Embassy alive." He lifted a shoulder. "The attack will not occur on Alanthian soil and will simply be written off as part of a global uprising. The press and the public will hold me blameless."

Angelica watched him shift, going into character. Actual tears hovered in the corner of his eyes as his voice shook. "They are going to kill my son."

He moved away from her and looked over his shoulder with a smirk. "Even though I despise those ravenous beasts, their timing is impeccable. I will, of course, move to establish order throughout the kingdom and root out the subversive elements bent on disrupting the peace and prosperity Alanthians have enjoyed throughout my reign."

Shivers of pleasure ran down Angelica's spine, brandy and desire fueling the fire in her blood. "Are you purging?" she breathed.

"Never let a good crisis go to waste."

Heat engulfed her, and she moved within inches of him. "That is dangerous, given the current political environment, but clever, ruthless, and brilliant. I love it."

Korah bit her neck and whispered, "How are preparations coming from your end?"

"Everything is ready," she murmured, sliding her hand inside his robe, "there and here."

Come Home – London – Reuben and Kayah

Reuben used his key to Kayah's London townhome, coming through the door with a chilly breeze, his olive complexion flushed with cold and exertion. "It is convenient, living so close to the Embassy. Did you plan that, Yakira?" He leaned in and gave her a sweaty peck on the cheek. "A perfect run."

"You Mossad boys are so fit, so sexy." She smoothed his black hair off his forehead. "Yes, I did consider how close it was to the Embassy. I thought perhaps I might catch a glimpse of you." She winked, settling into his arms. "You're late. How was your first day back?"

"Yehonathan is in residence and awaits Josiah's arrival in the morning. I am assigned to the unit that will retrieve them from the landing field." He shook his head and rolled his eyes. "The diplomatic negotiations that secured the rights, Yakira, you would not believe what it took."

Kayah looked up at him, raising a golden eyebrow in speculation. She was blonde again, resuming her identity as Dorothy ben Quincy, the Bostonian. "I can imagine."

"Prince Edward is under tremendous pressure to stay loyal to Korah, though privately he assures Yehonathan he will support an Alanthia governed by Josiah. The other Ruling Princes will take more convincing. They all attended that wedding back in January, and Yehonathan suspects Lucifer has visited each of them. They are scared. Egypt will not support Josiah's bid, and Greece is highly doubtful. The other five? I cannot say, but Josiah has much work to do."

"Global politics were not supposed to intrude on Dorothy and Isaac's life in Notting Hill."

"Banking and tea were to be the order of the day, yes?" Reuben drew himself up in a farcical pose of a British businessman, absurd in his athletic attire. "We did not get our month, did we?"

"No, we did not." Kayah's eyes went stormy green. They planned a month of seclusion, just the two of them, without work, politics, and global upheaval, but Gus ben Allen's murder changed everything.

"Are you hungry? I picked up a couple of doner kebobs while I was out."

"I'm starving." He grinned, pulling her against him. "I do like London. When this is all over, shall I request a permanent post here?"

"If only we could," she sighed.

"Why could we not? It is a good place, no?" Reuben rubbed his nose against her temple, inhaling her expensive shampoo.

"Leon will call in his favor, Reuben, and Josiah will need you. At least for the foreseeable future, we will be in the New City. I feel it."

He pressed his lips against her forehead. "That does not make you happy, Yakira? To reside in the New City again?"

"Josiah on the throne most assuredly makes me happy," Kayah whispered.

"There is much political risk for me to stay at his side. He knows that, even if we are like brothers."

Kayah laid her hand against his cheek, clammy as his body cooled from the run. "It is not right. If you were British, no one would have anything to say about it."

"But I am not." Reuben rested his head into her palm.

"No, but I would not have you any other way." She brushed a light kiss across his lips and said, "I love you."

His eyes widened in surprise. He knew she did, but she rarely said the words, which made them special. "And I, you. You will come with me next week when we go to Tel Aviv? I am to be in the advance guard again. I will show you my home."

Kayah stiffened, then pulled away. "I cannot. Right now, I am the only member of The Resistance not in hiding. Yet," she made a self-deprecating snort, "when am I not in hiding, Reuben?"

She spoke the truth. She was the primary suspect in a half a dozen active investigations in Alanthia. While the authorities lacked any evidence to arrest her, she lived under a cloud of suspicion and existed in the shadows. The woman he met last spring did not care; the woman standing before him today, did. She had softened, changed, though he suspected that she did not see it in herself. He did. But he also understood her reluctance to join him in Tel Aviv had nothing to do with The Resistance or her duty.

He tucked a lock of her hair behind her ear and asked, "Do you remember the morning we fought Erica?"

She adopted a cynical expression and said, "It would be hard to forget."

"Do you remember what you sang?"

Kayah lifted her head, going rigid, fighting the memory. She had asked Mack to play Gus' favorite song, and as she sang, a spirit swept over her with the music. She cried out to the Iron King, asking the question that plagued her since her first conscious memory, 'Who am I?' Sir Preston said he knew, but there was a deeper answer than who her parents had been, and that morning, surrounded by replicas of the bunker that sent her to prison, she thought she knew. But now she was no longer certain. "That was a fleeting moment in time."

"No," Reuben said, refusing to let her dismiss it. "It was not, and that is not how He works."

Kayah templed her palms and pressed them over her lips. "No. This is me we are talking about here. Mere days afterward, I killed a man, and you know what happened."

Reuben shook his head. "The Lord disciplines those He loves, those He has chosen. Have you considered that was His way of telling you that you must stop? That your new life requires it?" His gaze did not waver. He did not shrink from the subject of infinite importance.

She covered her face, unable to meet his eyes. "You did not hear what that evil spirit said to me."

"I did not, but nothing from the pit of hell ever tells the truth, Yakira." He took her by the shoulders. "Who do you believe, a demon, or the Most High and the man who loves you? Because that is your choice."

Kayah opened her palms and showed them to him, looking lost. "They are covered in blood."

"As are mine, but not the blood that you think."

She drew her brows down, her lips parted. "I don't understand."

"It is a mystery, yet one that has pulled man from the pit of hell and damnation since Calvary. It is the blood of the Lamb that covers you now. I was there, Yakira. I felt the Spirit. I see the transformation in you. Come home with me, go to the temple, then you will know."

Since meeting him in Bologna last year, Kayah felt the pull, experienced the change. They stood together in the townhouse she purchased, intent on a new life, away from the blood and intrigue, but forces greater than she, pulled her back into the mire, and she feared she would never crawl out. But Reuben bent over and offered his hand. He refused to abandon her to herself, to shame. "He will not smite me the moment my foot touches the Golden Kingdom?" she asked, and it was not a rhetorical question.

"No," Reuben said, shaking his head. "If King Korah, the most wicked man on Earth, were to repent and present himself in the temple with a contrite heart and in genuine faith, even he would be accepted. Yakira, it is the path to salvation the Iron King offers to all mankind, not just the so-called good people. That is why He commands men to make the pilgrimage, not for Him, but for us," Reuben declared, blazing confidence. "You will see, trust me, I know this is true."

She leaned into him, feeling his damp shirt under her cheek, warm and strong, the man who loved her. "I trust you. I will go."

He covered her, held her close, and whispered, "Is good."

Road to Rephidim – New York

The Resistance members in New York told no one they were leaving. They simply vanished. Thaddeus, dressed in running attire and pushing a stroller with Claire bundled against the cold, waved a casual goodbye to the doorman and jogged off toward the park. Mack, with whom the security staff had grown familiar, left wearing his dark suit and sunglasses, agent attire, nothing out of the ordinary. Esmeralda went to work, but at 9:30 am shut down her computer, told Camy she was not feeling well, and caught a train. Lavinia and Richard asked the guard at the front desk for directions to the zoo and departed, a mother and son on an outing. None of them returned to the Midtown apartment.

Since joining The Resistance, Thaddeus planned every detail of their potential escape. Using fake credentials, he paid cash for a large SUV and drove it straight to a parking garage three blocks from their apartment. He and Claire found the vehicle covered in a year's worth of dust and New York City grime, but it had a tankful of gas and turned over on the first crank, since the king's ransom he paid in parking fees included a weekly start. Thaddeus drove around the city and picked up his passengers at their prearranged meeting places. By 11:00 am, they were on their way to Rephidim.

Weeks after the attack in Thyatira Woods, the residents of Rephidim held a townhall to discuss the merits and drawbacks of opening a road in and out of the sanctuary village. Many argued the Iron King blessed Rephidim because it remained apart from Alanthia and its rebellion, and opening access made them no better than Bezetha, their sister village, who fell into temptation and was now indistinguishable from everywhere else in the kingdom. Others asserted that if the technology ban stayed in place, an emergency evacuation road would not bring Rephidim down. Tearful mothers argued their sons and daughters might visit more often if they had easier access, since the only way into the village was either on foot or on horseback. Tempers flared, voices raised, and both sides entrenched. Ernst ben Otto led the "no" side with booming rhetoric and dire warnings. He escaped Endor; his wife and daughter had not. Dr. ben Hagen led the "yes" side, making a compelling case for public safety.

In the end, the most convincing argument came from the least likely source, Esmeralda's mother, Julianna. She rose to address the town on trembling knees, unaccustomed to public speaking. She was a simple lady with a kind heart and apple cheeks, who made the most amazing Brown Betty anyone at the church potluck suppers ever tasted.

"I moved to Rephidim when Claude and I married in September of '73." She smiled shyly at her husband, who squeezed her fingers in encouragement. "I had just turned eighteen, and like some of you, I grew up in Bezetha. So, since I have lived in both places, I think I can speak on the subject."

A general murmur of agreement rose from those gathered. Julianna met Eve's sparkling blue eyes and continued, "It is the leadership here that makes us different. The men and women of Rephidim are good, upstanding, and God-fearing, who chose to live in the light. The people of Bezetha," she hung her head, "including many in my own family, have not."

Throats cleared, heads bowed, and people shifted in their seats. Every family in attendance had their rebels.

Julianna's cheeks blazed, but her voice rang with sincerity. "I held my daughter's hand as we watched her husband slowly bleed to death after the Endorites attacked. No road brought that evil to our door, yet it came." She turned to Ernst and said, "What would you have given that day for a road to take Thaddeus to safety?"

The measure passed by an overwhelming margin and construction began.

Thaddeus' SUV bumped along the farm roads in rural Pennsylvania, approaching Thyatira Woods. Securely strapped into car seats on the third row, Claire slept, while Richard peppered them with questions. When Mack informed him they were once again hiding from the bad guys, the questions became whispers but did not stop.

Thaddeus shot Esmeralda a sidelong glance that begged the unspoken question, 'Does that kid ever shut up?'

Esmeralda covered a smile and stared out the window, finding the dairy cows suddenly very interesting.

Lavinia understood her son's inquisitive nature, so she answered all his questions. She did not patronize, never lost her patience, and often gave complex answers he absorbed like a sponge.

"Mr. ben Todd, where will I sleep?" Richard asked.

Thaddeus looked in the rearview mirror at the little chatterbox and said, "Likely at Grandma Eve's. She's a very good friend of mine."

Richard drew his eyebrows down and crossed his arms over his chest.

Blessed silence filled the cabin.

A few minutes later, Richard started kicking the back of Mack's seat.

Mack twisted around, irritated. "Quit it."

Richard stopped but glared at his father.

"What's that look about?" Mack asked. Having learned the father's fine art of tuning out, he had not been listening to his son's incessant dialogue.

Richard bulled up at him. "You're dumping me."

Mack drew back. "What?"

"You're taking me to a grandma and leaving me to go fight the bad guys," Richard said, brimming with indignation. "I know how this shit works."

"Language!" Lavinia scolded.

Esmeralda and Thaddeus both tried not to laugh. Esmeralda was more successful than Thaddeus.

"Your momma's right, watch your language, and we're not dumping you. Part of fighting the bad guys is being patient, and sometimes you gotta lie low, like you did with Pappa Tony and Nanna Violet. This time we are staying together, at least for now." Mack would not lie. There was a distinct possibility that they might have to leave Richard behind for his own safety. "I expect you to understand that."

"Daddy, I am only 1345 days old. My frontal cortex is not fully developed."

Mack pointed at Lavinia. "This is your fault. That, right there, is your fault."

Lavinia laughed.

Thaddeus chuckled and called to the back, "You'll like Grandma Eve, Richard. She makes the best biscuits you have ever tasted, and pies, oh the pies."

Richard, who had a sweet tooth, perked up. His mother always tried to trick him, doing things like putting spinach in the brownies, but he could tell the difference. "Does she make apple pie with crumbles? That's my favorite."

"My mom does," Esmeralda said. "And my dad says it's lip-smacking good."

Thaddeus grimaced. "That is disgusting."

Mischief danced in Esmeralda's eyes, as she smacked her lips at him.

"Quit." Thaddeus shuddered and redirected his attention back to the road, searching for the hidden entrance. According to the hand-drawn map Claude sent, they should be approaching soon. "Keep an eye out for the road," he said, passing the map to Esmeralda.

"You've got about five minutes. It should be over that ridge." She shook her head and muttered, "I cannot believe they built it where they did. We will drive right past Endor."

"According to your father, they held quite a debate about it, but the primary purpose of the road was emergency medical evacuations." He rolled his shoulder in unconscious remembrance. "And the most direct route to New York is through Endor." He looked in the rearview mirror, directing his next comment to Mack. "You've got to give it to them. They've got balls."

"All boys have testicles," Richard blurted. "Mine feel like marbles when I squish them in the bathtub, but they don't have hair on them like my daddy's."

Mack turned crimson, Lavinia covered her eyes, and the ben Todd family laughed out loud.

Crush - Rephidim

The return of Thaddeus ben Todd to Rephidim prompted a village-wide gathering. The residents hugged Esmeralda, welcomed Mack with open arms, cooed over baby Claire, and embraced Richard and Lavinia as honored guests, but they rejoiced over Thaddeus. His ordeal shook them all, and to see him hale and hearty, instead of blue and exsanguinating, was a restoration worthy of celebration.

Richard hid behind his momma, staring at his new surroundings in wide-eyed wonder. Rephidim looked like a picture in one of his books, a fairytale land, where brightly dressed ladies gathered together to laugh and set tables full of yummy food. Everything sparkled, unspoiled by cars, trash, or sour-faced men. Even in winter, it felt warm, and there were flowers blooming everywhere and leaves on the trees. The grass tickled his fingers and felt soft like the barn cat's fur. There were lots of children playing, and he wanted to join them, but felt shy, so he peeked around his mother's legs and watched.

A dark-eyed little girl, wearing a red curly ribbon and a blue dress, skipped over and offered her hand. "Do you want to play?"

Richard looked up at his mother with serious brown eyes, questioning but hopeful. "Can I?"

She smiled and said, "Sure."

"What's your name?" he asked. "I'm Richard."

"I'm Betsy. I live over there." She pointed to a small house on the third row with a green door. "We gonna play hide and seek. Are you a good hider?"

Richard grinned and said, "I'm a good finder." He sent Lavinia an impish look and scampered off.

Mack moved beside her, rested his hand on the small of her back, and watched his son disappear into the throng. "He will be fine."

Lavinia backhanded a tear. "I've never let him go off by himself."

"He's not by himself, and I'll keep an eye on him," Mack assured her. "Go on over and meet Ernst ben Otto. He's the local historian. You'll like him."

Lavinia clenched her hands at her sides, an internal battle raging. She wanted to stick close to her son, to stand beside him, and protect him. There were older children in the group. He might be hurt. They might call him names or make fun of his accent, which was so different from their own. "Don't let them be mean to him." She turned, keeping a rigid spine, exercising more courage than she had when they went into battle with Erica.

Krish, the Indian Opie who worked at the mill, sidled up to Mack as Lavinia walked away, a dazed expression on his face. "Is that enchanting creature your wife?"

Mack turned, giving the man a warning glare. "She is."

Krish blinked and found himself under the spell of the lovely Lavinia ben Anthony, where he kept company with a hundred other poor souls before him. "Wow, she is beautiful."

"You still living over at Eve's?" Mack asked, suddenly doubting the wisdom of putting his gorgeous wife under the same roof with this doe-eyed, horny bastard.

Krish's mouth hung slack, and he could not take his eyes off Lavinia. "Uh-huh."

"Dammit," Mack said and stalked off, determined to see if he could find a house to rent.

Doctor ben Hagen hugged Thaddeus like he was a long-lost son, which startled Thaddeus, who had only a passing acquaintance with the man in the years he live in Rephidim.

"Oh, it does my heart good to see you, it truly does." The doctor enthused. "How are you? Have you recovered fully?"

It did not take a detective to read the situation. Thaddeus had vague memories of being shot but remembered nothing of the ordeal until he woke up in the hospital a day and a half later. He knew what the bullet had done to his body, but never asked about the details of his medical drama. But as the doctor beamed at him, Thaddeus realized he must have played a major role in keeping him alive. Suddenly ashamed, he realized he had never thanked the man. "I still have my arm and my life. Thank you, Doctor."

The country doctor flushed. "I did what I could, which was limited in a cave." The lines that bracketed his mouth deepened. "Your friend arriving with the plasma helped stabilize you. I'm just thankful we did not have to perform surgery in my office."

Thaddeus glanced at the small doctor's office and knew without a doubt he would not have survived if they had been forced to operate on him there. The best surgeons in the region, using the latest medical technology spent six hours working on him, and even they could not repair all the damage.

"We have upgraded the facilities since, and I've made several trips into New York City to refresh my skills." He looked down at his shoes and added quietly, "I never want to go through that again."

Thaddeus let out a hollow laugh. "That makes two of us."

Doctor ben Hagen raised his chin and pressed his lips in a grim smile. "It was a terrible thing that happened to you, Thaddeus, but much good has come from it." He gestured to the road where the SUV sat, parked beyond the fifth ring of Rephidim. "We had a baby present transverse breech last month, and we used the road. Mother and child are safe." He pointed to a young lady holding a bundle. "They might not have been otherwise. We have never had one of those here."

"Why do you think that is?" Thaddeus asked, troubled by the prospect. Life outside was brutal, but he always gained a measure of comfort knowing Rephidim stayed isolated and safe.

Doctor ben Hagen looked around and answered in a hushed voice, "The others do not see, and I do not say, but there is more sickness here than there used to be. We have three cases of cancer right now."

Thaddeus rubbed the back of his neck. "Since the attack?"

Doctor ben Hagen nodded, solemn and serious.

"Thanks for the warning. We will be on our guard."

Across the square he saw Eve, moving slow, but with a purpose. His heavy mood evaporated. "Excuse me, Doctor."

He jogged across the square, and she threw her arms wide. She looked thin, but her lively blue eyes sparkled with delight, and he could tell she had taken the time to put on her best pantsuit and do her hair. "Oh, welcome home, Thaddeus!" She fell into his embrace, and to his surprise, she began to weep.

It startled him. She felt frail in his arms, delicate. Instead of the great bear hug he usually swept her up in, he held her gently as she cried. "Eve," he choked. "Oh, Eve, why didn't you tell me?"

She looked up at him, her head tremor more pronounced, but the light of her indomitable spirit was still shining strong. "I knew you would come home, and I did not want to worry you. Now take me to meet my," her voice broke, "my granddaughter."

Thaddeus squeezed his eyes tight, holding back the tears, trying to compose himself. He blew out a shaky breath and smiled, "She is beautiful, just like you."

Eve nodded, her own tears glimmering, but she refused to wallow in sadness. "I knew she would be."

As he led her by the elbow, she whispered, "If you have a camera, sneak a picture of me with her. I want one." Then she winked and broke free, rushing toward Esmeralda and baby Claire. Eve did not plan to waste a second.

Part 17 - Uprising

February 2, 1000 ME

The Longest Mile - London - Kayah

Kayah heard the first explosion as she sat on her back patio petting Mr. Mumps. The noise startled the cat, who darted away, disappearing into a tall patch of fountain grass. Kayah jumped to her feet, the hairs on her body standing on end. Cursing herself as a fool for drinking tea and visiting with her cat while Reuben escorted the Princes to the Embassy, she ran inside. She should have known better, should have been prepared for violence. Korah was bound to make a move, and it did not surprise her he did it when the Princes were not on Alanthian soil.

She jerked open her closet door and pulled out a pair of gray pants and a thin, warm tunic, both the color of London. Dressed and heavily armed, she flew down the steps, intending to head for the Embassy on foot.

Outside, she heard a full-blown battle in the distance, screaming, gunfire, and explosions. She ran toward it with her heart racing. Out of the morning fog, a cloaked rider bore down on her, hoofbeats thundering on the ancient cobblestones. He unsheathed a wicked blade and raised his arm. Kayah crouched and fired, hitting the jihadist between his black eyes. His head exploded, ripping his hood back and throwing him from his mount.

With the grace of a cat, she leapt from her crouched combat position, grabbed the dangling reins, and pulled the horse to a halt. Pedestrians screamed and scattered while she fought to control the wild-eyed, prancing gelding.

Another pair of black-clad riders raced up the street, cutting down everyone in their path. Kayah mounted the horse and fired; the two terrorists fell dead. She galloped away, recalculating her route to the Embassy, suspecting more jihadists were coming her way. Sirens blared in the distance, and a portentous column of smoke rose from Kensington. Red buses careened through the narrow streets, crowding frightened commuters and early morning walkers. A carriage tipped over, blocking the road, as crowds and vehicles clogged her passage to the Embassy. Riding hard, Kayah dodged panic-stricken pedestrians, fleeing the chaos and blood. Breaking glass and the hissing trails of gunfire caused her to bend low in the saddle and spur the horse harder.

She knew a direct approach to the Embassy would be futile, if not fatal. They would be in full lockdown, and if she rode onto the grounds, they might shoot her on sight, but she had to get to Reuben, to make sure he was safe. If they attacked the caravan, if Josiah was dead, then so was Reuben. The smoke billowing into the London sky seemed ominous, its source near the route they would have taken from the airport.

For the first time in her adult life, Kayah prayed.

Urging the horse forward, she fixed her destination firmly in her mind, St. Govor's Well and the secret entrance to the Embassy. She barreled down Portobello and spotted a jihadist menacing a young mother and her baby. Kayah pulled her weapon and fired. Blood sprayed from his chest as his sword clattered to the sidewalk, spinning at the terrified mother's feet. The woman ran away, screaming and clutching her baby to her breast.

Someone shouted, and Kayah glanced around, as half a dozen mounted jihadists came at her from all directions.

But they did not know who they pursued.

She pulled the reins hard, stood up in the stirrups, and aimed. Her vision changed. Everything slowed down. Falling back on her training, she took a deep breath as her heart slowed and her senses sharpened. One rider pulled back, recognizing death when he saw it, surprised it was blonde and beautiful.

An icy February wind blew through the blood-soaked streets,

smelling of copper and fire. It lifted her hair in a golden halo, and Kayah ben Samuel blazed like an avenging angel. She stared directly into their black eyes before she sent them all straight to Hell.

When the last rider fell, an eerie quiet swept through the street.

Kayah ejected the clip from her spent weapon and loaded a new one.

An elderly woman in a blue wool coat stared up at her. "Oh, my! Who are you, dearie?"

Kayah took her seat, as a familiar cold calm settled on her shoulders. "Kayah ben Morte." She nodded toward a bakery. "Get inside. There will be more."

Without a backward glance, she spurred the horse and rode into the heart of the Battle of London.

No Mere Hacker - New City - Himari and Genevieve

"Is a sneaky bastard, eh?" Himari mumbled under her breath, using Filippo's accent. She did it regularly, figuring if she could not speak to him, she would let his words echo in her mind. Voicing them aloud, bound them to her heart. She would not lose him. That simple determination drove her, pushed her through the mind-numbing exhaustion of analyzing millions of lines of code, searching.

She discovered the intruder's tracks after taking four hours of restless sleep. First, she sealed the minute crack in the system, locked it down, and admitted with grudging admiration that whoever broke through their layers of security did so with near-supernatural skill, a chilling thought. Attempting to trace the intruder backward, the path it took her down elicited a groan.

"Auntie," Himari called, "we have a problem."

Genevieve looked up from her study of the journals Lavinia sent. Since the breach, she directed her attention to cracking the code, leaving Himari to her computer work. While she had value monitoring the systems, relaying messages, and was an indispensable asset to The Resistance, she was not a computer analyst. "Did you find it?"

"I did." Himari nodded, her skin sallow and pale, dark circles of fatigue bagged under her almond-shaped eyes. "Whoever it was, I think Erica has been there, too."

"Oh, my heavens." Genevieve left her table, coming to Himari's side.

"It came from here." Fueled with caffeine and adrenaline, Himari's finger shook as she pointed to a map. "Baker's Corners."

The old section of the city sprawled to the east of Prince Eamonn Park, home to thousands of small apartments, old businesses, and run-down hotels. Genevieve peered at the map and asked. "Do you know where?"

Himari rested her chin in her hand. "No. The hacker scrubbed his tracks into and out of the system. I did well to follow the path back as close as this. It's like footprints the tide has washed over, only a trace remains." She looked up with pleading eyes. "It is the best I can do."

"Then you set up the protocols necessary to keep them out. Have the alarms trigger if they try it again, just as you have with the Palace. You fought Erica and won. No hacker is a match for you, *shojo*."

"This was no mere hacker; this has shades of her." She pointed to the monitor on her left. "No one should have been able to breach our firewalls, no one. Alaina put three more levels of security on our systems, so we now have eight layers of encryption protecting us down here."

"There is more than encryption protecting us, and you know it. Do your best, but get us back online, we have a revolution to run." Genevieve turned, lest she reveal how Himari's words rocked her. "Get to work, Sunflower."

My Prince - London - Reuben

"Move aside. I must go!" Reuben ben Judah shouted to the guard blocking his path out of the Embassy. "I have done my duty, but my fiancée is one mile from here. I will go to see that she is safe."

"Stand down, Agent ben Judah," Prince Yehonathan ordered in a quiet voice.

Reuben whirled. "I will not! It is not safe for her. The entire city is at war. I will not abandon her to it."

"Kayah ben Samuel is perfectly capable of taking care of herself."

"Against jihadists, against a marauding horde?" Reuben stalked over to his Prince, heedless of the direct defiance or the consequences. "Have you forgotten what they took from me, that you would issue such an order?"

"Lower thy voice." Yehonathan drew himself up in effrontery. "Hast thou been amongst the Alanthians so long that thou hast forgotten how to address thy Prince?"

Reuben's nose flared, and he snarled back, "Has my Prince

forgotten thy love? Wouldst thou command me to cower in safety to await the news of my beloved's slaughter? Wouldst thou order it such if it was thy beloved in peril?"

Yehonathan raised a straight salt and pepper eyebrow and said, "Princess Rebekkah is not a trained assassin, Agent ben Judah."

The sound of gunfire and chaos drifted in from the street a hundred yards from where they stood. Reuben turned to Yehonathan, pleading, "The blood of Jews stains the ground of every continent on Earth. They will target her, my Prince. They knowest where we live, that I am a Jew, and she is my beloved. That is the manner of evil, how it operates. Whilst they cloak themselves in righteousness, they remaineth who they have always been. As I stand before thee now, our residence may be under siege. Kayah may be trapped." He fell to a knee, his head bent in supplication. "I beg of thee, release me."

"She is unworthy of thee." Yehonathan shook his head. "I am sorry, Agent. I cannot permit it."

Unholy rage erupted in Reuben. Supplicated on his knees, he wanted to drive his fist into the Prince's belly and rush the door. He raised his head and looked directly into Yehonathan's eyes, brimming with fury and desolation.

Yehonathan regarded him with cold, unblinking eyes and something inside Reuben broke; the loyalty and bond that held him to this man snapped. He rose, no longer seeking permission. "Then Yehonathan," he said, "you have my resignation. As you say, I have been among the Alanthians too long."

Only the sound of his boot heels filled the hall as Reuben ben Judah walked away, each step an echo, symbolizing the monumental, life-changing decision he just made. He strode through the corridors with his heart pounding, furious, but oddly calm. Climbing the stairs, he sought the man who had saved his life and earned his allegiance every moment they served together, his brother, his friend, his Prince—Josiah ben Eamonn of Alanthia.

Peter and Josiah met in the hallway, both shaken from the attack on their caravan, but full of resolve and prepared for their audience with Prince Yehonathan. The meeting was the first of a dozen planned for the next few days, and the chaos raining outside the Embassy walls lent a new urgency to their mission.

Reuben strode toward them, his face flaming, and without preamble, knelt at Josiah's feet and said, "I have resigned my commission with Mossad and from this day forward, I swear my allegiance unto you. You have my sword, my shield, and my honor. I am at thy service, bound to thee as my sovereign, Prince Josiah ben Eamonn."

He looked up, an Israeli ready for battle. "I know Kayah. She is out in this. I seek thy permission to retrieve her and bring her to safety. If thou willst not grant it, I ask thee to refrain from accepting my vow of service until I return."

Josiah drew back in shock at the unprecedented declaration. But he recovered with the instincts of a field commander, understanding the hotheaded nature of his friend and the passion that could drive a man to make such a vow. "Reuben ben Judah, my brother, I am humbled and honored by thy words and thy offer. We shall discuss this further with cool heads. But first," he smiled, "let us rescue thy beloved. We will not avenge more of thy family's blood."

Reuben rose and embraced Josiah in a back pounding hug. "Be it as you say, my Prince."

"Bloody Hell. Let me get my coat." Peter turned from the pair and retreated into his apartment where an Embassy servant was unpacking his belongings.

"Hand me the black jacket there." He shrugged it on and switched his Italian loafers for boots. He did not bother to change out of his silk trousers and cashmere sweater but took a second to remove his tie. Gratified to see his favorite weapon in its old case sitting in the corner, he picked it up and headed out to fight.

Reuben paced outside, looking resolute and fierce.

Josiah joined a moment later, kissing Davianna on her pale cheek. Peter glanced at Astrid's door and said, "Tell Red I will be back later."

She nodded and picked up Benny, who wiggled in her arms with delight. As the threesome ran down the hall, Benny's inquisitive bark masked their footfalls, and Davianna called, "Be careful."

Rain of Fire - London - Kayah

Kayah rode, leaving the jihadists in the distance, however she found new trouble as anarchists slithered out of their holes. Less intent on murder, they set their sights on destruction. Molotov cocktails rained down like meteorites. Pierced and tattooed thugs slung bats and shattered glass. A rock caught her in the ear, and her hand came away bloody. She fought the urge to shoot the stone throwing bastard but saved her bullets.

Kayah cursed the wall-to-wall buildings that offered no sanctuary for the fleeing horse. The streets of London became a gauntlet to run. She pushed the horse as fast as she dared, dodging debris, glass, and terrified people. Far from abating, the noise and violence escalated.

She cleared an alley in time to see a yellow compact car jump an embankment and sail across the intersection of Pembridge and Holland Park Avenue. Jihadists swarmed the overturned vehicle, pulled a bloodied and dazed young girl from the front seat, and slit her throat. Kayah reined hard to the left and spurred her horse toward Hyde Park.

Vehicle traffic ground to a halt. Cars crashed as panicked pedestrians ran straight into their paths. Police whistles and sirens drowned out the pounding hoofbeats and screams of the victims. Kayah heard nothing but her own breath and that of the horse. She took her mount down to a rapid trot. Posting up, she kept low over the saddle, scanning the area for threats.

She saw a gang emerge from a side alley, twenty thugs in scarves and gloves, dressed in black, intent on mayhem. An enormous man, in a shirt with the sleeves ripped off, raised a black flag with a jagged "A" inside a ring of blood. He aimed it straight at Kayah and shouted, "Get 'er sorted, mates!"

The leader…

She blew his head off from forty paces. It exploded in a shower of skull and brains, covering his fellows, who scattered like cockroaches.

"Come on, boy. Let's get out of here. I've had enough fun for the day," Kayah said to the horse, ducking low over the saddle. The second she did, a bullet brushed through her hair to the left. She pulled hard to the right and turned over her shoulder. The anarchists were regrouping. One of them had a motorcycle and a weapon.

Using her mount as a shield, Kayah slid off the side of her saddle. The trotting motion and the awkward angle made the shot difficult. She knew if the anarchist got a line on her, the motorcycle could outdistance her winded horse, and if he did, she was as good as dead. She expelled her breath, using the pommel to steady the weapon. Her pursuer lost his mask in the scuffle, or it had his friend's brains on it and he threw it off; she did not know which, but she could see his ugly fat face. He came into focus over her sights, pale gray eyes, a gap between his front teeth, a bulbous alcoholic nose. He looked like the prison guard, Stubby, the rapist. Kayah concentrated on the space between his front teeth and fired. It was the horse. Her aim was off.

Instead of blowing his teeth back into his skull, she shot him square between the eyes.

Motorcycle and weapon skidded across the road. His comrades did not spare their fallen mate a second thought. One of them, a dirty tattooed man in his twenties, snatched up the weapon and fired. His shot went wild, and Kayah did not waste a second giving him a better target. She pulled herself back into the saddle and kicked the horse again.

The green of Hyde Park beckoned like a sanctuary. "Come on, boy," she urged. Her thighs screamed, her chest tightened, and she gulped for air. It had been years since she rode, and her body sang a brutal song of burning pain.

She heard the motorcycle a split second before it overtook her. Her attacker came up fast on her left. She pulled her third pistol from the holster under her arm, turned and fired, nearly blind, instinctive. The rider clutched blood splatter from his neck and fell off the bike. This time, no one pursued.

She gave Kensington Palace a wide berth since the European Royal Guard had formed a human wall around the royal residence. Making a beeline for St. Govor's Well, a well-dressed gentleman ran in front of her. She had to veer sharply to avoid trampling him. Clutching his leather briefcase to his chest like a shield, he failed to notice her. He wore the look of a man who had just witnessed death and could not process what he had seen.

Kayah pressed onwards as the ancient well came into sight. Hope.

The winded horse stumbled, nearly unseating her. The sudden falter saved her life. A bullet grazed her left side. Had she been upright, it would have pierced her heart. She looked beneath her arm and saw three jihadists emerge from the trees. Their mounts were fresh, hers winded and stumbling.

One hundred yards from her destination, the horse took a bullet. Its knees buckled, and it went down hard. Thrown from the saddle, she sailed through the air. When she hit the ground, Kayah knew she was not going to make it.

Tunnels - London – Reuben, Peter, and Josiah

With the Embassy barricaded, Josiah and Reuben knew they had one way out. Deep beneath London lay a series of ancient aqueducts, rivers, and tunnels. Begun by the Romans in the First Age, buried by generations of growth, construction, wars and conflagrations, a secret passage from St. Govor's Well led to an underground entrance to the Golden Kingdom's Embassy. Reuben brought Josiah through the watery tunnel two-and-a-half months before, and that was how they planned to escape.

Peter, who was not privy to their unspoken plan, took it in stride, having spent a large part of his childhood hiding in such places. Armed and ready, the trio sprinted in a soldier's run through the dark tunnel with the sound of lapping water a foot to their right. Reuben led the way, his flashlight bouncing with every footfall, his urgency growing by the second.

"I will go first," Reuben said, pressing the ancient stone pattern that opened the well to the outside world. He squinted against the abrupt change in light. The sound of gunfire greeted them the instant the passageway opened. He swore in Hebrew and lifted his head above the stones to get a better look. Bellowing a mighty war cry, he fired, and his feet disappeared as he ran headlong into the fight.

Josiah moved to follow, but Peter grabbed his arm and pulled him backward. "No, Prince! You stay here unless I call." He bounded up the steps with his assault rifle poised and ready.

Josiah watched him disappear up the stairway in open-mouthed shock. A shower of bullets erupted from his cousin's weapon.

Josiah climbed the steps, not willing to cower while other men fought, but as he cleared the ancient well, silence reigned in Hyde Park. With his weapon still smoking, Reuben sprinted toward a bedraggled, but very much alive, Kayah ben Samuel. She struggled to her feet from behind a barricade of a dead horse. Three jihadists lay on the ground, mere yards away. Peter covered their retreat as Josiah came alongside, his weapon aimed and ready.

Reuben scooped Kayah up and threw her over his shoulder, running full speed back to the well, his face black thunder. "Get inside!" he yelled in Hebrew, his English deserting him in the crisis.

Josiah handed Peter his weapon, taking Kayah to free Reuben to close the passageway.

She wrapped her shaking arms around his neck, her breath coming in deep gasps. "Hi," she panted.

"Hi." Josiah guarded her head and descended the narrow steps. In the small confines, he smelled gunpowder, blood, and horses. Kayah reeked of war. "Are you wounded?"

"Not bad." She rested her head against his cheek. "Couple of close calls, though. I may be hit; you know how that goes."

"I do." Memories of Reuben's leg wound flashed through his mind. He had operated on a dozen soldiers who, in the heat of battle, never realized they had been shot. If she had a doubt, there was a good chance she was hit. "Get the light," he called as the passageway closed.

"Yakira, are you hurt?" Reuben shouted down the steps.

Josiah answered, the doctor taking command. "Not bad, Reuben, but I need to check her out. Let's get her to the Embassy."

Reuben leapt down the ladder, took Kayah out of Josiah's arms, and pressed a quick kiss to her pale cheek. Above them, the Battle of London raged.

Infirmary - London - Josiah, Reuben, and Kayah

The foursome burst into the infirmary, startling the nurse, who jumped out of her chair with a squeak. "The doctor is outside! I'll get him. Take her into an exam room."

"I've got her." Josiah's royal command brooked no argument. "She is one of mine. I will see to her care."

The nurse looked around, not sure how to react. Falling back on protocol, she made a respectful bow and demurred. "I am at your service, my Esteemed."

"Prince, inform Davianna we have returned unharmed. I will attend to her as soon as I am able. Have my medical bag sent." To Reuben, he said, "Agent, wait in the hall. Nurse, please join me." When neither man moved, Josiah barked, "Now!"

Laying Kayah carefully on the examination table, he stripped off his jacket and washed his hands. The nurse came in, bearing medical instruments and a clean coat. He shrugged it on with thanks.

Kayah huddled on her side, exhausted and sore, but her color was good and her breathing normal. Her gray tunic was torn and bloody. He lifted her shirt and saw the wound, singed and oozing, but not life threatening. He checked her pulse, rapid but strong. Her pupils were responsive, and she was lucid. Blood covered the side of her neck and face from a nasty gash on her ear that looked like it would require a stitch or two. "I'll step out while you get undressed. Nurse, stay with her."

Outside, he found Reuben guarding the door.

"She is okay?"

"Yes, she appears to be. I will do a full exam, but the worst of it is a laceration on her side."

Reuben covered his eyes, blowing out a lengthy breath. "She was out of ammunition. Three of those pigs were bearing down on her and she was out of bullets!" Josiah rested his hand against Reuben's shoulder. Reuben turned, his eyes desolate. "He would have left her out there to die."

"But she did not," Josiah countered.

Reuben dropped his chin to his chest, nodding.

"We are ready for you, Doctor," the nurse said from the open doorway.

Josiah patted Reuben's shoulder. "I'll be back."

Kayah was lucky, or better stated, she was fortunate because there was nothing lucky about the skill she exhibited on her heroic charge to the Embassy. The gash in her ear took two stitches, the graze on her side had to be cleaned of gray fibers but required only a pressure bandage. For the bruises on her elbows, knees, thighs, and ribs, Josiah applied arnica ointment and gave her a mild painkiller.

"You will be fine." Josiah pulled off his gloves when he finished. "Do you have any lingering injuries from the car accident?"

Kayah looked at him, confused, then realized he was referring to the story Reuben told him about her injuries in Vegas. "No, all healed up."

Josiah glanced at the nurse. "Will you excuse us, please?"

The nurse bobbed a curtsy and left.

"I wanted to thank you for what you did on New Year's Eve," he said, staring into her interesting hazel eyes. They were rimmed with blue, but the irises shifted from amber to green, depending on the light and her emotions. Even injured and tired, she was lovely. However, there was much more to Kayah than just a pretty face. She was an enigma, a complicated, complex woman.

"New Year's Eve?" she asked.

"Yes. If you had not stopped Korah, we would not be here right now. The whole escape would have fallen apart. There were many acts of bravery that night, but yours, Kayah, stands out in my mind as the greatest demonstration of cunning, intelligence, and courage. We owe you our lives."

He smiled and took her elegant hand in his. "As such, I will reward your valor by bestowing upon you a royal pardon. Any past transgressions you have committed are null and void. You are immune from prosecution for any crime you may have committed before this date. Your record will be expunged, and all rights as a full and upstanding citizen of Alanthia are restored unto you."

His unexpected pronouncement caught her completely by surprise. "A pardon?"

"Indeed." Josiah gave her hand a gentle squeeze.

Her chest heaved as she blurted, "Will you do the same for my friend Gus?" She closed her eyes against a swell of grief. "It would be posthumous, but they declared him incompetent. He was not."

Josiah's eyes crinkled at the edges when he smiled. "Yes, of course. Reuben told me about your friend. I am sorry for your loss."

Kayah nodded and sniffed back a tear. "I am pardoned?" she asked tentatively, exploring what that simple word would mean in her life.

"Yes, you are."

The authority in his voice and the regal set of his shoulders inspired a confidence that felt foreign but precious to her. He radiated integrity and honor, and in him, she sensed no deception. She never had. Moistening her lips, she looked down and said, "I need to tell you something."

"Go ahead." Josiah sat back in his chair, feigning relaxation, praying he would not regret what he had just done.

"Sir Preston ben Worley, your attorney?" She wiped her nose, meeting his eyes. "Do not trust him. Stay as far away from him and his machinations as you can." Kayah added in a barely audible whisper, "Auntie G says so, too."

"Well then, I will take it on good authority."

Kayah reached out a trembling hand. For three years, she skirted the edges of The Resistance. Taking part initially out of boredom, and because Lavinia was involved. She wanted to monitor things, to protect her friends, but she never fully committed. For Kayah, The Resistance provided an interesting diversion, but the cause did not burn in her heart. That changed when she met Reuben. Through him, she witnessed the type of love and loyalty that inspired a person to put their life on the line for something greater than self. In November, Sir Preston gave her a personal reason to fight for Josiah's restoration, but today, sitting with this man, she recognized all her earlier motivations amounted to nothing. He inspired true fealty, and as a fully restored citizen of her kingdom, she owed him her loyalty.

"My Esteemed," her voice caught, "thank you. You do not understand what this means to me. But I want you to know even if you had not… not granted me a pardon. I would still do everything I could to see you on the Alanthian throne. I pledge to you, my faithful troth."

Josiah's eyes registered his surprise at her unexpected declaration.

He took her hand and bowed over it. "I am honored to accept, Kayah ben Samuel. I consider it a great blessing to have you on my side."

Kayah flushed. "I have a certain set of skills, my Esteemed." The hint of an affectionate smile hovered. "I surmise you will not put them to use as others have in the past, and for that, I am grateful."

Josiah pressed his lips together, hiding his own smile. "Oh, that is regrettable. You made an admirable sidekick for Carsten ben Hansen."

She laughed, which hurt. Flinching, she said, "Reuben liked my boots."

Josiah had a sudden vision of her wearing those boots and a bikini. Heat rose up his neck and he moved to the sink to wash his hands. "I appreciate all you have done." He turned and gave her a smile. "And you were nice to my dog."

Her eyes widened.

"I did not forget, Kayah. You shocked me that night, but that was your plan, wasn't it?"

"I have my moments."

"I suppose you do," Josiah deadpanned. "Had I known you were Reuben's girlfriend, I might have figured out who was tailing me… and the girls."

"Congratulations on your marriage, by the way. They are all here? Everyone is safe?"

"Indeed. Speaking of Davianna, I must assure her I am fine. She will be worried. Though I suspect our mutual friend is keeping her company."

"Mutual friend?" she asked, tentatively leaning back on the narrow bed, exhausted.

"My dog."

"Benny?" Kayah lit up. "That's right, he is here. I would love to see him."

"We have dinner tonight with Prince Yehonathan, but I'll bring him down when I check in on you in the morning."

"The morning? You are going to keep me here all night?"

He lifted a shoulder and turned toward the door. "Just a precaution, Kayah, to make sure you have no internal injuries that have escaped our notice. Being thrown from a horse bears watching, and I need you in top form."

Their eyes locked.

"Get some rest. I am going to see about getting my kingdom back."

Shot of the Day

Junior photojournalist Alexander ben Dean knew he had to pay his dues at his new job, so while he was not thrilled with his assignment the morning of February 2nd, he took it without grumbling and figured he could grab a takeaway curry at that fantastic Indian joint in Notting Hill afterward. It was a fluff piece about the opening of a museum in the newly restored Darling House, where James Matthew Barrie penned the Last Age classic *Peter Pan*. He had only taken a few exterior pictures when the violence erupted.

He abandoned the museum and rushed into the chaos. The sound of gunfire drew his attention and his lens. He captured a beautiful blonde in a military-style crouch, aiming a weapon at a black-cloaked rider. Alexander snapped his photos in rapid succession, capturing the athletic grace of the woman as she seized the horse and swung into the saddle. On foot, he chased her down, using her hair as a guiding light amid the chaos.

He caught up as a group of terrorists surrounded her. When she rose in the saddle, he captured a surreal moment. A cold London wind swept up the street, lifting her hair, and showing her fine profile in silhouette as she aimed her weapon. Chills ran down his spine, while he watched her annihilate five more jihadists, each with a single bullet to the head.

Alexander knew, in that instant, he had the story of the morning, paying his dues be damned.

A crowd gathered around the blonde and her mount, seeking shelter. She spoke to an old woman and cantered away. He ran toward them, snapping as many pictures as he could without getting trampled. "What did she say?" he demanded, framing the old woman's careworn features and glazed expression.

"Blimey! She said 'er name was Kayah ben Morte. She saved me life, saved all our lives. Did you see what she did? I can't Adam and Eve it."

"Cheers!" Alexander called over his shoulder, chasing after Kayah ben Morte and cursing his lack of transportation. A riderless horse danced around the square, agitated by the noise and the stench of blood. He took inspiration from the woman, grabbed the reins, and took off.

A window blew out as he rode past a gift shop, and a mob of anarchists flooded the street ahead of him. He turned the horse around and escaped, protecting his precious camera. Alexander ben Dean knew he had gold.

By 5:20 pm, his editors agreed. London had a mysterious heroine, and they had a story.

When the World Erupts - New City - Himari and Genevieve

A scant two hours after falling asleep, the alarms in the bunker went off. Himari's eyes popped open, and she wanted to cry as her body revolted in protest, quaking in exhaustion, demanding sleep. When she rolled out of bed, her legs gave way, and she collapsed and lay in a heap for a moment, whimpering. Pushing herself up, she stumbled out of the room toward whatever fresh hell the world had in store.

Genevieve hovered over the monitors, moving like a crab between them. Himari sat down in a daze and killed the speakers with shaking fingers. "What tripped?"

"The residences," Genevieve growled. "All of them. Peccioli, Alaina's house, yours, all of them."

Himari began to cry as Korah's goons stormed her and Filippo's condo. "Please leave my paintings. Please leave my paintings," she sobbed. The market value of the series stretched into the millions, but it was more than the money, they were Himari's wedding presents from Filippo.

Tears fell unheeded down her cheeks, as she screamed with impotent fury as a man moved toward the erotic picture. "Look at this, boys!" the swine called to his fellow looters.

Genevieve grabbed Himari around the shoulders and held on, her eyes glued to the screen as the men ransacked Himari's home. "Lord, have mercy. Please stop this. Himari has been through enough. Please do not let them."

The condo's front door flew open with a crash. An otherworldly light filled the screen. Himari and Genevieve both turned away, blinded.

"You will not touch!" a woman ordered in a powerful voice. "Begone or I incinerate you to ashes where you stand."

Genevieve and Himari turned back to the screen. The woman swept her hand across the living room. The paintings flew back into place as the men slammed into the walls. She floated into the room, her hair loose and cascading down her back, moving like black water. She glowed with opalescent beauty, her skin flawless, her features perfect. When she opened her graceful arms, blue flames shot from her fingers and her eyes. "Go!" The camera shook with the force of her command.

The looters trampled each other in their haste, running out the door, crying, and begging for mercy. Himari noticed one had pissed himself. They knocked over a table as they ran, but before it fell and the Japanese vase crashed, the woman flicked a hand, and it righted itself. This seemed to irritate her, and she threw a bolt of blue fire, catching a straggler in the seat of his pants. He screamed and kept running. She slammed the door behind them with a flick of her wrist.

Standing in the silent apartment, the woman turned to the camera and smiled. "You are welcome, Himari." Then she winked and vanished.

Himari moistened her lips, staring at her pristine, empty condo, dumbfounded. "I promise, Auntie, you will never hear me doubt again."

Genevieve nodded, unable to speak.

Turning back to the other monitors, they watched the Alanthian purge unfold before their eyes.

The world caught fire.

February 3, 1000 ME

An Epic 24 Hour News Cycle

As violence swept the globe, stories of extraordinary heroism gave face to the carnage. These ordinary people and their stories anchored the abstract, giving heavy hearts a glimmer of hope. Even during the storm, there was light and valor.

Below the fold, on the front page, a full-color picture of Kayah greeted morning readers. Standing in the stirrups of her dappled gray gelding, outnumbered six to one, she aimed a weapon at the mounted jihadists. Commuters surrounded her, seeking protection, and the headline declared:

The Avenging Angel of Kensington Park

A brief story below the picture documented this mysterious heroine's deeds at the outbreak of the rioting. Continued on page eight, the London paper devoted a full page of the incredible photographs Alexander ben Dean captured as she rode across the city. Had she been a man, the story would have been worthy, but not particularly tantalizing. If she had been plain, it would have been a curiosity. However, Kayah was beautiful, and that made all the difference.

The photos looked like stills from an action movie from the Last Age, a gorgeous female badass, dispatching evil with expertise and skill. A director could not have choreographed the action better. It was epic. The paper sent a bevy of reporters to the scene to gather eyewitness accounts of the Kensington Park Angel's flight. They paid a fortune for three more photographs, taken by a young man with a shaky cell phone camera that depicted her clinging to the side of her horse, aiming a pistol at a motorcyclist.

The residents of Kensington Park Gardens recognized Dorothy ben Quincy, but they came from a class of society that did not speak to the press. While eccentric, she was quiet and fed the community cat. They shunned publicity, so they kept their knowledge to themselves. However, amongst their ranks, they discussed it with avid interest and speculation.

*   *   *   *

At the Embassy, Peter did not sleep well, accustomed to having Astrid by his side. He resented their separate quarters, and if there was not a full-blown riot raging outside, he would have thumbed his nose at stuffy old Prince Yehonathan and taken Astrid to the Ritz.

Rising at 5:00 am, jet-lagged and groggy, Peter dressed for a workout, and went in search of the elixir of life—coffee. He snuck out of his apartment, careful not to wake Reuben, who was bunking on his couch. Since he was no longer Mossad, he refused to sleep in their quarters. Peter thought with wry amusement that Astrid would likely find herself in a similar situation when Josiah discharged Kayah from the infirmary today. The absurdity of two couples sleeping in separate quarters across the hall from one another made him shake his head, yet he understood royal protocol and figured they could abide by their host's wishes for a week.

When he stepped inside the busy kitchen, he shocked the Embassy staff. After his mother died, he delighted in showing up in the Palace kitchens unannounced, though now he understood what a terrible inconvenience that must have been for them. However, he liked the cozy environment and the fawning housekeeper, Edith, who set up a little table in the corner of the busy kitchen and served him weak tea and blueberry scones. The staff grew accustomed to having him in their midst and went about their work.

Today, there was no little table for him to sit at, and he had long since outgrown weak tea, so he accepted a carafe of amazing Israeli coffee with thanks, took the freshly ironed paper, and retreated to a small nook, overlooking the floodlit gardens behind the Embassy. When he opened the paper, he nearly sprayed coffee all over himself. He scanned the article, unable to believe what he was reading, then went to wake the Angel of Kensington Park, chuckling at the irony of anyone dubbing Kayah ben Samuel an angel.

Said angel woke like the devil, highly pissed. "Leave me alone, Peter ben Korah, you little shit."

"Is that any way to speak to someone who brings you coffee and a delicious bit of morning news." He sat down in the chair beside her bed and offered her his cup.

"I hate you," Kayah grumbled through sleep-thickened vocal cords.

In the dim light, he saw the swelling in her face, noticed the bandage covering her ear. She winced and tried to sit up, holding her side, and attempting to keep her gown from gaping open. She gave up, laying back with a groan, and fumbled with the bed to raise it into a sitting position. Giving a speculative sniff, she snatched the coffee from his hand and settled into the pillows. "They know how to make good coffee."

"It is nice. What is that spice?" Peter opened the carafe and inhaled.

"Cardamom." Kayah closed her eyes and relaxed.

"Yes, that is it. Auntie G. makes cookies with it."

"Auntie G. is amazing." She cracked an eye open and glared at him. "She lets hurt people sleep."

"Reuben told me," Peter said quietly.

"Hmm, not one of my fonder memories. Next time you send me to kill someone possessed by a demon, give me a bit of warning, will you, puppy?"

Peter rubbed the stubble on his chin. "We know where it came from now."

Kayah cut her eyes toward him. "Where?"

"Greece."

Kayah stared into the cup and watched the tiny specks of cardamom floating on the surface. "Ah, I guess you are right. Mack sent us the video. I am sorry about your friend, Persa."

"Me, too." Peter pressed his lips together and exhaled through flared nostrils. "Speaking of Persa, it appears that she and James are not my only friends with extraordinary equestrian skills." He handed her the paper.

"Holy shit!" She dropped the paper in her lap, in utter shock, then picked it back up and stared at it, muttering, "Oh no, this is bad."

When she lowered the paper, a light gleamed in her eyes. "Actually… it's not. Your cousin pardoned me last night." She threw back her head and laughed, pointing at the headline. "An angel, me?"

"It gets better, check out page eight." Peter grinned.

She flipped to the full page dedicated to her mad dash.

He watched the play of emotions over her face, amusement, resignation, then disgust. When she finished, she schooled her features, composing them into her typical expression. The corner of his mouth lifted as he recognized the look, one that resided on his own face more often than not, bored cynicism.

"I will say, I was quite peeved at you recently. Though I suppose now that you are an angel, I must forgive you." He quirked a golden eyebrow at her.

She shot one back. "Peeved at me, whatever for? As you say, I am an angel."

"We both know there are two kinds of angels, Kayah."

She grew still, detecting the metal in his voice.

"You knew exactly where Josiah, Davianna, and Astrid were the night they were arrested at Massimo's and kept that information to yourself. Did you not, angel?"

Kayah settled back onto her pillows and crossed her arms, completely unrepentant. "Sorry, puppy, I made a promise."

"To Reuben?" Peter looked at her from beneath his long eyelashes.

She brought her shoulder to her pointed chin and shot him a coy smile. "Of course."

"Count yourself fortunate you were nowhere near me the day I found out. I will not go into depth or detail about what Korah did to Astrid, or the mind fuck he threw on Davianna, or the beating Josiah endured, but the information you held could have prevented all of it."

Her face remained impassive, though there was a slight flair to her nostrils that conveyed her distaste.

"Not to mention," he continued, raising his voice, "had we known where they were that evening, it would have negated the need to rescue them, an operation that put our entire organization at risk!"

She met his eyes, not flinching.

"However," he said calmly, "I have taken into account what you did outside my mother's room the night of our escape, your dispatch of that maggot Guan, and your rescue of Astrid's father. So, we are square."

The corner of her mouth began to lift.

But with shades of Korah, Prince Peter charmed and soothed then struck like a viper, turning dangerous and deadly. He leaned forward and hissed, "Do not cross me again, Kayah."

Kayah did not flinch, meeting him head-on. She respected him, was fond of him, and admired the skills he employed organizing and executing their operations. And while she did not wish to alienate him, she needed to set him straight, so with a rueful smile, she said, "My Esteemed, I hold you in highest regard. We have been allies, and will continue to be, for I would never seek to harm or betray you. But I have never given you a vow of loyalty, nor have I ever inferred such a promise." She paused, letting her words sink in. "I have sworn my oath to your cousin. It is to him I owe my fealty."

The anger in him faded as the wicked gleam in his emerald eyes vanished. He gave her a regal nod of assent. "Aye, as must we all."

Then he rose from the chair and said, "Your servant, madam. Enjoy the coffee."

*   *   *   *

While the world exploded in violence and chaos, newsrooms across the globe picked up the story of the Kensington Park Angel. When Himari brought the bunker back online twelve hours after the story broke, it had grown into a worldwide phenomenon. "Auntie, check this out! It's Kayah!"

Genevieve left her half-poured coffee on the sideboard and came to the monitors. "Oh, my goodness, look at her." She stared at the screen hard, then fell into her seat with a thud. Running her fingers through her hair, she fixated on the screen. "I swear, I am getting old."

Himari turned, surprised at her reaction. "Why do you say that?"

Genevieve covered her mouth, shaking her head. "I keep seeing ghosts."

"Huh?" Himari pointed. "That's Kayah, or it certainly looks like her."

"She's not often blonde, is she? Is that her natural color?" Genevieve asked, sounding haunted.

Himari grew very still. "Yes. She did not begin changing it like she does until we were older, until she left prison."

Genevieve covered her eyes, shaking her head in denial. "How old is she, Himari?"

"I'm thirty-four, which means Kai is thirty-five. Why?" Himari's voice cracked as she took in Genevieve's stunned expression. "What do you see? You are scaring me."

"That is why Sir Preston took such an interest in her!" She bolted from her chair. "Oh, that wicked, conniving old bastard!"

"What are you talking about?" Himari stood up.

Genevieve pointed at the picture, her finger shaking. "If she is who I think she is, she looks exactly like her mother."

*　　*　　*　　*

At 7:00 pm, New York time, another story supplanted the Kensington Park Angel and took over the news cycle, the unmasking of King Korah ben Adam.

Rising super-star reporter, Sondra ben Pierson, delivered a bombshell that rocked the world. Before he disappeared, Alanthia's Minister of Technology and Security, Stephen ben McSwilley, compiled video, photographic, and written evidence that exposed Alanthia's darkest secret.

No one knew Erica mined the Palace's secret archives and Korah's private stores for the evidence. It mattered little who put it together because it damned him. Corruption, torture, and satanic rituals, from the vicious to the mundane, painted a picture so contrary to the benevolent, handsome Alanthian ruler the public could barely fathom the depths of his betrayal and depravity.

By 7:30 pm, the pundits declared Korah's floundering, illegal reign was over.

Korah watched the news by himself, dozens of newspapers spread over his desk, a bottle of brandy by his hand.

He picked up the phone and ordered the Minister of Defense to quadruple the security forces around the grounds, then rose on shaking limbs and went to face his ghosts—alone.

Part 18 – Italians

May 12, 987 ME

Family Ties - Italy

Francesca ben Salvatore did not know why her brother bothered to knock. He burst through the door before she could answer, then again, that had always been his way. "Hello, Lorenzo. Do come in," she said sarcastically.

"Where is he?" Lorenzo ben Salvatore demanded, scanning the room.

"He is gone." Francesca rose from her chair. "I sent him away."

"They will kill him!" Lorenzo shouted. "You have signed his death sentence."

"It is you," she pointed a finger that was not perfectly steady, "who did that. When you bring him into the family—you kill him. Do you think I would let you do that? That I would stand by and do nothing and watch my son die like our father and our brothers?" She glared at him. "We had an agreement. You broke it, so he is gone."

"I did not break our agreement," he protested. "Roberto, he comes to me. He is a grown man and makes his own choices."

Francesca waved him away with disgust. "I know that life. Roberto, he does not. But you try to seduce him, no? You show him the money, the power, the women? But you neglect to tell him the cost, and now?" She set her jaw, fury pulsing off her with every heartbeat. "You would have him swear the oath, to take his blood and bind him to you and that life? No! I will not have it."

"It is too late for your interference! He has made his decision."

"And I have unmade it! You fill his head with false dreams, and in his eagerness to please you, he makes a mistake." She held up a palm in his face. "And it gets him a price on his head."

Lorenzo balled his fists. "They will not kill him if you let him come with me! I can protect him."

Francesca scowled. "From the Martinellis? Do not lie to me, *Fratello*. They have grown too strong, and since *Padre* and Isidoro died, we have grown too weak. You are living in the past! There is no parlay, no Duke to settle disputes between us. The balance of power has shifted, and under you, the Giovannis have lost."

Lorenzo stalked across the room, coming nose-to-nose with her. "You know nothing!"

"Get away from me!" Thousands of men would have cowered in the face of such rage, but Lorenzo ben Salvatore did not scare her. "You are worse than the Martinellis. You are a failure."

"How dare you say such a thing to me!" Lorenzo seized her upper arms, hurting her. "If you would have let Roberto come to me, I would have sent him abroad. He would have been safe! You think we have lost power in Italy? It is a strategy," he bellowed, shaking her. "And you are wrong. There is a parlay. I gave the Martinellis the piazzas and the vineyards, and they gave me the world. We are global now! Giovanni power is everywhere!"

She jerked away, refusing to rub her aching upper arms, refusing to second guess her decision. "Claudio and I, we agreed. We will take our chances and let him build a life away from here, away from the blood."

"Claudio?" Lorenzo snarled, rolling his eyes. "The barista decides what is best in these matters? You trust the espresso maker over your own brother?"

Francesca gestured around the small living room full of paintings. "My husband is more than a barista, and I trust him over you in everything. In the end, so did our son."

Lorenzo closed his eyes, shaking his head. "You have made a mistake, Francesca."

"I do not think so," she said, turning her back on her brother.

As Lorenzo rode away, Francesca murmured a prayer that her son would make a splendid life, away from the violence, away from her family, away from vendetta.

January 24, 1000 ME

A Long Trip, That Just Got Longer - New York - Filippo

Filippo navigated the snarled traffic of Midtown New York, studying the map, getting honked at, and trying to make out the numbers on the unfamiliar buildings. He crossed the kingdom alone, seeking space and time to think. But five solitary days later, he had no answers and had found no peace.

The only thing waiting for him in New York was a gallery show, an important one, not only for the clients and the exposure, but for what it might do for his heart. He hoped submerging himself in the art world might lead him back to the man he had been before he went undercover.

He finally spotted his destination but was forced to drive past the offices of Worley, Blake, and Standish, Attorneys at Law, in search of a parking space. Kayah lent him her townhouse for his stay, but he needed to drop by her lawyer's office for the spare set of keys.

Forced to park three blocks away, he shrugged on a heavy leather coat and a knit scarf Genevieve had insisted he take with him. He was thankful she had. The city was frigid.

Preoccupied and miserable, he almost missed it. Had he not spent the last five days remembering, he might have. Perhaps the walk caught his attention, because it was not the hair, that had changed, silver instead of jet black. Filippo stopped and stared bug-eyed as his uncle, Lorenzo ben Salvatore, descended the steps of Worley, Blake, and Standish, got into a waiting limousine, and drove away.

Author's Note

Thank you all so much for reading! I sincerely hope you enjoyed M5-Circle of Trust. These end of book notes are normally written within days of finishing the first draft, when the rush of excitement is still fresh. But M5 differed from all the other novels, so I thought I might mix it up and write this one just before publication.

If I had to choose a word to describe the process of creating M5 it would be paradox. It is the fastest first draft I ever wrote, and the book I worked on the longest. It contains some of my favorite scenes in the series, yet for most of its life, it was my least favorite novel. Sometimes I liked it, other times I did not.

When I became a writer, I decided that I would never rely on formula, take the easy way out, or betray my readers by writing implausible storylines or making characters too stupid to live! I am humbled by your patronage, grateful for your support, and cognizant that you have chosen to invest your valuable time reading these stories. It is a privilege that comes with a responsibility. So, a Millennium Series novel will never go to market if I do not believe in it.

I cannot say how many iterations M5 has gone through since December of 2018; fifteen is probably not an exaggeration. However, as with all worthy endeavors, perseverance sees you through, and M5-Circle of Trust has finally earned its place in the Millennium Series.

The original construction of this novel was strictly linear, which made editing incredibly challenging. No matter how many times I fiddled with the sections, I could not make the story flow properly. M5, by its nature, is a bridge book that connects the characters and timelines of the four previous stories. There is a lot going on and a ton of people to contend with. Everybody plays a part, and everybody gets a piece of the action. I also did not want to recap everything that had previously taken place and trust you all to remember the big plot points from the earlier novels.

The writer I am today would not even attempt M5. The writer I was in 2018 did not have a clue. But there is something extraordinary about the beginner, who embraces the initial burst of creativity and runs headlong into the adventure, where no limits or rules exist. The novice makes art for the sheer joy of it and believes all things are possible. I have tried to preserve that beautiful beginner's spirit, while taming this beast with a bit of structure and wisdom. In the end, I sacrificed the original linear construction, and grouped the scenes as well as I could to give the story a bit more flow and cohesiveness. M5 might never be perfect, but it was indeed ambitious, even if I did not realize it at the time. Ha!

And there are wonderful sections in this story. The threads of loyalty, love, and friendship weave such an interesting tapestry. "Best Father in the World", where Richard kicks the basketball, is one of my favorites. I had so much fun going on the other side of the door with Peter and Astrid in New Orleans and shooting with them in New Mexico. In every scene, they stole my heart anew. I cried with Himari and felt her bewilderment and heartbreak bleeding through the pages. I loved the fights at Peccioli, and all the little nuggets sprinkled among the pages. And then Kayah showed up…

I adore these complex, brave, amazing characters, and am honored to share them with you. We have so much more to discover, so many more adventures to experience. M6-The Royals is up next, and trust me, that book is going to blow you away.

Take my hand; I am going to tell you an amazing tale.

In Christ,
Staci
03/20/2023

PS – Can you do me a favor? Drop a review, tell your friends, like my Facebook page, share this amazing series with your reader groups? That is a kindness I can never repay. Thanks!